TERMINAL
JUSTICE

CRCFELLOWSHIP
BURNABY
604 527 7200

THE BARRINGSTON **BOOK ONE** RELIEF CHRONICLES

TERMINAL JUSTICE

ALTON L. GANSKY

WATERBROOK
PRESS

TERMINAL JUSTICE
PUBLISHED BY WATERBROOK PRESS
2375 Telstar Drive, Suite 160
Colorado Springs, Colorado 80920
A division of Random House, Inc.

ISBN 1-57856-023-3

Printed in the United States of America

2004

10 9 8 7 6 5 4 3 2

This book is dedicated to
the quiet and unassuming heroes worldwide.

Acknowledgments

My thanks go to Lisa Bergren and the folks at WaterBrook
Press for their support and wise counsel
and to my agent, Claudia Cross, for her insights and
encouragement. It's a blessing to be associated with
such a professional team.

Prologue

JUDITH RHODES DREW IN A LONG BREATH OF HOT dusty air and slowly held out her arms. Her heart pounded, her mouth was dry, her eyes watered in fearful anticipation. She nodded once and motioned with her outstretched hands, beckoning, imploring, encouraging. Overhead a blue sky radiated with the heat of an unforgiving sun, and only the droning of the ever-present black flies broke the still air. She nodded and motioned again, watching as the dramatic act of courage unfolded before her.

His name was Namui, a Somali national, and he was returning from the dead. Seated in a fiberglass folding chair, he stared uneasily at Judith. Slowly, apprehensively, he leaned forward, and with a courage that can only be found in the deep reservoirs of the soul, rose to his feet. Judith watched as the emaciated, naked man gently swayed like a sapling in the breeze. His skin was taut and stretched over protruding bones that looked as though they might erupt through the flesh at any moment. His eyes bulged as if in perpetual panic. A small tear of pain trickled down his cheek.

Judith knew the cause of this. She understood fully that hunger had caused this once noble man's body to begin to cannibalize itself, consuming him from the inside out. Famine-induced hunger tortured him, robbed him of the simple strength to stand and walk. Two weeks ago Namui crawled into the Barringston Relief camp and collapsed in front of Dr. Judith Rhodes's tent. When she first saw him, confused and straddling death, she assumed that his would be the next body in the mass grave twenty meters outside of

1

camp. She had been wrong. Rehydration treatment, medication, and, most of all, easily digested meals proved a strong enough lifeline to rescue Namui.

Tentatively, Namui took a step forward, rocked from side to side, then stepped forward again. It took five minutes for him to traverse the ten steps between them. *Ten steps*, Judith thought, *a fine effort*.

"Very good, Namui," Judith exclaimed, making no effort to hide her joy. "You will be a wonderful example to the others." That thought saddened Judith. There were indeed others in various stages of lingering death. She had seen it all and wished she had seen none of it. But this was her work, her calling. This was where she had to be.

Taking Namui by the arm, Judith gently led him back to the chair and helped him sit. "I'm going to give you another shot, Namui," she said in Arabic as she removed a hypodermic needle from a medical bag that rested on a rickety card table nearby. He nodded slowly. It was clear that the small physical effort had exhausted him.

Judith crouched by the chair, and Namui leaned to one side baring a portion of his buttocks. Gently Judith inserted the needle and pressed the hypodermic's plunger until the clear liquid was gone. She slowly extracted the needle and wiped the injected area with an alcohol-saturated swab. "You sit and rest for a while," she said gently patting his bony shoulder. "Tomorrow you can try again."

The deep rumbling of trucks rolled through the thick air. The sound made Judith's heart skip. Trucks could mean anything from the delivery of supplies to roving bands of bandits. The trucks were being driven hard and fast. Forcing herself to turn around, she saw what she had feared: unmarked vehicles.

Judith's heart rate climbed as men poured from the twelve trucks that thundered to a stop in the middle of the camp. Leading the caravan was a dark blue, late model Jeep Cherokee from which a familiar looking man exited.

Ironically she had read a briefing paper on him just the night before. Holding the pages near a gas lantern she had read the file provided by the Barringston research team. The file had included a fuzzy photo of the man. He was round faced with short-cropped hair that had more gray than black. His hairline had marched back from his forehead. His skin was smooth, and his full face revealed his well-balanced diet. The photo made it clear that the only hunger that this man knew was what he saw around him. A small crescent-shaped scar etched in his right cheek verified his identity. There was no doubt in Judith's mind: This was Mahli, a mysterious warlord whose very name was in doubt.

Judith's first inclination was to bolt, but there was no place to run and certainly no place to hide. Shouting a warning was useless, for only a handful of the camp's residents were capable of running; they certainly couldn't fight.

Mahli stood next to the truck and casually surveyed the camp until his gaze rested on Judith and the skeletal figure sitting next to her. He smiled and casually strolled toward them.

"Do you speak Somali?" Mahli asked in Somali. His voice was high and nasal. Not answering, Judith looked into his eyes and saw there a wickedness.

He grabbed her chin and pulled her face close to his.

"Do you speak Somali?" Judith recoiled at his touch and slowly shook her head. She understood the phrase and maybe a handful of others, but no more.

"Arabic?" he asked. "English?"

"Both."

"Good." He said in English, dropping his hand and resting it on a holstered pistol at his waist. "Who are you?"

"Dr. Judith Rhodes," she replied quietly.

"Doctor?" He laughed. "You should have stayed home and

made yourself rich off the illness of others. Here there is nothing you can do. Who is in charge?"

"I am." She fidgeted nervously with the hypodermic in her hand.

"You? A woman?" Mahli sneered. "No wonder the West is weak." Mahli glanced around the camp again. "I want the food and medical supplies," he said matter-of-factly. "You will help me."

"We don't have enough food as it is," Judith objected loudly.

"We have greater need," he said calmly.

"Greater need? These people will die without the food and medicine. If you take our supplies, you will be killing them."

"It is Allah's will." He shrugged nonchalantly.

"Do you speak for Allah?" she asked with obvious sarcasm. The thought of losing the camp's supplies had momentarily erased Judith's caution.

At first Mahli did not respond. He weighed Judith's insolence and then sighed heavily. "These people do not matter," he said with a wave of his arm. "These are the . . ." He paused, searching for the right phrase in English. "Worthless. They will soon fertilize the earth."

A wave of anger surged inside Judith. She had to stop this but had no idea how.

"We could use a doctor," he said softly. "Especially a doctor as attractive as you."

"What would your Allah say?" Her voice shook with renewed fear.

"We are all human and have our needs."

"I am of more use here," she said, quavering.

"We have many uses for you." He reached forward and caressed her cheek.

Judith closed her eyes and tensed.

"Look at me," Mahli shouted fiercely enough to make her ears ring.

Judith's eyes snapped open. What she saw chilled her. A hand, black and cadaverous, had grabbed Mahli by the wrist. She was paralyzed by the phenomenal act of courage. Namui, the man who moments ago had worked himself to near exhaustion walking three meters, was attempting to rescue her from her tormentor. It was a hopeless act, a futile act, and the most gallant act she had ever witnessed.

With a sudden scream of rage, Mahli viciously jerked his hand away from Namui. The sudden force of the movement was too much for the man's hunger-enervated bones. There was an audible snap, and Namui fell from the chair to the hard ground. Slowly he reached for his broken arm with his other hand. The jagged edge of his radius protruded from the skin. He let out a low and mournful moan that immediately brought Judith to tears. The omnipresent flies swarmed around the fresh, warm blood.

"Namui!" Judith screamed and started for him, but before she could take the two steps necessary to reach him, a hand grabbed her by the hair and viciously snapped her backward.

Judith looked at Mahli in horror. She watched his eyes narrow as he pulled the pistol from its holster. "No," she cried. Mahli pointed the weapon at the fallen man. Her mind shouted that it was foolish to resist, but Judith had stopped listening to her mind. She now heard only her heart, and her heart compelled her to act. She lunged, not to Namui's side, but at Mahli. She attacked with a courage forged of fear and love and struck with the only weapon she had at hand: the syringe.

Without thought and with startling speed, Judith swung the syringe at the face of Mahli plunging the needle through his left cheek. The hypodermic pierced the tender flesh and continued into his tongue.

Mahli howled in pain and swung the revolver around, striking Judith in the jaw. Judith heard her mandible crack. She fell to the ground, her hands covering her face. Mahli's scream brought his men sprinting to his aid, but he waved them off with a quick gesture. Judith watched as Mahli slowly reached up to the syringe and smoothly withdrew its needle from his face. He studied it for a moment then dropped it to the ground.

Mahli stepped next to the fallen Judith and gazed down at her in fury. She held her jaw, blood trickling from her mouth, dripping to the parched earth. With agonizing deliberateness, Mahli raised the gun and pointed its barrel at Namui. A second later the pistol's loud report filled the air. The flies buzzed into the air and quickly settled again.

Judith wept. She wept for Namui, whose journey had ended in an act of bravery and whose courage had been stopped by an act of cruelty. She wept for her impotence to stop the inhumanity.

Removing her hands from her face, Judith saw the barrel of Mahli's gun pointed at her. She said nothing as his finger tightened on the trigger.

ONE

DESTINY'S KNOT

August 2 to September 4

1

DAVID O'NEAL BOUNCED ON THE BALLS OF HIS FEET, absentmindedly ran a hand through his brown hair, and waited for the elevator doors to open. It had been a long time since he had had to look for work, and now at the age of forty he faced his first interview in years with anxiety. A normally confident and decisive man, he felt overwhelmed, intimidated—overwhelmed by the events of the last months that had strained his inner strength to the breaking point, intimidated by the executive job for which he was being considered. "Easy, man," he said to himself. "This is just a job interview, not brain surgery."

The doors opened and a dapper man in an expensive, dark gray, double-breasted suit immediately greeted David. David thought of his own suit, which was at least six years old and well out of style.

"I'm pleased to meet you, Dr. O'Neal," the man said, extending his hand. "My name is Peter Powell, and I'm the head of personnel. You may remember that we spoke on the phone. I've been asked to escort you to A.J.'s office."

David stepped from the elevator and shook Powell's hand. "Yes, I remember. It's good to meet you face to face, Mr. Powell."

"Please call me Peter."

Peter was a lean African-American man of average height with salt-and-pepper hair. He had an air of confidence and wealth about him. He certainly didn't seem like a midrange executive. When he spoke he maintained direct eye contact.

The two men studied each other for a moment, then Peter laughed a deep and genuine laugh. "Well, now that we've sized each other up, allow me to show you to A.J.'s office."

They started down the corridor to David's left. The floor was filled with plants and brightly lit. The corridor led to a large pair of oak doors. Engraved on the doors was an embossment of a thinking man holding a globe in the palm of his hand. David had seen a marble statue like it in the lobby; he assumed that it was the logo of Barringston Relief. They stood motionless at the doors for a moment before Peter knocked firmly.

"Come in," a voice said from a speaker in the ceiling.

"Shall we?" Peter said opening the door.

David nodded and stepped across the threshold. He was stunned by what he saw. The office was cavernous. Floor-to-ceiling windows on two sides afforded a magnificent view of the San Diego skyline and bay. The carpet was a rich cobalt blue and had a pale yellow pattern of squares with the Barringston symbol stitched in the middle of each.

In one corner was a sitting area bordered on three sides by leather couches. A large glass table dominated the center. In the adjoining wall was a large fireplace with a hearth made of black marble.

Opposite the sitting area was a matching glass conference table. The table was the largest David had ever seen. A laptop computer was situated at one end of the table.

In the center of the office was a desk. It, like the coffee table and conference table, had a glass top, which rested on two marble columns. A smaller table to the left of the desk supported a computer monitor and keyboard.

A.J. Barringston rose from his place behind the desk and smiled. David was immediately struck with the height of the man, judging that he stood at least six foot six. He was trim but by no means thin. Unlike Peter, Barringston did not wear a suit. Rather, he wore a pair of pleated beige pants and a powder-blue polo shirt.

His hair was black and pulled back into a ponytail. He was not at all what David had expected.

"A.J., I would like to introduce Dr. David O'Neal," Peter said formally.

"Come in, come in," Barringston said as he stepped from behind the desk and moved lithely to David, stretching out his hand. "I've looked forward to this. I can't tell you how excited I am to meet you."

David was taken aback by Barringston's effervescence and gregariousness. Taking Barringston's hand David said, "Thank you, Mr. Barringston."

"A.J. please. Call me A.J.," he interrupted. "Everyone calls me A.J. We are a big family, and we don't hang on formality."

"Uh, thank you, uh, A.J." David felt off balance. "Please call me David."

"I shall," he said with a laugh. "Let's sit down." Barringston moved toward the couches.

"If you'll excuse me, A.J.," Peter said, "I have a few things to attend to."

"Certainly, Peter," he replied. "And thanks for your help."

Peter turned and left, shutting the doors behind him.

"Isn't he staying for our meeting?" David asked, surprised at Peter's sudden departure.

"Oh, no," Barringston said with a lopsided grin. "If he didn't approve of you, then you wouldn't be here now."

"I see."

The door to the office opened slowly. A woman carrying a tray of cups entered the room.

"Come in, Sheila," Barringston said, bounding toward the door.

Sheila Womack was every bit as stunning as Barringston himself. She was easily six feet tall and her blond hair was boyishly short. She wore a pair of black straight-legged pants that accentuated her height. Her eyes were a rich azure blue. She carried a tray with a carafe and two coffee cups.

"I thought you might like some coffee," she said in a throaty tone.

David thought she had an odd air about her. She seemed reserved but not introverted or self-conscious. She projected poise and control but seemed, at least at first glance, to be tense, as if on guard against unseen dangers.

"Oh, Sheila," A.J. said with a sweeping arm motion. "Come and meet Dr. David O'Neal."

David stood and approached her. After setting the coffee on the table, Sheila offered her hand. It was large and strong and lacked the delicacy David normally associated with women.

"I'm pleased to meet you, Dr. O'Neal," she said straight-faced.

"It's good to meet you. And please call me David."

Sheila nodded slightly.

"Sheila is my personal aide," A.J. said. "Without her I wouldn't get anything done."

"Please let me know if there's anything else you need," she said.

"Thank you," Barringston said. "Would you like some coffee?" he asked David.

"Yes. Black please."

A.J. poured the coffee into china cups that were hand-decorated with Asian paintings.

"These cups," A.J. said with a broad smile, "were given to me by a family in southern China. They're very special to me." David dutifully admired them. "Now, down to business. What do you know about Barringston Relief?"

"Not as much as I should," David replied. "I would like to have come a little more prepared, but your invitation was rather sudden."

"No doubt," A.J. said, sipping the coffee. "We tend to move rather quickly around here."

"I do know," David continued, "that Barringston Relief is a charitable organization that distributes food to the hungry."

"We are much more than that," A.J. said, beaming.

"How so?"

"First, we are the largest food-distribution charity in the world. Last year we dispensed over 150 million tons of food, countless gallons of water, $40 million worth of medicine, and started thirty different schools worldwide. And we're planning to do even more this year."

David tried to comprehend the numbers, but he had nothing to compare them to. Nonetheless, they sounded impressive.

"But that's not what makes us unique," A.J. continued, setting his cup down and leaning forward in excitement. "There are many charitable organizations in the world, and most of them are excellent. We, however, are unique because every dime that is given to us, we give to the world. None of it, not a single penny, stays in the organization."

David glanced around the opulent room.

"I know what you're thinking," A.J. said with a laugh. "You're thinking that this office and, well, this whole building was paid for out of contributions."

"The top ten floors of this building are used by Barringston Relief. Rent and utilities are free. How? The thirteen floors below are used by Barringston Industries. My father started the company in the mid-forties and had great success. Barringston Industries builds structures throughout the world. All our expenses are underwritten by my father and his business. They even pay for our overseas offices."

"What are the"—David paused as he calculated the remaining floors—"other thirty floors used for?"

"We lease them to other businesses. Actually, the rent money from those floors almost pays for this whole building. My dad has been using other people's money to pay for what he wants for decades. Even at eighty-seven years old, he has one of the finest business minds around."

"Does your father still work?" David was having trouble picturing an eighty-seven-year-old man coming to the office every day.

"Oh yes," A.J. replied. "No one has the courage to tell him he should retire. He's a forceful old bird."

"So this building and everything in it has been paid for by your father's firm?"

"Much of it. Barringston Relief is not a purely nonprofit organization. You see, we do more than take food to the starving people of the world. We also develop ways of raising crops in arid, drought-stricken lands. We have a pharmaceutical department that develops medications for the treatment of diseases associated with hunger and plague. Some of these have commercial value. We market what we can and use the profits to further our relief efforts."

"But you do solicit contributions, don't you?" David asked.

"Of course," A.J. replied enthusiastically. "We do so for two reasons. First, because the task at hand is great. How many people, do you suppose, die every day from hunger and related diseases?"

"I don't know." David felt embarrassed by his ignorance, again regretting that he had had so little time to prepare for this meeting. "I would think quite a bit."

"Forty thousand," A.J. said seriously. "And most of them are children. The saddest part is that hunger is 100 percent curable. More than sixteen hundred people die every hour. Every day we waste, the equivalent of a small city perishes. David, we take contributions because it enables us to respond more quickly. We also take contributions because the world needs to know of the problem. Our public appeals are as much an effort to educate about world hunger as it is to eradicate it. We can't do one without the other."

"I didn't mean to imply impropriety," David said. "I only meant—"

"Of course you didn't," A.J. said quickly. "You need to know these things if you're going to be part of the team."

"What exactly would my duties be?" David asked, sipping his coffee.

"Peter didn't tell you?"

14

"He said that you were looking for a speechwriter."

"That's right. But not just any speechwriter. I need someone who understands the art of motivational speaking. I spend much of my time traveling and raising funds. But I have other duties that consume my time. I need someone who can improve my public speaking. Your background seems perfect."

David knew that A.J. must have reviewed the résumé he had faxed to Peter just yesterday.

"I'm afraid that I don't know much about hunger relief," David said apologetically.

"But you know about speeches. Your background and education makes us think that you would be perfect for the job."

The education part was certainly right. David held a master of arts in communication from the University of Arkansas. But he had been out of the discipline for nearly fifteen years and had not written a formal speech since graduation. It was true that until six months ago he had spoken publicly every week of the previous decade and a half, but preaching a sermon to a congregation of three hundred Baptists was considerably different from writing speeches for someone else to deliver.

"Travel is involved too." A.J. said. "As my speechwriter, you would be required to accompany me on all my travels. That means that you will be gone for about thirty weeks of the year."

"That's a lot of travel," David replied. "Truthfully, I haven't been much farther than Tijuana."

"If you're half the man we think you are, you'll adapt."

David had done a lot of adapting over the last few months, more than he wanted. But he had been given no choice. His life was turned upside down, and he adapted to survive.

"David, listen," A.J. said, leaning forward and speaking softly. "I know you've been through a great deal. Yes, we know. We don't want to invade anyone's privacy, but we deal with hundreds of millions of dollars, and we can't be too careful. The stakes are just too high. So we did a little investigating. When we found out you had left the church, we decided to act. I know that you have been under a great deal of pressure, and I don't want to add to it, but we think you're our man. We want you to be part of our team and part of the family. This may be a way to work out the transitions you're going through."

David said nothing. He didn't know whether to be angry or embarrassed. He had always been a private man, keeping his emotions to himself. To think that not only everyone in his former church knew about his problems, but now total strangers, was a difficult realization to swallow.

"David, you are a man of belief and conviction. You are a man who cares. You believe that God has called you to help change the world. That's why you chose the ministry as a profession. None of that has changed. You are still the same person, and you can still make a difference. David, I want you to make that difference with us."

David stared at the coffee cup in his hand. A.J. was right, of course. David had many times said similar things to people who were in the same position that he was in now. It was hard to leave the ministry, and harder still to be left by his wife. Perhaps a change would be good. And he certainly needed the job.

"If it's the money," A.J. said, "I can assure you that you will be well compensated."

"It's not the money," David said looking up. "You're right. I can still make a difference. If you don't mind being patient with me, I'll take the job."

A.J. leaped to his feet.

"Outstanding!" he said, clapping his hands together loudly. "Absolutely great. Welcome aboard, David. We're going to have a grand time together."

"Thank you," David said, standing. "When would you like me to start?"

"Is tomorrow too soon?" A.J. asked.

"Tomorrow will be fine. I hope . . ."

Once again the door to the office slowly swung open and Sheila entered.

"Yes, Sheila?" A.J. asked.

She was carrying a blue file folder. Her face was taut and shadowed by a dark cloud of emotion. She looked at A.J. the way someone looks at another to communicate a silent and important truth.

"I'm sorry to interrupt," she said, "but I thought you should see this." She handed him the folder.

A.J. took the file and opened it. The color drained from his face.

"Thank you, Sheila," he said with a forced smile. "David has agreed to join our team."

"Welcome," Sheila said coolly.

David didn't need his communication expertise to know that his presence was now awkward. Whatever was in the file had clearly upset them both.

"Thank you," David said. "I'm looking forward to working here."

There was an uneasy silence as A.J. stared at the file's contents.

"Well," David said, "I'm sure you have work you want to do, and I think I'm going to treat myself to a celebration dinner. So if there's nothing else . . ."

"Thank you for coming," A.J. said, clearly distracted. "I know that you're going to be a big addition to Barringston Relief."

"I'll see you to the door," Sheila said.

■ ■ ■ ■ ■

A.J. Barringston watched as Sheila closed the door behind David. "It's him, isn't it?" he said sullenly.

"We can't be sure, but—" Sheila began.

"I can. It's him. I can feel him half a world away." A.J. returned his attention to the file and removed its contents: a one-page memo marked, EYES ONLY and three photographs. The memo was unnecessary; the photos said everything. Each photo was an aerial snapshot of a burned-out camp—a Barringston camp. The brown earth was marked by areas of scorched ground where tents that had housed the feeble once stood. Ghostly wisps of smoke that had danced above the pyres were frozen in place by the photo. In the middle of one of the pictures lay two bodies, arms and legs strewn in awkward positions. A label identifying the bodies was glued to the photo. One read: UNIDENTIFIED SOMALI NATIONAL; the other: DR. JUDITH RHODES.

"Communications dispatched a helicopter from Mogadishu when Rhodes didn't check in," Sheila explained. "That's what they found."

"It's him all right." A.J. slammed the photos down on the desk. "He's gone too far." A.J. leaned back in his chair and rubbed his eyes. "Have Peter pull Judith's personnel file. I want to talk to the family. They shouldn't have to hear this over the television. Also, have Kristen hold a press conference."

"Anything else?"

"Yes. Where's Roger?"

"He arrived in Egypt last night."

"I hope he hasn't unpacked," A.J. said seriously. "It's time for him to take another trip."

2

DAVID ARRIVED FOR HIS FIRST DAY OF WORK AT 7:50. The traffic along Interstate 8 had been grueling and hadn't improved when he turned south on Interstate 5. It had taken him nearly fifty minutes to make the drive from El Cajon in the east county to downtown. If the Barringston building hadn't had a private parking garage, he would have been late for his first day on the job.

The night had passed quickly. David had indeed celebrated his new job with dinner at a small Italian restaurant in La Mesa. The meal was good, but he still felt uncomfortable eating alone. He had almost always had company when he ate out, if not his wife, then a church member. The last six months David had eaten all his meals alone, turning down the kind invitations from church members who struggled to maintain contact with him after his resignation. He loved those people, but he found it impossible to face them without an overwhelming sense of embarrassment.

He knew the embarrassment was misplaced; he had done nothing wrong. But his wife had left him for another man—a church leader at that. She left him, the church, and the city. She left him with the task of disclosing the awful truth of her infidelity to the congregation. He had to share the news of the abandonment. He did so in a quiet and uncritical way, making great efforts to appear strong and resilient, but those who knew him well knew that his mind and soul had been shattered.

The church had been supportive. The congregation poured out

their love in many ways; they also talked among themselves. They pleaded with him to stay on as their pastor. "No one can replace you," they said. But Carol, his wife, had been able to replace him. Frequently waves of insecurity and inadequacy washed over him like a tsunami overwhelming a coastal community. The debris left behind was not the residue of houses and shops but the flotsam of pride and dignity. He had trouble sleeping at night, and when he did sleep he had unsettling dreams.

Despite the efforts of several church members, deacons, and other local pastors, David closed himself off, building a fortress around himself constructed of fear, anger, and self-pity. For months David lived the life of a recluse, screening all his phone calls through his answering machine.

One day he received a letter from Barringston Relief. They said they had been referred to him by the alumni association of San Diego State University where he had done graduate work in speech communication before going off to seminary. The alumni office had been made aware of David's new status when he had, on a whim, fired off a résumé to his alma mater looking for a teaching position. Unfortunately, there had been no budget for it.

Reluctantly, David called the phone number listed in the letter. It took only moments for David to be connected to Peter Powell, the head of personnel. Peter had gone straight to the point: They were offering David a job as a speechwriter. David needed a job. The savings he had been using to support himself would be depleted in less than two months. As a pastor, his income had been livable but limited. He was far from being a man of means. Intrigued by the offer and pressed by need, he agreed to meet with Powell the next day.

Now he found himself at the start of a new career. He had always been goal driven, and the thought of undertaking a new project excited him. He felt privileged—no blessed—that he should find a job with such a noble purpose. Certainly it would be different from his work as pastor, but he was resilient. He could adjust.

Stepping from his car, he started toward the bank of elevators. A message left by Peter on David's answering machine had said that someone would meet him and take him to his new office. Before he could reach the elevators, the doors parted and a woman exited. Her hair was shoulder length and dark red, and her eyes were a deep blue, the deepest he had ever seen.

"David O'Neal," she said, smoothly stepping toward him. "I'm Kristen LaCroix, and I've been asked to show you around." Her walk was peculiar. She held her head high, chin elevated, and moved with a strutting gait.

David had studied body language most of his adult life. The topic had consumed him in college and graduate school, and he had found it useful in the ministry. David intuitively sensed that Kristen LaCroix was subconsciously attempting to divert his attention. He found her so stunningly attractive that diverting his attention from anything else would be easy, but years of conditioning prodded his subconscious to seek an answer.

He discovered the truth quickly and was embarrassed to find it so obvious. Kristen's unusual gait was caused by a physical defect. Glancing at her feet, David saw a prosthetic shoe with a sole that had been built up approximately two inches. Her right leg was shorter than her left.

"So you're my guide," he said, shaking her hand.

"I am." Her smile was flawless and bright. "Peter had planned to do the honors, but he's rather tied up."

"Well, then," he said, "I'm in your hands."

"How about a short tour?" Kristen asked as she led the way into the waiting elevator car. "It'll help you get your bearings."

"I'll take whatever help I can get." He watched as she punched the elevator button. The cab rose smoothly. The hum of motors filled the car. "How long have you been with Barringston Relief?"

"Just under five years. I was recruited from a public-relations firm in Los Angeles."

"Is that what you do here? Public relations, I mean."

21

"Yes," she replied succinctly. "I oversee all press releases, contact with the media, and related activity."

"You must enjoy it."

Kristen glanced at David with puzzlement. "On most days," she replied quietly.

David caught the look. "Did I say something wrong?"

"You haven't heard?" she asked. "You must not have seen the news last night."

"No. I ate out and then went home and read." There was an uncomfortable pause. "What happened?"

"One of our overseas personnel was killed," she said solemnly. "She was murdered by a terrorist."

"I'm sorry," David said quietly. That explained A.J.'s behavior yesterday. "Did you know the person?"

"Her name was Dr. Judith Rhodes. She had been transferred from Ethiopia to Somalia three weeks ago. As you probably know, Somalia is experiencing yet another drought and famine. Because of all the problems the UN had in 1993, few countries are willing to help. Dr. Rhodes asked for the transfer. She knew the dangers, but she asked to go anyway. I gave a short press conference last night. It was on the evening news."

"Do they know who the killer is?" David asked.

"We know," she said, narrowing her eyes. "Not officially, but we know."

The elevator stopped with a small lurch, and the doors opened. As they exited the elevator Kristen said, "We have an open communication policy here, David. There are very few secrets. That means that everyone associated with Barringston knows about Dr. Rhodes. In fact, they knew before the media. Our ranks are filled with caring people, and many of them are taking the news very hard."

David understood the implication. In times of grief, people often seem preoccupied and distant. He could expect a subdued mood.

"This is our school," Kristen said. "Actually, it's part of our school. This floor houses our elementary classes; the junior high and high school students meet on the floor above us."

"You actually have a fully graded school here?" David looked around. He was standing in a large and brightly lit foyer with a view of San Diego's high-rise buildings. A wide hall led from the foyer.

"Yes, and we're quite proud of it. It was A.J.'s idea. He felt that parents would feel more comfortable coming to work if they knew their children were nearby. This room is used for lunch gatherings. Parents can share lunch with their children if they want." Pointing down the hall, she said, "That corridor leads to the classrooms. The children are in class now, that's why it's so quiet. The other corridor leads to the library, science rooms, language labs, and other such things."

"So a Barringston employee's child can go from first grade through high school in this one building?"

"Actually, they can start in our preschool. We also have a full gymnasium in the building next door. The children who come to school here get the best in education. All our teachers are paid executive salaries and have studied in the best colleges. High school students are guaranteed jobs in the firm if they do well."

"Do you have any children here?" David asked.

"No," she laughed. "I have no children, no husband, and no dog. I'm not much of a collector."

"Collector? I've never thought of relationships as collecting."

"I'm sorry," she said smiling. "I don't mean to make light of marriage. It's just that I've never been drawn to it. I tend to be a little compulsive and self-absorbed. I wouldn't make a very good wife."

David nodded. "Being a spouse and parent isn't easy, and it doesn't come with an instruction manual." He thought about his own failed marriage. Like most abandoned spouses, he assumed the breakdown was his fault. He had played the what-if game to the hilt. *What if* he had been more sensitive? *What if* he had been home more? *What if* he had expressed his love more clearly?

He knew that no good came of those questions. He also knew from experience and training that there was little he could have done to prevent his wife's departure. The simple truth was that she had found someone she'd rather be with, and there was nothing David could do about it.

The tour continued. Kristen showed David the research library with its multiple computers and current and past issues of every pertinent periodical. What they didn't have, Kristen had assured him, they could get.

On the forty-seventh floor were apartments used by employees who liked to work late. Here they could catch a few hours sleep, shower, and return to work. The floor also contained the cafeteria.

David had been the most impressed by the research facility on the forty-ninth floor and the communications center on the fifty-second floor. The research wing looked like something out of a science-fiction movie. Scientists, in white lab coats huddled over computers, microscopes, glassware, and devices that David couldn't identify.

"The Barringston philosophy," Kristen had said, "is not merely to feed the hungry, but to provide the means for them to feed themselves." She went on to describe the drought-resistant grain crops that had been developed as well as high-protein beans, nuts, and other foods, many of which had patents pending. David also learned that medical research was done in conjunction with Baylor College of Medicine in Houston, Texas. Several revolutionary advancements had been made in rehydration, vitamin supplements, and the reversal of tissue damage caused by hunger.

The communications room was nothing less than amazing. Here David learned that every field-operation team was equipped with state-of-the-art satellite communications technology. Kristen had said that it was the world's largest and most sophisticated, privately owned communications system.

"Communications was the first to realize that something was wrong in Somalia," Kristen had said. "When Dr. Rhodes missed her scheduled check-in, they sent an investigative team from another camp. That's when they found her body."

"I'd never thought of relief work as being dangerous," David said softly.

"It's some of the most dangerous work in the world," Kristen replied. "You would think that people and governments would be glad for whatever help they could get, but that's not the case. It's true that the truly hungry appreciate what we do, but some of their countrymen resent our presence."

"And that resentment can result in violence?" David asked.

"Definitely." Kristen was becoming animated.

David thought a moment then asked, "Has Barringston Relief lost other workers?"

Kristen nodded. "Yes. To date, three other members of our team have been killed. Two died in Bosnia, and one was captured and killed in Somalia in late 1993. We also had six members kidnapped in Beirut, but they were later rescued."

The tour had lasted only an hour, but David's head was spinning. The more he saw of Barringston Relief, the more impressed he became. "Executive offices are located on this and the fifty-third floor. Your office is just down the hall here."

A few steps later they stood before an oak door with a nameplate that read: DAVID O'NEAL, PH.D. Kristen opened the door and let David enter first. The corner room was about half the size of A.J.'s office, which meant it was twice the size that David expected. Two of the walls were floor-to-ceiling windows that overlooked the bay and provided a spectacular view. An oak desk was centered in the room. The carpet was the same deep blue that he had seen in A.J.'s office, but without the embroidered Barringston logo.

"Will this work for you?" Kristen asked.

"This is more than I could have ever imagined," David replied in amazement. "This is gorgeous."

"You can arrange the office any way you want. Supplies are plentiful, including furniture, computers, and even art. Ava will help you get whatever you need."

"Ava?"

"Ava is your assistant. She can help you find what you need. She's also great at research, so make good use of her."

"Where is she?"

"In the office next door. All you have to do is punch the intercom button on your phone and say 'Ava.' She'll be paged in her office."

"A voice recognition phone?"

"Yes, and it works great. I, however, still dial my own numbers. I guess I'm just an old-fashioned girl."

"This is going to take some getting used to," David said numbly.

"Shall I get Ava for you?"

David shook his head. "No, I think I'll take a moment to look around."

"After you settle in, give me a call. We'll have lunch in the cafeteria."

David smiled. "I'll do that."

A sensation welled up in David, a long absent feeling—a hint of happiness.

■　■　■　■　■

Light from the near midnight moon struggled to pierce the tinted windows of the office, adding its muted radiance to the soft glow emanating from the two computer monitors. The subdued luminescence from the computer screens provided the room's only light. A lit cigarette dangled from the mouth of the operator, its end glowing red and trailing thin, gossamer smoke that rose leisurely into the air in a diaphanous dance about the head of the room's lone occupant.

The office was as silent as it was dark, disturbed only by the clicking and tapping of rapidly moving fingers on the well-used keyboard. Occasionally a vocalized "hmm" or "ah" joined the slight sounds. The typing stopped occasionally to allow the figure to tap the ash from the cigarette into a nearly overflowing ashtray to the right of the computer. The gray-black ash fell, missing the ashtray and joining the other bits of burned residue on the desktop.

"I know you're there," the voice said softly. *Clack, click, click, tap, clack.* "Come out, come out, wherever you are." *Clack, click, click, tap, clack.* "Just a little hole will do." Five minutes passed, then, "Gotcha!" The operator hit the return key, and a shrill warbling emanated from the modem. A moment later a computer billboard appeared on the screen: WELCOME TO AMERICAS BANK, GRAND CAYMAN. PLEASE ENTER YOUR ACCESS CODE. *Clack, click, click, tap, clack.* ONE MOMENT, PLEASE. True to its statement, a new billboard appeared a moment later. PLEASE CHOOSE YOUR TRANSACTION. Fingers flew across the keyboard with the right hand moving from keyboard to mouse to keyboard until three minutes later the operator turned the computer off, leaned back in a chair that squeaked in protest, inhaled deeply on the cigarette, and then blew a steady stream of smoke at the moon outside the window.

"With $300 billion transferred daily around the world, who's gonna miss a measly $200 million?" the operator asked the empty room.

3

ABSORPTION.

David had always considered his ability to get lost in his work a beneficial trait. It served him well in college, in graduate school, and at church. Many times he found himself so caught up in his work that hours passed without his noticing. Now he leaned back in his chair and rubbed his weary eyes. He had been on the job two days, yet it seemed no more than two hours. If it hadn't been for the occasional blurring of his eyes, he would have had almost no sense of time passing.

He sighed heavily. There was so much to learn, so much to ingest. David had set three goals for his first week of work: learn the computer system, review tapes of A.J.'s speeches, and watch the Barringston briefing tapes provided by Peter Powell. Now halfway through his third day, he had accomplished all those goals. He felt good about his new job and the nobility of the work, but he was also emotionally exhausted. The tapes of the relief work were graphic and untempered. They were nothing like the sanitized versions broadcast on television by other charitable groups. These tapes showed the ugly face of starvation in garish and undiluted detail. Through the tapes, David traveled to the Sudan, Yemen, the Philippines, Bangladesh, Mexico, and even the Appalachian Mountains. Through the lens of the camera he saw children dead of dehydration caused by diarrhea, mothers carrying long-dead infants, mass graves, and the barely mobile skeletons of once-robust men.

Over the last two days, David had reviewed all eight hours of tape twice, taking them home to study. The first time he watched them out of duty, the second time out of discipline. What impressed him most was the sacrificial work of the Barringston teams. Doctors, nurses, agricultural specialists, and more, walking through the morass of death and decay. Each day they faced the hideous image of despair, and each day they gave their all to beat back death. Their pictures never appeared in newspapers or on televisions. They received no glory or honor. They all struggled stoically against a seemingly impossible enemy.

Over the years David had met many missionaries who had left home and friends for distant lands to spread the gospel of Christ. He had always admired their dedication and willingness to forsake a more comfortable lifestyle at home. But until now he had never realized what one person would endure to help a nation of strangers. Yet here they were, living in tents, mending broken bodies, burying the dead, and standing toe-to-toe with death. Simultaneously, David felt a sense of pride at being associated with such benevolent souls and a sense of profound shame at not being one of the ones on the front lines.

While not attempting to sway the viewer with overt emotionalism, the video pulled no punches. One could not watch such poignant footage without being wounded in soul. One picture touched David deeply. It was of an emaciated child no more than six years old sitting on a woven mat with his knees drawn to his chest. He wore only a red-and-blue striped T-shirt. Lying on the mat next to him was his mother, who was clearly dead. Two Barringston workers came, rolled the deceased woman onto a pallet and took her away, presumably to a mass grave. The boy did nothing, said nothing. He didn't even look at the men who took his mother's corpse. Instead he stared ahead and slowly rocked from side to side. Death was no longer a stranger to this boy; death was what happened every day, and no energy could be expended grieving.

David struggled to push those thoughts aside; he had other

things to consider. At hand was his review of A.J.'s speeches. Several manuscripts were scattered across David's desk, surrounding the yellow legal pad on which he had been scribbling notes. On the other side of the office was a television, and on the screen was the frozen image of A.J. behind a podium. David sighed and stretched.

It took a moment before he realized he was being watched. In the doorway to his office was the head of a young man. At first it looked to David as if the head had miraculously grown out of the door jamb. His heart skipped a beat as his mind attempted to make sense of the apparition.

"Uh, hi," the head said.

"Hi," David replied with a chuckle. "You startled me." The head and the body it had been hiding behind the wall moved into the office.

"I-I'm sorry," the young man said with a timid stammer.

There was something different about this individual. It wasn't his appearance. He was nicely dressed in a pair of tan slacks and white polo shirt. He was taller than David, maybe six foot one, lanky, and about twenty-two years old.

"Are you all right, mister?" the young man asked with genuine concern. "You looked like your head hurt."

"I'm fine, thank you. My eyes are just tired from watching videos and taking notes."

"Oh, good," the boy said nodding his head.

David noticed that the boy made very little eye contact and stood with his head down. He also rubbed the thumb of his left hand with the thumb of his right.

"Is there something I can help you with?" David asked.

"No, I can do it myself."

The two stared at each other in uncomfortable silence. The young man's nervousness puzzled David. What was there to be nervous about?

"You can do what by yourself?" David asked patiently.

"Trash."

"Trash?"

"I'm here for the trash." The boy pointed at the wastebasket next to David's desk.

"Oh," David said with a laugh, "you must work with maintenance."

"I get the trash and put it in the big blue Dumpster downstairs." The boy was rubbing his thumb faster now.

It was all beginning to make sense to David. The young man was more than shy; he was mildly retarded.

"What's your name?" David asked, smiling broadly.

"Timmy. Timmy Simmons."

"Timmy, I'm David O'Neal, and I'm new here. I am certainly glad to meet you."

Reluctantly, Timmy stopped rubbing his thumb, brought his hand up to shoulder height and waved, "Hi, Da-Da-David . . ."

"David will be fine." He extended his hand. "Well, Timmy, shake my hand and act like you like me."

Timmy giggled and then quickly stepped forward and shook David's hand hard several times. For a moment, David feared that Timmy would pump his arm hard enough to dislocate his shoulder. "Hi, David," he said beaming. "I like you, David."

"And I like you," David said, rescuing his hand from Timmy's grip and stretching his fingers.

"Cool!" Timmy said. "Well, I gotta go now." He turned toward the door.

"Uh, Timmy?"

Timmy turned still smiling, "Yeah?"

"The trash," David said quietly, never letting his grin diminish. "You came here to take out the trash."

"Oh, yeah. I forgot." Timmy quickly made his way to the receptacle, pulled out the plastic liner, tied a knot in the top, and then left the room only to return a moment later with a fresh liner for the bin.

"Thanks, Timmy."

"You're welcome, David."

"Come see me again, okay?" David said.

"I will. I will."

"I see you've met one of my favorite people, David." The voice startled both David and Timmy. Standing in the doorway was A.J. He was smiling expansively.

"A.J.!" Timmy shouted as he embraced the man, nearly knocking him over. "Look David, it's A.J."

"So I see, Timmy."

"Easy, boy," A.J. chuckled. "If you're not careful, you're going to break my ribs."

Timmy let go but bounced on the balls of his feet to release his pent-up excitement.

"Looks like you've got quite a friend there," David said.

"Timmy's more than my friend, he's family," A.J. said, putting his arm around the young man. "I found Timmy living on the streets about two, no, three years ago. He was nineteen, homeless, and hungry, and two men were beating him for the sport of it. I rescued him and brought him here. He lives in one of our apartments and helps the janitorial staff."

The picture of A.J. rescuing Timmy from a couple of thugs didn't surprise David. A.J. seemed the rescuing type.

"I missed you," Timmy piped in. "You weren't in the office when I went to get the trash."

"I've been out to meetings, Timmy. I missed you too. Tell you what. Let me take you out for hamburgers tonight, and we'll stop by the arcade and you can play some games."

"Superheroes! Can I play Superheroes and drive the race-car game too?"

"If you finish your work, yes."

"Cool! Yes! Neat!" Timmy was ecstatic. "I'll get to work right away." Timmy stepped from the office but immediately bounded back in, hugged A.J., and then bounded back out.

"I don't think my ribs will ever be the same," A.J. said rubbing his side. "That boy is about as strong as they get."

"So I found out," David replied as he rubbed his shoulder.

"But the strongest thing about Timmy is his heart," A.J. said. "I've never seen anyone who can love so unconditionally and with such . . . enthusiasm." Both men laughed.

"So tell me, David," A.J. said, "how have your first two days at Barringston been? Are you finding everything you need?"

"I think I'm adjusting to corporate life, although I can't imagine any corporation doing what you folks do here."

"We are different, but then our work is different. Is Ava helping out?"

David nodded, "Oh, yes. She's great. In many ways she's been my guiding light."

"Good. She's one of the best. If you need anything, she can get it." A.J. looked at the manuscripts on David's desk and then turned to look at the television opposite the desk. He saw his image frozen on the screen. "So what do you think?"

"Think?" David asked. "Think about what?"

"The speeches, of course."

David hesitated. How frank should he be? He barely knew his new boss. A.J. could be the sensitive type who had trouble accepting constructive criticism. When David was a student in college, he encountered several students who responded so poorly to criticism that they would risk failing the course rather than give a simple five-minute speech.

As if he had read David's mind, A.J. said: "No need to hesitate, I can take it."

"It's not that bad, A.J.," David said with a chuckle. "Actually you're a fine speaker with a natural talent. Your timing is good; your voice is clear and not monotone. You display a measure of presence, and your body language is unambiguous."

"But . . ." A.J. prompted as he sat down opposite David's desk.

"But in all the speeches I've watched, about eight, I've noticed that you've left something at home. Passion."

"Passion?"

"Absolutely. Let me show you." David picked up the VCR remote and pressed the rewind button. A moment later the image changed to A.J. dressed in a black tuxedo standing behind an oak lectern that was too short for his height. David provided a running commentary while the tape ran.

"First, your voice. It's good, strong, and well projected. Your body language says you are both confident and sincere. The speech itself is pretty good, and you deliver it well. But there's no passion. What I see here is someone giving a nice speech about an important topic. What I don't see is someone who's devoted his life to the eradication of hunger."

"I see," A.J. said, but David noticed he was puzzled.

"Look," David continued as he leaned over the desk, "it isn't enough to touch the audience's mind. With material this important, your words and delivery have to reach *into* each person and squeeze their soul."

"Squeeze their soul," A.J. repeated.

"Absolutely," David began to pace behind his desk. The videotape continued to play unnoticed. "People are intellectual creatures, but they are first and foremost emotional creatures. If you touch their hearts, you touch their minds. The reverse of that isn't always true."

"But I don't want us to be one of those organizations that parade pictures of naked children with bloated bellies."

"That's not what I'm saying. Such motivations diminish soon after the pictures are gone. What I'm talking about is letting your inner man out."

"My inner man?"

"Look, one of the reasons I came to work here was your enthusiasm. When you were telling me about the work that Barringston Relief did, you were excited, enthusiastic, ebullient, and even effervescent."

"That's an awful lot of *E*s, David."

"Sorry, I tend to alliterate when I get excited." David took his seat and leaned over the desk. "That enthusiasm convinced me that not only is Barringston Relief unique, but so is A.J. Barringston himself. It's that sincere enthusiasm that convinces people to believe and to participate. It's not enough to stand before a group and tell them that thousands are dying daily. We live in a callous age. We see death and destruction every evening on the news, and it no longer moves us. Why? Because we saw it yesterday, and we know we'll see it tomorrow. Death is no longer novel."

"I see," A.J. said contemplatively. "That's why we can see a news report of a child being shot in a drive-by shooting and not be emotionally moved."

"Exactly. It's not that people don't care, but that they no longer know how to care. They . . . *we* have been desensitized to the shocking. What little understanding does get through only causes a sense of frustration and anxiety. But if you can stand before them and show them someone whose whole life has been changed by the belief that something can be done, then they will associate with you."

"What do you mean associate with me?"

"They will come to see that yours is a zeal they can possess. They will see that people can make a difference. But they have to see you pour out your emotion, exposing your heart to them. If you do that well, then you will become a lens that can focus the problem and the solution in the audience's mind. They will appreciate that. They will relish that. Knowing that hundreds die every hour is too much to take in, too much to believe. But to see one person totally committed to helping others is something that can be grasped."

"You don't think the people will confuse me with some evangelist, do you?"

35

"Not possible," David replied shaking his head. "Heartfelt sincerity is as obvious to the audience as insincerity. I'm not proposing that you act out a drama or put on a performance. I'm merely suggesting that you drop that armor of formality you put on before you give a speech and let the real A.J. shine forth."

"The real A.J.?"

"The A.J. I met in the office a few days ago. The A.J. who is gregarious and filled with passion. The A.J. who knows what needs to be done and how to do it."

"I'm no different from the next guy. Not really."

"A.J.," David said quietly, "you are vastly different from the next guy, and your inability to see that proves the point. I've only known you for a few days, but I've seen enough and heard enough from the others here to know that you are motivated by the needs of others and not personal advancement."

"You make me sound like a saint. I can assure you that I have needs and that I do think about them."

"Of course you do, but do they motivate you? Have they formed your life? Or have the needs of others given you direction?"

A.J. sat silently chewing at his lip and rubbing his chin with his hand. David wondered if he had been too direct, too pointed, and had now offended his new boss.

"I think I see what you mean," A.J. finally said. "But I worry about my ability to carry it off without seeming . . . forced."

"It won't be forced because you'll just be being yourself. As far as your ability to pull it off, well, that's what I'm here for, to write speeches and coach you."

"Do you really think it will be useful?"

"Useful and fun," David replied. "It's honest, open, and convincing. From what I learned from the videotapes on your work here, there is a need to convince people to act."

A.J. sat up in his chair. "What did you think of it?"

Now it was David's turn to sit silently. His mind filled with the images he had seen: poverty beyond imagination; debilitating diseases; young people whom hunger had made old before their time; the heroic efforts of people he did not know struggling to survive and the equally heroic efforts of Barringston staff members, doctors, nurses, language experts, and others giving chunks of their lives to help people in distant lands. The tape had touched David deeply, shaking him to his emotional core. He had known of famine, but he, like so many, had been too busy to pay attention.

"I think," David said softly, "I think I'm glad to be here helping you do something about the problem."

■ ■ ■ ■ ■

Ian Booth's office couldn't be called opulent, but then neither could it be called Spartan. It possessed just enough dark wood paneling, just enough art, and carpet just thick enough to be impressive but not gaudy. The office was a reflection of the man: prim, proper, and just right in every way, the way Booth thought an international bank president ought to be. Standing at his window that overlooked the rolling azure Caribbean Sea, he thought of his good fortune. Here he was, president of the Americas Bank, a bank that had grown from humble beginnings twenty years ago to an international operation handling money not only for individuals and businesses, but for countries as well. It was true that occasionally he had to deal with unsavory types, but every successful endeavor has its drawbacks. Besides, some of those unsavory types were weighed down with money and needed his help in placing their currency in safe and untraceable places. It was an important service for which people paid a handsome price.

A knock on the door jarred Booth from his musing. "Enter," he said in a strong voice made all the more authoritative by his thick British accent.

"Good morning, sir," George Barr said as he entered. Booth couldn't help noticing the facial expression of the bank's senior vice president. Barr was a capable man who seldom got ruffled or lost his temper. He lacked the aristocratic appearance of Booth with his graying temples, aquiline nose, and obsidian eyes, and who, despite his average height, projected a bigger-than-life persona. Barr was the kind of man that ladies described as roly-poly, an attribute that was heightened by his short stature and a head that had long since been divorced from its hair. Despite his height and lack of sophisticated bearing, he had a sharp mind. There was nothing that he didn't understand about banking. If there was a problem, Barr was called to facilitate a solution.

"Good morning, George," Booth said amicably. "If you don't mind my saying so, you look a little out of sorts. Didn't you sleep well last night?"

"Last night was fine, sir. It's this morning that troubles me. I was just informed by one of our internal auditors, who was conducting a routine audit of our special accounts, that something . . . disastrous has happened."

"Disastrous?" Booth questioned with an invisible shudder. Such words were distressing to the bank president who could remember the BCCI scandal that rocked all the banks in the Grand Cayman Islands. In 1991 the Panamanian government brought suit against the International Credit and Commerce Bank—generally referred to as BCCI—to recover money it believed it was owed by former dictator Manuel Antonio Noriega. It was alleged that BCCI had allowed Noriega to send millions of dollars abroad for safekeeping. One of the defendants was a British banker. The scandal made news in nearly every country of the world. Since Americas Bank provided the same services to its unique clientele, Booth had reason to be afraid.

"Oh, yes, yes. Disastrous indeed," Barr said emphatically. "We have money missing. We've been robbed."

"Robbed? Someone broke into the bank building?"

"Not physically, sir . . . electronically. They broke into our computer system and pirated away money."

"Not possible," Booth spat. "We have the best protected computer system created. Someone would have an easier time breaking into the queen mother's bedroom in Buckingham Palace than into our system." Despite his bluster, Booth knew that billions of dollars were transferred around the world electronically every day. Sooner or later someone would turn that to his advantage.

Barr shook his head slowly. "Last night someone successfully transferred funds from our bank and placed it somewhere else. We don't know where; we don't know how."

"But the alarms . . . the fail-safes . . . the tracking systems . . ."

"All circumvented, I'm afraid," Barr said sadly. "Ingenious, really. Quite ingenious."

Slowly Booth walked to his desk chair and dropped in it. "Do I want to know whose money they've taken?"

"It's not good, sir. They took funds from the largest account of the Silver Dawn."

Booth groaned. He wanted to swear, to scream obscenities until they echoed down the halls and out the doors to the ocean, but all he could muster was a simple, deep, guttural moan.

"Two hundred million American, sir," Barr replied to the unasked question.

Booth groaned louder. "The Silver Dawn? Two hundred million dollars?"

"Yes sir."

Leaning his head back, Booth exhaled loudly. "Of all the accounts, why the Silver Dawn?" The Silver Dawn was the most ruthless of the Irish terrorist groups and was known for its indiscriminate use of car bombs. Scores of civilians had died or been injured by their terrorism. They were not known for kindness or forgiveness. They would want more than their money back; they would want an explanation, an explanation that Booth didn't have. "We have to get that money back, right away, George. We must do that right away, or my life is worthless. Do you understand, George? Do you understand?"

"I understand, but how?"

Booth sat staring at his vice president. He had no idea how to gather two hundred million dollars, but he had a very clear idea of what would happen if he didn't.

4

SHE'S NOT THE BIGGEST, CAPT. ADRIAN ADAIR thought. *No, not the biggest and not unique, but she is nonetheless important.* Gazing from the bridge, Captain Adair let his eyes trace the lines of the thirty-year-old *Sea Maid.* To him the ship formed a beautiful shape as it plowed through the sea, pushing aside tons of water with its wedge-shaped bow. Many ships were larger than the *Sea Maid* with her 110-foot beam and just over 700-foot length. But she was his to command, all 18,000 tons of her. And now, making way at a brisk ten knots, Adair felt a sense of euphoria. Tomorrow they would dock in Mombasa, Kenya, and unload their cargo of grain, food staples, and medical supplies, which would then be transported by trucks to Somalia, Ethiopia, and other famine areas. It will be another mission accomplished, another voyage without incident. *Just the way it should be*, he thought.

Those who had sailed with Captain Adair over his twenty-two-year career had crowned him "Lucky" Adair. In more than two decades of service on the world's seas, he had never been injured, lost a crewman, or damaged a ship. The more superstitious sailors would never refer to him by the unlucky title of "Lucky," but they all wanted to sail with him. He was stern but never vicious. He prided himself on bringing his ship to port in better condition than when it left. If a sailor could understand that goal, then he could expect the respect of the captain; those who could not were not allowed on board again.

Now Adair, who loved the sea more than any man could,

41

purposely took in the scenery around him. The sun was setting in the west, painting the slate-gray sky with streaks of iridescent red and pink. Over the port side he could see the hill country of Mozambique with the meager lights of Moçambique, Nacala, and Memba struggling to push back the invading darkness. Off the star-board side was the island nation of Madagascar. Where the setting sun blanketed the hills of Mozambique in ever darkening shade, it bathed the mountains of Madagascar with its soft waning light.

The sea, any sea, was Adair's only love. He had never married, not wanting to put a wife through the misery of being attached to a man who seldom came home and who could never love her as much as he loved the rising and falling of a ship on the swells of the ocean. And in some mystical way, he felt the sea loved him back.

Under the *Sea Maid*'s hull were the waters of the Mozambique Channel. Four hundred miles wide and more than one thousand miles long, the channel was home to the humpback whales (which the Malagasy considered to be the spirits of the dead) who frolicked and gave birth to their young. Below the clear waters rested the coral-encrusted carcasses of ships that had, over the centuries, suc-cumbed to cyclones or pirates. Ahead of him lay the rest of the In-dian Ocean, pristine blue during the day, ripening to near blackness at night. Between him and Mombasa were the Comoros, a small is-land group formerly owned by the French.

"Mr. Salizar," Adair said with aplomb, "do we have a weather update?"

"Aye, Captain," Salizar snapped. "Weather remains unchanged. Satellite shows all clear. It should hold all the way in, sir."

"Very good," Adair replied. "Maintain speed and course." Adair studied Salizar. He liked the young officer. Like Adair, Salizar had graduated from the Maritime Academy and had demonstrated himself an able and trustworthy officer, always showing up at his station precisely on time. He never questioned the captain directly, but was unafraid to offer suggestions that might improve the work-ing of the ship.

"Captain," a voice said to his right. "If you have a moment, sir."

Adair turned to see his first mate, Rudy McGriff, standing with binoculars raised to his eyes and looking over the prow. "What do you see, Mr. McGriff?"

"Unsure, sir, but I think it may be a raft."

Raising his binoculars to his eyes, Adair scanned the distant waters.

"About half a mile out, sir," McGriff said without breaking his gaze. "Look to starboard."

"I have it." Adair studied the bright orange object bobbing on the sea. "I believe you're right, Mr. McGriff."

"In this dim light it's hard to tell if there's anyone in it."

"Let's assume there is," Adair said decisively. "Mr. Salizar, I take it there hasn't been a Mayday recently?"

"No sir."

"Helm!" Adair ordered. "All stop."

"All stop, aye, Captain." A moment later: "Engine room answers all stop, sir."

A moment later, Adair felt the ship slow as the friction of tons of water pressed against the now unpowered vessel. "Mr. McGriff, I would like you to lead a rescue team to that raft. Use the Zodiac and be sure to take a radio." Adair limited his command to that single order. McGriff was an experienced seaman and an exceptional first officer. He would know exactly what to do. "And please work as speedily as possible. I would like to arrive at Mombasa on time."

"Aye sir." Rudy snapped, turning on his heel, and hurrying out of the control room.

■ ■ ■ ■ ■

The rescue crew consisted of McGriff and two other men: Chief Boatswain's Mate Harry Adizes and Seaman Bill Shank, both Americans. Adizes, a powerfully built man in his mid-fifties, piloted the Zodiac toward the raft. Rudy had always admired Adizes for his knowledge, skill, and, most of all, his ability to command men. One word from the chief and men hopped to action. He was gruff, impatient, and able, the men said, to intimidate paint off the bulkhead.

Seaman First Class Bill Shank was as thin as Adizes was brawny, his rail-like frame covered in ebony skin, giving him the appearance of an anorexic teenager. In fact, the thirty-year-old was stronger than he appeared and quick. He possessed a lightning mind. The three men made the best possible team for special work like a rescue. They shared a mutual respect, but more important they shared trust. Rudy knew he would not have to nursemaid these men; they would do what needed to be done, and they would do it without hesitancy.

Raising the handheld radio to his mouth, Rudy was about to ask that the *Sea Maid* turn a spotlight on the orange raft when the spotlight suddenly shone brightly. Looking over his shoulder, Rudy saw the powerful beam of the ship's light piercing the ever-encroaching darkness. Rudy shook his head. *Just once*, he thought to himself, *I would like to be a step ahead of the captain.*

The drone of the Zodiac's powerful outboard motor diminished as Chief Adizes eased off the throttle and let the momentum of the boat carry it alongside the raft. Shank reached over the edge and pulled the raft close to the boat. Inside the raft were two African men dressed in casual slacks, white deck shoes, and off-the-rack T-shirts. The men were unmoving and apparently unconscious.

"No uniforms," Adizes said. "Must be off a pleasure craft."

"Most likely," Rudy replied. "Mr. Shank, if you would please."

Shank immediately and deftly jumped from the Zodiac onto the raft. Placing two fingers over each man's carotid artery, he felt for a pulse. "They're alive, sir." Feeling along the men's arms and legs, Shank performed a quick examination. "I'm no doctor, sir, but I don't see any blood and none of their bones seem broken. I wonder how long they've been out here?"

"Not long," Rudy said. "They're clean-shaven, so they couldn't have been out here more than a day."

"Then what's wrong with them?" Shank asked.

"I don't know," Rudy said. "You got any ideas, Chief?"

The chief was leaning over the boat and holding the round raft in place with a viselike grip on the hold rope that circled the top of the float. "No sir, not a one. They're not wet though, so they didn't spend any time in the drink."

"See if you can rouse them," Rudy commanded.

Shank gently turned one of the men on his back and gently slapped him repeatedly on the cheek. "Hey, buddy, wake up. Come on, man, we're here to help." The man groaned but didn't open his eyes.

Rudy frowned. "All right, Mr. Shank, you stay in the raft. We'll tie off and tow it back. We can take better care of them aboard ship than we can bobbing out here in the dark." A moment later, the Zodiac was headed back to the *Sea Maid* with the raft and its puzzling occupants in tow.

■ ■ ■ ■ ■

"Captain?"

"Yes, Mr. Salizar, what is it."

"Mr. McGriff reports that all are aboard safely and the Zodiac is secured, sir."

"Very good." Captain Adair nodded. "Helm!"

"Helm, aye sir."

"Resume course, all ahead three-quarters."

"Aye, Captain, all ahead three-quarters." A moment later, the low rhythmic hum of the ship's engines reverberated throughout the freighter. Looking at his watch, Adair saw that only twenty-seven minutes had elapsed since the ship had stopped all engines. "It looks like we'll be right on time, gentlemen. As always, right on schedule. In the meantime, I'll see how our new arrivals are faring."

With purposeful strides the captain left the bridge, walked down the flight of stairs to the main deck, and quickly made his way to a circle of crew gathered around the two men who lay on the deck. The ring of sailors parted as the captain drew near.

"We were just about to transfer them to the crew quarters, sir," Rudy said. "I sent Mr. Shanks and Chief Adizes for stretchers."

"You said on the radio that they appear uninjured."

"Yes sir. We don't know what's wrong with them. We think that they may have been on a pleasure boat that went down. Many inexperienced sailors lose such crafts without so much as a radio cry for help."

"It still seems odd," the captain said. "Maybe they're in shock."

One of the men on the deck groaned and mumbled.

"What'd he say?" the captain asked.

Rudy leaned over the man and listened.

"Dan . . . danger . . . talk to . . . captain . . . warn him . . . captain . . . danger."

A puzzled look crossed Rudy's face. "He's asking for you, sir. Something about danger."

"Danger, is it?" The captain looked at the gathering crowd around him. "Back to your stations, men!" The group scattered like mice. "Let's see if we can learn what this danger is." Adair crouched down and put his face close to the mumbling man. "I'm Captain Adair. Can you hear me?"

"Danger, warning, captain," the man spoke in English just above a whisper.

"What danger," Adair asked leaning closer to hear.

"You . . . are . . . in . . . danger."

"From what, man?"

Suddenly the man sat straight up, stood up, and faced the captain.

"Easy there," Rudy said. "I don't think you should—"

Rudy stopped midsentence as the other man quickly stood to his feet.

"What is this?" Adair asked forcefully. "This had better not be some game."

46

"It's not," the man said as he reached down the front of his pants and pulled out a small pistol. The other man did the same. "No game at all." The man rushed the captain and shoved the gun under his chin. "Be very still, Captain, be very still, or I will scatter your brains all over the deck. Do you understand?" Adair stared at the man through steely eyes and slowly nodded. "That's wise, very wise." The man's words were heavy with accent.

When Chief Adizes and Bill Shank rounded the corner with stretchers in hand, they froze for a moment and attempted to take in the situation. Before them, the two men they had pulled from the raft were holding guns on the captain and Rudy.

"What the—" Adizes was cut off before he could swear.

"Be quiet and come here, or I'll blow a very big hole in your captain."

Adizes and Shank slowly set the stretchers down and walked toward the group. In a single motion the first man spun the captain around and placed the gun in his spine. The captain winced in pain. The second man did the same with Rudy, except he shoved his pistol in Rudy's temple hard enough to force his head to one side.

"Stand by the rail!" the man ordered. "Both of you, right now, by the rail." Adizes and Shank complied. "Move over. I want you in front of me." Again they complied.

"Listen, mister," the chief said. "I don't know what this is about, but there's no need to do anything stupid."

"You're right. You don't know what this is about, and you never will." In a single fluid motion the man brought the gun from behind the captain and aimed it at Adizes. A moment later the echo of the gun's report bounced off the bulkheads and out to sea. The second round was fired a split second later. Adizes and Shank flew backward against the white rail of the ship and then slumped to the deck dead, their uniforms marred by a circle of red emanating from their chests.

"No!" Adair cried. "You cowardly—" He swallowed his next

words when the still hot barrel of the revolver was pressed deeply into his cheek.

"You were saying?"

Adair said nothing. Rudy stared unbelievingly at the lifeless forms on the deck.

"To the bridge, now," the man shouted and shoved the captain toward the stairs. "Run, run, run." The captain took off in a trot, keenly aware that the revolver was never more than a few inches from his back. He could hear the footsteps of Rudy and his captor behind him. Moments later the four men burst onto the bridge.

"On the deck, everyone on the deck," the man cried. The bridge crew—Salizar, the helmsmen, and a cabin boy who brought in fresh coffee—turned to see the man behind the strange voice. "If I have to say it again, your captain will die." The men instantly hit the floor. "You too," the man said, shoving the captain down. "Face down and don't move."

Stepping quickly over to the communications console, the gunman turned the knob that changed the frequency of the radio and picked up the microphone. "Mukatu here. Go."

"Received," the radio crackled.

"Mukatu? Is that your name?" the captain asked.

"Those that love me call me Mukatu, and those that hate me call me sir."

"Well . . . sir," the captain said, struggling to keep the anger he felt out of his voice. "I don't know what you hope to achieve, but this ship carries only food and medicine for famine relief, and judging by your accent it may well be your people who need the help."

"I'll worry about my people; you worry about keeping your mouth shut."

"If we could talk, we could work out something."

"No," Mukatu said. "I'll talk and you'll listen. I have a task to do, and you're going to help me do it. You will do so without question, comment, or hesitancy. If you disobey me, I will kill someone. Do you understand?"

"Yes," the captain said quietly, "I just don't understand . . ."

Mukatu fired a shot.

"My leg, my leg," the cabin boy cried, "you shot my leg." Mukatu brought his revolver up again and pointed it at the boy.

"No," the captain cried, "I'm sorry. Leave him alone; he's only sixteen."

Mukatu grinned. "I said no questions, no comments, and no hesitancy. Do you understand now?" The captain nodded slowly. "Good."

A bell sounded. Mukatu stepped over to the captain's chair and picked up a phonelike handset. "Yes." There was silence on the end. "Talk to me."

"Who is this?" the disembodied voice asked.

"This is the man who is going to kill your captain if you don't start talking."

"I wanted to tell the captain something."

"If you're wanting to inform him of the cabin cruiser that is pulling alongside, you're too late," Mukatu said bitterly. "But I do have some news for you. If anyone interferes with the men coming on board, I'll shoot your captain in the head and drop him overboard. Do you understand?"

"Yes sir, I understand." The voice was now shaky, which caused Mukatu to smile.

"Good. Now run down to engineering and tell them to shut off all the engines."

"Shut them off?"

"That's right, sailor. Shut them off. I want this ship dead in the water. And one more thing. No one is to approach the bridge, unless he wants the death of the bridge crew on his hands. Do you understand that?"

"Yes sir."

Looking down at the captain of the boat, Mukatu laughed. The laugh was deep and guttural, demonic in timbre. "What a cosmopolitan group we have here today. A Panamanian-registered ship, crewed by Americans and leased by an American, sailing in African waters. Today Africa wins and you lose. You see, Captain, as you Americans say, 'It's time to rock and roll.' "

■ ■ ■ ■ ■

Four hours later, Capt. Adrian "Lucky" Adair watched as the cabin cruiser made its way into the folds of darkness. He knew what would happen next because Mukatu had taken great pleasure in telling him. In fifteen minutes the ship would be shaken by the plastic explosives attached to the inside of its hull. The Indian Ocean would then fill the drifting freighter, sucking her down into its bleak depths. The crew would sink with her, not out of some ancient mariner duty, but because Mukatu had chained all twenty of them to the starboard rail.

5

THE PHONE'S HARSH RING REBOUNDED OFF THE white walls of the penthouse on the top floor of Barringston Tower. Through bleary eyes, A.J. looked at the clock by his bed. "Two in the morning?" he said groggily and then picked up the receiver. "Yes," he croaked, "what is it?"

"Sorry to wake you, A.J.," the husky female voice said. "This is Eileen Corbin."

Eileen Corbin was head of communications. "Just a sec," A.J. said as he cleared his throat. "Let me get my bearings." He swung his feet over the side of the bed and sat up, taking a few deep breaths. "Okay, go ahead."

"I'm afraid I have bad news."

"What? What's happened?" A.J. stood up and began pacing beside the bed.

"It's the *Sea Maid*. She's missing."

"What do you mean, *missing*? How can a whole ship be missing?"

"She didn't show up in Mombasa on schedule. Search teams were dispatched to her last-known location in the Mozambique Channel. So far they've found nothing. It's believed that she may have sunk. Even the U.S. Navy has dispatched a ship."

"Sunk," A.J. said, clearly agitated. "How? Storm? Collision?"

"No storm and no collision, sir," Eileen said evenly. "There was no Mayday either."

"Is there a chance she was commandeered?"

"Unknown, but in that area anything is possible. One thing is certain: Something is very wrong. The *Sea Maid* is captained by Adrian Adair, and he's never been late to port. The man's legendary."

A.J. sighed. "You said she may have gone down."

"We don't know for sure," Eileen said. "The area has substantial ship traffic, and no ship has seen her since sundown."

"The search teams are still looking?"

"Yes sir."

"Keep me posted. I want reports as often as you can give them to me."

"Yes sir. We have a couple of small aircraft delivering food and supplies in the outlying areas of Ethiopia. Do you want me to redirect them to help in the search?"

A.J. was silent for a moment as he thought the question over. "No, they're needed where they are. Besides, I think they're too far away to be of any good."

"Okay," Eileen said, then asked, "Are you all right?"

"As best as can be expected. Thanks for asking."

"I know you take these things personally."

"Am I that transparent, Eileen?"

"On you it looks good," Eileen replied. "Try to get some sleep, sir. I think you may need it."

"I'll see what I can do. Thanks for everything, Eileen." A.J. hung up the phone and began to pace back and forth across his bedroom. His mind raced with the possibilities: ship failure, collision, modern-day pirates. There was too little information to satisfy him. For him, not knowing was worse than knowing. Somehow he felt, he knew, that something sinister had happened to the crew of the *Sea Maid*. If that was the case, then he would make the perpetrators pay for their deeds. Somehow, someway, they would pay.

■ ■ ■ ■ ■

A.J. lay awake on his bed and gazed at the ceiling. He had been unable to fall back asleep after Eileen's call, and now, in the predawn hours, his mind churned with the twin thoughts of Dr. Judith Rhodes and now the missing *Sea Maid*. The photo of Dr. Rhodes he had seen a few days ago showed her lifeless body, but what the photo could not show was her character and courage. Nor did it reveal the terror she must have felt. A.J.'s mind filled in those blanks. Those pictures were not eased by the addition of the missing ship.

There would be no more sleep for him tonight. He needed to do something. He tried reading, watching television, and pacing around the penthouse, but nothing quieted his nerves. The harder he tried to relax, the more upset he became. The muscles in his neck tensed more and more. His stomach tightened and was beginning to ache. "I've got to get out of here," he said to himself. Looking at the alarm clock on the nightstand he saw that it was now 3:30. The sun wouldn't be up for several more hours, but it didn't matter; he decided to take his morning jog early.

Physical activity had always been a stress releaser for A.J. He had been active in sports, playing volleyball and basketball for both his high school and college teams. He had excelled at both sports, for which he was ideally suited. Being tall and strong had certain advantages, but, at least for him, they brought certain demands, not the least of which was the need for regular physical expression. Each morning at dawn, he would slip into his custom-fitted running suit and put in five miles. He wasn't sure why, but he did his best thinking when he was sweating. He was happy with that connection.

Fifteen minutes later A.J. exited the elevator that had conveyed him to the ground floor from the penthouse at the top of Barringston Tower. During the descent, he had begun his warmup stretches, working each muscle group. A few more minutes in the lobby and he'd be ready to take to the now empty downtown streets.

The early morning August air was warm and felt good to A.J. as he relocked the lobby door and dropped the key into the zippered pocket of his jogging suit. Less than a minute later he was on the sidewalk in a full jog, his long legs spanning about one and a half times what a man of average height could cover. Overhead the ever-present marine layer of clouds blocked out the moon and stars. The streetlights cast their eerie yellow glow on the ground in identical circles of illumination. A.J. ran through the washes of light and the spaces of darkness that lay outside their penumbra. From light to dark to light to dark again until the alternating hues seemed to flicker like an old movie. Soon he fell into an almost hypnotic pace, hearing only his breathing and the repetitive thumping of his running shoes on the concrete. He saw little except the empty way in front of him.

He blocked out the scenery that he had seen a hundred times before, choosing to focus on the murder of Dr. Rhodes. It ate at him like an ulcer. It wasn't right for noble people to be killed while helping others. It was a heinous sin; a sin that must be avenged. A.J. was determined that atonement be made.

A.J. ran and thought, and the more he thought of Judith Rhodes and the *Sea Maid*, the angrier he became. That anger fueled his movement. He ran harder, increasing his stride with each step until he could feel every muscle in his legs strain and pull like massive elastic bands. His breathing became noisy as he forced the air from his lungs in explosive exhalation and then inhaled deeply. The noise of his footfalls echoed off the surrounding buildings and storefronts.

He focused on the missing *Sea Maid*. Surely he could do something, but what? He had a great deal of wealth, power, and influence. But his wealth couldn't provide the help he needed, and his power was equally useless. His influence, however, might be of some use. He had, over the years, carefully and judiciously supported candidates for congressional offices. He could call on a number of congressmen and senators any time of the day.

"That's it," A.J. said to the empty air as he stopped his jogging. "Of course, I should have thought of this sooner." Panting heavily he bent over, resting his arms on his legs. He had no idea how far he had run or how long he had been jogging, nor did he care, for now he knew what he had to do. It may not help, but it was something. He would call Sen. Dean Toler who headed the Armed Services Committee and ask a favor. With the continuing stress in Iraq and Iran, there must certainly be at least one navy ship in the Indian Ocean, most likely there were several. They would have rescue technology that would surpass anything else in the world. Maybe Senator Toler could twist some arms and influence the navy to send out search-and-rescue crews. If they couldn't find the *Sea Maid*, then no one could. The question was where would they find the ship? On the surface or on the bottom? The last thought sobered him.

"Nice suit, man," a heavily accented voice said behind him. A.J. turned to see three young Hispanic men approaching him. They were dressed in similar fashion, each wearing flannel shirts buttoned to the collar and baggy black pants. Their hair was cut almost to the scalp, and one wore a red bandanna. A.J. recognized the garb as that worn by a local street gang. "Looks real expensive."

A.J. said nothing as he turned to face the gang members.

"I bet a man with a suit like that must carry a lot of cash," said the one with the bandanna. "How about it, man. You got money for me?"

"No," A.J. replied firmly. "I didn't bring my wallet."

"You wouldn't be lying to us, would you? We don't like liars."

A.J. knew he should turn and run. There was no doubt that he could outdistance them in short order, but he also knew that at least one of them had a gun. Instead of running, A.J. laughed.

"What's so funny, man?" the youth asked harshly, spitting out his words. "You laughing at me?"

"Let me get this right," A.J. said. "You don't like liars. A gang of thieves, bullies, rapists, and killers are okay, but liars are beneath you."

"You know what I'm gonna do, man?" the gang member said viciously as he pulled a .38 police special from under his shirt and pointed it at A.J.'s chest. "I'm gonna shoot you in the head, steal your money, and take your fancy running suit. Do you find that funny, man?" The hood then nodded to the other two gang members, who approached A.J. and took hold of his arms.

To the gunman A.J. said, "How old are you? Twenty? Twenty-one?"

"Old enough to blow your brains all over this street."

"Maybe this question is easier for your twisted little mind to answer: Are you the leader?"

"Yeah. So?"

A.J. smiled, nodded, then with astonishing speed he swung his arms back and then upward, breaking the grip of his would-be captors. With the same fluid motion he grabbed their faces in his large hands, and with all of his well-honed strength he smashed their skulls together with a sickening thud that echoed down the street. The two men slumped to the sidewalk unconscious. Without wasting a moment, A.J. turned sideways and rushed the gunman. A.J. heard the shot fired and saw the flash from the muzzle, but his sudden move to the side kept him from being hit. Half a moment later, A.J. had the gunman's outstretched arm pinned under his own left arm with the gun pointed behind him.

With his right hand, A.J. seized the gang member by the throat and squeezed enough to cause pain, but not enough to close his trachea or pinch off the carotid arteries. A.J. wanted him conscious.

"I don't like you or hoods like you," A.J. said viciously, his eyes wide and his jaw clamped shut so that he had to force the words through his teeth. "You are leeches who live off the blood and terror of others. You tear down the good that others do. Day after day I see your kind threatening and torturing the innocent, as if you have some right to take what's not yours. For you, my friend, that ends today." The hood struggled to free himself, but A.J.'s adrenaline-aided strength was too much for him.

Anger boiled in A.J., anger that was fueled by the death of Dr. Judith Rhodes and now the loss of the *Sea Maid*. His heart beat strenuously, and adrenaline seemed to pour into his veins by the gallon. He felt strong and alive and powerful. "The only question here is, do I kill you or just maim you? Do you know what the word *maim* means, my young friend?" The man struggled to free himself, but A.J. squeezed his throat until the man's eyes widened. "It means to mutilate, cripple, and disfigure. If that's too complicated, then let me say it in a way you'll understand."

In one rapid motion, A.J. turned on the balls of his feet, placed his hip into the side of gunman, and threw him headlong to the ground where his head bounced off the concrete. The gang member dropped the gun. A.J. grabbed his victim's hand, pulled his arm up, and twisted it forcefully until his attacker groaned. "This leaves you with one arm to redeem yourself. If I see you with a weapon again, I'll use it to kill you and everyone you love." A.J. placed one foot on the man's head, forcing it to the concrete, and his other foot on the man's side so that A.J. was standing on the assailant with his full weight. With a firm grip on the gang member's arm, A.J. pulled up and twisted with all of his strength until he heard the arm come out of the socket over the attacker's screams.

Moving from gang member to gang member, A.J. searched each and removed their weapons, which he tossed down a nearby storm drain. A moment later he was jogging back to Barringston Tower, feeling refreshed and in control.

Jogging always made him feel better.

■ ■ ■ ■ ■

Fingers lightly drummed on the computer keyboard, making little clicking sounds that echoed off the hard surfaces of the computer room yet without sufficient force to depress the keys. A hand moved from its place, picked up a lit cigarette from the nearby glass ashtray, and delivered its smoldering cargo to the mouth of the user. The operator inhaled the smoke deeply and blew a long stream of smoke at the computer monitor.

"Well, nothing ventured nothing gained," the operator said aloud and returned the cigarette to the ashtray. "Be fast now, be sharp." *Click, click, clack, click.* The whine of the high-speed modem joined the muted noises of the keyboard and the hard drive's buzz. The modem, the fastest and most efficient ever made, sent its digital message from the tiny room into the phone lines and three thousand miles across the country to the secluded CIA Satellite Reconnaissance Building in Virginia. Brightly colored billboards appeared on the screen offering routings to different computer systems. Wasting no time, the operator selected the screen button marked RECON and activated it with the mouse. Another screen appeared on the video monitor: "Q" CLEARANCE REQUIRED; ENTER ACCESS AUTHORATION. In red letters were the words: ALL TRANSACTIONS ARE REPORTED TO THE DEPUTY DIRECTOR OF THE CIA. ATTEMPTING TO GAIN ACCESS TO THESE FILES WITHOUT PROPER CLEARANCE AND AUTHORITY IS A FELONY PUNISHABLE BY FINES AND IMPRISONMENT.

The operator reached to the right of the terminal and tapped in a six-digit code on a small keypad affixed to an electronic device mounted in a briefcase. Immediately, the whine of the modem intensified until it sounded like a thousand ant-sized bees buzzing in frantic frenzy. The screen blinked. The image scrambled for a moment but returned to normal. The words ACCESS GRANTED appeared.

"Yes!" the operator exclaimed. "Good work, baby."

With a series of quick actions on the keyboard and mouse clicks, a menu of files appeared. "Where are you?" the hacker asked. "I know you're there. You can't hide from . . . gotcha!"

Quickly the user activated the FILE menu and selected DOWNLOAD. Another window, smaller than the others, appeared on the monitor. A long, empty horizontal rectangle indicated how much of the file had been transferred from the CIA computer to the user's terminal—10 percent . . . 15 percent . . . 20 percent . . . "Come on, come on," the operator said. "Go, go, go." The user picked up the cigarette and inhaled deeply, then, finding no solace in the action, quickly exhaled the smoke. Each second passed slowly as the file yielded its information in tiny binary bits. The user drummed fingers on the table and unconsciously jiggled a leg in a rapid up-and-down motion—70 percent . . . 80 percent . . . 90 percent. "Almost baby, you're almost there."

Suddenly the indicator window stopped, and a moment later the screen went blank. The operator smiled, knowing that the electronic theft had been discovered but that enough of the file had been copied. A few keystrokes later the connection was broken, and the computer was turned off. Looking at the device next to the terminal, the operator's smile grew into a laugh. The laughter came from the image of CIA personnel scrambling around trying to trace the origin of the call. They would fail. The same device that disarmed the security system also sent out false information about the call's origin. Before the sun would rise, CIA and FBI agents would be scouring the small town of North Pole, Alaska, for the computer genius that who defeated their fail-safe systems, but they wouldn't find what they were looking for—indeed, they were several thousand miles off course.

■ ■ ■ ■ ■

In a Georgetown home overlooking the Potomac the phone rang at 4:30 in the morning, waking CIA director Lawrence Bauman from a sound sleep. The caller's message was calm but cryptic: "We have a compromise in SRC."

"I understand," Bauman said stoically, camouflaging his churning stomach. "I'll be there within the hour. See if you can have a report for me." He hung up the phone and quietly swore.

■ ■ ■ ■ ■

It had been four days since Roger had arrived in Mogadishu, Somalia, and it was four days longer than he cared for. Each day had plodded along with a vexing slowness. The equatorial sun would rise over the deep blue Indian Ocean and ascend to its zenith, driving the air temperature over the one-hundred-degree mark. The air conditioner in his room struggled valiantly against the oppressive heat and humidity, but it could do little more than move tepid, stale air around.

An uneasy feeling washed over him. He hated this country, and he especially hated this city. His animosity was deeply rooted in one catastrophic day in October 1993 when he walked the city streets as a U.S. Army Ranger. He had been part of a detachment to aid and protect relief workers from violence-prone warlords who had been using the famine of that year to solidify their power. He and other rangers and special forces personnel had been charged with the task of capturing the vicious warlord Mohammed Farah Aidid. Heavily armed, he and the others hot-roped out of Blackhawk helicopters hovering over the Somali's headquarters. Everything that could go wrong did. Before it was over, eighteen Americans had been killed by Aidid's followers, and seventy-six had been wounded. It should never have happened, but it had, and Roger had the wounds to prove it. Aidid had never paid for his crimes, and that fact burned in Roger's stomach every day. Roger bore as many emotional scars as he did physical. A bullet can wound a soul as well as a body.

Gazing out the window, Roger took in the city that was Mogadishu. As Somalia's largest city and busiest port, the ancient town had served as the country's capital since 1960. It had come a long way since its founding by Arab merchants in the early tenth century. Over the centuries it had grown in importance and prominence, its excellent port being leased by the Italian government, which ultimately purchased the city and made it the capital of Italian Somaliland. Yet despite its potential, its Somali National University, and its ideal location on the horn of Africa, Mogadishu had fallen into disarray. The once bustling city of 700,000 was devastated by infighting, civil war, and clan hostilities in the early 1990s. On November 17, 1991, civil war broke out, leaving 15,000 people dead and 30,000 wounded in the city alone. Now the city resembled Beirut.

As Roger scanned the buildings from his window he could see the devastation brought by civil war. As usual, it was the innocent who suffered. "The problem with this old world," Roger said to himself, "is that it's populated by people." Roger lacked the optimism that his employer, A.J., possessed in such great quantities. No, Roger was a pragmatist who considered each day a success if he survived it.

Turning from the window, he walked across the small hotel room to the bathroom and splashed cool water on his face. *At least the water is running again.* He thought he heard something. Turning the tap off, he listened intently. This time he heard it clearly, a knock on the door. Grabbing a towel, Roger patted his face dry as he walked to the door and opened it.

"I was hoping it was you," Roger said as he stepped aside to let his guest in. "I'm going crazy here. What took you so long?"

"Somalia is not an easy place to move around these days," Mohammed Aden replied. "Only 15 percent of my country's roads are paved. That and the fear of being killed by rogue clan members make travel unpleasant." Aden, like many Somalis, was relatively short. His hair was cut close to the scalp, and he had a pleasant way about him. Fluent in English, the former professor at the Somali National University in Mogadishu was an important cog in the Barringston Relief work in Somalia. He was a bright man who worked with both the local and the nearly nonexistent national government to expedite food shipment. In many ways he was a diplomat who walked the narrow path of negotiation. He was a vital source of information on Somali activities that might affect relief efforts. He had more than once been accused of being a spy for the CIA, and he had more than once been just that.

"Since you're smiling, I assume you have had some success."

"I have," Aden admitted. "But we will need to travel, so pack your bags."

"We won't be coming back?" Roger asked suspiciously.

"Probably, but take your things anyway. You don't want them stolen, do you?"

"They won't be safe here?" Roger asked with a hint of sarcasm.

"Nothing is safe in Somalia," Aden replied coldly. "We will be traveling to the north via airplane, but we won't be going to the airport. An acquaintance of mine has a small private plane near here. He will fly us to Bohotleh Wein in the north."

"This friend is trustworthy?"

"As trustworthy as anyone can be during these times," Aden said. "You're paying him enough to be loyal. He flies anyone who can pay him, and he knows how to keep his mouth shut. We will take a car to Johar which is two hours north of here, then we will wait with my friend until well after dark. After that we fly to Bohotleh."

"Bohotleh?"

"It's a small town on the northeastern border of Ethiopia. One of your relief camps is nearby, so you can visit it if you want." Aden pointed at the small leather suitcase and briefcase near the wall next to the window and said, "We shouldn't waste any time. The drive could take longer than I planned."

"I sure hope you know what you're doing," Roger said.

"Knowing is the only way to survive in Somalia," Aden replied seriously.

Ten minutes later they were in a vintage Toyota Land Rover, bouncing over damaged pavement and dirt roads. Dust and heat poured in through the open windows. When Roger first entered the vehicle he instinctively reached for the seat belts; there were none. Aden caught the habitual act and smiled. "Seat belts are good in an automobile accident, but they slow you down if you must run for your life. Besides, the belt would only leave you bruised after the drive we are taking."

"Swell," was all Roger said.

The drive to Johar was easier than Roger thought it might be, but it did have short spans where the road had deteriorated to a series of oddly shaped potholes of various depths. Aden managed to steer around the worst of them, but he hit a few with sufficient force that smacked Roger's head on the ceiling and passenger door, causing him to spew a string of obscenities. Aden took it all stoically.

Two hours fifteen minutes and one flat tire later they arrived at their destination, an old barnlike structure on the outskirts of Johar. They were greeted by a tall, lanky Somali who shook hands with Aden first and then Roger. Aden and the man spoke in Somali for a moment, then Aden turned to Roger. "This is our host and pilot, Mohammed Arteh."

"Another Mohammed," Roger said, smiling at the somber-looking Somali.

Aden shrugged, "It is a popular name in an Islamic country. Come, I'll show you the plane." Aden walked toward the dilapidated barn and pushed back a large sliding door that groaned each inch of the way. In the barn was an old six-seat Cessna. That was all Roger could tell about the plane. Oil streaks stained the area around the engine cowling, and rust was visible on the wings and the body. Roger frowned.

"It will fly," Arteh said, noticing the look of consternation on Roger's face.

"You speak English," Roger said, a little embarrassed at his display of dissatisfaction.

"Yes," was all the pilot said.

"It looks like your bird here has been around the block a few times," Roger commented as he slowly inspected the craft. Not receiving a response, he looked at Arteh, whose face displayed a puzzled look. Roger realized that his colloquialisms confused the two Somalis. "Your plane, you've flown it a lot."

"Yes, many years," Arteh said, nodding. "It is a good plane. It will fly you to Bohotleh Wein."

Roger wasn't so sure, but it made no sense to offend his host and his only source of transportation. "I'm sure it will," he lied. "When do we leave?"

"We must wait until the moon is high," Arteh answered. "We will arrive at dawn. Landing in the dark is not good."

Roger chuckled nervously and looked at the ancient aircraft. "I don't imagine that it is."

It took just under five hours for the Cessna to cross the central desert region and approach the mountainous lands of the north. Wanting to make the best possible time to maintain the cover of darkness, Arteh crossed the Ogaden region of Ethiopia—a dangerous course. Roger felt fortunate that their trip went unchallenged by gunfire, something he attributed to Arteh's insistence that they fly under cover of darkness.

Now darkness was giving way to the rising August sun as it steadily scaled the sky over the Indian Ocean and cast long shadows from the mountains. Bohotleh Wein lay one thousand feet below them. Arteh circled the small and impoverished town looking for a place to land. Aden pointed out the pilot's window and said something in Somali. Arteh grunted and banked the plane in the direction indicated by Aden, all the while descending with stomach-churning speed.

"I've been meaning to ask you something, Arteh," Roger said as he leaned back in his seat in a futile gesture to reduce the precipitous descent angle chosen by the bush pilot. "Who taught you to fly?"

"I taught myself," he replied matter-of-factly. "Why?"

Roger looked at the rapidly approaching ground. "No reason, just curious." He swallowed hard.

At about two hundred feet, Arteh pulled back on the yoke and eased the creaking Cessna into an easy glide path. He had found what Aden had been pointing at: a small cluster of unpainted wood buildings about two miles from the heart of Bohotleh Wein that had a flat piece of ground that looked suitable for landing.

"That looks pretty smooth," Roger said, eager to be back on the ground.

"Maybe," replied Arteh.

"Maybe?"

"If there're no holes, soft spots, rocks, or animals in the way, we'll be fine."

"And if there is a hole, soft spot, rock, or animal, then what?" Roger asked. Arteh just shrugged and continued his descent.

The plane touched down and bounced back into the air. Seconds later it touched down again, this time rebounding only a few feet. The next time the wheels made contact they rolled freely along the hard earth surface. Arteh quickly stepped on the brake pedals, slowing the craft to a suitable taxiing speed. Turning the plane around, he taxied back to the buildings and switched off the engine, which coughed harshly and ejected thick oily smoke.

Roger took a deep breath and looked at the intrepid pilot. For the first time since meeting the enigmatic man he saw Arteh smile as he said, "Thanks for flying Air Somalia."

6

"AH, THE DEDICATED WORKER." DAVID LOOKED UP from the briefing he was reading and saw Kristen standing in the doorway to his office. "Hard at work, and you've only been here a week."

"It's an old trick really," David replied with a smile. "Simply spread out a few papers on the desk, rub your eyes until they're red, move a little more slowly than normal, and everyone will think you've been burning the midnight oil."

"What? Trickery from a man of your caliber?" Kristen returned the grin. "Somehow I don't think you're faking it."

"See, it works," David said. He was glad for the distraction. "Come in and have a seat."

"I'm not interrupting, am I?" Her voice was sweet and melodious, yet filled with confidence. David watched as she stepped into the office and made her way to a chair opposite his desk.

"Actually, I could use a break. How have you been?"

"I'm well, thank you, but like you I'm buried in work," she said looking at the papers strewn across his desk. "What are you working on?"

"A.J. has asked that I prepare a speech for the Washington Press Club and one for a fund-raiser here in San Diego. They're the first ones I'll have written for him, and I want them to be right."

"The press club is an important speech," Kristen said leaning back in her chair. "He speaks there about once a year. Sort of a standing engagement. He briefs the reporters and news executives on the hot spots of the world and hopes that it'll inspire them to keep the issue before the public."

"I've read the last two speeches," David said, pushing his chair back from the desk, "and that's the approach he's used each time. I think we can do better."

"Oh?"

"Sure. These reporters are some of the best. They can get whatever information they want. They need more than an update on world conditions, and they certainly need more than a reminder of how bad things are. They write about danger, evil, and the worst that life can deliver. I think we need to punch their buttons another way."

Kristen stared at David for moment and then said, "I wrote those speeches."

David returned her gaze and wondered how clearly his embarrassment showed. "I didn't mean to say the speeches were bad, I just meant . . ."

"Don't apologize," Kristen said laughing. "I'm no speechwriter, and I know it. Press releases, I understand, but speechwriting is beyond me. If the truth be told, I hated writing those things. In fact, I'm the one who pushed for a professional writer. It seems I was right."

"I really wasn't meaning to belittle your work; they are fine speeches." David felt the warmth of embarrassment touch his cheeks. "I tend to get a little overenthusiastic about these things."

"That's good. Enthusiasm is what we need. So what approach do you think the speech needs to take?"

David shook his head. "I'm not sure yet. It needs a strong emotional angle that the audience won't expect, but I don't know what that is."

"I'm sure it will come to you."

"It will, and when it does, I'll recognize it."

"How are you fitting in otherwise," Kristen asked.

"Fine. The hard part is the learning curve. I've been trying to get a feel for all the work that Barringston Relief does, but there's so much of it I feel a little overwhelmed. The statistics alone are intimidating, as are all the different countries where the work goes on. I don't know how you keep up."

"I've been at it longer. As time passes you'll get a better grasp on it all."

"I hope so. I really want to do a good job."

"Well, you've impressed A.J.," Kristen said, shifting her weight in the chair.

"I haven't done anything yet."

"Sure you have. You spoke the truth to him."

"Truth?"

"He told me about his visit with you the other day. He said you were candid with him, and he appreciated that."

"That's good. I was worried that I had offended him. Like I said, I tend to get excited about these things."

"You not only didn't offend A.J., you dazzled him. He said you saw things he would never have noticed, but more importantly, you corrected him. A.J. likes that sort of thing. He hates yes-men who only tell him what they think he wants to hear. Shoot straight with him, and you'll have a friend forever. He likes you, David, and thanked me for pushing for a speechwriter."

"That's a relief. I like him too. I've never met anyone like him, so filled with passion and devotion to others. He seems to be quite a man."

"You don't know the half of it," Kristen replied. "Wait until you see him in action. You'll have to run to keep up with him." She paused for a moment and contemplated the red polish on her fingernails. David noticed that the nail polish matched her hair almost exactly. "He's a hero, David. I hope you can help the world see that."

David said nothing but nodded his head. He watched Kristen closely. Was she in love with A.J. or simply an ardent admirer? In either case, she was right: A.J. Barringston was a hero, something the world needed.

"Well," she said, rising from the chair. "I just wanted you to know how pleased A.J. was with your meeting."

"I appreciate your coming by," David said as he, too, rose from his chair.

"You know," Kristen stated, "you do look tired. How about a break? Do you like European coffee?"

"Cappuccino, latte, that sort of thing?"

"Exactly."

"I love them. What do you have in mind?"

"Well, since you've been thrown into the fray of things and haven't been properly welcomed, I thought I'd take you out for a midafternoon coffee and maybe a sandwich."

David beamed. "I'm in."

"Great. I'll meet you at the elevators in fifteen minutes, and we'll go to Horton Plaza. I know a great coffee shop there."

"Fifteen minutes it is," David replied, rounding the desk to walk her to the door.

■ ■ ■ ■ ■

Roger strolled around the area where they had parked the Cessna. It seemed peaceful enough, making it hard to believe tens of thousands of Somalis had been killed or wounded in clan fighting, and most of those were innocent bystanders and children. Now as the sun slowly rose along its course, he could see the simple, austere but majestic landscape. In the distance he could hear the calls of animals. He knew that the land had everything from crocodiles to giraffes. It would be an interesting land to investigate; unfortunately this wasn't a safe land, despite what the peaceful early morning might imply. The simple truth was that a few thousand people would die today, and a few thousand more tomorrow, and there wasn't anything he, Barringston Relief, the UN, or anyone else could do about it. Well, not all of it anyway. There was something that could be done about one of the problems, the madman Mahli. Roger wanted to be the one to handle that particular problem.

Roger turned back to the plane and said, "Let's go." Wordlessly, Aden exited the plane, and the two began walking toward the small village. Arteh chose to stay with the Cessna.

Unlike the grass-domed huts that were popular throughout much of East Africa, this community was composed of a few dozen wood structures. People and a few goats were beginning to mill around. Women with pails and jugs made their way to a nearby well to gather what water they could. Men sat on the front doorsteps or talked to each other. Everyone stopped to watch as one black man and one white man walked away from the dirty little plane and toward their small community. Roger could read the suspicion in their eyes. In this land of turmoil, everyone and everything was suspicious.

While most Somalis were nomadic or lived in urban areas like Mogadishu, Marka, or Hobyo, a few farmed the arid yet fertile land in the river valleys of the Juba or Webi Shabelle. In good years they could grow sugarcane, sorghum, corn, bananas, and sesame seed. In drought years, especially those years when the clan civil war was excessive, the farmers made barely enough to survive. Aden had told Roger that this village was one of the few that were managing in the drought. They had no surplus, but they were able to grow enough produce to sell or trade for food and supplies. They were neither rich nor safe, but they were better off than any suburban or rural Somali had been in the last two years.

"This way," Aden said as they strode toward the small wood house closest to a parked truck. As they approached the building, the door opened and a woman with piercing eyes clothed in a dark brown wraparound dress stood in the doorway. Aden stepped to the door but said nothing. A second later the woman stepped aside and he entered the house with Roger close behind. Once they were inside, the woman closed the door. The house was one large room with a table and four chairs in the middle, a wood-burning stove and stack of firewood on one end, and sleeping mats on the other. It had no lights and apparently no bathroom. The early morning air was thick and fetid.

"Aden, you have returned just as you said you would," a raspy voice said in thickly accented English. Roger saw that the voice came from a lone man seated at the table. "This is the curious American?"

"Yes," Aden said. "He is eager to speak to you."

The man laughed. He looked old, and he wheezed as he breathed. Roger realized that the man looked older than he was. Most people in Somalia died before they reached their mid-fifties, and those who lived that long often looked as though they had lived much longer. "He's eager to know what I know. Is he willing to pay?"

"I am," Roger answered before Aden could speak. "If your information is good."

"It is true I can tell you where to find Mahli, but I don't know why you would want to do that. If you get too close, he will have you killed. Perhaps he will kill you himself."

"How do you know where he is?" Roger asked bluntly.

"I worked for him for two years. I had great responsibility." The man began to cough a harsh and grating hack.

It was clear to Roger that the man had a severe respiratory problem. Pneumonia? Cancer? He decided it didn't matter. "What's your name?" Roger inquired.

The man shook his head, "My name doesn't matter. What I know, that is what matters. That and what you can pay. I want ten thousand dollars American."

"You don't want Somali shillings?"

The man laughed. "No, I want American money. British pounds would be acceptable."

"That's a large sum of money," Roger replied incredulously. "What would you do with such a large sum of money?"

"Leave Somalia."

"Leave?"

"I need medical help, and our hospitals are now useless. And once Mahli finds out I've told you where he is, he will have me and my wife killed. After he kills you, of course."

"What makes you think he can kill me?" Roger said pointedly. "There's a lot about me you don't know."

"There's a lot about Mahli you don't know. He will kill you, and I will have my money. If he doesn't kill you, then Mukatu will."

"Mukatu?"

"See, there is much about Mahli you do not know." The man coughed loudly and roughly. "You Americans are stupid. You think you know everything. You know nothing. That's why Aidid embarrassed your mighty UN."

Roger felt his anger rise exponentially and wondered if it showed. "Ten thousand is still a lot of money."

"Eleven thousand," the man said calmly. "Agree or leave; it's time for my breakfast."

Roger was nonplussed, "You said ten thousand . . ."

"Twelve thousand," the man replied. "I do not wish to barter."

Lowering his head, Roger bit his lower lip as he struggled to contain his anger. After a moment's thought he said slowly, "I will pay you the ten thousand, but since I do not carry that much money with me I will need to make arrangements. Tell me where Mahli is, and I will see that you get your money."

The man exploded in laughter and continued laughing until he began coughing again. Once the respiratory spasm ceased, he said something in Somali to his wife. Roger turned to see that she had been laughing too. The woman took a few steps toward the door and opened it in a clear gesture that said time to leave. Roger walked slowly toward the door, his rage boiling inside of him. *This should not be this difficult*, he thought.

"We have come a long way," Aden said. "Surely we can come to some agreement." The man shook his head and motioned toward the open door.

When Roger arrived at the door, he looked at the age-creased face of the woman who was still smiling. Roger returned a sneer for her smile, placed his hand on the door, and shut it. He turned to face the man at the table.

"I thought you would see it my way," the man said, "but now it's fifteen thousand American dollars."

In slow deliberate steps, Roger approached the man, who placed his hands behind his head and leaned back in his chair showing every ounce of confidence he felt.

"Fifteen thousand?" Roger said. He stepped beside the seated man as he rocked his chair on its two rear legs. In a swift motion, Roger kicked the legs of the chair, sending the man crashing to the floor. He seized the front of the man's shirt with both of his hands, and in an almost effortless move lifted the stunned African from the floor, spun him around, and threw him onto the tabletop, pinning him.

"What are you doing—" the man started to ask, but his words were cut off when Roger seized his throat with his right hand.

"Shut up!" Roger yelled. Reaching into his pocket, he pulled out a stiletto which, at the touch of a button, unsheathed a six-inch blade. Roger placed the point of the knife in the man's right ear and pressed gently until the man squirmed. "I have spent too much time in your little backwoods country sweating under your sun and being eaten by your bugs. My patience is exhausted—gone! So now I'm going to tell you how this is going to work."

"Roger," Aden began, "I'm not sure this is a good—"

"Shut up!" Roger shouted again. As he did so, he caught movement in the corner of his eye. Snapping his head up he saw the man's wife approaching with a log from the woodpile. Roger glared at her through eyes that carried more meaning than any words—"One step more, and you'll be burying your husband tonight." The woman saw the message in Roger's eyes and stopped cold. Slowly she lowered the log and backed up until she made contact with the

73

wall. Quickly surveying the room, Roger saw Aden, mouth open in shock, watching dumbfounded at the sudden violence.

Roger turned his attention back to the prostrate man he had pinned to the table. "As I was saying," Roger uttered through clinched teeth, "my patience is gone. You will tell me what I need to know or I'll push this knife clear through your skull. Do you understand what I'm saying?" The man gave the best nod he could. "Where is Mahli?"

"Marka," the man croaked as Roger loosened his grip so that he could speak. Roger listened intently as the details of Mahli's whereabouts unfolded from the sickly man's lips. Still pinning the man to the table, Roger made him repeat the information, memorizing each point. Ten minutes later the duo left the wooden hut armed with the information they had sought.

Roger had stopped in the doorway and looked back at the frightened man who held his slightly bleeding ear. He felt a small sense of remorse for his actions, but mostly he felt anger at himself. He had lost control, and that was dangerous. He could have cost himself his mission.

"Ten thousand dollars," Roger said grimly, "that's what we agreed on, and that's what you'll receive. The money will arrive this week and will be brought to you—unless Mahli gets word of our little conversation, in which case I'll be back to visit, and I will be in a real bad mood. Do you understand?"

The man nodded gravely.

"Good."

■ ■ ■ ■ ■

Even in lunchtime traffic it took less than ten minutes for Kristen and David to drive from Barringston Tower to the multilevel, upscale shopping mall known as Horton Plaza. This was due in part to the close proximity of the two places and in part to Kristen's energetic driving style. Aggressively she maneuvered her late-model cherry-red Mazda Miata through the congested urban streets of downtown San Diego. She showed no hesitancy as she darted from one lane to the next, putting the little sports car through its paces. "I hope my driving doesn't bother you," she said impishly. "My mother hates to ride with me."

"God is my copilot," David answered, not wanting to reveal his growing sense of apprehension.

"I thought it was crowded in here."

It took a moment for David to catch the joke. "I'm not too nervous. After all, I didn't see any dents in the car."

"I have great insurance." Kristen pulled into a parking stall on the first level of the concrete parking structure. "Our lucky day," she said. "Usually we have to hunt for a space."

From the dark parking area the two moved into the open plaza of shops and restaurants. The sky overhead was bright blue; the cloud layer that California weathermen called "the marine layer" had been burned off by the warm summer sun. A cool breeze from the nearby bay blew along the walkway. Walking along the shops, they stopped at a bookstore to see the latest soon-to-be summer best-sellers and toured a store that specialized in science-related toys, books, and gifts.

As they strolled, David noticed how much more animated Kristen was than the first time he had met her. But the circumstances were different. Then they were total strangers, and while they knew very little about each other now, they were fellow workers—they now had common ground. David remembered the other reason for Kristen's reserved and somber attitude when they had first met: She had recently learned that Dr. Judith Rhodes had been brutally murdered in Somalia. As the public-relations officer, it was her job to deal with calls from the media. Now a week later, some of the strain had dissolved, allowing her personality to shine.

Near the center of the mall they came to their destination, a small coffee-and-sandwich shop. David ordered a turkey on rye with an iced cappuccino, Kristen a blueberry muffin and a mocha.

Finding a table outside the shop, they sat under the warm sun, watched the meandering shoppers, and ate their lunch.

"Tell me more about A.J.," David said as he sipped his coffee.

"What do you want to know?" Kristen dabbed at her mouth with a napkin. The sun glinted brightly off her dark red hair and illuminated her deep blue eyes.

"Anything that will help me do my job. He certainly seems unique—and I mean that in a good way."

"He is unique. I've never met anyone like him before. He is the most dedicated man I know."

"*Passionate* is the word that comes to my mind."

Kristen nodded. "He is that and more. He's a big man, and I don't mean his height. He's big in heart and in vision. The entire Barringston Relief organization originated with him. There's no other organization like it. Oh, there are other charitable groups, and many of them do a wonderful job, but A.J.'s vision included more than giving out food and building orphanages—all of which we do. He wanted to do something about the root of world hunger."

"The root of world hunger?" David thought for a moment. "If I understood the briefing tapes I've been reviewing, most famine areas suffer from political problems."

"That's right. While weather, deforestation, poor farming practices, and similar factors affect hunger and may even initiate famine, political problems prevent adequate help. If the problem were only nature, our job would be infinitely easier. We, along with other organizations and nations, can deliver enough food, water, and medicine to a stricken area. What we have trouble with are bandits and demented political leaders."

"How can A.J. change any of that?"

"It's not easy, and I don't pretend to understand it all, but he has made some headway. He travels to Washington several times a year to lobby congressional leaders. He's also developed quite a reputation as a humanitarian around the world and has befriended the leaders of many countries."

"It sounds like you know a great deal."

"Not really," Kristen said with a shrug. "What little I know comes from writing press releases."

David nodded and took another drink of his cappuccino. "You seem impressed with A.J."

"He is impressive, and I don't know of anyone who's met him who wasn't impressed."

"Well," David said, "he has sure made his mark with me. It's always a pleasure to meet someone who has strong beliefs and a clear vision. Our world could use many more A.J. Barringstons."

"Here, here," Kristen said lifting her cup in the air with mock formality. "To A.J. Barringston and those like him." David joined in the gesture, raising his cup and tapping it against Kristen's. The cups yielded no sound, so David uttered a single "Clink."

"Enough about A.J.," Kristen said. "What about you?"

"Me?" David replied. "What about me?"

"I'm not after any deep dark details," Kristen said. "But I would like to know more about you."

"Like what?"

"I already know the basics: your education, ministry, and that kind of stuff—"

"Oh?" David interrupted. "And how did you become privy to such information?"

"I wrote a press release about you for the local business papers. You know, the column about executives who have been promoted, moved, and hired. I sent a copy to you. Didn't you get it?"

"Possibly," David said with chagrin. "There are some papers I haven't looked at yet. It's hard to believe: One week on the job and I'm already behind."

"If you don't find it, let me know; I'll get you a copy." After a moment, she asked, "Do you miss it? Your church, I mean."

David stiffened a little and stared into his coffee cup.

"Did I say something wrong?" Kristen asked with concern. "I wasn't trying to pry; I really wasn't."

"No, you didn't say anything wrong," David replied quietly. "It's a hard question to answer. It shouldn't be, I suppose, but it is." He paused for a few moments before he spoke again. "Pastoring a church is a mixed bag. It was the easiest thing I ever did, and at the same time the most difficult. Some weeks there was more to do than could be done, and other weeks I would wonder if I earned my salary. It's been more than six months since I left the church, and I still don't quite know how I feel. I should, but I don't."

"Six months isn't all that long," Kristen said. "Time will give everything perspective."

"I do miss some of the people. I had some good friends in that church."

"Had?" Kristen said with surprise. "Are they not your friends anymore?"

"I haven't really thought about it."

Kristen leaned over the metal table. "When was the last time you talked to one of your friends?"

"Not since I left the church. I've been too embarrassed to face them since my wife left."

"Why should you feel embarrassed? If they're your friends, they'll stand by you. If they don't, they don't deserve your friendship. It's not like you have the plague. This sort of thing happens all the time. You know as well as I do that nearly 60 percent of all marriages fail. Why should you be immune?"

"Lots of reasons," David said shaking his head. "It's different for ministers. People have expectations. The work we do requires credibility without blemish."

This time Kristen shook her head. When she spoke, she spoke softly. "David, bad things happen to the best of people. That doesn't mean the person is bad, it simply means that you have passed through what others have. It means you are a human and you married a human. And one of them did a very human thing. It doesn't make it right or appropriate, just human."

David sat silently.

"I know I'm out of line here," Kristen continued, "but I see a lot of good in you and a lot of value. I've only known you for a short while, but everyone I talk to—Ava, A.J., Peter—thinks that you have a lot to offer. I agree, but I think you need to get on with the future. And that doesn't mean cutting your past friends off. Didn't they turn to you when they needed a friend?"

David nodded, "Yes, I guess they did."

"So turn to them now. I bet you'll find they're happy to hear from you."

"I'll think about it," David said.

"Isn't that what being part of a church is all about? Worshiping God and supporting fellow Christians?"

"Yes, among other things. It sounds like you speak from experience."

"I do. My church has been a big help to me. It's faith that keeps us centered, isn't it? One of the reasons I left my job at the PR firm in L.A. is the work Barringston Relief does. My old employer offered me a hefty raise to stay, but I needed to invest myself in the lives of others. I'm incomplete otherwise. I'll bet the same is true of you. Christianity doesn't make our lives easy, it makes them purposeful. Don't you agree?"

"Yes, I do."

"I don't mean to preach to the preacher, and I'm sorry if I've butted in where I'm not welcome. That certainly wasn't my intent. But you're a classy person, Dr. David O'Neal, and classy people shouldn't stew in their own emotions."

"Classy person?" David replied. "What should a classy person do then?"

"Buy a classy redhead another mocha."

"Hmm," David said scratching his chin. "If only I could find . . ."

"Don't say it!" Kristen exclaimed with a grin. "Or I'll make you walk back to the office."

"Hmm," David said again and rubbed his chin all the more.

"Hey!" she said. "I think I resent that insinuation." The two laughed.

7

"DON'T YOU EVER CLOSE YOUR DOOR?" A.J. ASKED jovially. "If you leave it open like this, anyone can walk in."

"A.J." David said enthusiastically. "Come in, come in." David stood and shook hands with his boss. "Leaving the door open is an old pastor's tradition."

"Wait a minute," A.J. said. "Do you mean a tradition for old pastors, or an old tradition for pastors?"

David laughed. "The latter, I think. When I first went into the ministry, I worked on staff in a large church. The pastor insisted that we keep our doors open so the parishioners would feel welcome and know we weren't sleeping. I've been leaving my office door open ever since."

"Nice sentiment," A.J. said as he took a seat opposite David's desk. "It doesn't appear to have hurt your work. These outlines for the press club and fund-raiser are outstanding. I especially like the front-line hero aspect."

"I was hoping you would. I feel confident that the press will see a new angle on this if they can focus on those who are in the field, doing the work. They're heroes and should be referred to as such."

"It will be difficult for me to talk about Dr. Rhodes," A.J. said somberly. "Every time I think about her death I get both angry and sad."

"That's the whole idea," David replied. "Speaking of her will help unleash that passion in you that we spoke of. Those are the emotions that you should feel. They're honest, sincere, and moving. Share them with your audience, and they'll listen."

"You're right," A.J. agreed.

"One thing I'm certain of is you. You have the ability to be an excellent speaker. You have presence, you have a worthwhile cause, and you have the best information. There's no doubt that with a little coaching you will rivet the audience's attention to your message and involve them in the cause. Let that passion show through. Let them see the anger, hurt, even the tears. But also let them see the hope and the vision you own. Let them hear your heart and see your soul."

"You must have been quite a preacher," A.J. said. "You're very convincing. You could have made a lot of money in sales."

"Thanks, but sales isn't my cup of tea," David said, reaching for the outline. "All I need to do now is polish this and make sure my facts are correct."

"They seem correct to me," A.J. said, surrendering the notes. "You know, David, I'm amazed at how quickly you're adjusting to all of this. Not everyone can deal with the ugliness of world hunger, but you seem to have taken right to it."

"It's a satisfying feeling knowing that I'm involved in something worthwhile," David replied. "But if there's anyone who should be admired it's you. I'm amazed at what you've built here and the work you do."

"It's not just me," A.J. said humbly. "I was lucky enough to have something to start with and good people to help. Barringston Relief is bigger than any one man."

David paused before speaking. "If you don't mind my asking, just how did you get involved in all of this?"

"I don't mind at all," A.J. replied leaning back in the chair. "It's a long story. Let's see if I can give you the *Reader's Digest* version."

"That would be great, if I'm not being nosy."

"Not at all. As you know, I'm wealthy. Well, more accurately, my father is wealthy. You'll have to meet him. he's one of a kind."

David wondered if Archibald Barrington could be any more extraordinary than his son. "He made his money in the construction business. He started building homes with his father after World War II. You can still see some of them in Linda Vista. They were small, inexpensive, and designed for military families. During those days San Diego was a big navy town. Still is somewhat, but then just about everyone was associated with the navy at Point Loma, the Thirty-second Street training area, and later at Miramar Naval Air Station. He struggled at first, but through hard work, perseverance, and an unusual ability to finish his contracts on time and under budget, he forged a reputation with the military community. Soon he was building subdivisions in other military towns. But he knew that kind of work wouldn't last forever and that he would need to branch out. My father's that way. There are times when I would swear that he could see the future.

"Anyway," A.J. continued, "when my father was thirty-one, his dad, my grandfather, died, leaving the construction business to him. It wasn't long after that that he began doing commercial construction. He started off with small offices and shopping centers, and once he learned the ropes and obtained sufficient backing he began doing larger work. He's built no less that ten of the high-rises in downtown San Diego and has done hundreds all over the world. That's where his genius lay. He saw the opportunities overseas. Soon he was building skyscrapers, office buildings, hotels, and the like in Iran, before the fall of the Shah, and in India, Saudi Arabia, and Pakistan as well as Western countries like England and France. I couldn't name all the countries that have a Barringston building in them. By the seventies, Dad had built an international company that was sought after worldwide. He also built quite a fortune."

"Did you work for him when you were growing up?" David asked.

"For a while, but I was rebellious. I had little interest in business or construction." A.J. chortled. "I still can't drive a nail into a two-by-four without bending it."

"Wait a minute," David interrupted. "Does that mean you bent the two-by-four or the nail?"

A.J. laughed out loud, "Touché, David, touché. I meant the nail. My construction skills were hindered by profound lack of interest. The only things I excelled in were spending money and having fun. I went to the best schools, Harvard and even the London School of Economics. I did well, but I didn't especially enjoy it. Unlike my brother, I was a wayward son."

"I didn't know you had a brother," David said. He realized that he hadn't known A.J. long enough to know much of anything about him.

"He's gone now," A.J. replied. "Died from a blood clot. He had been driving supplies for dad and had been spending a lot of time sitting in trucks. The doctors told us that a blood clot had formed in one of his legs and traveled to his heart. He was only eighteen months younger than me."

"I'm sorry. Were you close?"

"More than most brothers, I suppose. We were different in many ways, but we always had a good relationship. It undid me when he died. I dropped out of the London School of Economics and began to live the high life, spending a trust my father had set aside for me. It was an empty experience except for Cyn."

"Sin?" David asked, puzzled.

"Cynthia," A.J. said, chuckling at the misunderstanding. "I always called her Cyn. We met in London while I was in school. She was tall like me and athletic." David watched A.J.'s focus shift to the image in his memory. "She was beautiful, the most beautiful woman I had ever seen. She had long platinum hair that hung past her shoulders, green eyes so deep you could swim in them. And she had passion, the very kind of passion you've been talking about, David. She loved life, but she took it so seriously. We married while in school. When I dropped out, I forced her to leave too. She came from a banking family and had some wealth of her own. We spent my money and her money."

A.J. paused as he recalled the details. "We moved to Monaco for its nightlife and gambling—well, that's why *I* moved to Monaco. Cyn went because she was my wife. I thought it would be ideal. How many people can lead a life like that? But Cyn couldn't adjust. She needed purpose in her life, a reason for living. She begged to go back to school, but I was too self-absorbed to care. Our marriage deteriorated daily until there was nothing left. We argued constantly. I told her to loosen up and crawl off her pedestal, and she reminded me how I was failing to do anything responsible with my life. It went from bad to worse. I started having affairs, and she left me."

David made no comment.

"It's strange," A.J. said after a moment of clearly painful thought. "It amazes me how much good can come out of a bad situation. Even in the midst of hunger and disease, special people arise and relationships begin. That's what happened to me. After Cyn left me, I continued my party lifestyle, but it could no longer hold my interest. I was angry at the loss of my brother and the loss of my wife. I was angry with my overbearing father, who, I felt, could still control me across an ocean. So I talked a couple of friends into traveling with me. 'It'll be great,' I said. 'Just three buddies traveling the world.' That's what we did. Europe, Asia, South America, the Caribbean. I learned to love travel as a child when my father took me on trips with him. I loved it because it got me out of school, but I soon learned to love the travel itself. I've always found it therapeutic."

"Was it?" David asked quietly.

"No," A.J. replied sadly. "Not at all. The more I traveled, the lonelier I became. Cyn was right: I had no purpose for living. Living for myself was . . . inadequate. That's when it happened. One of my traveling companions had a brother in the military—air force or maybe marines, I don't really recall—and he wanted to visit him where he was stationed in the Philippines. So we went. While we were there his brother gave us a tour of the area. Seeing the brothers together made me feel worse, but there was nothing I could do about it except sink deeper into my despair. During the tour he said he'd show us the good parts of the Philippines. I asked if there were bad parts. 'Oh, yes,' he said, 'there are places you don't want to go.' 'Like what?' I asked. He told of a place called Smoky Mountain, a place of pure poverty. I was young and impetuous and convinced my friends to go there with me. We went the next day."

A.J. stopped abruptly and closed his eyes. "It was . . . life changing," he said slowly. "We convinced a cab driver to take us. He must have argued with us for fifteen minutes telling us that Americans like us shouldn't go there. 'You not like,' he kept repeating, but with a promise of a big tip he gave in. When we arrived he refused to get out of the car and pulled a handkerchief from his pocket and put it over his nose and mouth. Then he reached in the glove compartment and pulled out a small bottle of perfume and began spraying it in the cab. My friends and I got out and walked toward the mountain."

"Is it a tall mountain?" David asked innocently.

A.J. shook his head no. "It's not a mountain at all; it's a massive pile of trash—large enough for people to live on. It is, David, one of the most pitiful places I have ever seen. People, whole families, live on this gigantic mound of garbage. The trash dump is their world, and they spend their days looking through other people's discards in hope of finding food that's not too rotten to eat and bits of clothing to wear. Children run after the trash trucks and pick through the new piles of garbage, collecting things like paper and holding them as though they were valuable. A little girl was there. She wore no clothes and couldn't have been more than four or five. Her hair was matted and filthy; her little brown body was covered with dirt. I watched as she picked through the refuse, found a bit of apple, and ate it. She didn't even wipe it off, just put it in her mouth. A rat emerged from the trash next to her and bit her foot. I expected her to start wailing but she didn't even cry; she just swung her little arm at the filthy rodent. It was an everyday occurrence to her."

Tears brimmed in A.J.'s eyes. He no longer looked off into the distance but down at his folded hands. David said nothing, having no words. He watched the turmoil in A.J.'s life ooze from his being. Here was a man who saw an image he would never forget, one that would haunt his dreams and follow along behind him for the rest of his life.

Sucking in a deep breath, A.J. continued: "My friends immediately went back to the cab; one stopped long enough to vomit. But I stood there transfixed. The cabby honked the car horn, but it didn't move me. Here was the worst that life could offer. Here was a poverty so deep that my rich upbringing had prevented me from even imagining such conditions. The mind is an amazing thing, David, truly amazing. I stood there watching the little girl poking and prodding around the smoldering debris that gives Smoky Mountain its name. I saw—I swear I really saw—her grow up before me until she was a young woman who looked twenty years older than her true age, and she was"—A.J. choked back a sob— "was still poking around in the debris, and next to her was another little girl, just as naked and just as dirty, following in her mother's footsteps."

The image was so vivid that tears filled David's eyes.

"That was my catharsis," A.J. continued, "the epiphany of my calling. I saw that little girl and others like her living on the refuse of others and not being able to offer her children anything better. That's when I learned that I had no problems. Sure, I had lost a brother, and, sure, my wife had left me—the result of my foolishness—but these people had real problems, and maybe there was something I could do about it."

"You found a life purpose."

"I found my life's purpose," A.J. said, taking a deep breath. "I want to abolish all the Smoky Mountains in the world. By any

means and at any cost, they must be eradicated, and those who—"
A.J. broke off suddenly. "I'm sorry," he said as he looked at David.
"I didn't mean to upset you."

"No, please go on."

"There's not much more to tell," A.J. said. "We drove back to
our hotel, none of us speaking. I flew home to San Diego the next
day. I didn't know then what I would do, but I knew I would do
something. I called Cyn, but she wouldn't speak to me, and I can't
blame her. The divorce became effective that year. Since then I've
been building what you see."

"What about your father?"

"At first I went back to work for him, and then, as I realized
that I was going to devote my life to the eradication of pain and suffering, I asked for his help. I thought he was going to explode because I had always viewed him as a man driven to obtain wealth as
I had been a man driven to spend it. Instead, he put me in touch
with his key executives, contributed space, equipment, and utilities
in this building, and gave me ten million dollars to hire a staff and
start the work."

"Ten million dollars?" David said in disbelief. "All at once?"

"All at once—and a great deal more than that over the last two
decades. But he gave me something else. Guidance. I thought at
first that I could throw a few million dollars at the problem and it
would go away. It didn't take long before I realized that government
leaders and others would take my money and somehow the problems remained. It was going to take a great deal more than money
to solve the problem. My father helped me see that. He taught me
from his personal experiences abroad how to deal with small-
country governments and large organizations. He introduced me to
the movers and shakers in this country and a couple dozen others.
His name carries tremendous weight in some parts of the world. He
has been my guiding light."

David sat quietly and considered what he had just heard. As a
pastor, he had heard many interesting and moving stories, but this

one touched a sensitive nerve. Very few men could be this open about past errors. Yet A.J. had so easily unburdened his soul to a man who was still basically a stranger, a newcomer. *Men of this caliber are rare indeed*, he thought. David had always considered himself dedicated and giving, but sitting near A.J. made him feel that his light was a birthday candle compared to A.J.'s brilliant solar beam.

A bond was being formed between the two men., a strong and almost palpable bond. David had lost a wife to another man; A.J. had lost a wife because of his own actions. *Different causes*, David thought, *but the end result is the same, loneliness.* Looking at A.J., his tall frame folded up in the chair before him, David knew that he had found a friend and more than a friend—he had found a mentor.

■ ■ ■ ■ ■

"Chained them to the ship's railing?" The dark man with the crescent-shaped scar on his cheek said with a chortle. "You have always been creative about such things."

"It does have a certain flair to it, doesn't it?" Mukatu said, joining in the laughter. "That's one ship that will not be delivering its cargo of food."

"See, brother, how it all works together," Mahli said with a perverted grin. "We think, we act, and if we make no mistakes, we will achieve the great goal. Soon East Africa will be indebted to us, and we will have power and wealth. Our clan will be spoken of for centuries, and our names will be remembered forever."

"Assuming enough people live to remember," Mukatu said. "If we keep the food from too many, we will have no one to rule and no one to make us rich."

"There will be enough," Mahli replied firmly, shaking an uncallused hand at his brother. "There are always enough who survive. You leave the planning to me, and we will achieve all that we desire."

Mahli rubbed a hand over his head and looked at his brother.

In many ways they were much alike. People had assumed they were twins when they were young, but in truth Mahli was ten months older. Now they had aged differently. Both men were short by Western standards and slightly portly. Their skin was dark and clean. Age had left Mahli's hair intact, although he wore it cut close to the scalp; Mukatu's hair had abandoned him years ago.

"So we continue as planned?" Mukatu asked.

"Exactly as planned," Mahli replied, stressing each word. "Hunger is our ally, and we can't let anyone take away our powerful friend. Hungry people can't overpower you. A man has many desires, but those desires can be stripped away until only survival remains. A starving man cares nothing for freedom or gold, just food. He'll sell his country and his soul for it. That is our edge. That is our power. That is our victory."

"And when they are weak enough from hunger, we make our move," Mukatu said viciously.

"We become the leaders who bring salvation to the land," Mahli lectured. "We become the saviors of not only Somalia but our old enemy Ethiopia as well. We will bring the help they need, and they will be thankful. With the food we will bring peace from violence because we will have destroyed all our enemies. It will be a new age for us. With the food we have stored here in the warehouse and others like it scattered all over Africa, we can control the famine and the destiny of East Africa."

"If no one stops us," Mukatu said.

"No one will stop us," Mahli pronounced with authority. "The UN is a toothless lion that was run out of Somalia years ago. They have shown themselves incapable of meaningful action. If they choose to return, the other warlords will cause them enough trouble that they will not give us a second thought. That is why we let the other warlords remain; we may need them. Look what Aidid did to the Pakistanis and the Americans. We have a hundred times the weapons and support he did."

"And when we don't need them any longer we get rid of them," Mukatu said.

"That day will be a pleasure," Mahli said. "And you can have your choice of leaders to kill."

Mukatu nodded in approval, then a moment later said, "Is there more baked chicken?"

"Plenty of chicken," Mahli said. "As much as you like." Both men laughed, and the sound of their voices echoed through the warehouse in Marka that served as their headquarters.

8

DAVID TROTTED UP THE EXTERIOR CONCRETE
stairs to the second floor of the renovated house that was now
The Cove Experience. He paused at the top of the steps to take in
the view. Across the narrow street the Pacific Ocean glistened in the
cascading moonlight that painted the swells and waves of the sea
with a golden light. The aroma of the beach—a mixture of salt,
seaweed, and ocean breezes—hung heavy in the August night. The
evening was still warm despite the sun's setting an hour before. It
was a beautiful experience, medicinal for mind and spirit. There
was no wonder why thousands of people flocked to this area of
coastline every year. La Jolla Cove, with its underwater marine re-
serve, tide pools, and lovely beaches augmented with parks, was visited every day by tourists and locals alike. Some went so far as to
claim that the area had mystical qualities like Santa Fe, New Mexico, or Ojai, California. David had no leanings toward such New
Age dogma, but he did love this area, as all San Diegans did.

Turning back to the entrance, he entered the upscale restaurant, quickly spotted A.J. sitting by a window, and strode over to
meet him.

"Beautiful, isn't it?" A.J. commented as he gazed out at the
ocean. "This is one of my favorite places."

David agreed, nodding his head. "The restaurant is new,
isn't it?"

"Less than six months," A.J. replied. "I know the owner. He's
quite a story. Refugee from Cuba who came here a couple of

decades ago. Started working as a busboy in a Miami restaurant and worked his way up to management. Saved every dime he could and opened this place. Now he's making money hand over fist. Sports stars, major executives, and entertainers dine here."

David looked around. The restaurant was filled with antiques he couldn't identify, a design motif he couldn't name, and an ambiance that was new to him. But he was sure of one thing: This was an expensive place. "You sure have great taste in eating establishments."

"Wait until you taste the food; it's absolutely fabulous."

Opening the menu, David read through the fare. It took only a moment to discover the establishment's theme. The menu listed dozens of Mexican offerings, almost all associated with seafood. There were crab enchiladas, various fish tacos, shrimp salad with black beans, and other similar dishes.

"Crab enchiladas?" David said aloud.

"They're wonderful," A.J. said jovially, "I think I'll join you." Before David could speak, A.J. raised a hand and motioned to a waiter who scurried over.

"Yes, Mr. Barringston," the waiter said in heavily accented English.

"Caesar, we would each like an order of the crab enchiladas, a big bowl of salsa—green salsa—chips, a large glass of ice water with lime for me and for my friend . . ."

"Iced tea, please."

"Iced tea."

The waiter bowed, acknowledging the order, and scurried away. A moment later he was back with a bowl of chips and a soup bowl of green salsa.

"The waiter knew your name," David commented.

"I eat here whenever I can, usually with business owners I'm trying to wring donations from. Occasionally I bring a congressman or a senator. I like to leave a good impression. You have to admit this place can do that."

"It does," David agreed. "And you're right, the ocean view is impressive."

"I have a reason for this little get-together," A.J. said.

"I thought you might want to talk about tomorrow night's fund-raiser."

"No, we're as ready as we're going to be on that. The speech is great, and I've been practicing it as you told me to. I have another reason. You are a man of talent. I see that in the work you've already done, and I sense it too. You have taken to our unique work quite well. That leads me to my next point: A few of us are going abroad soon, and I would like you to go along."

"Me?"

"All of our key people travel to the areas where we work from time to time. It gives them perspective and motivation. I thought we might as well toss you in to see if you can swim. We'll be going to several countries in East Africa. I can promise that it'll be an eye-opener for you. When we first met, I mentioned travel, but if this is too soon . . .'"

The image of the little boy on the mat that David had seen on the videos of Barringston Relief's work flashed vividly to his mind. "East Africa?"

"As you know, that's one of the most troubled areas of the world right now and will continue to be for at least another quarter century. It's a fascinating area, but I have to tell you right up front that the trip will be unpleasant at times."

"I've never been abroad before," David said, "unless you count Tijuana. I don't even have a passport."

"We have people to take care of that. They'll give you a protocol book and arrange for whatever papers are needed. Just sign where they ask you to."

"When do we leave?" David asked, his mind filled with images of Africa.

"September 5, if everything goes as planned."

"That's only a couple of weeks, but I'll be ready to go," David said enthusiastically.

"You're not afraid to fly, are you?"

"Not in the least. I love to fly. I'm thankful for the opportunity and look forward to the trip."

A.J. shook his head slowly and said, "No one who's ever been to a relief area ever looks forward to it; they go because they must. But I appreciate your zeal."

"I didn't mean to imply that I thought this was a vacation . . ."

A.J. raised a hand and smiled. "I understand fully and there's no need to apologize. There will be plenty of adventure and many sights to see, but I want you to be prepared for the . . . more difficult parts of the trip."

"I'll be ready," David affirmed resolutely.

A.J. leaned back in the booth, smiled, and nodded. "Your life is about to change again, David. Change for the good."

The waiter arrived with two massive plates of crab enchiladas, which brought comments of delight from both men who then whiled away another hour with food, laughter, and appreciative glances at the silver-laced ocean.

After the meal, David strolled across the street and through the small green park to the concrete stairs that led down to the small sandy grotto that formed La Jolla Cove. A few people sat on the small confined beach and watched the ocean perform its mesmerizing dance. David removed his shoes and socks and walked through the still warm sand. The air was fragrant with the smells of the ocean, seaweed, salt, and nearby plants. The gentle roaring of three-foot-high waves as they crashed on the shore echoed off the southern sandstone cliffs. The few people on the little beach spoke in hushed tones as if showing reverence for the location and the sea's display.

Finding a spot that was as far from the others as possible, David sat on the ground. He knew that he'd have to clean the sand from his pockets later that night, but that didn't matter. He was feeling good, truly good, for the first time in months. He thought about the glorious opportunity that was his. Now he possessed a great job and was about to travel to distant lands, something he always dreamed of, but never did. Topping it all off, however, David had made a friend. A true male friend with whom he could bond and build a lasting camaraderie. There was no doubt in David's mind: His life had taken a turn for the better, and he was convinced that nothing would disrupt his newfound happiness.

■ ■ ■ ■ ■

The USS *Shepherd* rolled easily on the gentle swells of the Indian Ocean in such gradual fashion that even the most neophyte sailor would find the rocking pleasing. The rocking was even less noticeable in the cramped room adjoining Central Command, near the center of the ship, where two khaki-dressed officers, one standing and one seated, peered at a video monitor.

"Lighter touch, Greeny," the standing man said in a deep, resonant voice. "Caress the stick. Don't tap it, press it smoothly. Remember, it's not a video game."

Lt. Julian "Greeny" Greenbaum flexed the fingers of his right hand and gripped the molded plastic handle again. "Understood, sir. There seems to be a decent current down there."

"Always is," Lt. Comdr. Patrick Odle replied. "Ocean currents are the life of the sea."

"So much for 'Still waters run deep,' " Greeny said.

"More like 'Deep waters still run,' " Odle replied as he stood straight and stretched his back. "I'm getting too old to be crammed into closet-size cabins like this."

"Ah, but the company's great."

"The jury's still out on that," Odle remarked casually. "Got the feel of it now?"

"I think so," Greeny answered. "It's a lot different from the tank training."

Odle nodded. Just two months before he had been training young officers like Greeny in the use of underwater remotely operated vehicles, known as ROVs. With the advances in undersea robotics, remotely operated vehicles had become indispensable to both navy and commercial interests. Trained personnel could now sit comfortably aboard ship while guiding magnificently engineered submersibles hundreds of feet below them. Yet it took practice, a high level of concentration, and great patience to do the work properly. Odle had been charged with training officers and enlisted personnel in the maintenance and operation of submersible ROVs. The tank training Greeny spoke of was the first hands-on experience the naval trainees received. Each took a turn operating an older version of the current ROV. Later they moved up to drills in one of the East Coast bays that harbored some of the navy's ships. After their training, the sailors were stationed aboard ships in either the Atlantic or Pacific fleet where they would ply newly acquired skills in various jobs, from inspecting the submerged electronic submarine detection net to investigating hull damage caused to ships.

There was no one better to lead the training. The navy had educated Odle at Annapolis, where he earned his commission and a degree in marine engineering. From there he had devoted his time and the navy's money to the development of ROVs that could descend through the deepest waters and handle the most sensitive tasks. The minisubmersible that Greeny now struggled to control in the unexpected current was Odle's latest design, able to descend to eight thousand feet and maintain its functionality. One of the engineers had nicknamed it *Snoopy*, because of its stark white paint and its small black sensor emitter that looked like the nose on Charlie Brown's dog. "What do you make her depth, Greeny?"

"Fourteen twenty-six, sir," Greeny replied crisply. "Still no sight of her."

"We'll find her. Side-scan sonar gave us a good image and a firm location. She's there; we just have to get to her." As if confirming his prophecy, a small bit of debris appeared on the stark, sandy ocean floor. The high-intensity lights of *Snoopy* caused a glint on the edge of the metal shard.

"Got something," Greeny said excitedly. "Looks metallic." Without waiting for instruction, Greeny twisted the control stick to the right and slightly down. The electronic command was transmitted down the nearly one-third-mile length of cable to *Snoopy's* mechanics, causing the little submarine to bank right and point its nose down so that the piece of metal scrap was centered in its camera eye.

"Zooming, sir." The small metal shard suddenly grew larger as the zoom lens on *Snoopy's* camera tightened for a closer look. Under *Snoopy's* bright lights the reddish-orange piece of metal came into focus. "It's definitely metal, sir."

Odle nodded in agreement. "What else can you tell me about it?"

"It's new to the ocean bottom, sir. The surface seems to be painted, but the edges are clean, no corrosion. It hasn't been down here long."

"Good observation," Odle said. "What else do you see?"

Greeny sat in silence as he studied the image on the monitor. Then it dawned on him: "Its thickness. It's thick enough to be from the hull of a seagoing vessel."

"Exactly," Odle said. "I think we found our missing lady."

"Shall I collect the piece, sir?"

"No, let's keep searching until we find the rest of her. Is the VCR running?"

"Yes, sir.

"Then resume course, and keep her off the bottom. I don't want us stirring up clouds of silt that might bury something important."

Aye sir," Greeny snapped and directed the ROV back to its original course. Moments passed slowly as the two men studied the drab, barren otherworldliness of the ocean floor. Both men were confident they had found what they were looking for, but the bottom of the Mozambique Channel was home to many skeletal remains of ships current and ancient that had been placed to rest by pirates, storms, or war. The fresh appearance of the metal scrap gave them hope that their mission would soon be successful, and they would once again show the importance of ROVs in the modern navy.

Snoopy advanced slowly, seeing only the occasional bottom-dwelling fish. Five minutes later the seabed took on a new appearance, that of a cluttered floor in an auto shop. Bits of metal scrap and debris littered the bottom as far as *Snoopy*'s "eye" could see in the deep ocean's penumbral gloom.

"Steady on," Odle said in professional tones. The banter between the two men had quickly reverted to formal navy protocol. "Sonar, Mr. Green."

Greeny reached forward to the control panel with his free hand and activated the miniature sonar device. *Ping . . . ping . . . ping.* Speakers overhead sounded the familiar sounds of active sonar.

"Spin her, Mr. Green, and see if we can get sonar acquisition."

Greeny slowed *Snoopy* to a stop and then twisted the control handle so that the ROV turned on its vertical axis. A moment later the repetitive ping was joined with an echo. "Target acquired, sir. I read a large metal object forty-eight degrees starboard from present course. Distance"—Greeny paused as he checked his readings—"four hundred yards."

"Adjust your course, Lieutenant. Let's have a look at her."

Neither man spoke as the slow-moving ROV lumbered through the pressure-filled depths. Odle and Green had been charged with finding and investigating a missing ship—a ship that had disappeared with all hands. Such missions carried a mixed blessing: Fulfilling the mission brought professional satisfaction; knowing that lives were probably lost bathed the work in a somber light.

"There she is," Greeny said excitedly as the image of a large metal behemoth loomed on the monitor. "We got her."

"Easy, Mr. Green," Odle said firmly. "Let's play this by the book. Take her aft, and let's see what name's painted on her." Greeny complied by directing *Snoopy* to move laterally along the hull toward the rear of the sunken vessel. "She's listing hard to port."

"Looks like she impacted stern first," he said, his excitement supplanted by a swelling sense of apprehension. Seconds passed sluggishly as the little submarine pressed against the current. Moments that seemed like eons later, the two men saw the stern. One of the two propellers lay in the silt by the ship, the port prop was not visible anywhere. "What could separate the propeller from the shaft? And look at that hole."

The hole in the ship's hull was large, and it was clear that it came from an internal explosion. "Take her up and back," Odle commanded, choosing to ignore the question. Greeny complied quickly, and *Snoopy* responded without complaint. The image of the ship slowly shrank to allow a greater view of the stern. The white painted words *Sea Maid* soon appeared. Both men gasped, not at the name of the ship, for it was the ship they were searching for, but at the sight they couldn't have expected; a scene they had never seen before, not even in their nightmares.

Not waiting for a command, Greeny slowly caused the ROV to move closer to the vague apparitions that emerged on the screen. He did so, not out of courage or some latent macabre leaning, but for the need for emotional closure. He had to know if what he was seeing was real or imagined. He knew his superiors would ask questions, and he had to be ready with meaningful answers. So he pushed *Snoopy* forward, slowly forward, until he knew the truth with no shred of doubt.

The image of the ship was secondary now, shrinking in importance in the light of the hideous vision before him. Greeny retched.

"Easy, Lieutenant," Odle said, quietly placing a hand on the younger officer's shoulder. "Let's finish our job."

"Aye sir," Greeny croaked.

Picking up the hand piece of the ship's intercom system, Odle signaled the bridge. "We found her, sir," he said when the captain responded. "But there's something I think you should see." Turning, Odle looked at the ghastly image on the screen and imagined what was happening fifteen hundred feet below the surface as *Snoopy* hovered a few feet away from the *Sea Maid*'s crew. Their bodies floated like balloons tethered to the ship's rail, their sightless eyes staring into the abysmal darkness of the ocean bottom. Odle wondered about the kind of man who would do such a thing.

■　■　■　■　■

The twenty-by-forty-foot room was filled with an eclectic assortment of sounds: squeaks, thumps, swats, and grunting. A.J. took his place between the two parallel red lines that had been painted on the highly polished wood floor at the center of the court. "Ready?" he asked.

"As ready as I'm going to get," David replied, taking large gulps of air and expelling them in massive pants. A.J. looked at the twenty-foot-high wall in front of him, pulled his racquet back, and in a fluid motion struck the small blue rubber ball in a vicious serve. The ball rebounded off the front wall and careened back across the red lines, bouncing to David's right. David's swing connected with the ball, sending it sailing to the ceiling where it ricocheted to the front wall and then down to the ground. A.J. sprinted forward and gave the ball a gentle tap so that it barely touched the front wall before bouncing weakly on the floor, making it impossible for David to return. David stood at the back of the court in disbelief.

"That's game," A.J. said.

"Is it just me, or does this court get bigger with each game?" David asked as he walked to the back wall and sat on the floor, still gulping for breath.

"You're just a little out of shape," A.J. said kindly. "A few more games and it'll all come back to you."

"A little out of shape? I'm dying here. And you," David remarked, pointing his racquet at A.J., "are in great shape. Look at you! You're not even breathing hard."

"Nothing like racquetball to keep a guy in shape. It involves more than your body; there's a strategy to it."

"That's why I gave it up half a decade ago. I couldn't think and sweat at the same time."

"Don't kid yourself," A.J. said, joining David on the floor. "You show a natural talent. You simply have to spend more time here."

"If I spend any more time here," David said, wiping his brow, "you'll be burying your latest speechwriter."

A.J. chuckled. "Physical activity releases the stresses of both mind and body. We see a lot of abuse in the world, and that builds up emotional strain. I come here to work some of that off. I find I think better after hitting this ball around. Besides, the ball doesn't hit back . . . usually."

"Yeah," David said with chagrin. "I'm real sorry about that. I wasn't aiming for your head. How's the lump?"

A.J. rubbed the back of his head. "It'll heal," he replied. "How about you? How are you adjusting?"

"I'll get my breath back in a minute, but I'll be sore tomorrow."

A.J. smiled, "I meant, how are you adjusting to all the changes in your life? You've got to be going through some stress yourself."

"I'm managing okay," David squirmed.

"Getting used to living alone?"

"It has advantages."

"It has disadvantages too. Personally, I love living alone . . . now. But when my wife left, it took me forever to adjust. I hated to go home, because there was no one to go home to. Just emptiness and loneliness."

"But you adjusted?"

"I have a new wife now—my work. In most ways it's a poor substitute, but it's not without merit." A.J. stretched his long legs.

"Some people are cut out to live alone, others aren't. You strike me as one who prefers living with another."

"I never really thought about it," David said as he focused his attention on the strings of his racquet, straightening the misplaced ones.

"Does it make you uncomfortable to talk about such things?" A.J. asked.

"I suppose it does," David chuckled. "Odd, isn't it? I spent years in training and service to help others through their spiritual journey, which often meant counseling individuals and couples about their problems. And here I sit struggling with the same kinds of problems and I have no advice for myself. I guess I'm an emotional cripple."

"How many men do you know who aren't?" A.J. asked. "Very few of our gender can deal with their own emotions. People can say what they want about a nineties kind of guy, but we haven't changed all that much."

"You're right, of course," David replied. "But that still leaves the problem."

"Let me ask you this: If you could change anything about your life right now, before we leave this court, what would it be? Short of wishing that none of this ever took place, I mean. What would you change about yourself right now?"

David inhaled deeply and thought. "That's a deep question, A.J., and I'm not sure I have an answer."

"Give it a try. I promise not to chisel it in stone."

"Confidence, I guess," David replied quietly. "I have moments of total, abject insecurity. I'll be going along fine, working at the office, but then as I drive home, I'm seized by a feeling that I will never again be able to do something worthwhile. That everything that happened—my wife leaving, my resigning the church—is all my fault. My reason kicks in and says, 'Bologna, you're not at fault,' but I still feel that I am. And then there're my emotions."

"What about your emotions?" A.J. prodded.

"They're confused." David crossed his legs and leaned forward. Sweat dripped from the tip of his nose. "There're too many of them at times: anger, remorse, joy at my new job, regret, fear. They all pour in at the same time."

"I understand," A.J. said. "I felt the same way. We're very much alike, the two of us. We both have a need to do a work that is both meaningful and lasting, and we both lost our wives. I lost mine because of my self-centered stupidity, you were an innocent victim."

"Can anyone be innocent in a divorce?" David said solemnly.

"My wife was, and you are too. It's not fair. It stinks. But that's life." A.J. bounced the ball on the floor in a consistent rhythm. "Even if you were at fault, you still have a future. The way you feel now will pass. The more you face the future, the easier it will be to remember the past."

David said nothing. He felt uncomfortable sitting on the floor of a racquetball court discussing his problems with his boss. He wondered if it was wise. Employers seldom liked whining employees. Still, he knew that if anyone could understand, it was the man sitting next to him. A.J. had walked the path that David now found himself traveling and had succeeded in forging a new future.

"Do you remember," A.J. continued, "when you told me I had to get in touch with my passion when I give a speech? You told me to be free to express that passion, to bare a bit of my soul. Well, I'm giving you the same kind of advice: You need to feel free to . . . well, feel. Face those emotions, David. Ask them questions, challenge their right to be in your life."

"Challenge them?"

"Sure. Just because you feel something like guilt doesn't necessarily mean that you're guilty. Do a little self-discovery. You have too much to offer the world to sit around feeling sorry for yourself, David. We need you, buddy. And you need yourself. Does that make sense?"

"It does. Thanks."

A hard knocking sound reverberated throughout the court. Both men got to their feet. "It sounds like our hour is up," David said. "We had better surrender the court to the next crew."

"It's been a good hour. Let's do this again."

David laughed. "You're assuming I'll recover from this workout."

"You'll recover," A.J. said with a broad grin, "and not just from racquetball."

9

"YOU LOOK NERVOUS," A.J. SAID CALMLY. "I'M THE one giving the speech, and I'm not nervous."

"The problem of empathy," David replied. "I'm nervous enough for both of us. Besides, I'm not used to wearing a tuxedo and standing shoulder to shoulder with all these important people."

"You look good in a tux, and as far as being among important people, all I can say is that everyone is important. The only difference is that these people are rich. Which is a good thing, since I'm about to ask them for a lot of money."

"It looks like the Academy Awards around here," David said as he scanned the ballroom of the Harrington Hotel in Mission Valley, San Diego's newest and largest five-star hotel. The room was crowded with men in black tuxedos and women in glamorous gowns. In one corner of the room a band played dance music. David saw movie stars and starlets, so many that he thought all of Hollywood must surely be vacant. There were politicians from the western states: mayors, congressmen, and senators, all laughing and shaking the hands of those around them like farmers working manually operated water pumps.

"Come on," A.J. said, "It's time to press the flesh."

He began moving through the crowd, shaking hands with the men and hugging the ladies. David noticed that A.J. always had the right words to say. He also noticed how the women ogled as he walked by, and for good reason. A.J. was as dapper as they came in black tuxedo, white dress shirt with pearl posts, black tie, and his ponytail bobbing behind his head. The fact that the tuxedo was wrapped around a well-maintained and muscular frame only increased the aura around him. A.J. introduced David to soap-opera stars, movie moguls, and business tycoons, and he was suitably impressed with each person he met. A.J. introduced him as "the newest member of the executive team—a key player, an exceptional catch." After one introduction, a junior congressman from California asked if David wouldn't like to write speeches for an up-and-coming politico, but A.J. intercepted the question and saved David some embarrassment by saying, "Now, now, Congressman, I'm here to take money from you, not for you to appropriate members of my team." Everyone, including David, laughed.

The West Coast fund-raising banquet was off to a good start, and David was right in the middle of it. There were three more of these, David had been informed, one in Dallas, one in Miami, and one in New York City. Every few years additional fund-raisers would be held in London and Paris. Each one cost tens of thousands of dollars to promote and execute, but it was worth the cost since each brought in a hundredfold more in gifts and pledges. There was also the opportunity to meet members of the press, who were not only invited, but wined and dined. Most reporters fought to be assigned the task of covering a Barringston fund-raiser.

David followed in A.J.'s wake as he milled through the ballroom, greeting everyone in sight. David had shaken so many hands that his wrist began to ache. He was relieved when A.J. nodded toward the table where the Barringston staff were gathering and said, "It's time to get things started."

No sooner had the two approached the table than Kristen made her way to the front of the hall to a podium on a raised rostrum. She tapped the microphone a few times. David wondered why speakers had to do that.

"Ladies and gentlemen," she said loudly over the din of the crowd. The bedlam quieted to a roar, then to silence. "Thank you," she said. "I'm Kristen LaCroix, and I have the wonderful opportunity of not only working for Barringston Relief, but also the distinct pleasure of informing you that it's time to eat."

People applauded, and a couple of men who had become well acquainted with the fully hosted bar shouted "great" and even "amen," causing laughter to ripple through the gathering. Kristen smiled and said, "If you'll be seated, our servers can begin. I think you'll enjoy tonight's offering."

David watched as the crowd diffused to their tables. The room followed a specific design with the media near the front and the politicians to one side near the Barringston staff's table, which allowed a discreet distance between the two. A.J. had told David that this was more comfortable for officeholders, who liked to savor their meals without being quizzed. On the rostrum and to each side of the podium were tables at which sat A.J.; his father, Archibald; the mayor of San Diego; and the governor of California. David looked at the three men seated with A.J. at the front of the room and realized that they were the only people he hadn't met.

Kristen made her way to the table where David was standing. As David watched her, he was suddenly taken with her beauty. She wore an elegant full-length dress of a color that matched the blue of her eyes. Her shoulders were bare, except for the thin straps of her dress, revealing scores of freckles that he found both amusing and endearing.

"Shall we sit?" a voice said behind him. David turned to see Peter Powell smoothly seating himself in his chair. "It's rather difficult to eat standing up."

Other Barringston people sat at the table with him: Powell from personnel; Sheila Womack, A.J.'s personal aide; and others who David had yet to meet. Peter made the introductions: Walter Lays, Barringston's chief financial officer; Kathy Ellis, attorney; Eileen Corbin, head of communications; Gerald Oswell, department head of research and development; and Hector Chavez, who managed commodity distribution. Kristen sat next to David, an act he found surprisingly pleasing.

"Well, Dr. O'Neal," Kristen said, "how did I do? Not bad for a public-relations person?"

"Not bad at all," he replied. "You're a natural."

"Why, thank you. That's quite a compliment coming from such an esteemed expert," she responded playfully.

During the dinner the group talked freely. Several around the table mentioned the good things they had been hearing about David since his arrival at Barringston. He took the compliments in stride and said something about paying good money for people to pass on those favorable rumors. They spoke of last year's achievements and what they hoped their departments could do during the coming year. There was small talk about who was getting married and who was leaving the firm.

"Are all the department heads at this table?" David asked Kristen.

"Oh, no," said Kristen. "We're scattered all over the room. Each table has someone from the firm seated there. That way they can answer any questions people might have. It keeps A.J. from being besieged all night by inquisitive people. Some of our department heads are out of the country on business or back in Washington."

"This table is for the leftovers," Peter added.

"Speak for yourself," replied Chavez with a laugh.

Those who had not met David before took turns quizzing him on his background, his likes and dislikes, hobbies, and even the last movie he saw. Only Sheila and Eileen remained quiet, choosing to listen to the discussion rather than participate. Time passed quickly, and David became more and more comfortable, except for the stiff shirt collar that rubbed at his neck. Before long it was time for A.J.'s speech, and David became apprehensive again. He had coached A.J. extensively over the last two days, and he was now worried that he might have overlooked something important.

Kristen looked at her watch, then turned to look at A.J. on the dais. A.J. saw her and nodded. Excusing herself, Kristen made her way to the podium.

"Ladies and gentlemen," she said firmly, "I hope you enjoyed your dinner as much as I did." The crowd responded with polite applause. "Each year we at Barringston Relief are thankful for many things, but two things remain foremost in our minds. First is you, our supporters, who maintain a belief that we can make a difference in the world if we work together—" The audience interrupted with more applause. Kristen continued when the clapping ended. "And we feel most pleased about our opportunity to work with one of the greatest men in this generation, one to whom thousands owe their very lives, one who believes that all people have a right to life and happiness without poverty and disease—A.J. Barringston, founder and leader of Barringston Relief."

The crowd stood in ovation, the sound of their clapping reverberating around the hall. A.J. rose from his seat and took his place at the podium. Kristen stood by him leading the applause.

David held his breath.

The people continued their applause for another few minutes before taking their seats again. As they did, A.J. opened a small folder that contained his notes. He glanced at them for a moment then looked up and, purposefully, steadily, looked at each table in the room, yet said nothing. David leaned forward in his seat. A.J. was doing as he had instructed: "Don't speak until they are all looking at you. Build the moment, then build the momentum."

After a short time, A.J. smiled a larger-than-life grin and turned to face Kristen who had returned to her seat. "Thank you, Kristen," he said in a voice that gave the illusion of great power being checked, like a dam holding back a massive river. "Thank you for those kind words. You read them just as I wrote them." The audience laughed. "You did such a fine job with that introduction that the governor wanted to know if you were for hire. He said he wanted at least one person in the state to say something nice about him." The audience guffawed loudly.

"Perfect," David said under his breath.

A.J. began his speech.

"Over four decades ago, the famous adventurer and seaman Jacques Yves Cousteau dropped anchor from his research ship *Calypso*. The heavy metal anchor plunged into the dark waters of Atlantic's Romanche Trench until it struck the silty bottom of the ocean 24,600 feet below the surface. The anchor, which was attached to the ship by five and one-half miles of heavy nylon cord, did its job and held the ship in place. Cousteau did something unique that summer's day in 1956: He set the record for the deepest anchorage of a ship. He did something else that day: He gave us an illustration of the power of anchors to hold us back.

"Each morning when I rise from my bed, my thoughts immediately turn to the hundreds of heroes that are never noticed except by those whose lives they save. Their faces never appear in newspapers or on television screens across our nations. They serve because they have heard that quiet voice that speaks in the ears of every soul that has ever lived, a voice that says 'The world's problems are my problems. The pains and anguish of strangers are my concern.' These people are heroes of the highest order.

"But how do those brave souls who leave home and riches behind to serve in Colombia, the Yucatan Peninsula, in the slums along the Rio Grande in our country, or in the blood and muck of Rwanda and Somalia deal with life's horrors? They are able to do so because they have discovered the personal power that comes from releasing those anchors that keep us from moving forward. They have successfully severed the long and deep anchorage that tied their minds and hearts to less noble pursuits. And so they went to serve. That makes them heroes.

"Tonight I will not stand before you and display pictures of starving children with bloated bellies of malnutrition. Nor will I attempt to pull the emotional strings of your heart with tales of sadness and pain. Instead I will display before you a hero, a hero to match any found in the books of history, a hero to serve as a shining light in an ever-darkening world. I wish I could present this champion of justice and life to you today, but I cannot. I wish with every fiber of my being that she could sit at your table and regale you with tales of distant lands and changed lives, but I cannot. For this hero lies in the cold ground of her home state where she was buried a short time ago."

David watched intently as A.J. delivered his message in clarion tones. Even though he had rehearsed the speech several times, he was now experiencing the impact that comes from projecting his words to a captivated audience. With each moment that passed, David could see A.J.'s rising passion. He took his eyes off A.J. only long enough to gauge the audience's response. Each person sat in rapt attention. Even politicians who were used to finely crafted rhetoric could not shield themselves from the honest expression of emotion being displayed on the stage before them. A.J.'s voice drew David's attention.

"Today thousands of people mourn her murder at the hands of a criminal who still walks free. Those who will miss her the most are those who teetered on the edge of the dark precipice of lingering death.

"I wish I could tell you that her work is complete; that death from hunger and disease have left the lands in which she so unselfishly served. The sad truth is that those same people face greater famine, greater social turmoil, and greater disease."

A.J. paused and stepped to the side of the podium. He slowly, deliberately, scanned the audience, making eye contact with as many as possible.

"But we are not defeated," he said loudly. "No murderous madman can cause us to drop anchor. No famine or fear will bring about the defeat of those heroes who remain at the front lines of the battle, striking at death with the swords of food, medicine, and respect for human life. Despite the reminder of the ever-present danger they face in the hot light of day and cold dark of night, they push on. In my mind, they are the greatest heroes of all. They are champions of compassion; they are people of distinguished valor, whose lights will never be extinguished by tyranny, natural disaster, or civil unrest."

The audience broke into thunderous, spontaneous applause. A.J. waited for the clapping to die down and then resumed.

"Today I look across a sea of faces who have given of their time and who have in the past given of their resources. I look across this gathering and wonder if in this fine group is another hero like Dr. Judith Rhodes. I don't mean the kind who feels compelled to travel to the world's worst places to share the sunlight of hope. No. I mean the kind who will extend a helping hand across the plains and deserts and seas of our world, a hand that says, 'We support you workers of courage.'

"You see, despite all our good work, the need has continued to grow. My researchers tell me that the drought that has afflicted much of Africa will not only continue, but worsen to unprecedented levels. It appears that the weather will pirate away our reserves and our ability to be of help."

A.J. described in detail the problems that lay before them. He spoke of other heroes working in Ethiopia, Mozambique, and Burundi, as well as those in Asia and other parts of the world. He passionately linked each area of need with the names of Barringston Relief staff working in the area. With each minute that passed, his message became more passionate, more heartfelt. Every sentence impacted each listener with the full force of conviction. Tears came to the eyes of women and men. And still A.J. continued, pacing back and forth behind the podium, at times waving his arms in broad gestures and at other times poking the air with his long finger.

David watched in amazement. A.J. was surpassing every expectation. His deepest passions erupted with volcanic force, spewing his concern and belief throughout the room. Looking at the crowd, David saw they were captivated, mesmerized by the tall, powerful man in the tuxedo.

"Today we need those who rise from complacency to lend support. Today we need those who will say, 'I have some responsibility for what goes on in this world, and I will make a difference.' Who will rise to the occasion? Who will invest in the future of people they do not know and will never meet? Who will say with me, 'All people deserve life'?

"Each day I am reminded that the only reason I stand before you in a tuxedo today while millions are naked and exposed to the elements elsewhere is that I had the undeserved fortune of being born in this country, and they had the great misfortune to be born in the stricken and scarred lands of the world. Only the capriciousness of fate separates me from the child who fears that roving mobs of vigilantes may kill him because he's homeless, or from the starving Somali mother who this day buried yet another child.

"This one thing I know," A.J. said, almost shouting. "I could not choose my manner and place of birth, but I can choose how I will live my life. And I choose to live my life battling those elements—be they natural or human—that would scrape human life off this planet as one scrapes weeds off an undeveloped piece of property." The crowd responded with pounding applause.

"But I cannot do the work alone," A.J. said softly, dropping his head. "I wish I could. I wish that the task was that easy, but it's not, and you don't need me to tell you that. So I come before you as a beggar—a man with his hand out. Except I do not ask for myself. Thanks to the diligent and lifelong work of my father, my future is already secure. That is why I take no salary for what I do. But even the substantial resources of Barringston Industries are not enough to achieve the good we set out to do. We can put an end to the madness, however, if we pool our resources, if we draw together as humans who dare care for other humans. So once again I ask for your help and support. I do so with no sense of shame or embarrassment. Today I ask that you reach deeper into your resources than you've ever reached before, and that you give financially to this tired old world that is home to every one of us.

"Will you do that? Will you be one of the heroes this world so desperately needs? I think you will, because I know the kind of people you are and the kind of world you dream of. Dr. Judith Rhodes gave her life, spilling her blood on the soil of another land. I would like to know that she did not face terror in vain."

Stepping from the podium, A.J. took a few steps to his seat at the front of the hall, but before he could be seated the crowd stood in unison and exploded into near-deafening applause. A.J. scanned the crowd that cheered him and nodded, occasionally mouthing the words *thank you.* David watched as A.J. shifted his gaze to him and smiled and winked.

"Incredible," Kristen said. "I have never heard him give a speech like that. Absolutely incredible. David, you're a genius."

"I just wrote it," David said with genuine humility. "A.J. gave it life. He delivered it better than I wrote it."

It took an additional two hours of handshaking, backslapping, smiling, and chatting before David and the other Barringston staff could leave the hotel. It was now close to eleven o'clock, and everyone was showing the strain of the day. Several Ford minivans took the executives back to their cars, which they had left in the Barringston Tower parking garage. David, A.J., Peter, Sheila, and Kristen were the last to leave, and they rode together. Kristen sat next to David and Sheila next to A.J. The conversation in the van was light and good-natured, with each person complimenting A.J. on his speech. A.J. attempted to pass much of the credit to David, but David would have none of it, saying that the best words are useless if delivered inappropriately.

"I am curious, though," David said. "When I wrote the speech I mentioned nothing about worsening conditions in Africa, nor did I cite any statistics. Are things really that bad?"

"I added that information at the last minute," A.J. replied.

"Research handed me the report this morning. I wanted to run it by you, but my day was already filled. You're not offended, are you?"

"Not at all," David offered quickly. "It was a good addition and done perfectly."

"Good. To answer your question, yes, things are getting that bad. Climate conditions may be worse next year than they've been over the last ten. There will be too little rain, and therefore too little food for man or beast. We also have reason to believe that warlord activity and civil war will be increasing. I'm not free to tell you how I know, but the information is reliable. The UN is also aware of the developments."

"That means more work for us," Peter commented. "It's a good thing that nearly everyone present made a healthy contribution. Will it be enough?"

A.J. shook his head. "A thousand times that wouldn't be enough."

"So what do we do?" David asked.

"We do the very best we can and never lose sight of our objective of saving lives. If we can't save all of them, we will save some of them." A.J. looked out at the passing traffic and the tall downtown buildings. "You know, David," he continued slowly, "there are times when I sleep at night that I can hear the hoofbeats of your four horsemen of the apocalypse, and famine rides in the lead."

David nodded in understanding, "It's a shame we can't do more than provide food and medicine."

"Maybe we can," A.J. said softly. "Maybe we can."

■ ■ ■ ■ ■

Before going to his apartment, A.J. stopped by his office to check for messages and to leave his speech notes for his secretary to file. On his desk he found a small black plastic case, which he immediately recognized as a videocassette. A note written in the meticulous handwriting of his secretary read, "Special delivery from the office of Sen. Dean Toler." It was Senator Toler, head of the Armed Services Committee, whom he had asked for help in locating the missing *Sea Maid*. Apprehension flowed through him. Instinctively, he knew this was bad news.

One minute later, A.J. sat in shock as the macabre pictures of the sunken *Sea Maid* played across his television. The ghostly and grotesque images of the tethered crew floating in the dark waters sickened him, but one sight turned his horror into rage. Arrogantly scratched into the paint of a bulkhead were the foot-high letters that spelled Mahli and Mukatu.

10

"I'VE GOT SOME THINGS FOR YOU," PETER POWELL said as he stepped into David's office. "I know you're dying to have more stuff to read, but information makes the world go around, and it certainly makes Barringston Relief go around."

"Thanks, Peter," David said, taking the manila folder and the large white binder with the company logo prominently displayed on the front. He nodded at a chair and said, "Have a seat."

"It looks like you're settling in all right," Peter said, taking the seat opposite David's desk. "You look sufficiently inundated with paperwork. They must be keeping you busy."

"I've got a full plate, but it'll all even out once I learn what I'm doing."

"Judging by the response to A.J.'s speech, you already know what you're doing."

David chuckled, "Not really. The beautiful thing about a speech is that no one interrupts you to ask questions. You say what you want to say and then sit down. It works even better when someone else is delivering the speech. Have you heard how the contribution commitments are doing?"

"I have, and they're doing great. The accounting office is projecting that financial gifts from this last fund-raiser will be double the previous year. If the others go as well, we'll have a good year."

"Judging by what A.J. says about things getting worse, we're going to need it."

"Amen to that," Peter said solemnly. "Let me tell you what I just gave you. The folder is the paperwork you need to fill out for a passport, medical history, and travel log. The travel log is something we keep here so that we can keep track of where you've been. The medical history is self-explanatory, and the passport information is basic. You'll have to make the application yourself and get an ID photo, but that's easy. The binder contains information on the countries we'll be traveling to. I don't have a full itinerary, so some of it may not apply, or I may have to bring you more information."

David opened the binder. "You said, 'we'll be traveling.' Are you going too?"

"Yup, it's my turn again. My office doesn't have much to do with the actual work in the field, but I do make all the hiring decisions, except for senior management and department heads; A.J. makes all the final decisions on those. I do the research and bring recommendations. Since I hire the field workers, A.J. likes me to travel with him to check up on the welfare of our heroes."

The last comment, which was a clear allusion to the speech he had written, caused David to smile. "Do you enjoy the travel?"

Peter paused before answering. "*Enjoy* may not be the right word. While we often have the opportunity to visit some of the most fascinating places in the world, like Rome and Paris, our trips always end up in the . . . well, in more difficult areas. I can promise you one thing, David: You will see things that you will never forget."

"Personally, I look forward it," David replied. "I've never really traveled much, so this will be an experience for me."

"Just don't convince yourself that this is a pleasure trip or some vacation," Peter admonished. "We want you to go in with your eyes open." David nodded absentmindedly as he thumbed the pages of the binder. "You'll also find a protocol section in there. I suggest you read that several times. We may be meeting some very important people, and we don't want to get on the wrong side of them."

"I'll do it."

"David," Peter said seriously as he leaned forward. "I think you've already demonstrated how important you can be to this team, so I don't want you to make the mistake of taking this trip too lightly. We've taken others who couldn't bear what they saw. Several quit on the spot. I don't want that to happen to you. We need you, and A.J. needs you."

"A.J. needs me?"

"You've been good for him. I can see it already. Perhaps it's because you've both had marriages that failed. Perhaps he likes your humor. Whatever the reason, he likes you a great deal. And most likely you've made a dear friend for life—a powerful friend."

"Thanks for sharing that," David said sincerely. "It means a lot to me."

"I'm not trying to scare you, David. I want this trip to make you stronger, not shock you into leaving."

"I can't predict what the future holds, but I've enjoyed, no, more than enjoyed, relished my time here. This is more than a job to me; it's my second chance at a meaningful life. I assure you, I will be fine. As a pastor I had to deal with many people who have received the worst kind of news. I've buried adults, infants, and persons of every age in between. I've counseled those who have had loved ones murdered or killed by drunk drivers. I've seen sorrow before."

"That's good to know," Peter said firmly, "but remember that on this trip you'll see that kind of sorrow multiplied by the thousands."

"I'll be there for you and the rest of the team," David said resolutely. "I promise not to scurry off into the bush."

Peter nodded approvingly.

■ ■ ■ ■ ■

Over thirty-five hundred miles away Ian Booth, president of the Americas Bank, sat on the backseat of a rented Cadillac DeVille as it drove five miles under the speed limit along the coastal route north out of Georgetown on the island of Grand Cayman. The deep blue ocean and the verdant hillsides went unnoticed by the executive; his wide eyes stared ahead, not comprehending anything he saw. He was blinded by the terror brought to him by the four other men in the car. Two men, the driver and another, sat in the front seat. The other two men sat in the back with Booth, one on each side.

"It's no' the money, ya' understand," the man on his right said, his words heavy with an Irish brogue. "It's the principle of the thing." The man pulled a small knife from his pocket and began to clean his nails. Booth didn't have to turn to see the man, his face, ruddy and thin, was branded deep into his memory. "We do have an image to protect, ya' know. I mean, what would the others say?"

"I have done my best to do right by you," Booth said, his voice trembling. "I informed you as soon as I found out the money was missing. I kept nothing back. I've worked hard to find out who did this and to replace the money, but it takes time. It's not easy to siphon off two hundred million American dollars."

"No, I suppose not, boyo, but you understand my point."

"Time. All I need is . . . time." Booth's eyes filled with tears. "I've always been trustworthy. I've always delivered on my promises. I need more time."

"It's a sad thing, lad, I agree," the man said, putting the pocket-knife away. No longer seeing the knife brought Booth a small measure of calm, but he knew it was artificial. They were going to kill him, but not with a pocketknife. The man continued. "Truth be told, I rather like ya'. It hurts me to have to do this, but we have other people to consider. Folk in my position depend on their reputation. The Silver Dawn has a fine reputation in the world, one we work hard to maintain. It behooves us, laddy, to mind even the wee details. And ya' must admit, allowing two hundred million dollars to be stolen from our accounts is more than a wee detail."

"There must be some way," Booth rattled. "Some . . . way."

"Nah. We've given ya' weeks to work on the problem, and you've not solved it. We'll take it from here now. Ya' needn't worry 'bout it anymore."

"You're going to kill me, aren't you?" Booth was surprised at the brazenness of his own question. "You're going to take me somewhere and kill me."

The man nodded slowly, almost as if he was feeling genuine remorse. "'Tis a sad thing, Ian boy. I've grown to be fond of ya' and your family. This gives me no pleasure, even if ya' are a Brit. This is . . . well, 'tis business and that's all it is."

Booth tried to think clearly. "What if I just disappeared. You know, just dropped off the face of the earth. I can arrange that. I really can."

The man shook his head from side to side. "No, boyo. There's got to be a body and an investigation. That's part of maintaining our image." After a pause he continued, "Ya' sent your family away didn't ya', Ian boy?"

It was the one act that Booth felt proud about. The day he discovered the missing money from the Irish terrorist group, he booked a flight out for his family, said his good-byes with hugs and kisses and toys for his two small children, and sent them to the United States. His wife had family there, but she wouldn't be seeing them for a long time. Instead she would be staying in a home in the San Bernardino mountains in the small community of Big Bear. It was a lovely house, chosen in part for its secluded view of the lake and for its sequestration. The house, a three-bedroom cabin, had been purchased under an assumed name that matched the artificial identities he had had the foresight to create. Holding and laundering large sums of money for groups like the Silver Dawn had inherent risks that required prudent planning. That was one thing at which Booth excelled. It had crossed his mind to go with his family, but he knew the Silver Dawn would never give up until "justice" had been served. His family would never be safe until the money had been returned or he was dead. Only by sending his family away while he remained behind could he assure their safety.

"Are ya' listening, Ian boy?"

"Yes, I sent my family away."

"Ya' sent them away and ya' stayed behind—a brave thing, lad." The man paused as he looked out the window. "I suppose ya' sent them to that mountain cabin in the States."

Booth's jaw dropped open. No one could know about that. He had been too careful, too meticulous in his preparation. His racing heart beat faster, sweat appeared on his brow, and his stomach ached.

"Close your mouth, Ian. We're not interested in your family. I just wanted ya' to know that we make efforts to know everything about everyone who could hurt us. Your family will remain safe. At least from us. We're not monsters, ya' know."

"Thank . . . thank you."

"This will be fine," the man said to the driver. "Pull over here." The car veered to the right across the empty oncoming lane and parked behind a clump of trees that were growing near the edge of a cliff. The four men exited the car and waited as Ian Booth slid across the seat and stepped from the vehicle. The man who had been sitting in the front passenger seat pulled a small .25 caliber handgun from under his coat. The warm tropical air was heavy with humidity, and soon all five men were sweating. Booth, however, was perspiring for an entirely different reason. He had come to the end of his life. He had not been a religious man, but now he wanted so very much to be . . . if only there was a little more time, he could pray and maybe find the missing money. But the time was gone. It had ticked away until his days had evaporated, and now his life would end at the hands of men who valued their cause above anyone's life—his especially.

"Would you mind terribly," Ian said as tears streamed down his cheeks, "if I just jumped?" He finished his sentence by nodding his head in the direction of the cliff. "I'm not sure why, but I find that demise a little more . . . palatable."

The leader of the men shook his head. "Sorry, laddy. As I've said, there must be an investigation so that the papers will print a nice story about it. Our friends read the paper, ya' know."

The refusal made Booth's sorrow all the more profound. Not only would he die, but he would do so with no dignity whatsoever. Leaping to his death would have brought only a smidgen of honor, but at least he would be ending his own life and not surrendering it to others. It was a small point, and in a mind suffering less stress it would be no point at all—but it was all he had. It was the last thing he could do to exert some control over his life, and he would be deprived of this. It was so patently unfair. Someone had robbed his bank, and now he was going to be killed for it. Booth watched in detached horror as the man with the gun walked toward him and wondered if the thief was enjoying the money. It was an odd thought for a man seconds away from his execution.

The gunman pressed the cold barrel of the gun to Booth's forehead and pulled the trigger. In the distance, sea gulls, startled by a loud and unfamiliar sound, took to the air.

■ ■ ■ ■ ■

"So your journey was useful?" Mahli asked as he took another small bite of roasted goat and watched his brother, Mukatu, devour yet another portion of his meal, leaving spots of grease on his chin and cheeks, which he wiped away with the back of his hand.

"I found out what you wanted to know, but I could've stayed here and told you the same thing."

"Firsthand information is the best information," Mahli replied. He wondered how he and his brother could be so different. Both had had the same opportunities for education, far more than 99 percent of their countrymen could hope for. Both had taken degrees from a college in London, Mahli with honors and Mukatu with barely passing grades. Both had returned to help manage the banana export business that their father and grandfather had built, with Mahli working in the office and Mukatu with the men on the docks. Mahli liked to read; Mukatu liked to eat. Yet different as they were, they shared some traits in common: Both men were ambitious, loved wealth, hungered for power, and could kill without a second thought. But even in that there was a difference—Mahli killed to further his purpose; his brother Mukatu killed because he enjoyed it so much.

"It's like you said," Mukatu said, his words muffled by a wad of food. "Ethiopia is now worse than we are. The people there are weak with hunger and frustration. They die by the hundreds." This last comment was made as he stuffed a large piece of bread in his mouth. Swallowing hard, Mukatu continued. "The civil division is still strong, but there are fewer people who can fight. They are ripe for the picking."

"Good," Mahli said, dabbing at his mouth with a napkin. "Very good. You have done well, my brother. It is time we help our brother Africans in Ethiopia. Tomorrow I want you to have some of the men begin loading supplies to be taken there. Be sure that the boxes and medical supplies bear the right mark, the mark of our clan. I want them to know that this food comes from us."

"What about our people?"

"Send some of the trucks to the relief centers along the way, but only those that might see our convoy pass. They will think that we are taking food to other centers. You already have teams ready to do this?"

"Yes, we've been ready for weeks."

"Good. Begin passing the rumor too. Tell people that the UN and American food may be poison. Tell them it is the American's way of taking revenge for their defeat at the hands of loyal Somalis in 1994."

"Will they believe that?" Mukatu asked as he began wiping bits of food from his face with his hands.

"A starving man will believe anything as long as he can swallow it with fresh food." Mahli got up from the table and walked over to his brother and put his hand on his shoulder. "I have one other task for you. It involves more travel." Mukatu groaned and started to object. "It is necessary. Who knows, you might even get to kill someone."

Mukatu turned to face his brother. Both men smiled and then laughed.

■ ■ ■ ■ ■

In Marka, Mukatu began a hurried inspection of the convoy of trucks in one of the dozens of warehouses that housed food and medicine commandeered over the months. Some of the food had spoiled, but the grain and dried goods were still intact. There was some damage and loss due to rats, but the supply of food that remained usable was more than enough for present purposes.

Under a waning moon the trucks began to leave the warehouse and make their way toward the bordering nation of Ethiopia, as did others like them up and down the coast of Somalia. It would take most of the night for the trucks to travel the deteriorating roads, but by tomorrow's end they would be dropping bags of grain, boxes of medicine, and rehydration kits to various relief centers operated by independent groups. Mahli had insisted that the UN and Barringston Relief camps be avoided, the first because he wanted to distance himself and his plan from Western intervention, and the latter because the Barringston group would be leery of his efforts, especially in light of the recent double murder and theft in the Somali camp for which his brother was responsible. He knew the Barringston group had made formal complaints to both the UN and to the provisional Somali government.

The protests would do them no good, but still he must be cautious. His plan was in full swing, and details must be attended. Oversights could bring hindrances and inconveniences, maybe even defeat, though that was not likely. Mukatu respected his brother's intelligence even if he didn't always agree with his decisions. He was sure of one thing, Mahli was going to be the most powerful man in Africa, and he, Mukatu, would stand as his second. He could live with that.

■ ■ ■ ■ ■

As the sun rose high in the Ethiopian sky, Mukatu's truck caravan arrived at a small village near Mustahil, and Mukatu knew that other caravans would be arriving soon in Domo, Dolo, and other villages. As the trucks arrived, the food and supplies were freely distributed to villagers and relief camp residents, and so was the brothers' propaganda. The irony was not wasted on Mukatu. In 1974 Ethiopia and Somalia went to war over the long disputed Ogaden desert region. Now two decades later, he led a caravan of hope to both Somalis and Ethiopians. *This is one way to unite Africans*, Mukatu thought. *Make them owe you their lives.*

Of course, there had to be more to the plan than providing food. People could easily forget their saviors with proper motivation, as his own country demonstrated when many Somali nationals, pressed on by powerful clan leaders, attacked UN peacekeeping troops. Rock throwing and armed attacks led to injury and death for the Pakistani, French, and American workers. The corpses of foreign soldiers had been dragged through the streets. The difference, Mukatu supposed, was that the UN genuinely desired to help. Mahli and his followers wished only for control, and he would have it.

Famine was not new to East Africa. Somalia, Ethiopia, Sudan, and other sub-Saharan countries had experienced drought, civil unrest, and crop failures many times over the previous decades. Repetition dulls the mind, and perhaps that was the reason why the Western world had grown insensitive to the plight of East Africa.

No matter, Mukatu thought. *We don't want the interference that comes with the rich nations. We can help ourselves.* By *ourselves* he meant himself. It was famine's repeated returns that had taken Mukatu's soul. He no longer was shocked or grieved to see the decomposing bodies of people who had lost the battle to survive. Their presence along the road moved him no more than seeing a dead animal that had been struck by a vehicle. Nor did the bloated bellies of starving children, the open wounds of women, and the vacant, empty eyes of the men touch him. He was too far removed to notice the human agony or to feel the injustice of premature death. He had seen it before; he would see it again.

Wherever there were groups of people, the trucks stopped and distributed food. Those people who were well enough to help did so; those whose minds were not too fogged from malnutrition gave thanks to Allah and his servants. At each stop they gave more than food; they gave a warning: "Eat only African food. The American food is spoiled and poisoned. They want to rid the world of our kind." They also made sure that as many as could understand knew that the food was being provided by the African Unity Party. None had ever heard of the organization, but it didn't matter, they were giving them another day to live and that was appreciated.

The trucks that lumbered through the Ogaden could not alleviate the famine. The effort they made was purely show, but word would spread. Food was given to both Somalis living in the Ethiopian region and Ethiopians themselves. Each person greeted them with open arms and readily ate the food provided. Under Mahli's orders, the trucks avoided highly populated areas to avoid riots and injury. Such events, which they were undermanned to prevent, would injure their image and set back their cause. Mukatu knew that his brother would not overlook such details, not after half a lifetime of planning.

11

THE SMALL BEDROOM COMMUNITY OF EL CAJON was known in San Diego County for many things: its summer heat, its crowded streets, and the sea breezes that blew the smog into the surrounding box canyon, where it settled on residents like a thick brown blanket. This was especially true in the summer months, and David, who seemed more susceptible to smog than most, was feeling a slight pain in his chest with each breath. This made him all the more happy to be in his air-conditioned home. His simple three-bedroom, bungalow-style house sported the typical California stucco and decor. The home was far from fancy and would never appear in any magazines that displayed finely crafted and expensive houses surrounded by meticulously manicured lawns. David's lawn, he noticed with chagrin, was entirely too tall and filled with dandelions. He would have to mow the yard before he left for Africa, and he wondered who would take care of the house while he was gone.

The trip occupied his mind. As he sat at his dining table, he reviewed the protocol book. After viewing the tentative itinerary, David couldn't help but feel excited. He had been warned by others not to consider this a vacation, rather to consider it a journey that could be grueling physically and emotionally. Still, to travel to the land that he had read about as a child when he devoured books of adventure and intrigue that were often set against the geographical backdrop of the Serengeti Plain or deep jungles in Central Africa filled him with palpable excitement. Those stories brought images of tall Watusi, fierce Masai, pygmies, and headhunters. As a child, he had spent hours imagining himself as the great white hunter who traveled the jungles of the dark continent. But this trip was to be real and not fantasy. He would meet no spies nor hunt big game. He wouldn't travel to the dense jungle areas of Central Africa; instead he would see the sub-Saharan countries with their vast expanses of open plains and deserts.

David rubbed his left arm where he had received inoculations against malaria and other diseases to which he might be exposed on the trip. He knew he had been invited along as part of his education and maybe as a test. Seeing the relief work firsthand would certainly aid his work. It would allow him to infuse the knowledge of actual experience into the speeches and materials he wrote instead of relying on mere research. Yet he wondered if he was ready for such an exposure to the worst that life could deliver.

A fog of personal doubt settled over him. As a minister he had seen many unpleasant things, the worst being an eight-year-old child who had been killed by a drunk driver. Seeing the effects of the untimely and unjust death of the little boy had touched him deeply, but now he would be facing hundreds of adults and children who face untimely and equally unjust deaths every day. Was he the kind of man who could face such sights with the necessary balance of detachment and genuine concern—detachment to save his mind, concern to see the need?

Not for the first time, he felt a strong sense of personal doubt. It hovered above him like storm clouds on the horizon bringing flashes of lightning and peals of thunder. Some storms were worse than others, and David could never predict their severity. He had been plagued with incertitude since childhood, but he had always been able to overcome the pervasive feelings of impending failure and inadequacy through prayer and sheer determination. That had always worked during his years of school and ministry, but his wife's desertion had wounded that resolve, leaving his mental resoluteness slashed and bleeding. Now in a matter of days he would be forced to face, to really see, what caused most people, even those stronger than he, to avert their gaze.

Pushing back the protocol binder, David rose from his seat and went to the refrigerator to refill his glass. As he sipped the tea he felt a strong sense of loneliness that heightened his personal insecurity. When others were around there was a need to put on affectations of confidence, and the very pretense brought a notion of self-assurance. No one in David's church would have guessed that their pastor suffered from strong doubts about his ability and worthiness. They considered him the best pastor in the church's history, a man of direction and great ability. They never saw the cracks in the glass psyche of the man who was their shepherd. David simply did the job that needed to be done regardless of how he felt. But this evening he was alone, with no one around for whom he could perform his act.

Perhaps that was what he needed. Some company. But who? It surprised him only a little when Kristen's face appeared in his mind. He had enjoyed her quick wit and ability to laugh, while not sacrificing the meaning of her life to frivolity. Would she consider going out for coffee tonight? Storm clouds of doubt flashed and roared in David's head.

Returning to the dining table at which he had been working, David reached into his open briefcase and pulled out his staff directory. Thumbing through the pages he found her name, picked up the phone, took a deep breath, attempted to ignore the raging doubts he felt, and dialed her number.

■ ■ ■ ■ ■

Kristen answered on the second ring, showing genuine pleasure at hearing his voice. Now as David parked his car at the Mission Valley Shopping Mall, he felt a sense of cautious euphoria. He also felt guilty. He wasn't sure of the guilt's origin, or even of its purpose. This was not a romantic encounter, and even if it was, so what? He was the one who had been deserted. Did he not have a right to seek out a friend and companion, even if the companion was female? Of course he did. But why the sensation of nagging guilt. *Someday, David,* he thought to himself, *you're going to have to learn to give yourself a break.*

They had agreed to meet at the coffee shop next to the food court. The warm evening had brought droves of people out to walk by the shops, gazing at the wares, or to grab a quick fast-food dinner. When he arrived at the espresso shop he found Kristen sitting at one of the plastic outdoor tables. She saw him and smiled broadly.

"We've got to stop meeting like this," she said cheerfully when he joined her at the table. "People are going to think we have a caffeine addiction."

David chuckled, "It could be worse. What can I get you?"

"Latte with vanilla."

"Sounds good. I'll make it two." David quickly made his way into the little shop. The room was filled with a blend of aromas that emanated from the various brews and flavorings. At least a dozen people stood in line while the employees hustled behind the counter adroitly creating each cup of coffee to order. David admired their skill at handling the crowd. A few minutes later he exited the shop with two tall cups of steaming coffee.

"I got large cups so I wouldn't have to forge through the crowd again."

"You're a wise man," she said.

"Oh, I don't know," David replied. "It's still hot out, and here we are drinking coffee. But then again, I had a navy chief in my congregation who maintained that the only way to cool down in the heat was to drink something hot."

"That doesn't make sense."

"I didn't think so either, but I didn't have the heart to tell him. Besides, he could be right."

They each sipped their coffee and made simple comments about how good it was.

"I'm glad you had some free time tonight," David said. "I was feeling a little boxed in. Lately, I've been indoors, either at home or in the office or in the car. With a few exceptions, of course."

"I'm glad you called," Kristen stated. "I tend to get a little antsy before a big trip."

"Trip?" David asked with surprise.

"I'm going to Africa too. I assumed you knew. It's my turn to go again. In fact, I was studying the protocol book when you called. Have you been reading yours?"

David nodded his head. "Several times. I found it all very interesting, although I'm a little concerned."

"Concerned? About what?"

"If I read the program right, we will be meeting some important foreign dignitaries. That's out of my experience. It's probably out of my league."

"Nonsense," Kristen said firmly. "Those dignitaries are more nervous about meeting us. Americans can be mystifying to them. Besides, A.J. carries a lot of influence. He'll be handling all the discussions. We just show up at parties and the like."

"Parties?" David said, nonplussed. "They have parties in famine areas?"

"In some countries, yes. Remember, the political leaders are not the ones who go hungry, those in the outlying areas do. True, famine can and has reached some cities, but the seats of government usually fare better. You may be surprised at what you'll see. In fact, I know you will."

"You've been on trips like this before?" David said, taking another sip of his coffee.

"Two others. The first was to Mexico and the Yucatan Peninsula. The second was to South America, Brazil mostly. This will be my first trip to Africa."

"Do you look forward to it—the travel, I mean?"

She paused before she answered, letting her eyes follow people in the crowd. "Yes, I think I do, but not the way I look forward to something pleasurable. I look forward to the trip because of the way it changes me. No one goes on one of these trips and remains the same. We go places tourists never see. We travel to towns and villages that even the best travel agents have never heard of. It's like being ill and going to the doctor: You don't really *want* to go to the doctor, but you know that you will feel better if you do. You'll do fine, David."

"I hope so. A.J. and Peter have both told me that it can be rough, that I shouldn't think of it as a vacation."

"It's no vacation, that's for sure, but it does have its moments. The key is having the right eyes."

"The right eyes?"

"Yeah," Kristen leaned over the table and spoke animatedly. "It's like this. Some people go on these trips and all they see is the abject poverty and human misery. They see death and smell its stench. They sense frustration. Soon that's all they can see and feel. It overpowers them and fills their minds with despair. But there is more there than human misery; there is human triumph. I didn't realize this until my second trip, but then I saw the innate ability of people to survive. Not all make it, many don't—in some cases, most don't—but they try so hard and survive so much longer than anyone would think possible. I've seen starving kids hunted down who find ways of helping themselves and helping others like them. That's what gives me hope, David—that intrinsic good in people that makes them struggle to survive. That's why I don't give up. I have found that we can make a difference, that we can save lives, because those in need are willing to survive."

"You never despair?" David asked quietly. "You never want to quit?"

Kristen shook her head. "Not much more than two or three times a week," she quipped. "Sure, I have my moments of despair. We all do. I've seen A.J. in tears over situations, but we don't give up. Why? Because it isn't what we *feel* that matters, David. It's what we *know*, and we know that there are people alive today, working and having babies, because we were there. We can't save them all, but we can save some."

"So you're saying that it's all right that I have doubts."

"It's more than all right. It's normal. Doubts have their place: They make us reevaluate our present position. That causes us to think, to reason things out. And sometimes we come up with a better way of doing things. Doubt is fine as long as it is used as a tool and isn't adopted as a lifestyle."

"You're a fascinating woman, Kristen," David said. "You have a reasoned purpose, you're a person of faith and belief, you're filled with passion, you're witty, you're intelligent, and you have enough good sense to drink coffee with me." He continued the thought silently, *You're also undeniably attractive.*

"Why, thank you," Kristen said in her best Southern-belle imitation. "I have always depended on the compliments of strangers." The two laughed heartily.

"Would you like another cup of coffee, or would you like to walk around for a while?"

Kristen thought for only a moment, "What I would really like is to see a movie."

"A movie?" David said. "Well, it just so happens that there's a theater around here. Any particular movie?"

"No, but nothing too romantic. I don't want you to see me get all weepy eyed."

David rose from his chair and offered Kristen his arm, and the two walked toward the mall's theater box office.

TWO

DARKNESS
IN THE LIGHT

September 5 to September 28

12

THE TASK OF CONCEALING HIS EXCITEMENT WAS proving formidable for David. Not even the early hour could subdue the thrill of the trip he was about to undertake. It all seemed surrealistic. A little over seven months ago he was the pastor of a small Baptist church, but today he sat in the plush surroundings of a Learjet airplane. With him were his travel companions, A.J. Barringston, A.J.'s aide-de-camp Sheila Womack, Kristen LaCroix, Peter Powell, and two men David had just met.

The group had arrived at Barringston Tower at 5:00 that morning, each bleary eyed and clinging to a cup of coffee. As promised, A.J. had arranged a private breakfast in his office. The small group ate around the glass conference table making idle chitchat between bites. David forced himself to eat the ham-and-cheese omelette despite his stomach's protestations about the early hour. He was surprised to find that he became more alert with each bite. As the sun rose over the Pacific and cast long shadows from the tall downtown buildings, A.J. began the short meeting.

"Most of you know each other," he began, "with the possible exception of Gerald Raines and Leonard Wu, both of whom are with Child Touch Ministries and are hitching a ride with us to Ethiopia." David had heard of Child Touch and had seen their heartrending ads on television. They specialized in feeding and sheltering children, especially those orphaned by war.

These men, however, didn't strike David as the type who would involve themselves with orphans. It was a subjective opinion, he knew, and one that wasn't based on any more information than the personae projected by the men. Both seemed pleasant enough on the surface. Wu wore khaki pants, a dark brown polo shirt, and a casual pair of slip-on shoes, an outfit that seemed to match his youthfulness. David judged him to be in his late twenties, trim and thin of frame, fitting the stereotypical image of a Chinese. Raines, a stocky dark man with a pencil-thin mustache, appeared to be in his late forties and wore loose-fitting jeans, running shoes, and a long-sleeve dress shirt with the sleeves rolled up to the elbow. While the men differed in dress and age, they both possessed the same wariness, something David saw in their physical manners, clipped fragments of conversation, and the occasional exchange of glances that carried unspoken messages.

A.J. handed out a single piece of paper to each person. "This is our final itinerary," he said, "or as final as it can be at this point. We will be traveling over and into a few hot spots, so this may change. As it stands now we will fly to New York today, where we will spend the night." A.J. smiled, "My father insists that we take in a Broadway play. His treat, of course. Then we fly to Rome. I've arranged a two-day stay there so that we can all do a little sightseeing. David, you must see the Basilica. I know you're not Catholic, but I promise you'll be impressed. From Rome we will fly to Addis Ababa in Ethiopia for a three-day stay, then to Mogadishu in Somalia. All of this is subject to change—especially Somalia. We'll go if we can. If not, we will spend more time in Ethiopia. Are there any questions?"

No one spoke.

"Okay then. Our luggage should be loaded with the supplies, so all that remains is for us to hop into the van." With that, A.J. rose from his chair and started for the door. The others were quick to join him.

■ ■ ■ ■ ■

"Call it in the air," Special Agent Woody Summers said into the phone as he prepared to flip his lucky Kennedy half dollar into the air.

"Wait a minute," Stephanie Cooper retorted. "How do I know you'll tell me the truth? I can't see the coin over the phone."

"That's the problem with you CIA types, always so suspicious," Woody replied humorously. "I am a duly authorized keeper of the peace and protector of our country. I am a highly trained agent with many years of experience. I never lie."

"And I am a highly trained CIA operative who specializes in foreign terrorist groups, and I trust no one, especially special agents of the FBI."

"I'm crushed at your lack of confidence in me," Woody said with mock despair. "Have I ever misled you in any way?"

"We've never met before, so you've never had the opportunity to mislead me."

"We're getting nowhere fast," Woody said. "Heads I go there, tails you come here. Fair enough?"

"No, but flip the coin anyway."

Woody flicked the coin and let it fall on his desk where it bounced twice before falling flat. "It's tails. This must be my lucky day. If you leave soon you shouldn't encounter too much traffic."

"I'll bet it's tails. For all I know, it's standing on its edge."

Woody laughed. "I can assure you it didn't land on its edge."

"All right, all right," Stephanie said, resigning herself to the inevitable, "I'll leave in a few minutes."

"I look forward to it." Then in a horribly executed imitation of Humphrey Bogart, he added, "This could be the start of a beautiful relationship."

Stephanie groaned and hung up.

■　■　■　■　■

"You made good time," Woody said as he quickly assessed the woman in front of him. Stephanie Cooper stood five-eight and had brown, wavy hair that cascaded to her thin shoulders. Her face was lightly freckled and sported a slightly turned-up nose and keen dark brown eyes that reflected her quick wit and high intelligence. He felt an immediate attraction to her, but quickly dismissed it. He was, after all, a married man, and judging by the ring on the finger of her left hand, she was a married woman. Besides, this was business, and as much as he liked to joke around, he was very serious about his work.

"Nice office," Stephanie replied. "You FBI folk even get art on the wall."

Woody knew that Stephanie was taking stock of him. He was shorter than most men, but not unusually so. He had black hair and a thick mustache to match. "I added the art. It's a hobby."

"You paint?"

"Don't sound so surprised. I have a sensitive, artistic side."

"No doubt. I didn't think that computer jocks enjoyed the fine arts."

"That's a stereotype," Woody said glibly. "I know a computer jock who can even read."

Stephanie smiled. "You're quick, Agent Summers, I'll give you that. What say we get to work?"

"Have you had lunch yet?" he asked.

"Five minutes and already you're asking me out?" she asked curtly.

"No. My wife discourages dating on my part, unless it's with her. I haven't had lunch, I'm hungry, and I thought we could talk in the cafeteria."

"Oh," Stephanie replied, slightly abashed. "I get hit on a lot, and I tend to overcompensate. It's still hard for a woman in this business, you know."

"I can imagine. Is the cafeteria okay?"

"That will be fine."

Ten minutes later they were in the expansive cafeteria of Washington's FBI building. Woody was eating a turkey sandwich, and Stephanie was drinking a diet cola.

"Okay," she said with authority. "We know our assignment. We are to discover who has been breaking into the CIA computer. Since the crimes have taken place on U.S. soil, your agency is involved. That's why you're here. Since I specialize in foreign terrorism, especially technical terrorism, I've been asked to represent the Company. Tracking down criminals is your stock and trade, where do you suggest we start?"

Woody swallowed hard and took a drink of milk from the small carton on his tray. "We start at the beginning. What did they take and when did they take it?"

Stephanie laid open a file. "Over the last two years, one hundred and fifty attempts have been made to pirate CIA computer files. Only three have been successful. All of those occurred in the last year. Most of the attempts are by amateur hackers who think it might be fun to find a crack in our system. Other agencies like the Atomic Energy Commission, the Secret Service . . ."

"And the FBI," Woody added. "We get our fair share of hackers too. What makes the three successful attempts unique?"

"Success, for one thing. In each of those attempts the perpetrator was able to steal one or two files before our system could shut it down."

"The system shuts down the access by itself?"

Stephanie looked chagrined. "Normally, yes. But on these three occasions they had to be shut off manually. We don't know what the hacker's doing different, but it works—which surprises me."

"Why surprise?"

"With the level of encryption we use, I thought it would be impossible to gain unauthorized access to our computers."

"Nothing's impossible," Woody said stoically. "In fact, it's a misconception that the more our technology advances the safer we are. Actually, the more dependent we become on technology, the more vulnerable we become. Every new technological advance opens doors for new crimes and new terrors. No matter how sophisticated we are, there will always be those who can find a way to break through that sophistication. We think that we can build a technological barrier between us and the bad guys, but the bad guys are smart too. There will always be someone who will find or create a way to break a system down. Information was safer before the days of computers. In the old days, a person had to physically break into an office or home. Now any reasonably educated teenager with a computer and modem can access millions of files worldwide."

"But surely our systems are a little more advanced."

"True. That's why there have only been three successful attempts, and they were probably done by the same person. What did they take?"

"Satellite photos of East Africa."

"East Africa?" Woody said with surprise. "That is interesting. I would have thought that someone sophisticated enough to get into the CIA system would want more than satellite photos. What could they use them for?"

"They're from an orbiting platform that allows us up close and personal photos of almost any area in the region. It helps us keep track of ship traffic in and around the Red Sea and the Gulf of Aden."

"How close?"

"I'm not allowed to say."

"We are on the same team, you know," Woody said seriously. "I need to know so I can start thinking about who could use such photos."

Stephanie remained silent and unmoved.

"Okay," Woody said with resignation. "I'm going to assume that your little eye in the sky can read a newspaper on the ground. Now, if that's true, who would be interested in such photos. Any ideas?"

"We've been thinking about that," Stephanie said. "I talked to our people who specialize in the area, and we're coming up blank. There are no serious international terrorist groups in Somalia or Ethiopia. It's a troubled area, that's for certain, but most of the fighting takes place between rival tribes or clans. Somalia used to host a Russian military base years ago, but that base was given back to the Somalis. There is no present military value, although the northeast end of the country—the Horn of Africa—is situated at the Gulf of Aden, which provides direct access to the Red Sea. We have people looking into that possibility."

"But you said these were extreme closeups."

"I said no such thing. You inferred it."

Woody chuckled, "So I did. The files that were stolen, did they deal with the Gulf of Aden?"

"No. They were of Mogadishu and surrounding areas."

"What areas?"

"Other cities—Marka, Kismayu. All port cities."

"That's a famine area, isn't it?"

"Very much so."

"So we need to ask some basic questions: Why Somalia? Why those cities? Perhaps a clan leader wants information. But that's not likely. They probably already know where their enemies are. So who else needs closeup satellite photos? Someone outside of Somalia most likely. The UN? Nah, probably not. If they wanted that information, they'd just ask for it. Another country? Unless I've missed something, Somalia has little to offer another country but trouble. If not a foreign government or someone in Somalia, then we are left with businesses, associations, or individuals. Who does business in that land?"

"Not many companies. Most shipping done now is the receiving and unloading of foodstuffs. The recent clan uprisings that ran off most of the United Nations also ran off most foreign business. So I guess that leaves relief organizations and . . . and . . . what? I can't think of anyone else."

"There are still others, including criminal elements, so we have to keep our options opened. How many relief groups are working in Somalia?"

"Dozens," Stephanie said as she riffled through the file folder she had brought. Woody watched as she furrowed her brow, an act that made her all the more attractive. She withdrew a page of paper and started counting the names on the list. "We show about two dozen, including groups from France, England, Italy, and the United States."

"You're the expert in terrorist groups," Woody said. "Do you know any group that would be interested in a thoroughly beat-up country?"

"Some might be interested. Several groups might make some use of the direct sea access to Egypt or Jordan, but there are better ways and more friendly countries to set up a base of operations. Drug cartels don't seem too likely."

"What are the odds of my seeing those pictures?" Woody asked.

"That's not up to me, but I will check on it," Stephanie replied. "Why do you want to see them?"

"I'm not sure really. It may be a wasted effort, but sometimes clues come unexpectedly. It might help me get into the mind of our thief." Woody paused before he asked the next question. "Have you folks considered that you have a mole?"

"An agent selling information?" Stephanie said. "Why is that everyone's first thought? Most of the people who work for us are unselfish. I can assure you that the CIA is not filled with double agents like the media would have everyone believe."

Woody raised both hands in an act of surrender. "I'm not im-pugning you or the CIA, but we both know that organizations like ours have their share of people who can be manipulated, threat-ened, or just plain bought. You had Aldrich Ames who spied for Moscow for almost a decade. The man made $69,000 a year, yet he paid $540,000 cash for a house. He even had a suspicious lie-detector test. The British discovered too late that Harold Philby was working for the Russians. The Pentagon, the navy, every major in-stitution has had those in its ranks who sold out. And we at the FBI are not exempt. This is not a personal thing. The easiest way to get into a computer system is by buying the code. That's not the only way, but it is the easiest way, and we can't overlook it."

"You're right," Stephanie said. "We are looking into that possibility, but we think it's unlikely."

"You're probably right, but if we are going to catch the person who's helping themselves to your files, then we can't leave a stone unturned. Listen, go back to your office and see if you can get copies of those pictures. In the meantime, I'll keep this list of relief agencies working in Somalia and see what I can find out. What say we meet again tomorrow afternoon?"

"Agreed, but this time we meet at Langley. No more coin flips."

"All right," Woody said with a broad grin. "Fair is fair. I'll see you then."

13

"WELCOME TO ADDIS ABABA, ETHIOPIA," A.J. SAID AS their plane taxied toward the terminal of the Bole International Airport. "You are now in one of the oldest independent countries in the world, at least two thousand years old. I hope everyone is dutifully impressed."

"I didn't know it was so mountainous," David said with surprise.

"Good coffee-growing altitude," A.J. replied, and then speaking to the whole travel party he said, "Just a reminder to everyone: Our elevation is pretty high, so if you feel dizzy or have trouble breathing, be sure to tell someone right away. Don't overexert yourself for a few days. As your briefing papers told you, this is the rainy season, but the drought has cut into that. Still, we may see a few short rainstorms while we're here. Also, and I know I don't need to say this, but let me say it anyway: Don't travel alone or into any of the outlying regions. This country is still unstable, and even with its new government there is still tribal violence. Democracy has not eased the age-old tensions between the Afar, Tigrean, Oromos, and others. Things are better, but I would be more comfortable knowing that everyone was hanging around the hotel."

"What do we do now?" David asked.

"Leonard and I have to say good-bye," Gerald Raines interjected. "Someone from the Child Touch orphanage is picking us up. It's been great traveling with you. We appreciate the lift, A.J."

"My pleasure, gentlemen," A.J. replied. "Be careful out there."

"We will," Wu answered. The two men shook hands with the other travelers, gathered their luggage from the rear of aircraft, and quickly deplaned.

"Sheila has made arrangements for transportation to the hotel," A.J. said. "The National Tourist Office has provided cabs that will take us directly there. We'll rest while I make contact with the U.S. Embassy and our field teams. Now if everyone will find their Ethiopian visas we'll be on our way. Oh, one last bit of advice: Don't drink the water." Several of the team chuckled. "I'm serious. Tap water here is not potable, so don't drink it. Bottled water will be provided in your rooms. Now let's enjoy the land of Ethiopia."

■ ■ ■ ■ ■

The hotel was the best in Addis Ababa, but it still fell short of the five-star hotel they had occupied in Rome. The hotel was a metaphor for Ethiopia itself: grandeur and majesty, pockmarked with holes of poverty and conflict. The advice that A.J. had given on the plane was just what he had called it—a reminder. David, like each member of the crew, had been given a briefing book on each country they'd visit. The section on Ethiopia had contained all that A.J. had said and more. The country could be the poster child for world hunger. In the early nineties it had suffered one of the most devastating famines in contemporary history. David, tired from the travel and now suffering from jet lag, lay on the bed in his room, with the briefing book propped on his chest.

Ethiopia was a land filled with diversity. Its highlands accounted for almost half of all those found in Africa, yet it also had hot grasslands and the Great Rift Valley, which was still geologically active. He had been surprised to learn that 80 percent of the mighty Nile River's water came from the vast mountainous area of the country, yet the land had been frequented by drought and famine. There had been four famines previous to the one Ethiopia was experiencing now: 1972–74, 1984–85, 1987; and 1989–90. More than two million Ethiopians died of starvation during those years. If A.J. and his researchers were right, the present famine could

149

match the total devastation of the other three periods combined. According to the briefing papers, Ethiopia was as varied in people as in geography. More than eighty languages could be heard within its borders.

There seemed to be an unfairness to it all, David thought. A country as ancient and as ethnically rich as Ethiopia should be the crown jewel of Africa. Unlike all other African countries, Ethiopia had never been a settlement of Europe. It had always stood on its own. But recent decades had forced it to accept help from other countries to keep its people alive. What both puzzled and infuriated him was that none of the loss of life need have occurred. Sufficient food supplies could be delivered to the country in short order. The country possessed an international airport and, until the recent breakaway of Eritrea in the north, had two ports on the Red Sea. But neither weather nor terrain prolonged the famines, caused the large numbers of displaced people to flee across borders, or killed the innocent. No, it had been men who did such things. Men who could not live with one another because they were of different tribes. Men who felt the need to force changes on people as did the former leader of Ethiopia, Mengistu Haile Mariam, the young military leader who founded the nation's Communist Party and, with the help of the once Soviet Union, became the nation's president. Fourteen years later he resigned in the face of force. During his years in office he attempted many plans that led to the deforestation of land and the forced resettlement of a half million nationals who had been pressed into new and unwanted villages.

David and millions of others had seen pictures from Ethiopia on their television sets. But the images always seemed too far away to be true. Now David lay on a bed in a hotel in the capital of that country, and soon he would stand in the filth of abject poverty. He wondered if he was up to it. With that last thought still floating in his mind and compelled by jet lag, he dozed off to sleep.

He awoke to a banging on his door. At first he felt groggy and displaced. His mind struggled to place him in his own bed in his own home, but reason reminded him that home was thousands of miles away. The knocking on the door resumed and was accompanied by a muffled voice. "David, are you in there?"

"Yeah," he shouted, rubbing his eyes. "Just a second." Taking a few deep breaths to help wake him, David rose from the bed and went to the door.

"I thought you had died or something," Kristen said. "I must have been knocking for five minutes."

"I fell asleep," David replied groggily. "I must have really been under."

"It's the altitude," Kristen said with a grin. "People who aren't used to it tend to get sleepy."

"So that's what was wrong with my congregation," he said with a smile. "And I thought it was my sermons." Kristen laughed. "But maybe it is similar after all," David continued. "One has to do with thin air, and the other with hot air."

"I came by," she said, "to see if you wanted to go down to the restaurant with me and sample some native cuisine."

"Does native cuisine include hamburger and fries?"

"I sure hope so," she replied. "You'll join me?"

"I wouldn't miss it."

■ ■ ■ ■ ■

Across the eastern border of Ethiopia, past the dry Ogaden desert, in the Benadir region of Somalia lay the coastal city of Marka. The small city had been Roger's home for eight hot days. He, along with Mohammed Aden, had been staying in a small hotel near the warehouse district of the port city. Actually, Aden had made arrangements for the room. Roger crept in the room that night and only left it under the cover of darkness. It was his intent to remain invisible. This was one of Mahli's towns, and Mahli would have people on the lookout for the unusual—such as a white American.

"Find anything?" Roger asked Aden when the latter stepped into the hot hotel room.

"This is not easy, my friend," Aden said exasperated. "I can ask no questions of the people here for fear of alerting Mahli; I cannot simply walk up to the warehouse and peek in a window without being shot. And I am not trained for electronic surveillance."

"I'll take that as a no then," Roger said bluntly.

"I have had no more luck during the day than you have had at night," Aden replied. "But we know the information we received is right because of the number of guards and the weapons they carry. We are, at least, in the right place."

"Most likely, we're in one of the right places. Mahli probably has dozens of places like this scattered across Somalia. We just have to wait. Get some rest; we'll be going out again tonight. Maybe tonight we will be lucky."

Aden groaned.

■ ■ ■ ■ ■

The hotel restaurant served a fair dinner for a country in the midst of famine. The food was far from the well-prepared and tasty delights on which the hotel had once prided itself. Now it was content to serve sandwiches and thin soup—a meager meal in the West, a banquet for the rural people of Ethiopia and a half-dozen other nations in East Africa.

"Sorry there were no burgers," Kristen said, "but I suppose we should still be thankful."

"Amen to that," David said. "Besides, the food is less important than the company."

"Why thank you, Gentleman David. You are most kind."

"I aims to please, ma'am," David said jovially. "Does it seem like we're in Africa to you? I find it all a little hard to believe."

"We're here all right. But I know what you mean. It seems as though we could walk outside and see the San Diego skyline with all its lights."

"Let's do that."

"Go back to San Diego?"

"No. Let's go outside."

The night air had cooled as the sun set over the mountainous horizon and gave way to the flood of darkness. Scattered shards of starlight hung from the canopy of space like tiny ornaments on a gigantic Christmas tree. The moon, three-quarters full, was already high in the sky. A warm current of wind flowed leisurely along the street, moving bits of dust and dirt along its path. Cars, some in extreme disrepair, passed along the paved road in front of the hotel. David and Kristen meandered along the walk a few yards until they found a wrought-iron bench set back from the walkway and street. They sat and gazed at the ebb and flow of the city. Bicyclists rode along the street, dodging parked cars and pedestrians.

"It's hard to believe that we are in the middle of a famine," David said. "It looks almost like any other city."

"Cities are the last to feel the squeeze of famine," Kristen said. "Besides, we're in the highlands. The worst hunger is in the lower, hotter elevations."

"It's amazing to think that the same moon that shines on our prosperity in the United States shines on their poverty here," he said dolefully. "We are at the threshold of the twenty-first century and still struggling with such things. One would think we would be beyond such problems by now. But then I guess it's to be expected."

"Expected? Famine and poverty? Death and disease?" Kristen was astonished. "I don't think we should ever assume that such things are natural. It's unnatural in every sense. You surprise me, David. I never would have pegged you for a fatalist."

"I'm not," David said with a disarming grin. "You misunderstand me. I'm not defending the presence of poverty. I'm saying that it's not surprising. Look," he said, turning on the bench to face her, "humankind has achieved many things in the course of its history. We have put men on the moon and probes on Mars. We have developed machines like CAT and MRI scanners that look right into the human body. Doctors can even replace the heart and the liver. But with all of those advances, we still need police on our streets and locks on our doors. In fact, as time goes on, we become more violent and self-centered. There's a theological concept that explains why."

"You're talking about sin nature."

"Yes. Sin nature is defined differently by various scholars, but at its core is the idea that every person has a tendency to sin—to do wrong. That's not to say that we lack control of our lives or that we are doomed to give in to the evil that is resident in everyone; that is only to say that everyone commits sin. That's the real problem. That's the disease; everything else is symptomatic of the problem."

Kristen thought for a moment. "I've heard sin nature spoken of in church all my life, but I've never applied the idea to things like world hunger. It seems too simplistic."

"Simple answers are often right," David said, affecting a professorial tone. "My point is this: People have a tendency to act in their own self-interest, even if it means that others may suffer in the process. This remains true, unless something changes that tendency."

"Not everyone is evil?"

"Not in the sense that every child born will turn into some kind of monster. But everyone does view the world through his set of personal needs. That's why the real culprit in famine is not weather, strong contributing factor as that is, but people involved in power struggles and civil war. That's why prejudice exists even after ten thousand years of history have taught us how wrong and futile bigotry is."

"But there are also people who sacrificially give of themselves to help others. People like Mother Teresa and, well, even A.J."

"You're absolutely right," David said, "and I wouldn't hesitate to add you or Peter or all the people who are working hard to save lives right now. Please understand, sin nature doesn't mean that everyone is as depraved as they can be, only that everyone must deal with the inclination to sin."

"What's the solution?" Kristen asked pointedly. "Will there always be hunger and crime?"

"The blunt answer is yes. There will always be crime and hunger, and with that the opportunity to make a difference. From the Christian point of view, the world will continue as it is until Christ comes again. That's when the whole system changes. Until then, we must continue to fight the good fight. You see, not only is everyone affected by sin nature, but there is in every person the image of God. We all know the difference between right and wrong, and God has given us the opportunity to choose between the two. That's why we are faced with the paradox of a world that can produce both Gandhi and Hitler; men like A.J. and men like the one who killed Judith Rhodes. Same world, same people, different results. All based on choice."

Kristen turned and looked at David. "I've been a believer for a long time, David, and my church has always been important to me, but I've always struggled with the presence of evil and suffering in the world. Every day I go to work, and even though I am safe and comfortable in my office, I'm keenly aware of the people who live on the edge of disaster. On Sundays I go to church and try to make sense of it all."

"I wish I could give you pat answers to those kinds of questions, but there aren't any. There has always been pain and suffering; theologians and philosophers have argued over their source and meaning for centuries."

"It's good to have someone to talk to about it." Kristen returned her gaze to the moon. "Do you know how some businesses often have a statement of purpose?"

"Yes. Many churches have them."

"My favorite Bible verse is such a statement. Let's see if I can still quote it. It's from the gospel of Luke and it goes something like this: 'The Spirit of the LORD is upon Me, because He has anointed Me to preach the gospel to the poor; He has sent Me to heal the brokenhearted, to proclaim liberty to the captives and recovery of sight to the blind, to set at liberty those who are oppressed; to preach the acceptable year of the LORD.' I find my motivation in that verse. It's good knowing that God cares."

David sat in silence, enjoying the night, the company, and the conversation. A few minutes later he said, "May I ask you a question?"

"Sure."

"Why haven't you ever married?" David asked, then quickly followed the question with, "I don't mean to pry. If I'm being too personal . . ."

"No," Kristen interrupted. "Not at all. The answer is simple: No one has ever asked me." David furrowed his brow. "You look puzzled. Surely it makes sense to you."

"Unless I've missed something, like your being an ax murderer or something, then it makes no sense at all."

"Look, David," Kristen said firmly, "I don't kid myself. Men aren't interested in flawed women. I see them look at me from time to time. They look at my face, then they look at my feet and turn away. Guys just aren't interested in dating a cripple."

David laughed.

"What's so funny?"

"I'm sorry. I'm not laughing at you. I've never thought of you as a cripple. Here we sit in the capital of Ethiopia talking about world events. In a day or two we will be walking in a famine area. I think you're being unfair to yourself."

"You know what I mean."

"No, actually I don't. Anyone who would dismiss you as undesirable because one leg isn't a perfect match with the other is the cripple, not you. You have been blessed not to be shackled to such shallow people. Any man—any decent man—would be interested in you."

"Does that include you?" Kristen asked pointedly. David hesitated, took a deep breath, which he exhaled noisily, and then looked back at the moon. "See what I mean," Kristen said coldly. She started to rise.

David reached for her and placed a hand on her shoulder. "Don't go. You don't understand. I know how my reaction must seem to you. Trust me, it has nothing to do with you; it has everything to do with me." Kristen leaned back on the bench again. David bowed his head and spoke quietly. "I was caught off guard. I'm not very good at this. I didn't date much in school. I married young, and she left me abruptly. I'm gun-shy."

"Of what?"

"Of relationships, I suppose." David turned in his seat to face Kristen. "I don't quite know how to feel. Being left by one's wife is difficult for any man, but for a preacher it's worse. It brings up all kinds of sticky questions. Today people marry and divorce freely, but for pastors a failed marriage is the ultimate failure, at least in the eyes of many."

"Why? You're human too."

"True, but knowing that doesn't take away the ghosts of failure that haunt my mind. The truth is, Kristen, I find myself extremely attracted to you, and I don't know what to do or think about it. You fear rejection because of a birth defect, I fear rejection because . . . well, because I'm afraid I won't be able to handle another dose of it."

They sat in silence. Cars passed them noisily, pedestrians walked along conversing in Arabic, Orominga, or Amharic, and the moon rose steadily in the sky; neither noticed, each lost in thought and uncertain what to say or do in the awkward situation. David felt ashamed and confused, and he could sense that Kristen felt undesirable and unwanted.

"What do we do now?" Kristen asked, her eyes fixed on the moon. "Do we sit frozen in our own worlds?"

David turned his eyes from the moon to Kristen and took a long look at her. Her eyes glistened with restrained tears, her red hair swayed gently in the breeze, the streetlight and moonlight reflected off her smooth and tender skin. She was lovely, captivating, Helen of Troy setting on an iron bench in Ethiopia. David felt himself being drawn to her. His skin tingled and his stomach seemed to turn over. His mind raced and his emotions churned. He didn't know how he felt about her, but he knew he wanted to touch her. Slowly he raised his hand and touched her cheek. A tear rolled down to meet the slightly trembling hand that so mildly and cautiously stroked her skin. She drew in a ragged breath as he slowly, almost imperceptibly leaned forward and closed his eyes, not knowing what to expect. Would she pull away? Would she think him forward and slap him?

He waited a single moment, a moment that seemed ages long. Then something soft, moist, and tender touched his lips. He could sense her, smell her skin and hair. Her lips welcomed his in a gentle yet hungry fashion. Those lips received his kiss and returned it in kind. The embrace was slow and easy and communicated more than mere thought; it communicated a flood of emotion.

When their kiss ended, the two looked at each other. He stroked her hair in long easy caresses.

"We may be breaking the law, you know," said Kristen. "This is a largely Muslim country. Such . . . personal interaction . . . may be offensive."

"It was worth the risk," David said softly.

"What does this mean?"

"I have no idea, but I'll remember it forever." The two returned their attention to the rising moon.

A tall, silent woman stood in the doorway to the hotel lobby watching the young couple in the evening light. After seeing them kiss, Sheila Womack stepped back into the hotel.

■ ■ ■ ■ ■

"Good news," A.J. said as he hung up the phone. "Eileen tells me that Roger has made contact again and that they've finally located Mahli in the port city of Marka. It took days, but Roger came through."

"And the bad news?" Sheila asked as she sat on the edge of the hotel bed.

"You know me so well, don't you?" A.J. replied somberly. "The bad news is what we expected: Mahli never travels alone. In fact, he's constantly surrounded by his men. Heavily armed men, I might add."

"What's the plan?"

"Patience. Roger will maintain his observation until he finds a way to get to Mahli or finds some other way of settling the score. I can assure you of one thing, Sheila, Dr. Rhodes's death will not go unpunished, nor will the pain and agony of the good Somali people. Mahli will pay in some way. He will pay a very expensive price."

Sheila nodded in silent agreement then said, "There's something else you should know. David and Kristen are . . . becoming close."

"Great!" A.J. uttered exuberantly. "They both need a little companionship. It should make them happy and all the more useful to us. It's about time Kristen took an interest in men."

"He concerns me," Sheila said seriously. "He picks up on things."

"David? You worry over nothing. It's true that David is as bright as they come, but he's a team player. He knows the importance of our work, and he won't let anything interfere with it."

"If he knew it all, he wouldn't approve."

"But," A.J. said forcefully, "he won't know it all. He's not the kind to join us in our . . . extra efforts, so he must never know of our other activities. I'm not going to tell him. I know you're not going to tell him, and neither is anyone else. We all have too much to lose, and there are too many people who stand to gain." He walked over to the bed where Sheila was seated and kissed her forehead. "Stop worrying that gorgeous head of yours. You have bigger fish to fry."

"It's my job to protect you from both outsiders and insiders."

"And you're doing a tremendous job. I couldn't feel more secure," A.J. replied lightly.

"You're not always easy to protect. You leave without telling me where you're going, and you're too trusting."

"When have I left without informing you?" A.J. asked feigning hurt feelings.

"August 17 you went jogging in the early morning hours and were attacked. An eyewitness told a newspaper reporter that a tall man with a ponytail beat up three gang members and then continued jogging as if nothing happened. That sounds a lot like you."

"All right," A.J. said, throwing up his hands, "you got me. I'm guilty as charged. I was upset and couldn't sleep that night. But you have to admit, I don't do it often."

"A.J.," Sheila said rising from the bed, "you are the most lovable and loving man in the world, but that affects your judgment. That's why I'm here. I'm a skeptic and a pessimist. I trust no one but myself and you. It's my job to help balance your optimism and enthusiasm and to keep you safe. But you have to take the things I say seriously."

The conversation fell silent, and then A.J. took Sheila into his arms and said, "I do take you seriously. I need you, not just for protection and balance, but I need you because of who you are. Knowing you're close by means more to me than words can express. Don't be angry with me." A.J. held her close and tight. A moment later, Sheila returned the embrace.

14

"YOU WATCH FOR A WHILE," ROGER SAID AS HE rolled over on his back, extended his legs and pointed his toes, stretching until every muscle in his neck, back, and legs was taut. He held the position for ten seconds then relaxed. He sat up and moved his head in easy circles, working out the kinks in his neck. "The roof of this warehouse may be the ideal surveillance spot, but it sure is uncomfortable."

"I don't think it was designed for humans," Aden said seriously. "Personally, I'd rather be in my bed at home instead of watching for a man who may or may not be in the building across the street."

"He's there," Roger said resolutely, "and if he's not, he will be." He rolled over on his belly again and raised a pair of binoculars to his eyes. Slowly he scanned each window as he had done a hundred times before, but he saw nothing. "We know he has offices in the basement. At least that's what your informant said."

"Maybe he was lying," Aden said as he rubbed the back of his neck. "You were pretty rough on him. He may have been lying to save his own skin."

Roger shook his head. "I believe him. There are too many guards posted around here. I'm surprised there's not one on this roof. They're either careless or comfortable."

"But we haven't seen him in days," Aden replied tiredly. "Perhaps he went back to Mogadishu."

"Maybe. I suppose it's possible that he has an underground entrance to the place. He'll make a mistake, and when he does I'll be there to . . . wait a minute." Aden brought his own pair of binoculars up. "The front door, someone's coming out. Is that . . . him?"

Aden studied the dark figure closely before he answered. "Close. It's his brother, Mukatu."

"Judging by the bag he's carrying, it looks like he's planning on going somewhere." Roger watched as a blue Jeep Cherokee pulled up in front of the warehouse. "Are he and his brother close?"

"Yes. Both are sadistic, but Mukatu is more so."

"I wonder . . . ," Roger said, his voice trailing off as he watched the car pull away. "Come on," he snapped as he got to his feet while remaining in a crouch. "Let's go."

"Go where? But what about Mahli—"

"Come on! I don't want to lose him." The two men moved quickly along the roof to the back of the building where a rope ladder had been neatly coiled. After a quick glance over the low parapet to be sure no one was in the alley below, Roger threw the ladder over the side. Without hesitancy, he sat on the parapet and swung his legs around so that they dangled over the alley. In an easy fluid motion, Roger was on the ladder and racing toward the ground. A moment later Aden, who was more accustomed to discussing matters over a table than to scaling the sides of buildings, fumbled awkwardly as he searched for the first rung of the rope ladder. Finding it, he eased himself over the side and cautiously climbed down the ladder. "Couldn't you take a little bit longer?" Roger said sarcastically. "Now we might actually catch up to him."

"Look," Aden snapped, "you're the former army ranger; I'm the misplaced teacher, remember?"

Roger ignored the comment as he reached for nylon ropes that hung on each side of the ladder. With a firm pull on each cord, the knots that secured the ladder to vent pipes on the roof slipped their grasp and the ladder fell to the ground, folding in on itself. Roger grabbed it and began to run down the alley with Aden close behind. They wove their way through the small maze of passageways formed by the various buildings and warehouses. Three minutes later they stopped at the side of an old Peugeot sedan.

"I'll drive," Roger said bluntly.

"Won't they see us following them?" Aden asked apprehensively.

"Not if I can help it," Roger replied. The vehicle pulled away from its resting place. Roger turned the lights on and drove slowly through the back streets until he was sure he was at least a half-mile from Mahli's building. Then, as he steered onto the main street to follow Mukatu's car he switched off the lights and pressed the accelerator. The little car's engine responded accordingly, and soon Roger and Aden were bouncing down the rough road in pursuit.

"Isn't it a little dangerous to be driving without lights?" Aden asked as he attempted to catch his breath after their little jog.

"It's a lot less dangerous than driving with them on," Roger replied easily. He, unlike Aden, was not winded by the run to the car. "Unless you want to meet Mukatu face to face."

"No thanks. He's a piranha. I have no desire to meet him."

"That's odd, I think I would enjoy meeting him—alone and in a locked room."

Aden looked puzzled. "I thought you were after Mahli, not his brother."

"I'm after all of their kind."

"Kind?"

"Guys like that have kept your country in poverty and forced children to die on the streets. They kill people who come to help. They are the worst kind of human being. They are cancers, and the best thing that could happen to your country is to have those cancers removed." Roger spat his words with vehemence. "I want Mahli, and I'll get him. I may have to go through his brother first. Consider it a bonus."

Within five minutes they spotted the red taillights of Mukatu's car. Roger slowed to follow at a discreet distance, unnoticed by the vehicle in front of them. The disjointed two-car caravan traveled north toward Mogadishu but soon turned off onto a side road. Roger let his Peugeot fall even farther back so that the taillights ahead of them were barely discernible.

"How far from Mogadishu do you think we are?" Roger asked.

"Not far," Aden replied, "maybe thirty kilometers."

"Any idea where he's going?"

Aden thought for a moment. "There are some large oceanfront homes nearby. Some business owners and government officials live there. Maybe that's where he's headed."

"Follow them with your binoculars," Roger ordered. "I want to know how many people are in the car with him." Aden brought the glasses up to his eyes and struggled to keep the Jeep in sight, a task made difficult by the bouncing of the car. "See anything?"

"It's hard to see much in the dark and at this distance, but it looks like there are four occupants," Aden said as the car hit a pot-hole with a jarring impact. "That doesn't make it any easier," he snapped. "I don't know what I'm doing here."

"You want me to pull over and let you out?" Roger quipped.

"No thank you. I'll see it through, although I don't know why."

"You know why," Roger said firmly. "You're involved because you are a man of principles and because you believe that people in your country have a right to live without fear from guys like Mahli and Mukatu. Besides, Barringston Relief has been good to you. You have food, money, and a place to stay. That's better than 90 percent of your people. You don't want to give that up, do you?"

Aden ignored the remark and kept his binoculars on the Jeep Cherokee. "They're slowing," he said loudly.

"Don't shout! I'm in the same car as you."

"Sorry. They're pulling off the road. We had better slow down." Rather than step on the brake, which would activate the brake lights and increase the possibility of being noticed, Roger dropped into a lower gear. The car slowed immediately with a lurch. Ahead they could see the taillights of the Jeep glow brighter as the driver stepped on the brakes. The car was slowing and turning. Roger dropped to the lowest gear and let the car coast to a near stop. He then pulled up on the parking-brake handle until the car ceased moving.

"Looks like they're done for the night," Roger said quietly.

"What do we do now?"

Roger looked around. In the dim, moonlit night he could see the ocean to the east and a set of small rolling hills to the west. "We'll hide in those hills. Maybe Mahli is here, too, and if so, then we can take our next step."

"And just what is our next step?" Aden asked seriously.

Roger looked at the man for a few seconds. "I don't know yet. But I will."

■ ■ ■ ■ ■

Seated at the small desk in his hotel room, A.J. listened patiently to the ringing that was coming over the handset of his phone. Three rings later the Barringston Relief automated voice mail answered. A.J. punched three-two-two-three. A moment later a voice made tinny by the overseas satellite link answered.

"Yes?" The voice was slow and groggy.

"Good morning, Eileen," A.J. said cheerfully. "You sound positively radiant."

"I don't radiate until after noon," she said gloomily. "I hate mornings. What time is it?"

"It's nearly midnight, which means that it's almost eleven in the morning there, so wake up. The morning's almost gone."

"It's still before noon, and I didn't go to bed until six this morning."

"Been busy, I take it?" A.J. said with a chortle.

"Enough to keep me off the streets."

"Let me get to the point, so that you can have breakfast or lunch or whatever. Have you heard from Roger?"

"Last night. Is your phone working okay?" Eileen asked. It was a code to determine the security of the line.

"I have the encoder on," A.J. said as he looked at the small black plastic device that had been designed to look like a CD player. "I assume your outgoing line is secured."

"I turned it on last night. I had a feeling you'd be calling," Eileen said nonchalantly. "Anyway, Roger made his usual contact through the satellite, but this time he had news. First, the bad news. He hasn't seen our man yet, but—and here's the good news—he has found a new location. The old one is still a valid place to watch, but the new place may be even better. Roger was maintaining surveillance on the warehouse when he saw Mahli's brother leaving. Apparently, he travels more than Mahli."

"Probably to protect him. Where did he go?"

"A seaside villa between Marka and Mogadishu. It's heavily guarded, so sneaking in is out of the question, but Roger feels that Mahli is either there or will arrive there over the next few days. He has set up a surveillance spot with Aden. He feels secure, but he's complaining about the heat. There's nothing to do but wait. How are you doing?"

"We're all okay. Anything else I need to know?"

Eileen didn't answer at first.

"What is it, Eileen?"

An audible sigh preceded Eileen's words. "The president of the Americas Bank was found dead a few days ago. He had been shot in the head. A story ran in the *New York Times* and on the AP service."

A.J. felt his heart race and his stomach turn. "Do you think it had anything to do with the . . . the money transfer?"

"Yes, but don't take this too hard. It's not your fault. It's his for being involved with terrorist groups. He knew that he was dancing with the devil."

A.J. said nothing for a long time.

"You still there, A.J.?" Eileen's voice was laced with concern.

"Did he have family?"

"Yes."

"Are they well off?"

"I suppose so, he was the president of the bank, and we know that he skimmed money."

"Check it out," A.J. said sharply. "His family shouldn't have to pay the price for his sin or ours. Also tell Roger to keep it up, but to use his best judgment. I'll keep in touch."

"Will do. Are you going to be all right?"

"I'll be fine, thanks." A.J. hung up the phone, disconnected the electronic scrambler, and returned it to its compartment in his luggage bag. His mind raced with the image of a man with a bullet in his brain. It was true that Ian Booth was far from an ethical man, but he was neither violent nor vindictive. He didn't deserve to die at the hands of terrorists. A.J. felt remorse and guilt. It wasn't the first time that he had ordered the appropriation of someone else's funds to finance Barringston's work around the world. But he had always been careful to steal only from those who were outside the reach of the law, from those who made the world more violent and dangerous. He had no qualms about electronically stealing funds from the Mafia, terrorist groups, and oppressive dictators, but only if he was sure that the ramifications would never affect the innocent. Booth's death was a failure, and there was nothing he could do about it.

Life was neither simple nor predictable. He himself was a complex stew of intellect, desire, motivation, and emotion. He felt no remorse when the evil leeches of the world died, even if they died at his bidding. There were men who deserved death and for whom A.J. wouldn't waste a second thought. There were people like Mahli and Mukatu who killed the brave and noble Dr. Rhodes in the middle of the work to which she had so unselfishly dedicated herself. Adding insult to that act was the sinking of the *Sea Maid*. Mahli and men like him deserved to be planted in the ground where they belonged—their dead bodies fertilizing the earth. But the innocent were another matter. They deserved life, a reasonable life that A.J. struggled to provide. Now, because of his decision, a family mourned a lost loved one, a father, a husband, a brother, a son. It was not for Booth that he mourned, but for his family.

This knowledge caused A.J.'s adrenaline to kick in. Sleep was out of the question. He paced back and forth between his bed and the small desk at which he had been sitting. He had been pent-up too long. He missed the physical release of jogging, racquetball, and working out. It was the inability to exercise as he wished that bothered him most about traveling in difficult lands.

Stripping his shirt off, A.J. lowered himself to the floor and began doing push-ups, lowering and raising himself time after time in a slow steady rhythm. At first his muscles protested the strain, but soon they were loose, and he was feeling the exhilaration of his power. With each push-up, he withdrew further and further into himself. His eyes were fixed on a tiny spot on the dirty green carpet between his hands. Soon he saw nothing but that spot, heard nothing but the beating of his heart, and felt nothing but the stretching of his muscles. One push-up was followed by another. He didn't count. The number of push-ups didn't matter, only the mind-numbing work, only the searing muscular heat to be conquered. This would clear his mind. This would ease his tension. This would allow him to face one more day and to do those things that no one else in the world was willing to do.

■ ■ ■ ■ ■

The late afternoon sun reflected off the tinted, double-pane windows of Mahli's seaside manor, leaving the interior protected from the unrelenting and stagnant August heat, a heat the locals called *tangambili*, a Somali word that meant "two sails." It is said that during the hot months a boatman needed two sails to catch enough breeze to move forward. Mahli stood by the window gazing introspectively out at the rolling surf. Behind him, seated at a large dining-room table, was his brother, Mukatu, who unlike Mahli was still eating. Before him was spread an array of fruits, lamb, and sweet bread.

"What do you see out that window, brother?" Mukatu asked, his mouth full of meat.

Mahli turned for a moment and regarded his brother. They were as close as any brothers had ever been, but they were so different. Mukatu lived for the moment, for the present enjoyment or thrill, but Mahli lived for what the future held—the future he would help mold.

"I see the past and the future."

"You see all that in the waves? You are a wise man."

"I was thinking about our country's past," Mahli said, returning his attention to the rolling, blue Indian Ocean. "The ancient Egyptians call this the Land of Punt, and they sailed here in their ancient vessels and returned home with incense and myrrh to use in their temples. Then came the Phoenician traders, followed by the Greeks and Romans. Then Arabs and Persians joined the parade. The Arabs took our resources for their homes and gave us Islam for our souls. The Portuguese came and conquered until they gave way to the Italians who built the triumphal arches, but they too left in defeat. Then the British arrived, but they left three decades ago. Somalia always comes back to Somalis. Allah gave us this land, barren as it is, and no matter who takes it, it returns to us."

"You are indeed a philosopher, my dear brother," Mukatu said as he reached across the table and took a large pinch of leaves from a bowl and placed them in his mouth. "There is no doubt that Allah gave you the brains of our clan. Care for some kat?"

Mahli again turned to his brother and watched him chew the mind-altering plant. He knew the cathinone in the leaves would soon make his brother feel relaxed and blissful. This was good, he thought, because his brother would be easier to control. "No thank you. I prefer to leave my mind the way it is. You do know that kat is addictive, don't you?"

"As you have told me many times, brother, but as Father always said, 'Kat is not a luxury; it is a necessity.'"

Nodding his understanding, Mahli turned again to his pondering. His father had been right. The hardship of living in Somalia required a release. There was so little water, so little farmland, so little education, so few resources. Somalia was always the last to receive what every other country took for granted. The nomads still wandered the wilderness as they always had, despite the efforts of the Marxist government of President Mohammed Said Barre, who tried to settle the nomads into farming communities. But the nomadic life was too deeply rooted in their genes to surrender to a more anchored existence.

That was the problem, wasn't it? Mahli thought to himself. Change was difficult to make. Change, real and abiding change, could not be legislated. That had been tried many times, but always to no avail. Camel herders still herded their camels as their great-grandparents did; children still learned the Koran from their long, wooden prayer boards; famine still came; drought still came; and the desert still advanced. Some change had occurred. Somali families knew how to hide from Ethiopian military aircraft. They learned that during their two-year war with Ethiopia in 1977 and 1978. It was that war that had taken Mahli's father, and since they lost, also stole a good deal of Somali pride. During that war men learned to use more than knives to defend themselves; they learned to fire Russian-made weapons at their enemy. Ironically, they fought Russian-led troops from Cuba. They graduated to missile launchers and artillery, which came from the United States. But those were small changes. The heart of the people remained the same.

More needed to be done. Somalia could no longer remain the doormat for other countries. Somalia had to learn to stand on its own. But rival clans, lack of education, and lack of resources had kept the country mired in the past. *I will change that*, Mahli thought. *I will bring a new day, not only for Somalia but for all of East Africa.*

"May I ask a question, brother?" Mukatu asked.

"You just did," Mahli replied with a grin.

Mukatu giggled, and Mahli could see the kat was already working on Mukatu's mind, dropping its mist of euphoria on every brain cell. "You're right. Now may I ask another question?" Mahli started to tell him that he had once again asked a question, but thought better of it. It was clearly a joke with no end.

"Certainly."

"Why sink the ship?" Mukatu asked, shoving more kat into his mouth. "It makes no sense to sink a ship filled with food. "

It was a sensible question, but the answer might not seem sensible to Mukatu, whose mind was still alert but definitely clouded.

"It seems confusing, doesn't it?" Mahli said as he strolled from the window to the table. "The answer is in our goal. We wish to change our corner of the world. But change is difficult. That is what I was thinking a moment ago. Change must be forced. The world looks at us as unloved and ignorant stepchildren; as backward people who don't know enough to take care of ourselves. They don't think that we can feed our own or educate our children. We seem stupid and impotent to them. Some of our own people think that way too. But we will change all that, you and I." Mahli began to pace around the table, his hands folded behind him, his head bowed in thought like one of his professors in college. "We provided food not only to our own people but to Ethiopians. The world sees this, and they think that at last someone is in control. The Ethiopians see that we help them of our own free will and with no strings attached. We ask for nothing in return—at first."

"Do you really think Ethiopia will join the alliance?"

"Yes. The world thinks we are a vicious and ungrateful people who turn weapons on those who lend us help. Mohammed Farah Aidid saw to that when he killed Pakistani and American soldiers when they brought food and medicine."

"You've not had any problem with killing," Mukatu said firmly.

"You do not understand, brother. Perhaps you chew too much kat," Mahli said. "Death is required to make these noble changes.

The difference between Aidid and me is that I see to it that those deaths are not attributed to me. The world follows heroes, not monsters."

"So if the world knew . . ."

"It won't," Mahli snapped. "This plan will work as long as each of us does his job and we don't make any mistakes."

"I haven't made any mistakes," Mukatu said defensively.

"No, you haven't, and if you will let me do the planning, you won't make any in the future either." Mahli softened his tone. "There's a great deal in this for you, my brother. A great deal of power and a great deal of money."

"Here's to power and money," Mukatu said with a broad, leaf-stained grin.

Mahli picked up a glass of water, raised it in a toast, and said, "To *our* power and money."

■ ■ ■ ■ ■

"What are they doing now?" Aden asked as he lay on his back in the dried grass under an acacia tree.

"They're toasting their soon-to-be-success," Roger said, stretching his back. "I wish I had thought to bring a tripod for this dish; I'm getting tired of holding it. At least I thought far enough ahead to pack it in the car."

"You've been holding it on and off for hours," Aden said wearily. "Don't you think you have listened enough?"

Roger laid the parabolic listening dish down and switched off the electronics. "For now. But I still don't know their next move."

"Did they admit to downing the ship?" Aden was incredulous.

"That they did," Roger said. "And they don't feel the least bit of remorse. It's all part of their plan."

"Plan? What plan?"

Roger explained everything that he just heard through the advanced listening device.

"Unbelievable," Aden said. "I doubt it will work. There are too many variables, too many personalities to consider. He'll never be able to convince Ethiopia to be part of an alliance. Our country has never been on good terms with them. The whole idea is absurd."

"The most effective ideas in the world are absurd. That's why they work; no one has ever thought of them. Besides, it doesn't matter if the plan is possible or not. Mahli thinks it is, and he's killed to make his dream a reality. That makes the validity of the plan secondary, don't you agree?"

Aden sat silently for a moment then said, "Yes, I suppose so."

"Review your history, Aden," Roger said, sitting up and twisting his head around to loosen the muscles in his neck. "If you were to outline Hitler's plan on paper it would be laughable, but he pulled it off. If, in the thirties, you asked if Japan might attempt to conquer China and surrounding regions as well as to attack the United States, you would dismiss the whole concept. But it happened. Think of the most vicious dictators in the world. Did they arrive at their power because they were geniuses? No, but they believed they were. That's all it takes. Mahli and his no-good brother are no different. His plan may not be feasible, but I'm betting that he's willing to kill an awful lot of people to prove that it is."

"Your point is well taken," Aden acquiesced. "So what do we do now?"

"Wait. Listen some more. I'll report back to my people later, but until then we wait for opportunity to come knocking."

"What will opportunity look like?" Aden asked seriously.

"I have no idea, but I'll recognize it when I see it. No doubt about that. And when I do . . . that's when I act."

"I feel that I should tell someone in my government."

"What government? The last vestiges of corporate leadership fell twelve months ago when this famine started." Roger was animated. "You'll tell no one. This is something I can take care of, something I will take care of." Having said that, Roger rolled over on his stomach, picked up the listening dish, and aimed it at Mahli's compound again.

15

THE LARGE FOUR-WHEEL-DRIVE VAN PULLED UNDER the canopy at the front of the lobby. The driver exited the vehicle, opened the passenger door, and waited, his body erect and his head held high.

"Off we go," A.J. said as he led the small procession to the vehicle.

The driver, a tall, thin man with a perpetually murky expression, drove slowly along the paved road, occasionally steering around a pothole that might jar his passengers. He spoke not a word, but hunched over the steering wheel and squinted myopically down the road.

They passed through the heart of Addis Ababa with its high-rise and mid-rise office buildings from which Marxist banners once hung. The center of the city was much like any other major city in an industrial nation. Its streets were broad and paved. Cars, many of them vintage Volkswagens, Volvos, and Mercedes, lined the curbs. It was clear that some of them had not moved for quite some time. They passed a Mobil gas station, a large bank building, an Ethiopian Orthodox church, a mosque, and hundreds of pedestrians.

David found the pedestrians the most interesting. Many wore Western garb and would fit in to any city back home. Others, especially the Muslim women, wore either white shawls over their heads and shoulders or heavy black coverings that revealed only their eyes. Unlike cities in the States, all the pedestrians were slim;

174

there was not a single overweight person among them. None seemed especially famished, but it was clear that food was still a rare commodity even in the largest city of Ethiopia.

Once outside the city, the scenery changed from concrete commercial buildings to open country with green trees and brown, coarse grass. Here, David saw pedestrians too, but unlike those in the city, these were dressed in clothes that were old, faded, dirty, and often torn. Mothers carried children on their hips and wore bandannas over their heads, tied in knots behind. He also saw a small village of huts with brown-thatched roofing. The people walked aimlessly, their hopes of subsistence farming dashed by the persistent drought. David looked across the seat at A.J., who gazed sadly out the window.

A.J. gave more specific directions to the driver. When he heard where A.J. wanted to go, his murky expression darkened all the more.

"I know the area," he said cautiously. "It is bad, and the road is not good. At least fifty kilometers are rough dirt road. I'll take you back to the hotel."

"No," A.J. uttered firmly. "You will take us where I've told you."

The driver scowled, said something in Amharic, which David took to be other than a compliment, and pressed on. It wasn't long before the driver's prophecy became reality. The body of the long van squealed in protest of the cracked and eroded pavement. The passengers bounced off one another and the interior of the car, at times hitting their heads on the ceiling. David turned to ask the driver to be more careful, but saw that he was already intently peering over the steering wheel and doing his best to steer around the worst of it. The jarring they were receiving was the result of the driver being forced to choose between the lesser of the two evils.

"They should put this ride in at Disneyland," Peter said. "I don't think I'll be able to walk when we're done." David empathized with Peter. His back hurt, especially over his kidneys.

"Could be worse," A.J. said. "We could be driving your car."

"How much longer?" Kristen asked.

"My guess would be another hour," A.J. replied. "I think we'll all live."

David had his doubts. Not only did his body hurt, but his stomach as well. David was prone to motion sickness, especially as a child. As an adult he could ride in planes and cars with only minor discomfort. This, however, was asking his stomach for more than it could endure. He wondered if anyone else was suffering as much as he. Kristen looked thoroughly shaken, but still together; Peter was jostled and clearly uncomfortable. Only A.J. and Sheila seemed unfazed. Sheila simply gazed out the window as if lost in thought.

The remaining time passed with agonizing slowness, especially after the van veered from the maintained road onto a dirt lane. The vehicle's air conditioning spared them the September heat, but it could not spare them the bruises they received with each new teeth-jarring bump.

■ ■ ■ ■ ■

The camp was located in a small village of thatched huts and canvas tents. It was very much what David had expected. The sun had passed its zenith and was following its daily downward path, lengthening the shadows.

Strolling down the central lane of the camp, he listened as A.J. gave the team a briefing: "We work with many of Ethiopia's ethnic groups. We feed and provide medicine to the Sidamos, Oromos, Somalis, Amharas, Afars, and the Tigreans. We do so year in and year out. Even in nondrought years, five million Ethiopians depend on the half-million tons of grain provided by other countries. Experts call that a 'structural food deficit.' That means there's a gap between the food the country produces and the food it needs so that its people don't starve. But that's only part of the problem. There are other matters that must be addressed."

"What else is there?" Kristen asked. She had a video recorder raised to her eye and was panning the compound.

"That road we were just on is a perfect example of the problem. Ethiopia needs more than food; Ethiopia needs a way to distribute that food. Of all the countries that face chronic famine, this one is in the best position to end the suffering. It has a new and responsive government, the second largest population in Africa, and possesses a wonderful geography that if properly harnessed . . ."

David ceased to hear the discussion as he wandered from the group. A little boy, a profoundly pitiful little boy, had caught his eye. He was no more than five years old and was seated on the ground between two tents, playing with a small rubber ball. David was fascinated with the lad who seemed oblivious to the world. The boy moved hardly at all, but sat in the dust with his legs spread before him, holding the small rubber ball in his tiny black hands.

David didn't know why, nor could he tell when it happened, but his senses became more sensitive. Noises and voices sounded louder, even the wind, warm and thin, seemed to take on a new life. The tents of the compound seemed whiter, the sky seemed bluer, the smell—the stark near-putrid odor of poverty—seemed more intense. Even the ball that the little boy held in his hand took on new detail, revealing the abuse of years in its elastic hide.

The ball was painted with gay colors of blue and red triangles and stars. It reminded David of a ball he had as a child. It had been his favorite toy, and he used to sit quietly on the carpeted floor of his parents' home and stare at it just as this young boy was doing. There was something therapeutic in the presence of the toy. David had been able to project himself through his imagination onto the surface of the small sphere. In his mind it became a new world, a place all his own. It was something David did when he was sad or troubled or if his parents had scolded him. As he grew older his toys changed, but his imagination worked the same. It was then that David realized that all little boys could perform the same feat of magic—mentally projecting oneself to an imaginary world devoid of pain, frustration, and fear. That's what this little boy was doing. He was mentally disengaging from reality, if just for a short time.

As David watched the lad, a younger child approached. There was enough of a resemblance between the two to make David believe they were brothers. The younger boy, whom David judged to be about three or four, waddled on bare feet to his brother. He was crying, wailing in desperation and deep-seated fear. There was a loneliness in the cry, a tone of utter despair that no three-year-old should feel.

David recognized this emotion too. As a child not much older than the crying boy, he had become separated from his mother in a department store. To his young eyes the shelves of goods and the long aisles seemed an impregnable maze. He cried out for his mother but heard no response. He wandered to the end of one aisle and looked down the rows of shelves. People, tall as trees to him, walked past without comment. Panic set in, and David, in abject frustration, sat down in the aisle and wept deep and bitter tears. He had been left alone; he knew it. His mother had forgotten him, and he would forever be surrounded by strangers. He had wanted to go home, to his room, to his bed, to his family. But now he never would. He had been as sure of that as he had been sure of anything in his life—until he heard his mother's voice. "Why are you crying?" she had asked. "I wasn't that far away."

Perhaps that's all the little crying boy needed. Perhaps he just needed someone to take him by the hand and lead him to his mother. David could do that. After all, they shared a common bond. They both had felt the fear of loneliness, of a premature separation from their mothers. As an adult, David knew that problems like this were really a function of an overactive imagination, but the emotion was nonetheless real.

David decided to help. Moving farther from the others, he walked the short distance to the small lane formed by the rows of tents with the Barringston Relief logo stenciled on them. He was unsure of what to say. Most likely the boys could speak no English, but surely they would understand a smile and a gentle touch. As he approached the children he looked down the corridor between the tents and saw that the boys were not alone. A woman dressed in a white halter top and a brown ankle-length skirt was reclining on a mat. She lay still and unmoving, and David was puzzled how she could sleep through the shrieking and the sobbing of the youngest child. Surely she could hear the cries of her own child.

Smiling at the two boys, David stroked each of them on the head and said gently, "It's all right, guys. There's no need to cry. Mother isn't far away." The five-year-old looked at him through vacant eyes, the three-year-old continued to wail in long and loud ululation.

Stepping past them, David approached the reclining woman. She lay on her right side, her head resting on her outstretched arm. She lay still, unaware of David's approach. Squatting down beside her David said, "Excuse me."

The woman didn't respond. She was young, perhaps in her early twenties, and her sunken cheeks and thin arms gave testimony to weeks of malnutrition. "Excuse me," David said again, but still no response. He reached out and gently touched her frail arm. The woman rolled over onto her back, not by her own movement but because of David's gentle touch. A swarm of flies took to the air. The sight of the woman caused David to bolt upright and gasp. The woman stared at him through one partially opened eye that could no longer see. Her body was rigid, and the pernicious effects of rigor mortis had set in, causing her to sneer through the constricted muscles of her face. She was dead, something her children understood long before David.

He stared in disbelief at the corpse before him and felt his senses shutting down. A few moments ago every one of his senses had reached levels of new awareness; now they were rapidly closing in an attempt to preserve sanity and to lessen the emotional shock that raced through every fiber of his body and every avenue of his mind. The crying of the boys faded into silence; the light of the day dimmed; the air became heavy and unbreathable. David closed his eyes, but not before seeing scores of flies settle on the body again.

"David?" A distant and dim voice said. "Are you all right?"

David felt no need to respond; he remained motionless, silent, and kept his eyes tightly shut.

"David!" The voice said louder, and then the words took on an authoritarian tone. "Open your eyes, David. Open them right now and look at me."

He felt his body being shaken. "Now, David!" It was A.J.'s voice. He knew that voice, he trusted that voice, so David opened his eyes, but instead of looking at the man in front of him, he let his eyes drift back to the woman's corpse. "No, David, I said look at me."

The sounds were returning: the crying, the speaking, the buzzing of flies. David looked up at the tall man in front of him and blinked several times. Tears were beginning to run from his eyes, unexpected tears that streamed down his face. He blinked again, clearing the moisture from his eyes, and saw A.J., concern deeply etched into his face, looking back. David stared into his eyes and saw strength and power and resolve, all coated in a blanket of tears.

"Are you with me, David?" he asked firmly.

David nodded weakly. "I'm sorry. I feel like an idiot. I . . . I don't know what my problem is."

"Nonsense," A.J. said, physically turning David around and walking away from the dead woman. "It's to be expected. This is your first trip and your first contact with this kind of death. I remember my first time clearly: I threw up several times. At least you held on to your breakfast."

"The day is not over yet," David replied weakly. He felt hot and wiped the perspiration from his brow. "I thought she was sleeping. I wanted to help the kids. I had no idea . . ."

"You're an admirable man, David," A.J. patted him on the back. "You showed some wonderful qualities in that little act."

"I don't feel very admirable."

They stopped by the two children. The youngest had stopped crying now that he was surrounded by people. "You got involved. Most people just hang back, but you took steps. Sure you got a shock, but next time you'll be prepared." The others had joined them by the row of tents. A.J. continued, loud enough for everyone to hear. "People die here, David. A great many people die, but a great many live. This is not a place of death. Death occurs here, to be sure, but this is a camp of life. These two children, thanks to the heroic efforts of their mother, will continue to live. It's important that you focus on that, David. We grieve for the dead, but we fight for the living. That's why we're here."

"So you don't think I'm a complete idiot?" David asked meekly. He looked at Kristen, who was covering her mouth with her hand.

"Not in the least," A.J. pronounced. "Men of your quality are rare. I'm glad to have you along." Reaching down, A.J. lifted up the youngest boy and held him in one arm. Then he held his hand out to the boy with the ball, who stood to his feet. "Now let's see if we can find Dr. James Goodwin, the camp's leader."

■ ■ ■ ■ ■

The sun was dropping behind the highland mountains and staining the sky with gold that turned to pink that in turn deepened to red. David, Kristen, and Dr. Goodwin strolled down the lane that was formed by the rows of tents on either side. A.J., Sheila, and Peter were still in Goodwin's tent, resting and reviewing the doctor's notes.

"I wanted to talk to you apart from the group," Goodwin said with a slight but noticeable Irish brogue. "I felt the need to apologize to you."

"What on earth for?" David asked.

"For the incident with the young lady . . . the deceased. We normally don't allow the dead to lie around like that. We're still checking, but it seems she had just arrived and died where you found her. We were unaware of her arrival. Still, I feel badly."

"No apology is necessary," David replied quietly.

"We work hard here. Our battle is unending, our resources limited, and our help sparse, but we fight the good fight, and we make a difference."

"I can see that," David said. Then he asked, "Is this a large camp compared to others?"

"Small, actually. We expect that it will get larger as time goes on, but we're not nearly the size as those in the more arid regions like the Ogaden in the east or the Welo district north of here. We do the same work, but they do more of it."

"How long have you been here?" Kristen asked.

"In Ethiopia? About two years. I started with a group called Doctors Without Borders, but later joined Barringston Relief. I wanted to do this work full time, and A.J. welcomed me."

"How long do you plan to stay?" David inquired.

Goodwin paused before answering. He looked around at the pitiful city of tents and its emaciated populace. "Until there is no more work to do. I'll probably die here. This is my home now. My work is here, my research is here, my heart is here."

"Research?"

"Oh yes," Goodwin said proudly. "One of the reasons I joined Barringston is to research the effects of hunger and hunger-related diseases. Some of what we learn here is used in other lands, and not only among the hungry but among those with diseases that affect the body like hunger."

"Don't you ever despair?" Kristen asked directly. "Don't you ever feel like giving up?"

Goodwin laughed, "Daily. Some look at me with pity saying, 'What a shame he has to give up so much.' But what have I given up? Traffic? High malpractice insurance? These people have given me more than I could ever hope for. They are a proud and noble people. They know how to stand strong, and they also know how to love." As if on cue, a small group of children ranging in age from five to ten rushed toward Goodwin shouting, "Doctari, Doctari." They surrounded him and hugged him, the smallest clinging to his legs. He spoke to them in Amharic and reached into his pants pocket to extract small round candies.

"How many people are in this camp?" David asked.

"Around four hundred. Tomorrow it will be more. The next day, more still." Goodwin pointed to a tent. A man and two children sat in front of it eating a rice-and-bean mixture from a battered wooden bowl. "Do you see that man? We almost lost him. He arrived two weeks ago, barely able to walk. He was carrying his youngest son on his back. I don't know how he did it, but he did. We immediately administered vitamin shots and rehydration packets. We brought him and the boys food three times a day, but he wouldn't eat. Instead, he hid the food so his sons could have food later. He was hoarding in case we ran out of supplies. It took me three days to convince him to eat. At first I had to threaten to take the food away from his children. We would never do that, of course, but I had to precipitate an emotional crisis in the man to force him to eat. Now he helps us deliver food to the others."

"Amazing," Kristen uttered. "You would think that I would know all this, but I had no idea beyond what I read in the reports."

It was clear to David that he had no idea of the magnitude of need or how personal the grip of hunger was. He found himself inundated with guilt and remorse. "You know," he confessed, "I used to think that I had problems, that my life was difficult. You know—bills, lack of appreciation at work, a wife who left me—but now I see that I have never truly had a problem in my life. Inconveniences, yes, but never a real problem."

The remainder of the day was long and grueling. David and the others were more than observers in the camp, they were workers, each performing a needed function. Late that evening two covered, one-ton trucks roared into camp loaded with bags of rice, sorghum, beans, and other commodities. David was surprised to see a huge quantity of carrots. Dr. Goodwin informed him that many Ethiopians suffer from xerophthalmia—night blindness—due to a lack of vitamin A. David had noticed that the eyes of many of the adults were milky and lackluster. Each person received vitamin shots upon arriving in camp, but medication often ran out. The carrots not only provided the much-needed vitamin, they also served as a food supply. "Carrots are new to many of the people," Goodwin had said, "but they soon learn to love them. They say they're *batam teruno*—very good."

The trucks were unloaded, and meals were prepared and distributed to long lines of hungry Ethiopians. Those too weak to stand in line were brought food. David walked the camp with A.J. to help distribute meals. In some cases adults and children were too weak to hold their bowls or to spoon the lifesaving sustenance to their mouths. Tears welled in David's eyes as he watched A.J. Barringston, millionaire son of a billionaire industrialist, cradle an elderly man's head and slowly raise a spoonful of food to his mouth. Soon David was doing the same. He found the job as fulfilling as anything he had ever done in his life. Yet other tasks had to be done: Thirteen people had died that day, five children and eight adults, and their bodies had to be removed from camp. Each corpse was wrapped in a white sheet and loaded onto a truck and taken to a designated burial area. The awful irony weighed heavily on David: People had traveled at great physical expense only to die in the midst of help and nourishment.

After their walk through camp, David and Kristen sat on fiberglass folding chairs outside Dr. Goodwin's tent. A.J., Sheila, and Peter were still in the tent discussing the camp's future needs. Goodwin had joined them.

"You look exhausted," Kristen said.

"I feel exhausted," David replied. Rubbing his eyes he looked skyward. The large summer moon was floating high in the sky and casting its ivory light down on the camp. "Our moon is back."

"You were right when you said it was difficult to believe that the same moon that shone down on our prosperity also looked down on their poverty." Kristen shifted in her chair and stretched to loosen the kinks in her tired body. "This has been a day I will never forget."

"Amen to that," David said wearily. "I don't know how Goodwin and his staff do this every day. It must exact a horrible emotional toll. But then again . . ."

"Then again what?"

"The work does bring huge satisfaction, doesn't it?"

"I don't know," Kristen replied. "To be truthful, I'm too tired to feel much of anything, except for admiration."

"I know what you mean. That A.J. is something. The way he jumped right in unloading the truck, hand-feeding some of the worse cases, and even carrying the bodies of the dead out. And he's still working. I've never before met anyone like A.J."

"I think there are many like him; they just don't know it," Kristen said seriously. "You say you've never met anyone else like A.J., but I have. You have the same passion, David. You just don't know it yet."

"Oh, no," David disagreed. "You saw my strength when we first got to camp. I almost lost it when I saw that dead woman and her two crying children nearby. It was almost more than I could bear."

"Anyone would have reacted the same way," replied Kristen emphatically. "You heard A.J.; he reacted the same way. And as I recall, you didn't lose it. On the contrary, you unloaded the trucks, moved the bodies, fed the invalids right along with A.J. I saw it in you today, David. I saw the power to make a difference. I saw the genuine concern, not pity, nor revulsion, but heart-deep concern. Most people are so overwhelmed by what they see that they can do nothing, but you jumped right in there, right up to your elbows."

"You can't compare me to A.J., he's a great man. I've achieved many things in my life, but nothing like he has. I'll be lucky to get through this without freezing up again."

"Once again you're being too hard on yourself. Give yourself a break. Look around you, this is a walk through the edge of hell. No one can prepare himself for the impact that such a scene can make on the psyche."

"Still—" David began.

"Still nothing," Kristen interrupted. "You have more going for you than any other man I've ever met, but you keep weighing yourself down with personal doubts and insecurity. You're like a butterfly that's too afraid to leave the cocoon." She paused before speaking again, and when she did, she did so quietly, almost reverently, "I wonder what lies deep inside the man named David O'Neal. I wonder what's locked away inside his mind and soul. But most of all I wonder what it is he fears?"

"Fears?

"What would you call it? You yourself have admitted to being insecure. That was your confession not mine. How would you be different if you weren't constantly second-guessing yourself?"

David didn't answer at first. Kristen's words were striking home and striking hard. Her words came not with anger or even frustration, but with genuine concern that arose from something she deeply believed. He wondered if she was correct in her assessment of him. Maybe he had been too hard on himself. Maybe he did allow insecurity to anchor him in the past, allowing him to move into the future after only Herculean efforts on his part and on the part of others. And if she was right, what could he do about it? He had been taught in seminary psychology classes that that kind of mental programming couldn't be changed overnight, and he had seen it for himself in the hundreds of people who had turned to him for help. In many ways, Kristen was doing for him what he had attempted to do for those in church—incite him to make good and godly changes in his life.

"Are you all right, David?" Kristen asked softly. "Maybe I was out of line. Sometimes my mouth begins to work without the full benefit of my brain. I'm sorry if I hurt you."

Is that what I feel? David asked himself. *Hurt? No, not hurt. Not emotional pain, but something.* He looked into the clear night sky and gazed at the moon once more, then he turned to face Kristen who sat next to him. She was close enough that he could see the moonlight bounce gaily off her moist eyes; he could smell her distinctive scent. He looked into her eyes, fell into the beautiful deep-blue orbs. He let his eyes trace the lines of her face and take in each feature, light eyebrows, delicate nose, smooth cream skin, full lips. His gaze stopped on her lips, and he remembered that moment in front of the hotel in Addis Ababa when those lips, soft, pliant, warm, and welcoming, touched his. *Perhaps,* David thought, *it is time for me to emerge from the cocoon.*

He leaned forward slowly, fearful that she would pull away. Anticipation churned within him. His heart beat faster, and his breathing quickened. He was at the threshold of closeness, close enough to feel the life on her skin, yet too far away to touch. It was the magnificent moment when hope is less than a half-breath away from actuality. He wanted to stop right there, to hover in that ethereal plane of expectancy.

Then guilt, like some monster from the deep, broke the surface of his consciousness. The guilt did not come alone: It brought fear. What if they were seen? What if this attraction was only the fruit of exotic places and difficult circumstances? What would happen if it didn't work out and she rejected him? Could he deal with it? Was this proper and appropriate behavior? He sensed the questions, felt them more than thought them. It took less than a second for the fear, doubt, and guilt to fully emerge and begin forcing the cocoon shut.

But an image came to mind, an image of the beautiful monarch butterflies that he used to catch as a child in the back canyons where he grew up. He saw the butterflies in his mind as clearly as he had seen them when he was a boy. He felt the infinitesimally light touch of their legs on his finger where they would sometimes land. He remembered studying their elegance and their radiant orange-and-black markings. Monarchs didn't come around San Diego as much as they once did. Perhaps it was because of the city's remarkable growth, the rise of pollution, and the decline of raw, open land. Or perhaps they were having trouble breaking out of their cocoons.

The last thought propelled David forward. He closed the slight distance between their lips, and the kiss that started as seed in his mind blossomed into the fruit of pleasure, joy, satisfaction, and ex-citement—powerful, dynamic excitement. The ocean serpents of fear, guilt, and doubt sank below the waves of David's mind as the tender sweetness of the embrace grew. If it would have been pos-sible, David would have spent the remainder of his life in that mys-tical moment. His cocoon crumbled into dust.

16

"SHALL I GO FIRST?" STEPHANIE COOPER SAID INTO the phone as she shuffled through the papers on her desk.

"Sure, go ahead," Woody Summers replied. "Ladies first, I always say."

"How quaint," Stephanie said sarcastically. "Here's what I came up with. Now understand that this material is difficult to verify, and it wouldn't hold up in court. For that matter, it wouldn't get us a search warrant from any judge. Nonetheless, here it is. Like you, I started with who would want to electronically pirate satellite picture files from our computer databases? This turned out to be more difficult to answer than I first believed. If the satellite photos were of military bases, troop movements, or even shipping activity, we might think it was a terrorist group or a foreign government. But since the material stolen had to do with Third-World countries with no military or economic value, the question became convoluted. Why would anyone want pictures of Somalia or Ethiopia?"

"Did you double-check military bases there?" Woody asked. "You said that the Russians have or had a base there."

"I also said that they gave it back to the Somalis. Actually it happened a little differently from what I initially said. The Russians had a few bases along the Gulf of Aden and the Bab el Mandeb that leads in and out of the Red Sea, but the Somalis gave them over to us when the Soviets supported Ethiopia in its war with Somalia. The bases are pretty much useless these days. Knowing that, I then asked what's happening in Somalia that could interest anyone

189

enough to commit a felony? The only answer I came up with is the famine."

"This is groundwork we've already covered," Woody responded wearily. He wondered if all CIA agents insisted on recounting ideas already agreed upon.

"I know, but be patient," Stephanie snapped back. "The people most likely to be interested in famine in foreign countries are the UN, contributing governments, and private relief agencies."

"We know the UN wouldn't break into your computers, nor would any country contributing to the relief efforts. That leaves us with private relief agencies—and one you haven't mentioned."

"I assume you refer to a person or persons who feel the need to avenge the death of military personnel."

"It's possible," Woody said firmly. "Such things are not un-heard of. And it wouldn't be just our country either. Pakistan and France took some pretty heavy hits. And what about someone in Somalia itself? Maybe someone there is planning a coup."

"Doubtful on all counts," Stephanie replied. "Revenge is a powerful motive, but the object of that revenge, Mohammed Farah Aidid, is out of the game since he died a few years back. As far as a Somali group or individual doing the deed, well, why? To what end?"

"It's not necessary for us to know the why, just the possibilities so that we can investigate."

"Let's face it," Stephanie said. "Somalia is not a technologically sophisticated country. The computer break-in would have required advanced knowledge and equipment."

"True, but they could have bought it."

"Granted, but I still don't like it. It just doesn't make sense."

"I suppose you have a hunch."

"A reasoned guess. Listen, Woody, the only people who have a strong enough motive for accessing our files are these special relief organizations. They have an interest in protecting their people and saving the lives of the nationals."

"But which one?" Woody asked abruptly. "There are a couple of dozen such groups over there now, especially with the latest famine."

"More like scores of them from our country and the rest of the Western world. But I have an idea which one it might be. One organization is large enough and powerful enough to pull off the crime. And they have been in the neighborhood of other questionable activities."

"Such as?"

"Such as Colombia. There was a drug lord by the name of Manuel Herzog who was on the verge of building the largest cocaine cartel the world has ever seen. One day he went to see his daughter in a school play, but he never arrived. He was found in the jungle two days later with a broken neck—a broken neck he didn't get falling down. One of our case workers, a former army ranger, saw and recognized an old army buddy in a nearby village. The man's name is Roger Walczynske, and he's known to work for Barringston Relief."

"It could be coincidence."

"Of course it could, but there's more." Stephanie's excitement caused her to speak faster. "Normally I would write the killing off to a competitive cartel, but Walczynske's presence in the country couldn't be verified through passports, hotel registry, airline tickets, or any other means. It appears, on the surface at least, that he stole into Colombia."

"That's still pretty weak."

"Hang on. In Cambodia, a year ago, several political prisoners were rescued. They had been tortured by the Khmer Rouge for years. They, along with their families, were smuggled out of the country. Most settled in Europe, and one of our people had the opportunity to debrief them. They described a man who meets the physical description of this Walczynske. Altogether, there are fourteen documented events where a person associated with Barringston Relief was in the area of a crime."

"They're everywhere," Woody protested. "We could say the same thing about the CIA."

"You could and you'd be right, but I know that the Company had nothing to do with those particular events."

"You're still on thin ice."

"I warned you up-front that this was skimpy at best, but I think it's a viable lead. Don't you?"

Woody exhaled noisily into the receiver of the phone. "Yes, I do. Mind you, I'm not saying I agree with presupposition, but, and I can't tell you how much it hurts me to say this, I don't have anything better. I hope you're wrong."

"Why?" Stephanie was puzzled.

"Because I've been contributing to Barringston Relief for several years. It was my wife's idea at first. They do a wonderful work."

"I never took you for the type to respond to impassioned pleas to ease world suffering."

"It shouldn't surprise you," Woody said defensively. "Two types of people go into the FBI: those who want action and those who want to make a difference."

"And you're of the latter."

"I like to think so," Woody said firmly.

"I like to think so too. So what do we do now?" Stephanie asked pointedly.

"That is the sixty-four-thousand-dollar question, isn't it?" He paused in thought. "You're right about not having enough evidence to get a search warrant, but it's worth a try. I've had some luck with Judge Willimon. He's been known to grant warrants with little reason, but not without something. The question is whether we can make the little we have look like more. If we do get the warrant, we'll need to proceed carefully. Barringston Relief is underwritten by Barringston Industries, and they have enough bucks to tie us up in court so long that our great-grandchildren will be called to testify. Not only that, he is well connected to people in the Senate and the House. So let's tread wisely. Let's start with simple surveillance on the building and the key employees, especially the organization's head, Archibald Jr."

"Can't do it," Stephanie interjected. "He's out of the country. Went to Africa days ago. East Africa, I might add. At present he's in Ethiopia."

"Isn't that interesting? Should I ask how you came by that little bit of information?" Woody inquired with mischief in his voice.

"We have our ways," Stephanie quipped. "It's not all that difficult—I called and asked to speak to him. His staff told me he wasn't in, and they also told me where he was. Part of their public relations, I guess."

"Do you have any way of keeping track of him over there?"

"Not really," Stephanie replied. "The CIA is not nearly as ubiquitous as some think."

"Do you know if our mysterious friend, Walczynske, is with him?"

"No," she said bluntly. "Given time we might be able to track him down, however."

"Let me see what I can do about that warrant. I wonder if we could recruit an insider, someone who may know what's going on."

"It's worth pursuing," Stephanie said. "As long as he or she doesn't give us away."

"Let's get started," Woody said. "I'll check on the warrant; you see if you can find more on Roger Walczynske. And let's make sure—"

"We move carefully," Stephanie finished. "Got it."

■ ■ ■ ■ ■

To David the Ethiopian morning seemed matchless. The sun had only been up for an hour and was quickly expelling the darkness with radiant light that bathed the high cloud-shrouded mountains. The air was cool and clear. It was one of the advantages of being in the highlands of Ethiopia instead of the low desert regions where temperatures routinely rose above the one-hundred-degree mark. Still, David knew that the day would be warm and the thin air a challenge to breathe. He also knew the day would bring another encounter with the wretched souls who populated the camp. More people would die, people who would have seen their last sunrise and taken their last few breaths of the pure air. Yet David knew that he would be able to face the poverty and pain successfully, not because he had become callous but because he had crossed over from shock to involvement.

Kristen's words the night before had struck him deeply, but instead of wounding him they caused him to look back on his life and, more important, his faith. After walking Kristen to her tent, which she shared with Sheila and two other female workers, he had returned to his own tent. Lying on his cot, he stared at the canvas ceiling. It fluttered at the whim of a light African wind and reassessed his own existence. Kristen had been right, he told himself. And seeing the enormous needs of others had prompted him to once again be thankful for all that God had given him. He knew that he had received far more than he had ever been forced to surrender, and it would be the height of hubris and an affront to God to wallow in sorrow.

There was nothing to do but get on with the act of living. As he lay on the cot feeling the cool night air creep in through the flimsy tent walls, he recalled a passage of Scripture he had preached on many times in his fifteen years of ministry: Jesus' feeding of the five thousand. The miracle was simple in its approach but dramatic in its effect. The details of the event were as clear in David's mind as if he had actually been there to see the fainting masses of the faithful who had followed Jesus a great distance without food. He could hear in his mind the disciples' question as they asked what should be done and Jesus' cryptic response: "You feed them." Three powerful words that seemed to make no sense. "You feed them." How? With what? The answer to those questions became clear when Jesus miraculously transformed the lunch of a young boy into food for thousands.

"You feed them." David heard the words of one of his own sermons come back to him: "What is little in our hands is abundance in the hands of Jesus. What seems impossible to us is routine with God. The secret is to take what we have at hand and surrender it to Jesus. That's when the difference will be made." It was time for David to listen to his own message, to heed his own admonition. That night, with a wind that carried the cry of a hyena on its wispy billows, Dr. David O'Neal reacquainted himself with his God and with his purpose.

Now outside his tent he took in long breaths of cool air and sipped coffee made by the camp cook. The day seemed brighter and filled with more light. It struck him as strange that he should feel so good in a camp so filled with pain and hopelessness. Maybe he could do something to ease the suffering and lift some of the despair. He knew he couldn't do it all, not today and not tomorrow, but bit by bit he could help a few, and that was important.

A.J., Peter, Sheila, Kristen, and Dr. Goodwin looked weary from yesterday's work as they walked toward David.

"Good morning," A.J. said. "How are you today?"

"Outstanding, but I'll get better."

"That's good . . . ," A.J. paused as the oxymoronic phrase sank in. He looked at David for a moment, then at the plastic cup he held in his hand. "You get that in the cook's tent?" David nodded. "I think I need some. Let's go to breakfast."

The group, less Kristen and David, moved toward the large tent that housed some of the food supplies.

Kristen gazed in puzzlement at David for a moment. "Are you feeling all right?"

"I feel more than all right," David said, beaming a large addictive smile. "Thanks to you." He stepped toward her, kissed her on the forehead, and placed his arm around her shoulders. "Shall we join the others?" The speechless Kristen smiled and nodded. Five steps later she placed her arm around his waist.

Breakfast was Spartan by Western standards but munificent in the famine area. It consisted of *injera* flatbread, coffee, rice, and powdered eggs. The twelve workers ate breakfast early so that they would be free to begin the morning food and medicine distribution. It was a time of needed human contact with those who understood the need and dignity of the work in which they were involved. Depression, anxiety, and homesickness were not uncommon among the remarkable workers, and any chance to receive encouragement from one another or from outsiders was welcome. It was also a time to conduct business, communicate problems, make plans, and designate the work for the day.

"What will we do next?" Kristen asked. "Are we off to Somalia?"

"No," A.J. said, shaking his head. "That was part of the original plan, but I'm not certain that would be wise right now."

"Has something happened?" Peter inquired.

"Things are a little unsettled, but nothing to get worried about. Unless something changes radically, we'll stay in Ethiopia," A.J. explained. "I plan to make arrangements for a helicopter to fly us into the more severely impacted areas."

"What do we do today?" Peter asked.

"I'm sure they could use some help around here," A.J. said. "You and I need to meet with Dr. Goodwin about his need for future workers. I'll be trying to make some contacts back in the States about a few things. Fortunately our satellite link is working well. Any messages you want sent home?" No one did.

■ ■ ■ ■ ■

After the breakfast meeting David and Kristen walked from the tent to begin their work. "You sure seem . . . open today," Kristen offered. "Did you have a revelatory dream last night?"

"Sort of," David grinned. "Actually I just spent the night thinking about what you've been telling me. You are right, you know. As right as rain, as my mother used to say. I have been too consumed with myself and not with others. I often preached about living outside ourselves and about practicing the Christian faith as a way of life rather than as a set of beliefs. I decided that it was time to start living the way I wanted to feel instead of the way I actually felt. I have known for years that emotions are blind and unreasoning and that I shouldn't let them control my life. I'm grateful to you for helping open my eyes again."

Kristen's first response was to stop. David stopped too. She looked at him with wonder and joy in her eyes; she reached out and hugged him deeply. The embrace was short but meaningful and conveyed thoughts that could not be spoken. It struck David as odd that such a good and healthy affection as love should blossom in the surroundings of despair. But such is the mystery of life.

■ ■ ■ ■ ■

The growing darkness was appreciated by the weary Barringston travelers as they sat in front of their tent drinking water. The sun had dropped below the desert horizon, but the September heat in the lowlands of Ethiopia was still oppressive, and they longed for the cooler nights of the highlands they had left behind over a week before. Fewer trees provided shade, and only low-lying hills broke the monotony of the surrounding land.

They had left Dr. Goodwin's camp by helicopter and were given a guided tour of the Ethiopian mountain country. The pilot had flown down the deep and wide chasm through which the rapidly flowing Blue Nile rushed. The locals called the river Abbai, and it fed directly into the mighty Nile as it flowed north into the Mediterranean Sea. The pilot, an Ethiopian from Addis Ababa who spoke clear English, gave a nonstop monologue on the sights. He flew over several Ethiopian churches, some carved into the sides of cliffs or out of the hillsides. Many were cross-shaped, a configuration that could be seen clearly from the air. David was surprised to learn that Ethiopia had a longer Christian history than any European country. He wanted to visit one of the churches to see the priests who maintained such ancient traditions, but he knew that would have to wait until a future trip. As they flew over one church, they saw a line of priests in colorful vestments and acolytes dressed in white.

The pilot then flew over several small villages that were comprised of round thatched-roof huts called *tukuls* surrounded by groves of eucalyptus. Many villages were deserted.

The pilot steered east and did his best to ease the bumps caused by the rising thermals from the desert floor. "I don't know why you want to come here," he said seriously. "It is cooler and the living is easier in the mountains. Here there is nothing but starvation."

"That's why we want to come here," A.J. said. "That compound over there is one of mine. I want to see how they're doing." The pilot nodded and made his way to a spot one hundred meters from the last row of tents to keep the inevitable spray of dust and sand kicked up by the craft's high-speed rotors away from the camp.

Eight days later the band of travelers had visited six camps and worked in four, starting first in the heart of the near desolate Ogaden and moving closer to the Somali border. Everyone was proud of the work they had done, but they were near physical and emotional exhaustion. The days had merged with the nights and the night had melded into days, yet they did their work stoically and without a whisper of complaint.

Kristen, when she wasn't helping the camp staffs, maintained a photo diary that included video for possible public relations use later. Peter interviewed the paid staff to see what personal needs they had and what help could be provided to make their work easier. A.J. met with the head of each camp, planned strategy, made decisions, and ordered supplies through the satellite link. Sheila stayed close to A.J., offering only a few words of communication from time to time.

David continued to relish the work, although he, like the others, was taken aback by the extreme need of the people in the Ogaden area. Many of them were refugees from the famine in Somalia and had traveled a great distance across the dry, unforgiving land to one of the feeding centers on the Ethiopian side of the border. Their plight seemed infinitely worse than what David had seen in the highlands. The children displayed the swollen abdomen, the vacant eyes, the mucous streaked noses and lips of those who had been forced to take hunger as a travel companion. Half of all the children David saw had lost at least one parent to the famine. Some, especially the young, walked aimlessly around the camp with dirty fingers perpetually pressed into their mouths as if some minute bit of nourishment might be derived from their own skin. The lucky ones were cared for by an older sibling.

Camp life no longer seemed harsh to David. They had shelter, water, and an open latrine. Everything else was superfluous to the business of basic survival. David involved himself in every aspect of camp life. He served up dishes of cornmeal and rice-and-beans. At times he was called upon to spoon-feed those too weak to feed themselves, gently holding their heads up to drink water or chew soft food. He followed the doctor or nurse from tent to tent, area to area and aided in whatever way he could. Daily he helped remove the corpses of those who had fought valiantly but had been crushed by the overpowering weight of hunger.

David sighed heavily, closed his eyes, and stilled his mind to all thoughts, allowing the evening breeze to caress his perspiration-coated face. His muscles were sore from lifting bags of food and lifeless bodies; his face, neck, and arms were stung from a deep sunburn; his eyes felt gritty, his lips were cracked and dry; and sleep beckoned him to a few hours of oblivion. Despite his physical condition, he had never felt more alive or productive.

"Is it just me or are fewer people arriving in camp?" Kristen asked softly, not wanting to break the welcome hush of evening.

"I hadn't noticed," Peter said, rubbing his eyes. "It's hard to tell."

"I've noticed the same thing," Amy Person said. Amy was the camp director, a registered nurse with an advanced degree in health and nutrition. She was a sturdy woman in her early fifties with wavy black hair heavily streaked with gray. "It's puzzling. It's not likely that we are running out of people."

"Maybe it's just a fluke," A.J. said casually. He was crouched down in a folding chair, staring up at the night sky pregnant with stars. "It will probably return to normal tomorrow."

"Perhaps," Amy said, "but it's odd. Not only that, a few people had to be coaxed into eating. They acted like the food was rotten or tainted."

"What are you thinking about, A.J.?" Kristen changed the subject.

"A billion billion stars," he replied dreamily. "So far away, every star so very far away, yet we can still see them. They give us their light at night and ask nothing in return. They hang like tiny drops of water suspended in space, or like strange little eyes watching all that we do."

"You wax philosophical," David offered. "You are a man not only of action, but of thoughts as deep as the ocean."

"Now who's waxing philosophical?" A.J. asked with a laugh. "How are you dealing with all of this? You still okay?"

"I'm sunburned, sore, and dead tired. I've never felt better."

"He's a worker," Amy said. "Sure you don't want to leave him here when you leave?"

"Not a chance," A.J. said. "He's got work to do back in San Diego. He's going to make sure that people continue to give to the cause so that we can keep things flowing. That's just as important. If he doesn't do his job, you can't do yours."

"It was worth asking," Amy replied. "Fresh workers are so hard to get—" Amy stopped short when she heard footsteps behind her. Turning she saw three men walking abreast, purposefully toward the small circle sitting around the gas lantern. Unable to identify the trio because of the lantern's glare, A.J. sprung to his feet and tensed, an action that was quickly duplicated by Sheila.

"A.J.," a familiar voice said. "It's Roger."

David watched as the alert tension quickly drained from A.J.'s and Sheila's bodies. "Roger, I'm glad you could make it. Step into the light; let me get you some water." As the three men crossed the threshold from darkness into light, David saw that he recognized two of the men: as the two workers with Child Touch Ministries who had accompanied the Barringston group for the first half of their journey. The third man was a stranger to him.

"Let me make the introductions," A.J. said jovially. "Amy, this is Leonard Wu and his coworker Gerald Raines, both of Child Touch Ministries. They traveled to Addis Ababa with us. And this is Roger Walczynske, my trusted and longtime friend. He does on-site research for us and has been spending these few last days in Somalia." Amy shook hands with Wu and Raines as Roger did the same with the others.

"We haven't seen you since the airport," David said, a little confused. "How did you get way down here?"

Wu answered, "Our office changed our itinerary. We spent a few days in Addis Ababa and then flew to Mogadishu in Somalia. We have a few orphanages and a small medical center there. While we were there we bumped into Roger. When he told us that he was headed here, we asked if we could join him."

"It's no good traveling out here alone," Raines added. "We need to stick together you know."

"I need to speak to you when you can spare the time," Roger said to A.J. Their eyes locked in silent communication.

"Sure," A.J. said glibly. "I was thinking of strolling down to the latrine. It's a lousy location, but we can talk on the way."

■ ■ ■ ■ ■

The two men did not speak until they were out of earshot of the rest of the group. "You look positively grim, Roger. I take it that the news is not good."

"Mahli is still out of reach," Roger started slowly. "Their security isn't sophisticated, but the sheer number of guards makes it impossible to get close enough to do anything." A.J. reached out and touched Roger on the shoulder, communicating his support and understanding. Roger inhaled deeply. "That man has to die, A.J. He positively, absolutely has to die the most painful death possible and his carcass left for the hyenas."

"He will, Roger," A.J. said quietly. "He most certainly will." Turning back to the group, A.J. shouted for Sheila to join them. "I want Sheila to go with you, Leonard, and Gerald. It's time to put an end to this nonsense forever."

"Won't you need her?"

"I'll be fine," A.J. said tersely. "It's more important that she go with you. You're going to need another pair of eyes and hands. Mahli's too slimy to catch single-handedly."

"I'm sorry, A.J." Roger was downcast. "Mahli returns to the compound periodically, but it's hard to know when. I've followed him back and forth several times, but there's never an opportunity. Wu and Raines have been a big help with the surveillance. They have also been able to verify that it was Mahli at the Judith Rhodes camp. The satellite photos place his car there, but . . ."

"No need to apologize," A.J. replied. "Patience is what's required here. There's no sense in getting yourself killed. How's Aden holding up?"

"I sent him home when Raines and Wu showed up. He was never comfortable with all this. He's not cut out for this kind of work."

"I'm not surprised. Still, he has been helpful to us." When Sheila joined them, A.J. said, "I'll be taking the crew back to Addis Ababa tomorrow. We start back home in the morning, Sheila. I want you to go with Roger—"

"But—" she began to protest.

"No buts," A.J. said firmly. "I'll be fine. I need you to put an end to Mahli. Now here's what I want you to do . . ."

17

"I, FOR ONE, AM LOOKING FORWARD TO A REAL BED," Kristen said as she slumped in her chair. "My back wasn't made for canvas cots."

"It doesn't take long to appreciate the small things in life, does it?" David took a sip of dark bitter coffee and glanced around the hotel's café. "This place looks far more lavish now than when we left."

The two sat in a silence shrouded with weariness. Despite the fatigue brought on by their arduously slow journey back to Addis Ababa, both were too wired to sleep.

"You look positively contemplative," Kristen said as she looked at the changed man in front of her. He had, like her, only been in Africa a short time, yet he looked stronger, his skin was darkened by the sun, and he carried himself with more confidence. "What's floating around in that mind of yours?"

David chuckled and rubbed a freshly shaven chin, a chin that had until that day sported a thick covering of black stubble. "Fog mostly. I was just thinking about that Roger fellow; he sure came and went quickly."

"Sometimes things happen fast."

"But he left right after his meeting with A.J. I would think he would have spent the night and rested up some. He sure seemed in a hurry."

"And . . . ," Kristen prompted.

"I don't know," David rubbed his eyes. "He definitely had something on his mind. Something was bothering him."

"You could tell all that in the few short minutes you were with him?"

"That and his body language when he and A.J. walked away."

"You can tell that much about a person by their body language?"

"Sometimes," David replied. "It's more of an art than a science. The anthropologist Desmond Morris once said that body language is more truthful than words. Our physical actions constantly give clues about our thoughts and emotions. You can't read someone's mind, but you can learn a few things about that person."

"Such as?"

"Okay. Do you see that couple over there eating lunch?" David nodded to a middle-aged couple sitting about thirty feet away. Kristen nodded. "Where do you think they're from? I mean, which part of the world?"

Kristen looked at them for a short time and then said, "I have no idea. They're white, so they could be from the United States, Europe, South Africa, Russia, just about anywhere. There's really no way to tell."

"You're right, there's no way to tell *exactly*, but I can tell that he is from Europe and that she is from America, probably the Midwest."

"I don't buy this for a moment," Kristen said skeptically. "You haven't heard them speak, so you can't tell by their accent. I don't see how you can be so sure—unless you peeked at their passports."

"Not at all," David said beaming. "What is the man eating?"

Kristen looked backed over at the couple. "Pie. Probably apple pie. Why?"

"Which way is the pie pointed?"

"Pointed? You mean the front of the pie? The part away from the crust?" David nodded. "To the side, I guess. He's eating the pie from the side."

"When you eat pie, what direction does it point?"

"I've never thought about it. It points at me."

"There you go. Americans point their piece of pie at them and begin eating from the front of the triangle to the crust. Europeans turn their pie so that it points to the side and begin eating the pie at its side. Now notice the woman. She's not done with her main course. Watch how she cuts her food." Kristen did her best to study the woman without appearing to stare. "What do you see?"

"She holds the fork in her left hand and her knife in the right. She cuts the food, sets the knife down, and transfers the fork to her right hand to eat."

"That means that she is most likely from America, or at least her parents were. Transferring the fork from hand to hand is typically American."

"How do I know you're right?" Kristen grinned mischievously. "You could be making all this up."

"Simple," David replied. "Ask them."

"You don't think I will, do you?" Kristen slid from her place in the booth and approached the couple. David watched as the couple eyed her suspiciously at first, then smiled. A moment later she was back in her seat with a slight pouting expression on her face. At first she said nothing.

"Well?"

"All right, *Doctor* O'Neal," she said, playfully emphasizing his title. "He's from Manchester, England, and she grew up in Hutchinson, Kansas. Next you're going to be telling me that you can discern their driver's license numbers."

"No, and that's the whole point. All a student of body language can do is make broad generalities about the person being observed. In court situations, attorneys are trained to watch for a change in a witness's blinking pattern. A person who blinks normally and then changes to a rapid pattern is very likely lying, as is someone who keeps touching his or her nose or mouth. The sharp-eyed attorney sees this and presses the point all the harder.

He can't prove the witness is lying, but he can make adjustments in his questioning.

"That's my whole point with Roger and, I might add, Gerald and Leonard. I can't tell you what they're thinking, but I can tell you that they were agitated, maybe even frustrated. About what, I couldn't hazard a guess."

"Got your curiosity stirred up, David?"

"Something is definitely up. Shortly after his meeting with Roger, Sheila, and the two from Child Touch Ministries, A.J. announced that Sheila would be returning to Somalia with Roger. Doesn't that strike you as odd?"

"No, not really. Sheila has been with A.J. a long time. She's a capable person."

"I'm sure she is, but the suddenness of it all, makes me wonder."

"Maybe it's Somalia. It's not a nice place right now, and A.J. said that things were unsettled. Maybe there's some trouble at one of the camps."

David was somber. "It seems that every corner of the world has some problem, some tremendous need."

Kristen nodded. "That's why A.J. takes some of his key executives on these trips. Outside the comfortable offices of Barringston Tower it doesn't take long to see how difficult the work is and who the real heroes are."

"They are indeed heroes. The people I've met working in these camps have changed my life and my world-view. I know that I'm going home in a matter of days and will be sleeping on my bed, but they will still be out here doing the hard work."

"And the noble work."

"And the noble work," David agreed. "I wish everyone could see what we've seen. Maybe things would be different. Maybe more people would become involved."

"That's our job, isn't it? Making sure the word gets out. You do it through the speeches you write, and I through public relations.

It's important for you to know that you are doing hero's work as well. True, you and I are not out here every day, but what we do helps make it possible for others to be here day in and day out."

David wearily nodded his assent. "You're probably right, and I'm too tired to go on," he said in exhaustion. "All of this is catching up to me. If I don't get a nap soon, I'll end up sleeping under the table."

"We can't have that, now can we?" Kristen rose from her seat. "Take me home, James, and don't spare the elevator."

David laughed, rose from his seat, and escorted Kristen from the café.

18

THE IRONY OF THE MOMENT FORCED A SMILE TO Roger's lips. He gazed down at the sprawling, walled compound and watched as Mahli's guards scampered into the courtyard raising their AK-47s, AK-80s, and RPGs at the helicopter that hovered eight hundred feet overhead. Roger felt no concern, no apprehension that a score of deadly weapons were pointed at him. He knew they wouldn't fire, he had seen to that. The men in the courtyard would take a steady bead on the helicopter, but they wouldn't dare squeeze a trigger—not as long as the man, a man they all recognized, hung precariously out the open door of the craft, his mouth taped shut, his hands tied with nylon cord behind his back, and a rope around his waist tethering him to a metal brace under one of the helicopter's seats.

Roger diverted his gaze from the ground with its animated host pointing up to the terrified passenger. How different he was now. When they first met he was pugnacious, crude, and aggressive, baring his teeth like a mongrel dog and spitting his words out with bile-laced hatred. Now Roger imagined that he could hear the man whimper in terror, attempting to plead for mercy through the wide duct tape that held his lips immobile. He felt no pity for the man, for he knew that he was responsible for the death of many people. Roger had no pity, no remorse. Instead, he felt alive, really alive. He could feel his blood course through his veins and sense the pounding of his heart even over the thudding of the rotors above him.

It had been far easier to capture Mukatu than he would have

thought possible, a task for which he would like to have taken full credit, but the basic idea had come from A.J.

Frustrated at the conditions that had held success just out of reach, he had decided to strike back at the man who had cruelly and senselessly killed Dr. Judith Rhodes. Analysis of the satellite photographs pirated from the CIA's computers had been useful. They had hoped to be able to trace Mahli's activities from the camp to his hiding place.

The photos also proved helpful in an unexpected way. Each file had contained at least a dozen digitally enhanced photos of Somalia, especially Mogadishu and the surrounding regions. Reading the photos, which had been delivered to Roger by Wu and Raines, proved difficult. He had seen such photos many times during his stint in the army, but he had never been called upon to interpret the data. That had always been done by experts who pored over the photos with a fine-tooth comb. Roger could make out certain landmarks, but little more.

The combined expertise of Raines and Wu proved beneficial. Like Roger, they had been career military men who had become disillusioned with the American military structure. Also like Roger, they chose to work for those who could pay well, and A.J. paid them very well. Raines and Wu, both highly trained intelligence experts, had spent hours sitting in their hotel rooms analyzing the satellite images. The images were exceptionally clear with high resolution, having been taken on several of Somalia's many unclouded summer days. In the pictures individual vehicles could easily be made out. The space-borne cameras could have provided even greater detail, even to the point of reading license plates, had they been set to do so. But since no U.S. troops were active in the area, the cameras had been set to take images of larger areas.

Painstakingly comparing a sequence of photos taken over a period of weeks, Wu and Raines discovered a commonality. One photo showed the Barringston Camp on the Webi Shabelle at Giamama where Dr. Rhodes had been murdered. The image had been taken shortly after the attack and plunder. The men could see the still image of smoke rising from the burning structures and tents. They could even see the tiny black dots that were the camp's inhabitants standing in various open areas. Another photo taken at the same time, but with a wider angle, revealed a line of trucks leaving the camp. At the rear of the convoy was a dark blue four-wheel-drive car that Wu recognized as a late model Jeep Cherokee, ironically, the same kind of vehicle he himself drove back in the States.

"It makes sense," he said. "The cars are durable, able to travel rough roads, but still fairly luxurious inside. That's the kind of car I would expect these guys to drive. While their men get their kidneys shaken in the trucks, these guys enjoy a tape deck and leather seats."

The discovery of the vehicle would have been little more than an interesting insight if it had not appeared in other photos: once in front of the warehouse that Roger had staked out a few weeks before, and twice in photos of Mahli's compound.

"So we have more evidence that Mahli was involved in the murder of Dr. Rhodes," Roger said matter-of-factly. He remembered that he and Aden had followed Mukatu in a similar car, most likely the same car. "We were sure of that from the beginning. How does all this help us?"

Sheila answered the question. "We look for his car. I doubt anyone but Mahli and Mukatu drive that thing. We can better track them now. We continue the surveillance of the compound. When that car leaves we activate our plan."

"And what plan is that?" Roger asked.

Sheila explained in detail.

The plan worked perfectly. Raines and Wu kept vigil over the compound day and night, pulling back when guard patrols came near. Two days later they were rewarded when the Jeep suddenly appeared on the dirt road that led from the spacious walled retreat. A short radio message later, Roger, Wu, Raines, and Sheila sprang into action. Positioning a stolen, slightly battered Mercedes along the road fifteen miles from the compound, Sheila raised the hood and waited until she could see the Jeep's dust trail. As the Jeep approached, she squatted by the car and stuck a knife in the front left tire, making a long, jagged gash. Air rushed out noisily, but Sheila ignored it. She remained stooped over as she pretended to struggle with the car's jack. As the Jeep approached, she stood abruptly, flashed a toothy smile, and waved. The car stopped a few meters in front of the Mercedes, and four men exited. Three of the men carried AK-47s at the ready, and their eyes scanned the surrounding area. Seeing nothing, they relaxed somewhat and pointed their weapons at the ground. Mukatu walked toward Sheila with the three men in tow.

"My tire's flat," Sheila said sweetly in Arabic. "I can't get the jack to work."

Mukatu approached her brazenly. "How is it that a white woman like you speaks Arabic?" he asked tersely.

"Diplomatic corps," she replied softly and stepped back from him, averting her eyes in feigned fear.

Mukatu looked at the tire, the raised hood, and then back at Sheila. The fact that she was the tallest woman he had ever seen did not intimidate him. Instead, his face revealed that he found her strangely erotic. He stepped closer and inhaled deeply, taking in her fragrance. Slowly he reached up and wiped away a trickle of perspiration from her cheek. In response, she parted her lips seductively.

"I need help," she said softly. "I would be as grateful as a woman can be if one of you could lift that heavy spare tire out of the trunk."

Mukatu eyed her warily but found himself staring at her lips. "Go," he ordered. "Get the tire." One of the men shouldered his weapon and walked to the back of the car. The trunk lid was ajar, and he opened it quickly. He saw neither the man in the trunk nor the 9mm pistol aimed at his chest. A whisper of a sound was emitted as the pistol fired. The silencer stifled the sound of the shot, but it couldn't diminish the thud of the bullet crashing into the guard's sternum and forcing all the air from his lungs, nor could it quiet the sound of the man's body striking the hard dirt road.

Mukatu and his men snapped their heads toward the back of the Mercedes and then back to Sheila, who had already reached under the hood of the car and snatched up her own 9mm pistol from underneath a rag. Both guards raised their automatics, but both died instantly as rounds from Sheila's gun struck them in the forehead. Mukatu feebly turned to run, but he could not evade being pistol-whipped. He fell face first to the ground with a scream of pain. With astonishing speed and strength, Sheila flipped Mukatu from prone to supine. She sat on his chest. He screamed obscenities in Arabic until she placed the hot barrel of the gun between his eyes.

"Shoot! Shoot!" he screamed. "I'm not afraid to die."

"I have something better planned for you," she said calmly.

Roger, who had climbed out of the trunk, suddenly appeared and looked at the dead men on the ground. "You are one tough date," he said coolly.

"Just tape the little man's mouth," she replied curtly. "I don't know how much longer I can listen to his pathetic whining." Roger complied quickly, slapping a nine-inch-long strip of three-inch-wide gray duct tape across Mukatu's mouth, silencing the steady stream of obscenities. He twisted and pulled the African's hands, sending a scorching pain down the man's arm. Sheila stood and stepped back. With her weight removed, Mukatu screamed a muted cry through his taped mouth and kicked viciously at Roger's arm in a desperate effort to free himself, but Roger was prepared. He cranked Mukatu's arm farther until pain forced the African to roll on his stomach. Roger quickly dropped a knee on Mukatu's neck and pulled his arms behind his back. With Sheila's help, Roger bound his hands with nylon cord.

Sheila and Roger gazed at their captive as he lay facedown in the warm dust of the dirt road. Their disappointment required no words. Mukatu was a catch to be sure, but he was not Mahli. That fact complicated matters.

"We should have known," Roger said. "Mahli would have traveled with more of an escort, not just three guards."

"Well, we can't throw him back," Sheila said severely. "What shall we do with him? Kill him and leave him for the buzzards?"

Roger thought for a moment. "No," he said finally, "I have a better idea. Let's take him home."

"What?! After all we went through?"

"Trust me," Roger said with a smile. "If we can't get to Mahli, then maybe his brother can deliver a message for us. Let's take his Jeep. I'll explain on the way." Five minutes later they were headed to Mogadishu.

The helicopter had been rented in advance as a contingency escape vehicle should one be needed. Now Wu, seated in the pilot's seat, worked the controls to keep the craft hovering in position. Roger kept an eye on the crowd gathering below through powerful binoculars. Raines sat in the jump seat, a sniper's rifle held firmly in his right hand, waiting for Mahli to step into the courtyard. Sheila sat next to him. Each wore a headset that allowed them to communicate over the pounding of the rotor and the whine of the engine.

"Do you think he'll show?" Wu asked. As if on cue, Mahli stepped from the building.

"Target!" Roger shouted. "Doorway. Doorway."

Instantly Raines snapped the rifle to his shoulder and brought the sights to bear on the small group of men clustered in the plaster-covered doorway.

"Got 'em," Raines said calmly. Expelling his breath slowly, he positioned the rifle's crosshairs over the right ear of Mahli. The distance and the uncertain platform of the slightly swaying helicopter made the shot nearly impossible, but worth a try. Slowly squeezing the trigger, Raines waited for the sharp report of the weapon. Then he saw a man push Mahli back into the building. Raines swore. "His guard dogs pushed him back in the house. I've lost my shot."

"I don't think they're going to let him out," Wu said. "And we can't stay up here forever."

Roger slammed his fist into his hand. "We had him, and he got away. This guy leads a charmed life."

"He's luckier than his brother," Wu replied.

"I'm going to get him, you know," Roger said distantly. "Not today, maybe. But someday soon, I'll cut that little man's throat."

"What do we do now?" Raines asked, still looking through the scope. "I think he's watching through a window, but two people are shielding him with their bodies. It's a risky shot, but I can get one of them before they scatter. I can't guarantee that it'll be Mahli. Not at this distance."

"He's going to come looking for his brother, you know," Sheila said. "It won't take long for Mahli to put two and two together. That will change the rules of the game. We'll be the hunted instead of him. He knows about us now, and he has hundreds of followers."

Roger stared out the window, thinking. He turned to face Sheila and gave a two-word order: "Drop him."

There was no hesitancy in Sheila's action, no pause for thought. In a quick, effortless motion, she withdrew a switchblade from her pocket, sprang the blade into its locked position, and cut the rope. Roger watched Mukatu twist and turn as he dropped to the ground. Dust swirled around the body.

"Go, go, go!" Roger shouted into his mouthpiece. Wu banked the craft and forced the controls to the stops. The helicopter roared to life and headed over the blue ocean. Raines leaned forward to look out the open side. The stunned crowd stared at the body. Then, as if they shared a corporate conscience, realized that the helicopter was now a viable target. A roar of gunfire erupted in a futile attempt to shoot the craft from the air. Roger turned in his seat and looked out the open door in time to see the bright discharge-flash of a rocket-propelled grenade being launched.

"Hard right! Hard right!" Roger shouted.

Wu responded immediately, pressing the right pedal hard and simultaneously jerking the control stick to the right. The helicopter lurched right. A half-second later the grenade shot by them. Wu righted the craft, began a zigzag course, and rapidly changed the craft's altitude.

Five minutes later Roger knew they were out of firing range from the compound. He imagined the scene they had left behind: Mahli standing over the bloody crushed body of his brother and swearing at the unknown men who had killed him.

"That's for Judith Rhodes and the *Sea Maid*," he said.

■ ■ ■ ■ ■

Mahli paced methodically along the perimeter of the warehouse office in Marka. His supporters had insisted that he leave the compound for the more easily defended commercial building. After watching his brother fall to his death from the helicopter, he had burst into a frenzy of emotion, rushing from the building, seizing a weapon from one of his guards and firing wildly at the rapidly fleeing helicopter. When he saw that the craft would make a safe exit, he fired the weapon into the walls of the compound until every round had been expended. He then turned to look at Mukatu's crushed and lifeless body. He had seen death, indeed he had caused death, not of just a few, but of countless people. This corpse was different from all the others he had seen. Different not because every bone had been broken, nor because the torso was flattened beyond recognition by the fall, nor because the grotesque sight crushed Mahli's resolve and stripped away his fearlessness. It was different because Mahli knew that the one person for whom he actually had feelings was gone. Irritating and self-serving as Mukatu could be, he was still his brother, and no one had the right to take him away.

Later, in safer quarters, Mahli could think of nothing but revenge.

"I want them," he said again, and his words echoed off the hardwood walls of the warehouse. He had uttered those words many times over the last two days. "I don't know who they are, but I want them. They will pay with their blood. Their screams will be heard all over Somalia." He paused to look out an ocean-facing window. The pause lasted only long enough for Mahli to replay the haunting image of his brother plummeting to earth, his body twisting futilely against the air. Mahli had seen the terror on his face, his eyes wide. Each time the image played in his mind, the fire in his blood flared to a seething, searing caldron of bitterness and hatred. And each time the scene increased his resolve and commitment—a commitment to revenge. Two clarion truths rang through his tormented mind: He would make his plan work, and more people would die.

THREE

IT'S A SMALL WORLD

October 2 to January 15

19

FALL ARRIVED EARLY IN WASHINGTON, D.C., TO THE
great relief of the population who had quickly grown weary of the
late summer's sweltering heat. The brisk night air followed by mod-
erate daytime temperatures had alleviated the corporate crankiness
of the city. Taxi drivers were more patient, policemen smiled
occasionally, and power-company engineers worried less about
brownouts. Children started back to school and counted the days
until the Christmas break. Woody Summers and Stephanie Cooper
sat in stylish leather chairs and stared out the window at the grass
plaza that framed one of the landscaped areas of CIA headquarters
in Langley, Virginia. Woody drummed his fingers on the arm of the
chair, and Stephanie rubbed her hands together.

"How long has it been?" Woody asked, twisting in his chair. "It
seems like hours."

Stephanie looked at her watch. "Fifteen minutes. Stop squirm-
ing, will you? It's not like meeting the pope, you know."

"How many times have you met with the director of the CIA?"

"I met him once," she replied coolly.

"When was the last time you met with the director of the CIA
and the director of the FBI—together—at the same time?"

"I get your point, but getting fidgety doesn't help," Stephanie
said rubbing her fingers together all the more. "You're ready and
I'm ready. That's all that matters—"

Stephanie's words were cut short by the entrance of CIA

director, Lawrence Bauman, and FBI director, Gus Padgett. She and Woody stood immediately.

"Good morning," Bauman said good-naturedly. "Please sit down."

Padgett took a seat to the side of Bauman's large cherry desk, positioning his chair so that he could see the two agents as well as Bauman. "I understand you two have some information for us. Both Director Padgett and I are interested in tidying up this little mess, but I all the more. It doesn't do our image any good to have people browsing through our computer files as if they're walking through some five-and-dime store."

"Understood, sir," Stephanie replied smartly. "We have made some headway in the little time we've been afforded, and I think you'll find what we have interesting."

"Let's hear it then." Bauman waved a hand and leaned back in his chair. "My schedule is tight today, so cut to the chase."

"Yes sir. Agent Summers and I reviewed the files that were copied and found that most of them dealt with satellite photos of Somalia, mostly Mogadishu and the surrounding areas. This puzzled us at first. We kept asking who would want photos of that region? It has no true strategic value; U.S. troops are no longer there; the Russians want nothing to do with the nation; we can think of no terrorist group that would find that information useful. The bottom line is that Somalia has nothing but violence, famine, and misery."

"That was our first lead," Woody added. "We wondered who would be interested in a country brought to its knees by hunger."

"That's the avenue we pursued," Stephanie continued, the tempo of her words accelerating as her excitement increased. "Agent Summers suggested investigating some of the relief agencies working in the area. Dozens of them are there from all over the globe, but few possess the means to gain access to our system. Agent Summers did the preliminary work on the U.S.-based agencies; I did the investigative work on the foreign companies."

"And what did you find?" Padgett asked.

Woody replied, "We found a likely candidate. Barringston Relief."

"You're joking," Bauman snapped. "Doesn't Archibald Barringston's boy run that operation?"

"Why, yes," Woody said, slightly stunned at the director's knowledge.

"Archibald Barringston is a powerful man," Bauman said stoutly. "He's well connected with people on the hill, and even with the president himself. He's a heavy contributor to senators and congressmen from both parties. If you implicate him, a great many people are going to get their feathers ruffled."

"It's not Archibald Barringston that concerns us, sir," Woody replied. "It's his son, or at least someone in his son's employ. You see, Barringston Relief is the most active relief agency in the world. There's hardly a country that doesn't have someone from Barringston wandering around."

"We found operations in Thailand, Cambodia, Bangladesh, India, South America, half of Africa, and even China."

"China?" Bauman questioned.

"Yes sir. They have a group secretly working in some of the rural areas."

"Gutsy," Padgett said.

"Exactly," Woody intoned. "And that's why we suspect them. They often work on the fringes of the law. Not necessarily our law, but the laws of the countries in which they work. And there's more. Barringston Relief is incredibly sophisticated in structure and in technology. They work closely with several universities to develop hybrid plants that grow quickly and mature with a minimum amount of water. They recruit researchers right out of the best colleges. They also have one of the most sophisticated computer systems being operated by a private firm. They own two Cray computers, which they bought shortly before the Cray company went belly up."

"Do you know how expensive a Cray is?" Bauman asked in disbelief.

"I do, and I also know that several military complexes use them," Woody said evenly. "These guys have money. Archibald Industries underwrites them, and they also raise millions of dollars annually through donations. Not only that, but they own several patents on agricultural products that generate substantial income."

"Okay," Bauman said. "So they have a sophisticated computer system. So does IBM, but that doesn't make them our bad guys."

"True, sir," Stephanie jumped in. "But they have something else . . . or maybe I should say, someone else."

"That's right," Woody interrupted. "They have two people on their staff who have the knowledge to orchestrate the computer break-in: Eileen Corbin and Raymond Reynolds. Reynolds is a former Defense Department programmer. He wrote some of the programs that we use in the FBI and that you use every day here at Langley. But Eileen Corbin is the most interesting. In the computer world she is considered a peripherals goddess. Her great love is the fabrication of hardware. She was written up by all the computer magazines, and computer manufacturers were offering her six-figure salaries. At the height of her career, she was arrested for hacking into the computers of major businesses, stealing accounting files, and selling them to other businesses planning hostile takeovers. She made a fortune before an accomplice turned state's evidence. She spent six months in a white-collar prison. After her release, she went to work for Barringston Relief and has been there ever since. She is fully capable of creating a device that can ram so many codes into our computer entrance and recognition protocols that it grants access."

Bauman rubbed his chin in thought and then looked at Padgett. "What do you think, Gus?"

"Interesting, but do we have evidence?" he replied. "It's one thing to know that she is capable, and another thing to prove she's culpable."

"True," Bauman replied. "Do you have enough evidence for an arrest?"

Woody lowered his head before he answered. He had been dreading this question. "No sir, I do not."

"There's more," Stephanie interjected. "This goes beyond our own problems here at the CIA."

"How do you mean?" Bauman asked, furrowing his brow.

"We know that Barringston, or one of his people, has the means, the motive, and opportunity to commit these intrusions," Stephanie began. "We believe that such an act is in keeping with his method of operation. I told you that his group is active all over the world. Some of his people pop up in strange places. I spoke to some of our caseworkers overseas and discovered an interesting coincidence: Many disturbing events have happened when a Barringston Relief employee was around—a particular employee."

"Oh?" Bauman said.

"One of our caseworkers in Cambodia saw and identified a man he had served with in the army rangers. He tried to speak to him, but the man refused to acknowledge his call. He disappeared into the crowd. Two days later, thirty political prisoners were aided in their escape from a Cambodian prison camp. Sixteen guards were killed in the escape."

"I remember that," Bauman said.

"According to witnesses, three Americans led the escape. Our agent thinks one of them was Roger Walczynske, his former army buddy."

"Roger Walcz . . ." Padgett struggled with the name.

"Walczynske," Stephanie offered. "I pulled his file. Exemplary service, including service in Somalia during the last famine. He was involved in the attempted capture of Mohammed Farah Aidid. He lost several friends in that operation. It made him bitter, and he left the army."

"It made many people bitter," Bauman said sternly. "I assume there's more."

"Yes, but being mindful of your schedule, let me say that this same man has been spotted two other times: at the killing of a drug lord in Colombia and at the attempted assassination of the leader of the Irish terrorist group the Silver Dawn. The last one failed."

"If I recall," Bauman said, "no one has heard from the Silver Dawn for a while. They're just now becoming active again."

"That's correct, sir," Stephanie agreed. "I should have said that the last one was only partially successful. The man was wounded severely, as were several of his lieutenants."

Bauman looked at his watch, "I have to meet the president shortly, and he'll ask me about all this, so give me a quick summary. What should I tell him?"

Stephanie didn't hesitate. "Tell him that we believe that Barringston Relief is responsible for the intrusions into the CIA computers, and that they may be responsible for acts of terrorism against other countries."

"But you can't prove that," Padgett said quickly.

"That's why we would like to have permission to tap their phones and to recruit someone on the inside to gather information," Woody said.

Padgett shook his head. "That's a tall order. What you have told us makes sense, but I doubt you can convince a judge to give you a warrant to tap their phones. As for an infiltration, well, that's risky business."

"It's all we have," Woody said firmly.

Padgett and Bauman looked at each other. "All right," Bauman said. "For my part, I'll try to find a judge to convince. And infiltration? Just be careful, very careful. If what you say is true, then our actions may have repercussions around the world."

"I know it'll shake up the hill," Bauman added. "The Barringstons have a great many friends. You had better make sure that you have all your ducks in a row, or this thing will blow up in our faces."

"Understood," Woody and Stephanie said simultaneously.

■ ■ ■ ■ ■

"Where did you get these?" Stephanie asked as she turned another page of the small sheaf of papers she held.

"Some questions are best not asked and even better not answered," Woody replied with a wry grin. "Actually we did nothing untoward. Barringston Relief is a large corporation and as such must file certain documents with the government. The list you have was compiled by the IRS. Like every business with employees, Barringston Relief must file W-2 forms on each of its employees. All we did was obtain court permission to access those files."

"There are hundreds of names here." Stephanie sounded dismayed.

"There are, and as you can see by the dates next to the names, most of them have been on the payroll for a long time."

"Is that a problem?"

"Could be," Woody replied. "There may be a loyalty factor to consider here. The longer employees stay in a firm like this, the more they feel they have invested. Retirement, medical, position, and so on. But we've found one person who might be persuaded to help us. He arrived less than three months ago, he holds an executive position, and he possesses one other factor that could prove important: He's a minister."

"How do you know that?"

"We took a look at his previous tax forms. As you know, Form 1040 has a place for occupation."

"You're thinking that he will be open to our questions because of a strong sense of morality?"

"Exactly. It's not a sure thing, but it couldn't hurt."

"I'm not so sure," Stephanie replied, shaking her head. "The few ministers I know are pretty independent thinkers. It's possible that he may see all of this as bordering on deceit. If he does, then you're sunk."

"We'll convince him," Woody said with confidence. "We have to; he's our only chance for inside information."

"I hope you're right."

"There's one way to find out," Woody said. "Let's go see him."

"In San Diego?"

"That's where he lives," Woody said. "I could ask an agent from the San Diego office to talk to him, but I think it would be better if we did it ourselves. We're familiar with the problem; the San Diego office isn't."

"I've always wanted to go to San Diego," Stephanie said.

"Then pack your bags. I'd like to get there as soon as possible."

20

OCTOBER STROLLED QUIETLY INTO SAN DIEGO, AS IT did most years. The days became cooler and shorter, the nights cooler still and longer. David stood on the small walk that led to his front door, watering a lawn with too many brown spots and a ragged edge. Even before he had left for Africa, the lawn had been a challenge. He spent many hours mowing it, trimming it, feeding it ammonium sulfate, spraying it for bugs, and watering it, but like an unruly child the lawn insisted on growing unevenly and yielding its green beauty miserly. Still, it was his lawn, and David felt the need to maintain it the best he could, if for no other reason than his neighbors' sake.

Unsuccessful as he was with growing a lawn that could grace the cover of *Home and Garden* magazine (or in this case *House and Scrub* magazine), he did enjoy the simple act of watering. Like most yards in his neighborhood, his was equipped with a sprinkler system, but David often watered by hand. There was something therapeutic about unwinding a hose, turning on the bibb, and watching water spray from the red plastic nozzle. One could not hurry through such a process but wait patiently as the spray fanned out and cascaded over the grass carpet.

There was something magical about that inconsequential and routine act. For David at least, and he suspected for others, too, much more than water flowed from the hose. Anxiety and tension often were drawn out of his body in a stream that joined with that of the water. His wife had never understood this and had often accused him of wasting time at the end of the day. But David knew that he was far from wasting time, he was investing time, time that allowed him to visit with himself, an art lost in modern society.

Now he had no wife to impugn his lawn-watering meditations. He could stand on the concrete walk all night and listen to the magnificent orchestration of water whistling out of a plastic nozzle. This evening the water music was especially endearing and was carrying his mind away to a peaceful place. He understood the power of being alone on an early October night.

The sound of a car door slamming jarred him back to awareness. He directed his attention to a dark, nondescript sedan parked at the curb in front of his house. A man—young, relatively short but solidly built, with a thick dark mustache—stood by the driver's door. He wore an expensive looking dark blue suit, a sharply pressed white shirt, and a red "power" tie. A woman exited from the passenger side. She was dressed in a fashionable gray pinstriped suit and had brown shoulder-length hair and a very pleasant face. She carried a small black purse slung over her shoulder. The man looked at David for a long moment, studying him as if he could pull thoughts right from David's brain and suck them in through his eyes. A moment later the man smiled and gave a small wave. The two approached, being careful to remain on the walk and not step on the wet grass.

"Can I help you?" David asked, hoping that the yuppie-looking couple were neither Jehovah's Witnesses nor one of those Amway couples.

"Mr. O'Neal?" the man asked. "Dr. David O'Neal?"

"I'm David O'Neal," he replied, suddenly aware that the two people walking toward him had nothing to do with cultic evangelism or soap. They had a special bearing about them that revealed an inbred pride that came from professional training. *Which area of the government are they from? Police detectives? IRS?* David thought it interesting that he felt a stronger apprehension of the latter over the former.

"Great," the man said. Reaching inside his coat, the man removed a small leather case, opened it, and displayed an identification card. "I'm Special Agent Woody Sullivan of the FBI and this is—"

"Stephanie Cooper," the attractive woman interrupted. "I'm with . . . another agency."

"FBI?" David exclaimed. "You've got to be kidding."

"No sir," Woody assured him quickly. "Federal Bureau of Investigation. But don't worry; you're not in trouble."

"All the same," David said seriously, "something must be up to bring you out here."

Woody glanced at Stephanie then back to David. "Could we talk inside, sir? I think you can help us with a rather touchy matter."

"Me? How?"

"Inside would be better," Woody insisted.

"Certainly." David quickly cranked the nozzle off and put the hose away. "Come in," he said, shaking the water from his hands. Inside, he motioned to the couch, and his guests sat down. He offered them coffee, which they accepted. David disappeared into the kitchen and emerged a few moments later with a pot and three ceramic mugs. "I started the pot about half an hour ago, so it should be fresh. I brought some sweetener and milk if you want it." David took a seat in the lounge chair next to the sofa.

"Thank you," Woody said. "I hope we haven't caught you at an inconvenient time."

"No, not at all."

"Good," Woody replied with a smile. He sipped his coffee. "This is very good. This isn't your basic store brand, is it?"

David understood immediately what the agent was doing. He was attempting to establish common ground by chatting amicably about a shared interest.

"It's a new brand I'm trying," David said, playing his part. "The beans are from Central Africa. I bought them at a local coffee shop." Before Woody could reply with another question, David interjected, "But I don't think you're all that interested in coffee. What can I do for you?"

"Right to the point, eh? I like that." Woody put his cup down. "All right then, let's get to it. I, that is, we need your help."

"My help?"

"Yes. From time to time law-enforcement agencies enlist the help of private citizens in the investigation of certain crimes. Sometimes those citizens have information that is helpful or they are somehow related to an investigation. We believe that about you."

"You want my help in solving a crime?" David leaned back in his chair and slowly took a sip of his coffee. Something wasn't right here, but he didn't know what. The two people appeared sincere, but it was too early to tell. "I really should have done this before, but could I have a closer look at your identification?"

"Certainly," Woody said. "Take all the time you need." David took the leather folder and studied the picture-identification card. It looked authentic, but David wouldn't have been able to recognize a forgery anyway. He was buying time, attempting to learn as much as he could while simultaneously gathering his wits. A moment later he handed the ID back.

"Ms. Cooper?" David looked at her and waited. She seemed fidgety at first, reluctant to comply yet unwilling to refuse. She reached into the small purse and removed a similar folder. David felt the blood drain from his face. It was one thing to have the FBI sitting on your couch, a big thing, but to have the CIA in your living room smacked too much of the Cold-War spy movies that Hollywood had been so fond of producing in the seventies.

"Unreal!" David said with a nervous chortle. "Tell me you're joking."

Stephanie smiled sweetly. "I'm not joking. The identification is real, and so am I."

"But the CIA!" David struggled to believe what his eyes were telling him. "What . . . I mean who . . . that is, how . . ." He took a deep breath. "Let's start from the beginning. Why don't you tell me why you're here and how it is you think I can help you."

"Fair enough," Woody replied lightly. "We've been working on a case that has at its heart our nation's interest and our nation's security. I know that sounds a little hackneyed, but it's true. What I'm about to tell you should remain confidential. Since you are a former minister, I feel that you understand the importance of things spoken in confidence. Is that true?"

"I've kept my share of secrets," David acknowledged, wondering how they knew he was a minister.

"I take it, then, that we can count on your understanding and confidence."

David made no commitment and said, "I'll keep your confidence unless I feel that to do so violates my conscience."

"Let me cut to the quick of the matter. Someone has been electronically breaking into a certain computer system in the CIA and taking classified material. Their approach is efficient and effectively elusive. We haven't been able to catch them in the act or get a fix on the perpetrator, but we have been able to narrow our suspicions to one primary suspect."

David began shaking his head. "I know only the basics of computers. I can use a word processor, make my way around a decent database, but that's where it ends."

"We don't suspect you," Stephanie said. "We suspect someone you know."

"Who?" David asked pointedly. "I don't know anyone who could do such a thing."

"Very few criminals," Woody said, "especially criminals involved in technical crimes, tell their acquaintances what they've been up to. You definitely know him, and know him well." Woody paused to judge David's response, but David sat still, his eyes fixed on the FBI man. "You recently went to work for Barringston Relief, is that correct?"

"It is, as you know," David replied cautiously.

"Barringston Relief is a large organization, and one that makes extensive use of technology." David immediately thought of the research labs and the advanced satellite communications. "We know that some of the top computer systems people in the country work for Barringston Relief, including Eileen Corbin and Raymond Reynolds. Are you aware of these people?"

"If by *aware* you mean have I met them, the answer is yes," David commented evenly. "I met Mr. Reynolds when I first went to work. He set up the computer in my office and gave me a brief introduction to the network. I met Eileen Corbin at a fund-raising dinner. That's all I know. I've never spent any time with them or had any discussion with them. In fact, I've never been in their offices."

"That's fine," Woody said, picking up his coffee mug and sipping the dark liquid. "We didn't think you had. To be perfectly honest, we're more interested in Mr. Barrington himself."

"A.J.?"

"Yes, A.J."

David furrowed his brow in genuine confusion. Why would they be interested in A.J.? "Let me get this right," David said, raising his hand to his face and pinching the bridge of his nose. He spoke in measured tones. "You think that A.J. Barrington is somehow connected with the computer piracy of CIA files. Is that what you're implying?"

"Exactly," Woody replied.

Leaning back in his chair, David looked at his uninvited guests. He studied their faces as they studied his. One thing was clear. They genuinely believed what they were saying. It was then that David surprised both his guests and himself—he began to laugh. Not a snicker or chortle, but an unrestrained guffaw that repeated itself in loud repeating peals that rebounded off the walls of the living room.

Stephanie Cooper was aghast. "This is a serious matter, Dr. O'Neal. We're speaking of matters of national security."

David peered through tear-filled eyes at the somber woman in the business suit. Her distress made him laugh all the more. "I'm sorry," he said, wiping his eyes, "but the idea is so . . . so ludicrous, so out of character for A.J. that I can't help myself."

Woody leaned forward on the couch, staring at David in a manner that left no doubt about his current emotional state, and said in a tone a full octave lower than his normal speaking voice, and with a timbre dripping in intensity. "Dr. O'Neal, this is no joke, and we are no fools. This is not an assertion we make without reason. If you think you can gather yourself long enough to extend the courtesy of listening, then you will better understand our point."

"No," David snapped, his laughter relinquishing its position to a new and just as surprising emotion—anger. "No sir, I don't think so. How dare you speak to me in that tone. I don't know what you think you know, but I know a great deal. I know that A.J. is my friend, not just my employer. I know that I have observed this man's compassion, a compassion that surpasses any I've ever seen. I've traveled with him through some of the harshest terrain in the world and have watched him gladly endure hardship and the ugly face of mortality. I've seen him hold starving infants so thin and emaciated that they were glass fragile. I've seen him weep over the pain he's seen. No sir, you can't waltz in here and pretend to tell me about A.J. and imply some impropriety on his part. I'll have none of it. Do you hear? None of it!"

Silence flooded the room, filling the space with tension and suspicion. Stephanie broke the spell. "Dr. O'Neal, your loyalty is commendable. Most of the people we are forced to work with have no understanding of that concept. It's a pleasure to meet someone who values friendship. But I believe you have more going for you than loyalty. I think you're a man who knows how to weigh information given him. I want to give you the opportunity to do just that—to weigh the information. We came here for your help. It's possible that we are way off base, but there's a good chance that we're not. And since this is a matter of national security, then I would think that a man of your intellectual caliber and loyalty would at least invest a little time in listening to our point of view."

David sat silently considering her words. He was overreacting and he knew it. Both the laughter and subsequent anger surprised him, shocked him with their intensity and abruptness. And there was a national interest to consider. What if these two strangers were right? What if there was something untoward happening at Barringston Relief? Certainly A.J. wasn't involved, but that didn't mean that some employee hadn't found some rationalization for using the company's computers to access the CIA. He had always considered himself a rational man who purposely eschewed useless displays of emotion and opted for a reasoned approach. He wasn't always successful, as in this outburst, but he always returned to the pragmatic course.

"Okay," David said quietly. "I apologize for my reaction. I'm listening."

Both Stephanie and Woody relaxed and leaned back on the couch. Stephanie took the lead. "There have been several successful attempts to download files from one of our, that is, the CIA computers. I can't give you all of the details or explain how the individual circumvented our security systems. Those details aren't important to our discussion anyway." David wondered if she was concealing information or just flat didn't know how the break-in was achieved. "The files that were stolen were unique. In fact, it was their peculiarity that first made us think of Barringston Relief. You see, what was stolen were surveillance photos of East Africa, Somalia in particular. You just got back from Africa, didn't you, Dr. O'Neal?"

"Yes," he responded, wondering how they knew that and what else they might know about him. "But not Somalia. We had planned to go there, but we spent all of our time in Ethiopia. None of us, including A.J., went into Somalia."

"We're not saying that he did," Stephanie continued. "The

point I'm trying to make is this: Why would anyone steal satellite photos of Somalia, unless they had some vested interest in the country?"

"I couldn't say," David replied. "The world's a big place and filled with people who might find the area interesting."

"Doesn't Barringston Relief have employees in Somalia?"

David nodded, "Yes, and in Ethiopia, Sudan, Tanzania, and nearly every other famine-stricken country, including those outside of Africa."

"Isn't it true that one of your field workers, a Dr. Judith Rhodes, was killed in Somalia?" Stephanie inquired.

"Yes. That information was on the news some months back. It's common knowledge."

"Do you know a man named Roger Walczynske?"

The sudden change in direction shocked David. Suddenly his mind was filled with the image of the cool Ethiopian night as he, A.J., and the others sat around a gas lantern discussing the day's events. He recalled how Wu and Raines had shown up in camp with a man introduced as Roger.

"I met a man by that name in Ethiopia, but I spent no time with him. I can't even recall if I shook hands with him or not. He came into camp and left soon after. A.J. said he did on-site research. That's all I know."

"Let me fill in a couple of the blanks," Stephanie said seriously. "Roger Walczynske is quite the world traveler. We have eyewitness observations of him in Colombia, Cambodia, Brazil, and a dozen other places. He seems to like troubled areas of the world."

"If he works for Barringston Relief," David interjected, "then I would expect him to be in such locations. Especially if it's his job to gather information for future work."

"Agreed," Stephanie said with a weak smile, "but there's more to it than that. It seems that wherever Mr. Walczynske has been, trouble followed."

"What kind of trouble?" David furrowed his brow.

"Assassinations of military leaders, government officials, gang leaders, drug traffickers, and so on." Stephanie leaned even more forward and lowered her voice to a conspiratorial level. "All the events happened to unsavory people who could be linked to the very kinds of activities Barringston Relief battles: hunger, human rights, children's rights, and so on. We can't prove it yet, but we think that Barringston Relief, or at least a few people in the organization, are taking matters into their own hands."

Shaking his head, David said, "You're trying to tell me that A.J. and this Roger are taking action against people whom they perceive as the cause for human-rights violations. Is that right?"

"Exactly right," Woody replied. "But that's not the issue here. Personally, I think the world has been done a favor by having some of these people taken care of. That's my opinion, you understand, and not the opinion of the FBI or CIA. The point is that someone in your firm, most likely the top man himself, is overseeing these operations and gathering whatever information is needed, even if that information has to be stolen. In this particular case, photos of Somalia were illegally downloaded from the CIA to help find whoever it was that killed Dr. Rhodes."

"This is too implausible," David uttered with exasperation. "At best this is pure conjecture. You're impugning a man's reputation based not on facts but on coincidence. There are huge gaps in your logic, gaps so large that not even imagination can fill them."

"He, or at least someone in his organization, has motive, means, and opportunity," Woody snapped. "We can't tell you the details, but it took some pretty sophisticated equipment and know-how to pull off that little hacking job. Barringston Relief has top-of-the-line computers and electronics. We know that."

"So does IBM, MIT, a dozen defense contractors, scores of countries, and who knows who else," David snapped as he leaped from his chair and began to pace.

"But none of them has as clear a motive," Woody said. "Besides, we're not attempting to convict Mr. Barringston or Mr. Walczynske while we sit here in your living room. What we're doing is asking for your help in proving our theory correct or incorrect."

"I don't see how I can do that." David sat down again. "And I say that for several reasons. First, I think you're dead wrong about A.J. Second, I'm the new kid on the block, and I'm still trying to find my way around. I can count on my fingers the number of people I can call by name. And lastly, I'm a speechwriter. I don't have access to anything confidential. You need to get someone else."

"You're the only one we can trust," Woody said. "It's precisely because you're new that we came to you. That and the fact that you used to be a minister."

"What's that have to do with anything?"

"Everything," Stephanie said. "To be perfectly truthful with you . . ."

"Haven't you been up to this point?" David asked.

Stephanie was nonplussed. "I don't understand."

"You said that you were going to be perfectly truthful with me," David replied firmly. "In interpersonal communication that's known as a qualifier. It implies that up until that statement you have been less than truthful with me."

"We haven't, Dr. O'Neal, believe me." Stephanie sounded hurt. "I know this is difficult for you. If you had agreed to help us too readily, then we would have thought we had made a mistake. The very fact that you are so resistant to what we're saying is proof of your character. That's why we chose you."

"And the fact that I was a minister."

"Yes," Stephanie replied. "I was taught from the time I was a child that ministers could be trusted and that they were honest people. Not perfect people, but honest. Let's face it, most ministers don't go into that line of work for the money. They do it because they feel called of God to do His will and to help others. Am I wrong?"

David sat silently for a moment and wondered if she was attempting to manipulate him. "No, you're not wrong."

"Assume we're right for a moment," she continued. "What if A.J. or someone close to him really is breaking into CIA computers—and, by the way, if they can break into ours, they can break into anyone's—wouldn't you as an honest and upright person want to see that stopped? It is an illegal activity. It's a felony and could fall into the category of traitorous activity. Whoever is doing this could be harming himself and others."

"Still, I don't see . . ."

Woody raised a hand and stopped David in midsentence. "Let me ask a question of you, Dr. O'Neal. It's a bit philosophical, but I think you'll see where I'm headed. Here it is: Is it ever right to do wrong?"

"What's that have to do with—"

"Humor me this one time, Dr. O'Neal," Woody insisted. "Is it ever right to do wrong?"

David exhaled loudly and then repeated the question in his mind. "The answer depends on your worldview, I suppose. Those who hold to situation ethics would say that one's ethical paradigm shifts in accordance with varied situations."

"Is that your view?" Woody prodded.

"No, of course not," David replied quickly. "There must be a set standard for behavior that is absolute, otherwise any behavior can be rationalized. I've always held that the Bible is the only true standard by which to gauge a person's behavior."

"Does the Bible teach that wrongs can be right?"

"No, absolutely not," David replied. "But the answer to your question is not that easy."

"Well, then," Woody said, "is it ever wrong *not* to do right?"

David didn't answer. He recognized tricky and convoluted ground when he saw it. Any answer he gave here could be used as a tool to compel David to participate in the investigation. "What are you getting at?"

"Just this," Woody said. "We have a set of guidelines that we as enforcement officers must follow. They're the same guidelines that every citizen in this country must follow. They're our country's laws. These laws are not perfect, but they provide a needed set of rules for civilized behavior. As one who understands the need for a standard of behavior, I'm sure you are aware of the need for social law. Someone in your firm may be—and I emphasize the phrase *may be*—breaking the law to right a wrong. We are not allowed the luxury of determining if the wrong they commit is justified or not. We must act because the law is being broken. Do you understand what I'm saying?"

"I do," David answered.

"We need your help to uphold the law," Woody intoned. "We suspect A.J. Barringston, but you might be right about his innocence. You may very well clear his name and keep him from becoming entangled in a legal mess that would sully his name and the work of Barringston Relief. If he is guilty, then you will help uphold the law of the land, the same law that makes us civilized. No matter how well intentioned the perpetrator is, he must not be allowed to do wrong even for the sake of that which is right. And for us not to pursue the matter would be like the man who does wrong by refusing to do what is right. Help us, David. Help us solve this problem."

"I don't know," David replied quietly. Woody's argument made sense and put him in a difficult spot. They were right about his moral character and calling. If someone was misusing the technology at Barringston Relief, and if he did nothing to help stop it, then he would be tacitly approving the crimes. Yet to become involved might mean betraying a trust. But shouldn't there also be a loyalty to morality? Suddenly, David felt weary.

"Think about it, please," Woody said softly. "Here's my card; call me when you come to a decision. If you decide to help, I'll tell you what you can and cannot do." David slowly took the card. "Is it ever right to do wrong? Is it wrong not to do right? I'd be interested in hearing what you think."

Woody stood and walked toward the front door, Stephanie

following close behind him. "Thank you for your time and the coffee. No need to see us out. Just think about all that we've talked about. Your country can use your help."

David remained in his seat, unmoving but not unfeeling. His stomach was tight as if someone had just punched him. He felt angry, weary, honored, offended. But most of all, he felt confused.

■ ■ ■ ■ ■

When David attended Golden Gate Seminary in Mill Valley, California, he had an ethics professor, Dr. Linkhold, who delighted in challenging his students with difficult questions. More was the case than not that the class would erupt into spontaneous debate about social and ethical issues that had plagued thinkers for generations. The students, many too young and too brash to realize that simple answers usually came from simple minds, would proffer solutions after investing only a few moments thought. "The way I see it, professor," some student would say in tones made heavy with pseudo-intellectualism, "there can be only one answer." The professor would smile patiently, scratch one of his large wrinkled ears, and ask, "How can you see when you have failed to look at the problem long enough to recognize its origin or discover its nuances?" More discussion, often heated, would follow. In the end, the students would leave the class that day as full members in one of two groups. The first group was composed of those who were positive that their answers were right and beyond any real challenge. The other group was composed of those who felt confused and frustrated at not being able to find one simple answer to the ethical question. David was always numbered with the latter.

This evening David entered the debate again, but this time without the roomful of seminary students. This time he lay alone in bed, wide-eyed and sleepless, questions ricocheting around in his head. Is it ever right to do wrong? At first, he had been tempted to answer in the brash manner of the undisciplined students in Professor Linkhold's class, but he knew that hasty answers came from hasty thinking and often led to immense error. The purist would answer strongly that it is never right to do wrong. But don't we do that all the time?

Once David's former wife, Carol, had come out of the bedroom sporting a new outfit she had bought at a department store in Mission Valley. She paraded down the hall and into the living room like a model on the runway of a fashion show. To David, it was quite simply the ugliest outfit he had ever seen. David was no fashion plate himself, but he knew enough not to mix yellow and green into any form of stripe or pattern. She asked, as David knew she would, if he liked it. No, David didn't like it. He found it revolting, ill designed, gaudy, garish, and more. The question left him in a bind. Technically, if he said yes he would be lying. If he said no he'd be running the risk of decapitation. He chose the former answer, rationalizing that he had spared her feelings. Hadn't he committed a wrong to do a right?

Perhaps, but the question Special Agent Summers had asked David went far beyond an untruth told to avoid a spousal conflict. It went to the heart of his suspicions that A.J. was involved in illegal activities and that his involvement might be driven by his desire to alleviate sorrow and pain. It was one thing to tell an untruth about someone's appearance and quite another to commit a crime against one person to save another. Is that what A.J. is doing? Is he capable of harming someone?

It was a hard question, and as Professor Linkhold used to say, "Hard questions lead to other hard questions until all that your reasoning has achieved is a Gordian knot." David hadn't known what a Gordian knot was, so he looked it up in an encyclopedia in the seminary's library. He discovered that the phrase was named after King Gordius of Phrygia who tied an extremely complex knot that none could untie. Alexander the Great, prompted by an oracle that promised that whoever could undo the knot would be the next ruler of Asia, attempted to untangle the puzzle. He failed, so Alexander simply cut it with his sword.

That's what David needed, a sword with which to cut through

the problem. The only sword that he had found that could cut through the problems of life had been the Bible. Reaching for the Bible that he kept on his nightstand, he began to read at random, looking for an example to follow, a command to commit to, or some bit of wisdom to guide him. Minutes dissolved into hours as he lay with his head propped up on the pillow reading. He read through Proverbs and a dozen psalms before he drifted off to sleep, the Bible resting on his chest.

As he slept he dreamed of a huge knot with people tied to its surface. Strands of the knot's cord were wrapped around heads, arms, and trunks. The people, all of whom David knew, cried for help. Kristen was begging to be released, Timmy shrieked in terror, and A.J. reached out to him. Interwoven in the strands were Stephanie Cooper and Woody Summers, each beseeching David to act quickly to release them. David rushed to Kristen and began to pull on the cord that was wrapped around her waist, but as he pulled, Timmy screamed out in pain. It was clear that the more he struggled to free Kristen the tighter he made the knot on the others. He might free one, but not without killing another. In his dream, David began to pray. He prayed for a sword to cut the knot. But no sword came. He would not be as lucky as Alexander the Great.

21

"AM I BORING YOU?" KRISTEN ASKED.

David snapped his head around and cast a confused look at Kristen, who sat in one of the leather guest chairs in his office. The midmorning light cascaded in through the window and danced lightly on her red hair. "I'm sorry, what did you say?"

"I asked if I was boring you," she replied firmly. "I've been talking, but you haven't been listening."

"I'm sorry," David offered. "I didn't sleep well last night—too many weird dreams." There had been many of them, but the dream about the Gordian knot was the only one he could remember in the light of day, perhaps because the dream recurred several times in the night. He struggled with the image. Not that it was difficult to interpret. He didn't need to be a psychologist to know that his dream was a reflection of his confusion and anxiety over what Woody Summers and Stephanie Cooper had said. The image of those whom he cared about being restrained in a tangle was his subconscious fear of hurting them while attempting to help another. If he chose to do nothing, his friends would remain trapped forever; if he made an effort to help, he would cause greater harm. He was wrong no matter what he did. That was how David felt about Agent Summers's request for help.

"You're doing it again," Kristen said sharply. She studied him for a moment and softened her tone. "Something's bothering you, isn't it?"

"Just a thought or two bouncing around in my otherwise

empty head," David said, waving a hand in a dismissive gesture. "That's all."

"Can I help?" Kristen asked. "I'm a pretty good listener."

David chuckled, "I know. But there's really nothing you can do. Besides, it's not a crucial matter." He watched as Kristen's face darkened with disappointment. "Don't go looking like that. It's not that I don't trust you, it's just that I can't put my thoughts into words. It's sort of a philosophical question, really." It wasn't a matter of trust, for David had come to have a profound faith in the woman who sat on the other side of his desk. The weeks of close contact in Africa had seen to that.

"I'm bright, I can handle it."

"There's no doubt there," David agreed, beaming a broad smile. "You're one of the few people I wouldn't want to match wits with. But again, I wouldn't know where to start. I'm just in a mild funk. There's nothing to worry about. Really."

Kristen pondered his words as if she were looking for a key that would unlock the door to David's secret. "Okay, if you say so, but I think you're holding out on me."

"Honest, I'm not." David raised his right hand like a witness taking a court oath and signed an *X* across his chest with his left. Kristen was clearly unconvinced, and David feared that he might be hurting the budding relationship that they were nurturing. She had been patient with him and understanding to a fault. She had not pressed for a deeper commitment on any level but had allowed things to move along under their own power. "All right," he said, "but this isn't going to make much sense to you. I'll give you a question that was asked of me. Are you ready?"

"Ready. But first, who asked you the question?"

"I can't say yet," David replied. "It would confuse the issue."

Kristen pursed her lips then smiled. "If you say so. Shoot."

"Is it ever right to do wrong?"

"Ooh, a deep question," she said, rubbing her chin. "I suppose the answer depends on what you mean by right and wrong. If you're asking if it's wrong for a poor man to steal bread for his starving children, that's one thing. If you're asking if it's wrong for a businessman to lie on a loan application to expand his business so that his family might become richer, well, that's another matter all together."

"I think we're dealing with the former," David replied.

"In that case, I'm not sure there's a good answer. We might well ask if the poor man would be wrong for *not* stealing the bread if his children died of malnutrition. I think you know that there is no easy answer to this kind of question. No matter what answer you come up with, someone will chime in and say, 'Yeah, but what about . . .' and then change the parameters a little bit."

"There must be some answer, some solution," David interjected. "The world can't operate on a scale of sliding absolutes."

"Not only can it, David, it does." Kristen moved to the edge of her seat as she became more emphatic. "I know I'm talking to a minister who knows a great deal more about morality than I do, but you don't have to live very long before you realize that the world is not fair. Justice is more difficult to get if you're a minority. That's not an opinion, it's a fact that has been demonstrated many times. Is this because there is a deep, dark conspiracy against minorities? Probably not. It's simply the way things work right now. The same can be said for certain gender issues. Women still make less money for the same work as men. Why? Because there's a sliding scale of absolutes."

"But that's not right," David objected. "Everyone should be treated equally."

"Agreed. And not only do I agree, but everyone you ask will agree. So why is the problem still there?"

"Because we don't live up to our own ideals and laws."

"Exactly, and that creates an inequitable society in which some have advantages and others are deprived of opportunity. Now let's get back to your question: Is it ever right to do wrong? Technically, the answer is no. Practically, the answer is yes. Ultimately, the answer is that it depends on the situation. I suppose it all hinges on motivation."

"Motivation?" David inquired.

"Sure. If I break the law for no other reason than to enhance my personal wealth or social standing, then I'm wrong because my motivation is selfish and may come at the expense of others. If, however, I break the law to save your life, then maybe I've done something good even though I've technically become a criminal."

David raised his hand and rubbed his eyes. Normally the question would be a fun and intellectually stimulating discussion, one in which he would eagerly participate. But now he was dealing with real people in real situations, and like it or not, he was being asked to participate in the discovery of A.J.'s guilt or innocence. Kristen hadn't disappointed him. Her answers were thoughtful and direct. He wanted to tell her the whole story. He wanted to say, *Listen, Kristen, the funniest thing happened last night. I was watering my lawn when an FBI agent and a CIA agent came by to have coffee and tell me that my friend and boss may be guilty of stealing satellite photos. What do you think about that?* But there was no wisdom in that, and what that decision lacked in wisdom it made up for in danger.

"Does any of that help?" Kristen asked, her eyes fixed on David.

"Maybe. Let me think about it for a while."

"You're still not going to tell me what's troubling you?"

"I can't. Not yet anyway. Please trust me on this."

"Trust has a price," Kristen replied with a playful grin. "You want to keep secrets, then you have to buy me lunch—today."

David laughed. "Lunch it is. That's a price I'm more than willing to pay." He fixed his eyes on her only to discover that she was staring at him. As their eyes connected, David felt a sudden rush of warmth and the image of his lips meeting her lips in an unexpected soft kiss under the moonlight of Addis Ababa flooded his mind. An afternoon lunch with Kristen was just what he needed.

■ ■ ■ ■ ■

Lunch had been the perfect diversion. Kristen had wanted Chinese, so she and David made their way to a small place on Broadway, across from the Wells Fargo Bank Tower. They ate with chopsticks and discussed matters of absolutely no importance. It was as if she sensed the depth of his turmoil and had determined to distract him for as long as possible. When they left the restaurant, they did so hand in hand, an act that made the world look brighter and infinitely more optimistic to David.

Back in the office, David struggled to push the accusations of impropriety to the back of his mind. He tried to focus on his work, but his thinking kept drifting back to one thought that burned in his mind: Agent Woody Summers would be contacting him and demanding an answer, and David had no idea what he would tell him.

Despite the exertion it took to concentrate, the time passed quickly, and David was surprised to see that the sun was already setting. Most of the staff would have left, each gone home to family and friends. But David didn't want to leave. If he went home, then that same dark sedan might pull up in front of his house and Agents Summers and Cooper would emerge to put more pressure on him. They were wrong, and David knew it. The problem was proving it without hurting his relationship with A.J. Surely there must be some way to demonstrate A.J.'s innocence. Perhaps he should simply talk to A.J. and tell him about the investigation. But what if Agent Summers was right? If David spoke to A.J., would that make him an accessory? David felt stymied.

"Hello, David."

Looking up at his open door, David saw the thin frame of Timmy, a plastic trash liner in hand and a huge smile on his face. "Hello, Timmy," he said, "I haven't seen you in a couple of days."

"That's 'cause A.J. took me to the Wild Animal Park," Timmy said with pride. "He couldn't take me to Africa so we went to the Wild Animal Park instead."

"Was it fun?"

"It was neat." Timmy exuded excitement. "We saw lots of animals and stuff, but I ate too much candy and ice cream and got sick on the tram." David tried to picture A.J. dealing with a nauseated Timmy. "But I got well real quick."

"That's great, Timmy."

"And the next day, A.J. took me to Sea World. Have you ever been to Sea World?"

"Yes I have. Last summer—"

"They got lots of neat stuff there too. I like the penguins and the puffers the best."

"Puffers?" David asked, confused.

"Sure. They're like penguins, but different."

"Puffins," David said, nodding his head. "I like the puffins too. Did you see them swim?"

"Yeah!" Timmy clapped his hands together, but the sound was muffled by the plastic trash bag. "It was like they was flying underwater. I bet I could fly underwater." Timmy raised his arms like wings on a plane and ran through the door into David's office making zooming sounds. "Well, I could if I could swim."

"We'll have to teach you to swim, Timmy."

"Yes!" Timmy jumped up and down twice. "Neat. Will you teach me, David? If it's okay with A.J., will you?"

"If it's okay with A.J.," David agreed.

"Cool! You wanna see what else I got, David?" Timmy reached into his pocket and pulled out a key chain with a single strange-looking key attached. "It's got Shamu on it. Here, look." Timmy handed the inexpensive chain to David. "A.J. bought it for me at Sea World. Isn't it neat?"

David took the small silver chain with a tiny plastic killer whale dangling from it. But what caught David's eye was not the ornamental orca but the key at the end of the chain. It resembled an ordinary office key, except that the back portion where the user would hold the key was covered in black plastic and had a small microchip embedded in it. Most of the offices in the Barrington Tower had doors that couldn't be locked and, therefore, keys weren't needed. But apparently a few doors were special enough to require a key for access. This made sense to David, but why would Timmy have such a key? "This is pretty terrific," David said. "And this key is neat. What kind of key is this, Timmy?"

"It's my key. I need it to get into the rooms to empty the trash. That's my job, remember?"

"I remember, Timmy," David replied, giving the key back to him. "And you do a good job too. Do you empty the trash for the whole building?"

"Oh no." Timmy scowled and shook his head. "There are too many rooms. I just work on A.J.'s floors."

"You mean the floors used by Barringston Relief."

"Yeah, but only three floors," Timmy said proudly. "Floors fifty-one, fifty-two, and fifty-three." That made sense to David. Taking out the trash for all the offices in a fifty-three story building would be a monumental task for anyone, and especially difficult for Timmy.

"So that key lets you into all the offices?"

"Uh-huh," Timmy agreed. "It's a neat key, but I like my new key chain even more."

"I bet you do," David said. "Tell me, Timmy, what do you do after you empty the trash?"

"I put it in this big barrel," he replied, motioning to the large, green plastic trash barrel that sat on a cart with small, black rubber wheels. "Then I get in the elevator and go down to the basement and put the trash in the big Dumpster. Then the trashmen come in a big truck that makes lots of noise and take the trash away."

"Then what?"

"Then I go to the cafeteria and have dinner. The cooks always have my food ready for me. Unless A.J. takes me to Burger King or the Pizza Palace. But tonight A.J. is at a meeting so I have to eat alone."

"You know what, Timmy," David said casually. "I'm going to

work late tonight. Why don't you come up here when you're done with your work, and I'll join you for dinner in the cafeteria. How's that sound?"

"Neat," Timmy exclaimed, bouncing on the balls of his feet. "I'm going to get to work right now so we can go eat." He moved quickly over to the side of David's desk, where the waste bin was located, pulled the full bag out and replaced it with a fresh one. "I'll be back soon, okay?"

"Okay." David wasn't sure what he planned to do after his dinner with Timmy, but he knew he had to do something. Maybe he could do a little investigating on his own.

■ ■ ■ ■ ■

David and Timmy stepped from the elevator and made their way down the corridor of the fifty-second floor. They had spent the last forty minutes in the cafeteria chatting over a dinner of fried chicken and apple pie, which Timmy had gobbled at an alarming speed. The cafeteria, which stayed open late for those employees who were putting in long hours, was nearly deserted except for two couples seated near one of the large picture windows that overlooked the bay. The San Diego skyline was twinkling in the distance, and David could see a large gray navy ship in the harbor. David and Timmy chatted about things that excited the young man—video games, television, and comic books. It was during the conversation that David noticed how fond he was of the child-man. Timmy was a true innocent who went through life sucking up all the joy and pleasure he could find and doing so with no malice toward anyone. He was quick to laugh and express his pleasure over the simplest things. David offered him a cup of hot chocolate while he drank coffee, and this prompted a quick clapping of the hands and a little jump for joy in his seat. Seeing such innocent expression of pleasure demanded a smile from anyone nearby.

But Timmy's innocence also caused David guilt. He needed Timmy to help him do something that might not be viewed favorably by others. Timmy had a key, a key that would open most if not all of the doors on the top ten floors of Barringston Tower. David needed that key but he couldn't, wouldn't ask Timmy for it. Timmy had been entrusted with it, and it was patently unfair for David to ask the young man to betray that trust. Still, David felt compelled to do something. He couldn't stop going home because he feared that the FBI and CIA would show up to pressure him to service, yet he couldn't dismiss them out of hand. *What if what they say is true?* David kept asking himself. *What if someone from Barringston Relief is accessing the computers at the CIA? What if that presented a danger to the country? Surely it wasn't A.J., but what if someone, an employee, was using the Barringston computers to commit the piracy?* Such thoughts led David to take the next step. It was a little step, but something that made him feel that he was, at least, attempting to do right.

"Are you sure you don't mind?" David asked Timmy.

"Nuh-uh," Timmy replied. "But I wanna watch *Star Trek* on television tonight. Okay?"

"Okay. I promise this won't take long." The two walked down the hall until they came to a door marked COMMUNICATIONS. David remembered it from the tour Kristen had given him on his first day of work. "Do you need a key to get in there?"

"Nope. There are always people in there."

"Lots of people?"

Timmy shook his head. "At night there are only two. They listen to the space radio."

"Space radio?" David inquired. "You mean the satellite communications?"

"Yeah. From space." Timmy turned the doorknob and walked in with David close behind. One wall of the room was filled with electronic devices that looked like VCRs. David had seen similar devices in the homes of his church members who had satellite television. The black boxes with blue LED indicators were the receivers and decoders. Judging by the number of units, the communications division must be tied into a dozen different satellites.

"Hey, Timmy," a resonant voice called. "You've already been here, man. Don't you remember?" The voice came from an obese man with sagging jowls in the corner of the room. He was leaning back in a large, heavily padded executive chair and was reading the comic section of the *San Diego Union.*

"Hi, George," Timmy said with a wave. "No, I didn't forget. I want to show David something." The man looked David over quickly. David didn't recognize him, but he hadn't expected to. The last time David was in this room was at the beginning of the work-day, not three hours into the evening. A different shift would be working at night.

"Okay," the man replied. "Say, I forgot to ask you earlier. Did you like that new Nintendo game I loaned you?"

"Yeah, it's real neat, but I can't get past the second level."

"That's okay. Just keep trying; you'll get the hang of it." The man turned to David. "Are you new around here?"

"I started a few months ago," David said, trying to sound pleasant. "Are you here all alone?"

"Yeah. Normally, Hector is here too, but he's got the flu. First casualty of the fall."

"Can you work alone?" David asked, hoping he didn't appear too inquisitive.

"Sure," George replied, riffling his paper, "it's all automated. I'm just here in case something bad goes down. Like the Dr. Rhodes thing. Occasionally, someone in the field needs an answer right away, then I can get pretty busy putting people in contact with other people. But most of the time it's pretty laid back."

A beep emitted from the computer console. "Uh-oh, I must be a prophet. Here comes a call now." George threw his paper on the floor and turned his attention to the monitor. "It routes itself, you know. All I have to do is make sure there're no glitches. If there are, then I take the call myself and start playing telephone tag with whoever wants to reach whomever."

"Well, we won't bother you," David said. George waved nonchalantly. "What's down here, Timmy?" David pointed down another hall that led from the communications room.

"Offices," Timmy replied.

"Are those the offices with all the computers?" David kept his voice low. Timmy nodded. Casting a glance back at George and seeing that he was engrossed in watching the communiqué's connections being made, David walked down the hall. The hall was short and had two doors on one wall. One door had a small plastic sign that read DIRECTOR, COMMUNICATIONS. The other door had a similar plaque that said PRIVATE. Have you been in here before, Timmy?"

Shaking his head, Timmy said, "Uh-uh. It's locked."

"I'll bet that special key of yours will open it. Want to try?" Timmy shrugged, pulled out his key that dangled on his new Shamu key chain, and inserted it in the lock. Nothing happened. Timmy turned the key again, but still nothing. "Strange." David said quietly.

"Not really," a husky, dry voice said.

David snapped his head around and looked down the corridor. Standing there with her arms folded across her chest, a cigarette dangling from her mouth, was a middle-aged woman with a streak of gray in her hair. Her eyes were squinting against the rising stream of smoke that emanated from the tip of the cigarette. Standing behind her was George.

"You can't open it because the room is private—just like the sign says."

"Oh, hi, Eileen," Timmy said, smiling. Eileen didn't return the smile. "This is my friend David."

"I know who he is, Timmy," Eileen said firmly. "What I don't know is why he's trying to get into a room where he doesn't belong."

Timmy dropped his head. It was clear that he had picked up the anger in the woman's voice. "I was just . . . just . . ."

"That's all right, Timmy," David offered as he put his hand on Timmy's shoulder. "She's not angry with you. She's angry with me."

"Why?" Timmy wondered aloud. "We didn't do nothin'.."

Eileen inhaled deeply on her cigarette and blew out a long blue stream of smoke. David felt the odd compulsion to remind her that smoking in office areas was illegal in California, but he didn't think she'd care.

"Actually, Timmy, I let my curiosity get the best of me. It's always been a problem of mine. Something about closed doors piques my interest."

Neither Eileen nor George moved.

"That's my office you're attempting to break into."

"That door says director of communications," David said meekly. "Isn't that your office? We didn't go in there."

"I have two offices," she replied curtly. "Not that it's any of your business, now is it?"

"Of course not," David replied defensively. "But I think you are misunderstanding my intentions here."

"I'm not misunderstanding anything, Dr. O'Neal." She approached David and Timmy slowly until she was only three feet away. David could smell the tobacco smoke, and Timmy coughed. She held out her hand and said, "May I have the key, please?" David removed the key from the lock and meekly handed it to her.

"My Shamu key chain," Timmy cried and stomped his feet.

"There's no need to upset the boy," David said firmly.

Eileen Corbin took the cigarette from her mouth with one hand and raised the key chain to eye level with the other. "Do you want your key and key chain back, Timmy?" she asked coolly.

"Yes, it's mine," he stammered. "A.J. gave it to me."

"Timmy," Eileen said, "this key is a big responsibility. You must always make sure that you use it only in those places where you work. Do you understand?"

Timmy's eyes were brimming with tears. "Yes. Yes, I understand."

"All right, I'm going to give this back to you, but I want you to promise not to do this again."

"I promise. I promise." Timmy was hopping from one foot to the other with his hands stretched out before him.

"Here you go," Eileen said and dropped the key into his palm.

"Thank you, Eileen, thank you." Timmy stepped forward and hugged her quickly but backed away when the smoke caused him to cough.

"Go back to your room," Eileen said, "and watch some television. Okay?"

"Okay." Timmy was gone a moment later.

"I suppose you have a few things to say to me," David said.

"Nope," Eileen replied perfunctorily. "That's not my job. I'll leave that up to A.J." David felt his heart stop. "I will, however, invite you to leave and not come back into my department."

David flushed and left without a word.

22

MAHLI STUDIED THE MAN IN THE MIRROR. HIS shirtless torso was slightly hunched, his eyes red with fleshy pouches beneath, his brow wrinkled. He had lost weight. Not because of the famine but because of weariness.

"Tell me, Noonan," he said to the young black man who stood just outside the bathroom door. The man was in his early twenties, tall, robust, and fiercely loyal. He had worked for Mahli since he was seventeen and had distinguished himself by doing what he was told without question. That undiminished obedience extended to his firing a .30-caliber machine gun from the back of a technical— a truck with a high-caliber machine gun mounted on the back— into a crowded gathering of a rival clan.

"It goes just as you planned," the young man said with a voice that seemed too shrill for his age and build. "On your orders we began to roll out truckloads of food from Marka, Mogadishu, Hobyo, Hafun, and Kismayu. The food was distributed near existing foreign-relief camps. The people are very grateful."

"And the flyers?"

"Distributed with the food, but many cannot read, so we shouted the news to them."

"Do they believe?"

"Many do now; many more will soon." The young man broke into a huge grin. "Soon everyone will know that the foreign food is tainted and that only the food you provide is trustworthy."

Nodding, Mahli returned his gaze to the mirror. Two weeks ago he had not stood with a stoop, nor had his face been marred by as many wrinkles. But the days were taking their toll. The planning and supervision had been tiring work, but that didn't bother him. What weighed heavy on him was the memory of his brother kicking and struggling as he plummeted to the ground. The image played over and over in his mind. Someone knew how to find him and to deliver their message by killing his brother, Mukatu. There had always been that risk, but Mahli had assumed that he could and would strike back immediately. But he couldn't. He had finally figured out that the only group who would be so brash as to challenge him was Barringston Relief. The attackers had all been white, and that ruled out rival warlords. They were the only ones with sufficient reason and resources to do the deed. He had killed that white female doctor months ago, and now the Barringston people had exacted revenge. His theory was verified by the man who had rented the helicopter to the foreigners. He confessed, after a torturous hour of questioning, that Americans had rented the craft and that they paid in American dollars. Mahli killed the man himself.

His first impulse had been to slash and burn every Barringston camp in Somalia, but while that would make him feel good, it would also turn the tide of public opinion against him. He had worked too hard and too long to destroy his path to power and riches on impulse. He would take his revenge. He didn't know how or when, but fate would give him the opportunity. And when it did, he would make his brother's murderers squirm and die. He would savor every minute of that glorious day.

"You have done well," Mahli said, causing the young man to grin even wider. "Now go. I want every step of the plan to work perfectly. I hold you responsible. Succeed, and I will make you rich and powerful. Fail, and I will cut the heart out of every one of your family members." The man's grin evaporated immediately.

■ ■ ■ ■ ■

There was a sick feeling in David's stomach, an emptiness that had been suddenly and fully flooded with bile. But David knew he hadn't been stricken with influenza or any other disease, unless guilt could be defined as an illness. From his seat behind the desk, he looked across his office to the tall figure standing in the doorway.

"May I come in?" A.J. asked calmly.

"Of course," David replied meekly, struggling to maintain eye contact.

A.J. walked slowly into the room and took a seat opposite David. As he sat, David noticed that he didn't sit upright as he usually did. For that matter, A.J. looked tired, vapid. He slumped his tall frame in the leather chair and gazed at David.

"I need to talk to you, David," he said in hushed tones. "I think you know what about."

David nodded slowly and sighed heavily. He felt his face blush red. "Yes, I can imagine. If it makes things easier, I can have my things out of here by the end of the day."

A.J. looked puzzled then shocked. "Out? Do you mean quit?"

"I thought that you might be thinking of firing me."

"Oh, no," A.J. said shaking his head. "Nothing so extreme. We need you, David. I need you."

"But my behavior—"

A.J. stopped him with an upraised hand. "Enough, David. I didn't come here to fire you or scold you. I didn't even come here to ask you what you were doing. I assume you had your reasons."

"Well…"

"No, David, I don't want to know. All I want to know is this: Can I trust you? That's important to me—very important. You and I have traveled a lot of ground over the last couple of months. We've been halfway around the world and back. That creates a bond that's hard to break." A.J. squeezed the bridge of his nose with his hand and sighed. "I've been under a great deal of pressure lately, David. Sometimes the work is made unbearable by all the pain, hunger, and violence. It's a heavy burden, a crushing burden at times. I'm able to endure it because of the people in this building. It's their combined strength and purpose that makes it possible for me to get up one more day and do battle. I trust the people in our organization. I trust them with my life, and I trust them with the lives of the innocents who depend on us for an extra day or two of life. And—David, this is very important—I have to know that I can trust you in all matters and at all times."

"I'm not sure where to begin or what to say," David offered.

"Just tell me that I can trust you. I believe in you. I just need to hear that I can trust you in your own voice."

"But don't you want an explanation?"

"No, that's not necessary."

Forgiveness. That's what A.J. was offering. Unmitigated, undiluted, unpolluted forgiveness. The kind of forgiveness that doesn't demand explanation, only repentance. It was the same kind of absolution modeled in the Bible, the same kind of forgiveness about which David had preached so many times. Now A.J. was offering it freely and without limits. How anyone could suspect A.J. of criminal behavior was beyond David.

"Yes, A.J., you can trust me."

A.J. smiled a broad but strangely weak smile. "I knew I could, David. I knew I could." With that, A.J. rose and walked out the door. The sight of the normally convivial man meandering away stoop shouldered fanned the fire of guilt in David's belly. He decided then that the FBI and CIA were on their own. David would do nothing to further their illusion. If they wanted inside help, they would need to find it elsewhere.

■ ■ ■ ■ ■

A.J. lay down on the couch in his office with his arm over his eyes to block the overhead lights.

"Did you fire him?" Eileen Corbin asked acerbically.

"No," was A.J.'s brief reply.

"It would be wise," she said. "He could present a danger to us in the future. I have incriminating equipment in that room. Anyone with a little computer knowledge could have accessed it."

"I'm not going to fire him," A.J. repeated.

Sheila, who sat in one of the leather chairs near the couch, glanced at Roger then back to A.J. "I have to agree with Eileen. I don't trust that preacher."

"I do," A.J. said. "Besides, firing him would only make us look guilty. He has demonstrated his courage and loyalty. I won't cut him adrift for one bad display of judgment."

"I still think—" Eileen began.

"No, and that's final," A.J. snapped. "Now leave it alone."

"What could he have been looking for?" Sheila asked. "And who was he working for?"

"The FBI and CIA," A.J. said calmly.

"What?"

"The FBI and CIA," he repeated. "We broke into a CIA computer. They know it, but they don't know who did it. They suspect us because the pictures we stole were of areas in which we have work and in which one of our workers was killed. Since the crime occurred on U.S. soil, the FBI must investigate. David's the new kid on the block and a former minister to boot, making him the likeliest candidate for recruitment. They probably played on his patriotism, speaking of national security and the like. David is a sensitive soul who easily responds to such appeals. Those people can be very persuasive if need be."

"How do you know all this?" Eileen asked.

"Because it's what I would do in their place," A.J. replied wearily. "It's not especially creative, but the plan is functional. Now he will turn them down flat before he will attempt to betray us again."

"How can you be sure?" Roger inquired.

"Because I know David. I know him better than he knows himself. I didn't build Barringston Relief by making bad decisions, you know." Silence prevailed. No one wanted to challenge A.J.'s judgment.

Roger broke the silence. "I want to go back to Somalia and finish my mission."

"I know you do," A.J. responded evenly. "I admire your zeal, but the answer is no. We got our point across when you and Sheila booted his brother out of the helicopter. I want Mahli's head as bad as any of you, but things have changed. He's feeding the hungry, and he's the hero of the land. I know he's no hero, and I know that he has some devious plan cooking in that twisted mind of his, but if we off him now we could destabilize the whole region. We'd be shooting ourselves in the foot to make ourselves feel better."

"He's also telling the people that our food is poisoned," Roger insisted. "They're leaving our camps and refusing our help."

"And if we kill Mahli now, will that reinstate the people's belief in us? Now is not the time to kill Mahli. There will be a time, and I promise you that you can do the job. But not now. Now if you folks don't mind, I need a few moments to rest. I haven't been sleeping well of late." A.J. rolled over on the couch, turning his back to his three friends.

"Oh," A.J.'s now muffled voice intoned. "I want you all to leave David alone. Is that clear?"

"I'm not sure that's rational," Eileen said.

"It's not, but leave him alone anyway. Got it?" They acknowledged his command. "Good. Thank you. I love you all. Now go away."

23

DAVID WAS AMAZED TO SEE HOW FAST THE WORLD could change. Four months ago he and a handful of others from Barringston Relief had walked what was often dangerous ground in Africa. In Ethiopia they had seen heartrending scenes; Somalia, which they had not been able to visit, was a hotbed of civil war and warlords, a hotbed accentuated by hordes of homeless starving people. All that was in September of last year, now a new year had arrived and was only two weeks old.

The new year brought interesting news, at least according to the San Diego edition of the *Los Angeles Times*. Sipping coffee and nibbling on an English muffin, David sat in his now usual booth in his now usual restaurant and leisurely perused the paper as he did each workday. In a special section of the paper called "World Report," he read a lengthy article on East Africa. None of the news was news to him since he received briefings almost daily from the communications department of Barringston Relief.

Still, seeing the changes in East Africa delineated in print caused him to feel a sense of awe. Somalia, Ethiopia, Eritrea, and Kenya had agreed to participate in a loose confederation of states. The confederation was nonbinding and sealed by nothing more than a few handshakes, yet observers were hailing it as a hopeful sign for the beleaguered area. Civil strife between the countries had settled to small skirmishes; leaders talked to each other and even worked together on a few projects. The advance was a fragile one as all the naysayers were quick to point out, but the change was nonetheless significant enough to be noticed. Also noticed was the short man with a crescent-shaped scar on his cheek, a man named Mahli.

Longtime observers of the region, including those in the UN and in the CIA, knew that Mahli had been a dangerous and powerful man in Somalia, a leading warlord who may or may not have been responsible for the sudden disappearances of other warlords. Yet the public had taken to the man who was being heralded as the hero of East Africa. They, the public, had developed that unique ability to see only a portion of the truth about a man. The fact that he may well be a killer was never talked about. What was spoken of shocked those who knew more about Mahli than what the paper printed: *Time* magazine was considering him for Man of the Year, and rumor had it that Mahli might even receive the Nobel Prize for peace. The more David learned of Mahli from interdepartmental memos and briefing sessions, the more outrageous the last consideration was. The thought of Mahli receiving the same award that Mother Teresa had received years before seemed ludicrous.

"You're still here." David looked up to see Kristen standing beside his booth.

"Uh-oh, I've been caught," he said with a smile. He rose from his seat and kissed her lightly on the cheek. Her arrival was no real surprise. While not an early riser like David, she did on occasion crawl out of bed early enough to join him for coffee. When she did, David felt that the day became a little brighter, the sun a little higher, and the sky a little bluer. Any impartial observer could see that he was falling in love with her and she with him. Still they were a cautious pair, neither willing to push the relationship too fast.

"Would you like some coffee?" David asked.

"Like? I demand it." Kristen replied quickly. "And you're going to pay for it."

"Me?"

"It's all your fault, and you know it."

"What is?" David chortled. He could hear the teasing tone in her voice.

"These bags under my eyes, that's what. I don't know why you insist on going to the late movie anyway."

"It's all a matter of logistics, my dear," David answered. "By the time we both leave the building, get to our respective homes, change clothes, go to the finest eating establishment in town—"

"It was Coco's," Kristen interrupted.

"—and then wander across town to the movie theater, it's late. I'm an innocent victim of circumstance. Besides, you loved the movie."

"True."

"And the popcorn."

"Truer still."

"Lots and lots of popcorn."

"It's a vegetable," Kristen interjected quickly. "So give me a break."

"What about that box of malted milk balls?" David teased. "Are they vegetables too?"

"If you're not careful, Dr. O'Neal, I'm going to kick you in the fanny . . . with my heavy shoe."

"Okay, okay," David surrendered. "I'll buy the coffee, but only because I like you."

"And because you're afraid of the shoe of death."

David laughed. "Actually, you look wonderful today. Do you want some breakfast?"

"No. I'm still full of popcorn and candy. Breakfast of champions, you know."

"So I hear."

"Besides, I need to get to the office. I've got a feeling I'm going to be busy today, considering the news."

"How do you think A.J. will take it? He's no fan of Mahli."

"I don't know anyone in their right mind who's a fan of Mahli. The man is a murderer. We can't prove it, but we know he killed

Dr. Rhodes. A.J. hasn't forgotten that. Now that the president has invited Mahli to come to the States, A.J. is going to be in a foul mood—and rightly so."

"Do you think he'll issue a statement?" David asked.

"I doubt it, but I'm going to be getting calls from the media. I need to be there to run interference. Besides, I'm sure A.J. is going to have a general staff meeting about all of this, to reassure the troops, as it were."

"Why do you think the president did what he did?" David asked. "I mean, asking Mahli to come to the United States?"

"Who knows," Kristen said seriously. "Maybe he doesn't know about Mahli. Maybe he knows but doesn't care. Maybe he knows something we don't and feels compelled to take this action."

"Surely the CIA knows about Mahli. That's their job to know, isn't it?"

"Perhaps, but not necessarily," Kristen said as the waitress brought her coffee. Kristen shook her head when offered a menu. "Remember, Somalia isn't strategic, and the famine has pushed back its development. The CIA may have limited involvement there. They may not know."

David thought of Stephanie Cooper, of her determined attitude and her resolve. Both Stephanie and Special Agent Woody Summers had visited David twice over the last three months; both times he refused to speak to them other than to turn down their request for help. "But they must have done some research before they extended an invitation to a warlord like Mahli. They wouldn't expose the president to danger."

"Mahli won't be dangerous over here," Kristen said. "He needs the endorsement of the U.S. to enhance his world image. That's the only reason he would come over here. In Somalia he tells the people the Americans are poisoning the food to get even for what happened in 1994. He'll return to Somalia and tell the people that he has made the food safe once again and that he has influenced our country to be more sympathetic to their plight. We'll send supplies directly through Mahli, and he'll be a national hero. That's my best guess anyway."

"You've been giving this a lot of thought."

"I have." Kristen drank deeply from the coffee cup. "Personally, I think someone ought to shoot the little—"

"Kristen!"

"—the little man as he steps from the plane. If someone wants to hire an assassin, I'll contribute to the cause." Once again David thought of Agents Summers and Cooper. This was the kind of thing they had been talking about.

"That's pretty harsh, isn't it?" he asked seriously.

"No harsher than the way he treated Dr. Rhodes," Kristen opined.

"We don't know that."

"No, we don't, but if I were a betting woman, I'd bet the mort-gage to the house and the pink slip to my car that that's what happened."

David said nothing, for there was nothing to say. Mahli was probably as evil as Kristen had said, and there wasn't a member of Barringston Relief who didn't want to see him gone. That realiza-tion saddened and worried David. It also brought up a question that he had forced to the back of his mind: Is it ever right to do wrong?

"Anyway," Kristen continued, "be ready for a full staff meeting. I'm sure A.J. will have a few things to say to us all."

"How do you think he'll respond to the news?"

"It probably isn't news to him. A.J. is well connected in Wash-ington, so he probably had some warning, a day or two at least. But to answer your question directly: He's most likely livid and frus-trated. I wouldn't play racquetball with him today. He's likely to fire the ball through the wall, or maybe even through you."

David had begun to play racquetball with A.J. at least twice a week since early October. He did it at first to alleviate his guilt over disappointing A.J. with his failed little espionage adventure, but after a few weeks David began to enjoy the sport. He had improved markedly as the weeks passed, enough so that he could actually gain up to ten points before A.J. reached the game-winning twenty-one.

"I'll take your advice and stay off the courts for a couple of days. It wouldn't do for me to be run through with a little blue ball."

"True. Besides, I like you the way you are," Kristen said in soft alluring tones. She reached across the table and squeezed his hand. "You know I was only kidding about the movie last night. I really do enjoy going out with you—even if you do eat my malted milk balls."

David laughed and lightly caressed her hand. They gazed at each other for a moment, David staring deep into her blue eyes. Her eyes were so rich, so captivating that he felt he could fall into them in endless, blissful descent.

"You had better walk me to my car," she said moments later. "People are going to start wondering about us."

"What people?" David asked romantically. "There're only the two of us in this universe."

"You do wax poetic."

"You bring it out in me."

"I still think you had better walk me to my car. And if you do a good job of it, I might even give you a little kiss."

"You're on."

■ ■ ■ ■ ■

Kristen had been correct about the staff meeting. When David arrived in his office he found a memo with IMPORTANT emblazoned across the top. The memo itself was short, only a paragraph long, and announced a mandatory meeting at eleven that morning. All other appointments were to be rescheduled.

"This promises to be interesting," David said aloud.

At 10:50, David walked into the cafeteria, the only room large enough to hold all the Barringston workers at once. Scores of people were already seated around tables, and many more were pouring into the room. David looked for Kristen but didn't see her. He did see Eileen Corbin seated with Sheila. A man who looked familiar to David was with them. It was Roger Walczynske, the man whom David had met briefly in one of the relief camps in Ethiopia. He had arrived with George Wu and Gerald Raines. David could recall A.J. walking away from the others with Roger. George, Gerald, and Sheila had joined them a few minutes later, and then they all, except A.J., left together. A.J. had explained that Sheila was going to Somalia with the men to talk to some of the camp workers. Sheila had come back to the States about a week after David and the others had returned. He had not seen Roger since that night in Ethiopia. David also noticed that they all looked glum, depressed, and even angry.

When A.J. entered the room, the constant drone of conversation ceased. Timmy was with A.J. and sat at a table near where A.J. was standing. Once seated, Timmy began to play with a handheld video game. A podium had been set up in the corner of the cafeteria.

At precisely eleven o'clock, A.J. stepped behind the podium. "Good morning," he said. A few dozen people responded; the others smiled or nodded their heads. "Thank you for being here and being prompt. I shall not take up much of your valuable time." David felt proud of the way A.J. had grown in his public speaking. A.J. had taken immediate control of his audience, was making good eye contact, and was enunciating clearly and powerfully.

"I'm sure most of you have heard the morning news," he continued. "My sources in Washington have verified the story. The president has indeed invited the Somali warlord Mahli to visit the United States." Murmuring rippled through the crowd. "To some of you that name may mean nothing; to others it means a great deal. It has been no secret in this building that Mahli may have been responsible for the death of at least one of our noble doctors in Somalia. I personally suspect him of other crimes. We are saddened by the president's invitation, and I plan to telegram our concerns immediately following this meeting. I do not criticize our president, for he may not—must not—have the full story. As you know, Mahli has been active of late and seems, at least to the eyes of many, to have achieved some good in his land and in other African countries. We are thankful for the good he has done, but we remain dubious about his motives and about his plans for the future." Heads in the audience nodded in agreement.

"Nonetheless, we will continue our good work around the world, including Somalia and Ethiopia. So far as we are allowed, that is. It is important that we not lose heart and . . ." A.J. paused as his eyes caught a movement out of the corner of his eye. David, seeing A.J.'s glance, turned to watch as Kristen hurried into the room and headed for the corner where A.J. stood. He stopped speaking until Kristen had made her way to him. She whispered in his ear. A.J. scrunched his face in a puzzled and surprised expression. "I'm sorry for the interruption, but it seems that I have an . . . interesting phone call: the president."

The crowd chuckled, a few gasped, and one man shouted, "He must have heard you talking."

A.J. laughed with the others and then motioned to Peter Powell, who was seated nearby. "Peter has a few things to share with us about our new health and dental insurance. I'm sure you're going to like the changes, but there are some details you need to know. Peter, come and use this time to share those issues. In the meantime, I'll go see what the president wants. I promise to come back and fill you in." A.J. stepped from behind the podium and quickly walked from the room.

Kristen, who had seen David when she entered, walked over and sat next to him. "The president," David said. "I'm suitably impressed. I bet he really wanted to talk to you."

"Flattery always works with me, but this time I have to tell the truth. He wanted to speak to A.J."

"What about? Do you know?

"No. Haven't the foggiest. I started to ask, but it's hard to formulate questions when you're stammering." She made a face, crossed her eyes, and said in a voice an octave higher than normal: "You wish to speak to A.J. Barringston? Certainly President Gain, I mean Mr. Pain, I mean President Laine."

David guffawed loud enough to be heard across the cafeteria. Several people turned and looked at him.

■ ■ ■ ■ ■

A.J. walked purposefully but unhurriedly to a nearby office. The office was shared by several accounting clerks. He snatched up the nearest phone and dialed the access code that would open the line that Kristen had secured. The code was part of the Building Utility Security System that protected everything from the elevators to the computer network. Many of the calls made and received at Barringston Relief were sensitive and required protection from prying ears. The coded system allowed executives to put someone like a high-level diplomat on hold without fear that someone would pick up the line accidentally, or not so accidentally.

"Mr. President?" A.J. said evenly.

"Mr. Barringston, I presume," Gillian Laine said.

"Yes sir, Mr. President. I'm sorry to keep you on hold. I was in the middle of a staff meeting."

"I should apologize for calling at such an inconvenient time, but I need to ask a favor."

"A favor?"

"First, let me say that I have been a big admirer of both you and your father. I appreciate the excellent work your organization does, and I also appreciate your father's help over the years. As you know, he's been a big supporter of my administration."

A.J. knew that and also knew when he was being set up with a compliment. "Thank you, sir. The kind words mean a great deal to me and to my staff."

"I mean every word of it. Now, down to business. I assume you know that we have invited the Somali warlord Mahli to the United States for a little face-to-face chat."

270

"I am aware of that, sir."

"What you may not be aware of is this: He's made two requests."

"Only two."

"So far," the president replied, overlooking the gibe. "The first request is to see Disneyland. He studied in England years ago and learned of Disneyland from some students. I mentioned that Walt Disney World would be closer, but he insisted on California. I think it's because of his second request."

"Oh?"

"He wants to meet with you."

"You can't be serious . . . sir"

"Serious as a mortician, Mr. Barringston. He was clear about this one point. He wants to meet you: A.J. Barringston. Apparently he's familiar with your work in the area."

That's not all he's familiar with, A.J. thought and wondered if Mahli had figured out that he was responsible for his brother's death. If so, this could be a setup for revenge. "Mr. President, I have grave reservations about Mahli and his motives. I'm not sure he has the best interest of his people at heart."

"Let me make sure you understand my position here, Mr. Barringston. I know that Mahli is far from the ideal leader. I'm sure he's motivated by desires that are less than noble, but I work with senators and congressmen about whom I can say the same thing. Mahli may not be a great man and he may not be a saint, but he is in place to make a difference, and he has achieved some amazing things."

"Are you aware that he's telling people that food supplied by Americans is poisoned?"

"I am aware of that," Laine responded. "I am aware of a great many things, but my advisers and I think that we can save some lives and restore some stability in East Africa. Mahli is the key to that. I want to impress him with our sincerity and convince him that our supplies are not poisoned."

"I'm sure he already knows that," A.J. said evenly.

"Look," the president said, "I can't force you to help us on this, Mr. Barringston. I can't draft you into the service of your country. But I can ask for your help, and I'm not ashamed to ask for the favor. How about it? Can I count on your help?"

A.J. closed his eyes tightly and wished that the decision was not his. Then an idea began to form in his mind. It was more of a feeling than a full-fledged thought, more of an inkling than a revelation, but it was there nonetheless. "Yes, Mr. President, you can count on me."

"Outstanding," Laine exclaimed. "You're a fine American, Mr. Barringston. Someone from my office will fax you the details. It might be nice if you brought two or three of your executives with you. It should prove to be a good photo op for your work. Allow me to say thanks for your help. I knew I could count on you to be there for me."

I'll be there, A.J. thought, *but it won't be for you.*

■ ■ ■ ■ ■

"He's out of his mind," Roger shouted. "Disneyland? Oh for the love of . . . I can't believe it. Here, right here in our country, Mahli is going to walk around and play tourist, and he's going to do it at the taxpayers' expense."

"I didn't like it either," A.J. said solemnly. "At least not at first."

Sheila, who was seated on the couch in the meeting area of A.J.'s expansive office squinted questionably at A.J. "What do you mean? You've got something up your sleeve, don't you?"

"Ah, Sheila," A.J. replied with a broad grin, "you know me too well."

Walking over to the couch, Roger sat down. "Tell us."

"If we will set our anger aside for a moment, we may be able to see the silver lining in this little gray cloud." A.J. paused for effect. "You are aware that for the first time in years we will know exactly where the elusive Mahli is going to be."

"You're thinking of killing him?" Roger inquired eagerly. "Killing him right there in Disneyland? But he's going to be surrounded by security—Secret Service I would guess—and Disney-land is a very public place."

"And wouldn't killing him like that bring down Barring-ston Relief?"

A.J. said nothing, but let the idea take root in their minds. A few moments later, Eileen Corbin, who had been sitting quietly throughout the meeting smiled and said. "Actually, Disneyland can be one of the least crowded places in the world. I think I see where you're going with this."

"Well tell me," Roger demanded.

"I will, Roger," A.J. said. "I will. But we are going to have to get busy on this. There's a great deal to do."

24

SPOONING A MOUTHFUL OF NEW ENGLAND CLAM chowder into his mouth, David read intently the *Newsweek* in front of him. The magazine had devoted much of its space to the question, "What shall we do in East Africa?" There was an article on Ethiopia, Somalia, and other regions as well as opinion pieces on the role the United States should play in the famine-stricken land. So engrossed was David that he didn't see the approach of two people who seated themselves in the booth where David was having his lunch.

"Please excuse the rude interruption," Special Agent Woody Sullivan said as he and Stephanie Cooper took their places on the opposite side of the table. "We didn't want to interfere with your lunch, but you are becoming more difficult to contact."

"That's intentional," David said coldly. "I have told you on several occasions that I have nothing to offer you and that I believe you are barking up the wrong tree. A.J.'s no criminal."

"And we've told you that we have sufficient reason to suspect him or someone high up in his organization," Stephanie countered.

"That's nonsense, pure and simple," David snapped. "Now, if you don't mind . . ."

"There's something I want you to see," Woody said, placing a standard-size brown file folder on the table. "This information came via Stephanie's office. I should warn you that it's shocking."

"I'm not the least interested in what you have to show me,"

David said, ignoring the folder. "The last time I listened to you, it very nearly cost me a friend, not to mention my job."

"We didn't ask you to break into the communications room," Woody said firmly. "In point of fact, it was a stupid idea. Attempting to sneak into Eileen Corbin's office was your idea. You began without our instruction."

"But it's what you wanted."

"No, it wasn't," Woody said. "It's possible that some special equipment has been secreted there, but you're not trained to recognize it. Even if you did get into the office unnoticed, you would not be able to discern one electronic system from another."

"Then what did you want me to do?"

"We were going to ask that you keep your ear to the ground," Stephanie jumped in. "Watch A.J. and the others. See if he acts strangely or, better yet, shows you satellite photos. If you see them yourself, or at least hear about them in some meeting or hallway conversation, then we might be able to convince a judge to give us a valid search warrant. Then we could take a look for ourselves. That's all."

"My word might not be enough for a warrant," David commented dryly.

"That's right," Woody said, "but then it might. Granted, it's a shot in the dark, but it's worth the effort."

David leaned back, crossed his arms in front of him, and shook his head. "You're grasping at straws, and for what? Someone snatched a few photos."

Without hesitation, Woody reached across the table and opened the folder. Inside was a color photograph of a man on the ground. A dark circle stained the ground around a mass of material that David assumed had once been the man's head. David drew in a breath sharply and quickly turned away. "What . . . what . . . why show me that?"

"The man's name is, was, Ian Booth," Stephanie said coolly.

"He was president of an offshore bank called the Americas Bank. For the most part he was a pretty nice guy, or at least his friends and family thought so. But like many offshore banks, his dealt with some unsavory characters—in this case, a terrorist group called the Silver Dawn, a recalcitrant conglomeration of Irish dissidents. Booth helped them launder money from their supporters. Someone stole a hefty chunk of that money. We've been able to determine that the computer hacker who broke into the Americas Bank used the same technique that was used to compromise the computers at the Company." David noticed Stephanie's use of the euphemism, and figured she did so because they were in a public place. The word *company* turned fewer heads than *CIA*.

"How can you know that?" David asked as he gingerly closed the folder. "How can you tell the break-in was the same?"

Woody shook his head and said, "Look, Dr. O'Neal, I'm sure you're a real smart guy, but you have admitted that your knowledge of computers is limited. I'm an expert in the field. I could spend the next two or three days explaining it to you, but I don't have the time. Just believe me when I say that we are 90 percent sure it was the same person using the same ramming technique."

"I still don't see what that has to do with me or Barringston Relief."

"It's like this," Woody continued sternly as he leaned over the table. "Every action has a reaction. Ever heard that?"

"Isaac Newton said it," David answered. "It's fundamental physics."

"It's more than physics, Dr. O'Neal, it's honest-to-goodness life. Whether they intended to do so or not, whoever stole that money cost this man his life. I'm sure it wasn't part of the plan, but the act nonetheless orphaned Booth's kids and widowed his wife. No act stands alone, David. Every act has a reaction, and that leads to another reaction. A man is dead because of someone in Barringston Relief."

"How can you hold anyone responsible for the death of this

banker?" David argued. "If what you say is true, this man's death is an unfortunate accident."

"I'm surprised at you," Woody said quietly. "Would you also say that a drunk driver is innocent because he didn't intend to kill a child who was walking across a street? The laws of our society disagree."

"Of course I wouldn't say that," David objected.

"It's the same thing," Woody insisted, pounding the table with his finger. "A man is dead because of computer piracy. I don't know why the money was stolen. Maybe it was stolen to buy food and medicine, which seems noble enough except the money wasn't free. It came blood stained."

"You can't prove this," David said, but his words lacked force and conviction.

"That's what we're attempting to do," Woody said. How many more Ian Booths have been killed because of what someone in your organization is doing?"

David shook his head in disbelief but said nothing. He felt ill, as if the clam chowder had soured in his stomach. The garish and grotesque image of the mutilated head had been etched so deeply in David's memory that he no longer needed the actual photo. No amount of mental exercise could excise the picture's ugliness from his brain.

"There's more," Stephanie said.

"I don't want to hear it," David mumbled.

"I'm sure you're aware of the meeting that your boss has been asked to attend," she continued anyway. "The one with the Somali warlord Mahli."

"What about it?"

"Come on, David, think! Stolen satellite photos of Somalia, a Barringston doctor named Judith Rhodes brutally murdered, Mahli's brother flung from a high-flying helicopter into his brother's front yard." A puzzled expression crossed David's face. "You didn't know about that last part, did you? A man in Somalia provides us with information, a former teacher. Ironically, he's Barringston Relief's contact in the country. He filled us in."

"What are you saying?" David stuttered. "Are . . . are you saying that A.J. had something to do with the death of Mahli's brother? It can't be, I was with him or near him throughout our whole African trip. We never went into Somalia."

"Oh come on, David," Stephanie said coldly. "Didn't you tell us that you went down in the Ogaden area of Ethiopia? Didn't you tell us that you saw Roger Walczynske there and that he and A.J. had a private conversation?"

It was starting to make sense to David, and he didn't want it to. He wanted to shoot down their arguments like a trained lawyer would shoot down the testimony of a witness, but all the bits were hanging together. The pieces fit like a jigsaw puzzle, and with the addition of each piece the picture became clearer. "It's all circumstantial evidence."

"Circumstantial evidence is strong enough to get a person thrown in jail, Dr. O'Neal," Woody added. "It all comes back to that one question: Is it ever right to do wrong? If Ian Booth could speak to us today, I bet he'd have an opinion about the matter."

"I don't . . . I don't know what to say." David was shellshocked. "I don't know what I can do."

"That's all right, David," Stephanie said sweetly. "We know what to do."

■ ■ ■ ■ ■

The halls of Barringston Tower were quiet; the lights in most of the offices had been turned off. Only a few employees were working, the janitorial staff and those in the communication department. A.J. stood alone and watched the red and white lights of the traffic on the street more than fifty floors below him. He envied the people in those cars. He knew many of them were headed home to cozy dinners or to restaurants with friends. Some would watch television, others would read books, and still others would dance with those whom they loved. They were building memories that would warm them in the colder days and nights of the future.

A.J. had none of that. His warm and comforting memories had all been scarred by death, disease, and violence. The image of Judith Rhodes rose in his mind and bobbed on the swells of his emotion. Other images joined hers, images of emaciated people refusing food because an insanely ambitious man had told them that the food was poisoned. He saw the faces of hollow-cheeked youth who would never know what it meant to fall in love, learn a trade, or hear their own children laugh. He saw again the poignant drama of mothers holding dead infants to their withered breasts. The images moved across his mind like a videotape, but unlike a videotape A.J. could do more than see and hear the pitiful scenes. He could smell the decay of death and sense the heavy weight of despair.

The red from the taillights and the white from the headlights blurred as tears filled his eyes. The sadness was profound, the guilt so heavy that A.J. felt he might collapse. People brought the pain, not the weather, not the soil, not the sun or the wind, but specific people whose moral conscience had been consumed by voracious greed for power and wealth. Those people, people like Mahli, who kill on a whim and let thousands die to further their cause were nothing more than dogs made mad by rabies; they were animals that preyed on the weak. They were subhuman and unworthy to exist on this earth. They were dark, ugly souls, trolls who terrorized passersby.

Such men had to die.

A.J. Barringston, founder of Barringston Relief and defender of the innocent, wondered when his metamorphosis had taken place. Once his only goal had been to provide lifesaving food and medicine. But some people worked against him and blocked him in every way. Because of people like Mahli, many others died. People like Mahli couldn't be allowed to interfere with the greater good. He would stop them at any price.

A.J. wondered when he had changed from relief worker to

militant, ready to kill those animals. Was he becoming just like them? he wondered.

■ ■ ■ ■ ■

David awakened to the sound of his own voice—screaming. He sat up in bed, sweat rolling from every pore, his breath coming in ragged gasps. He looked slowly to the other side of his bed and exhaled noisily when he saw it unoccupied. It had been a dream, only a dream, the most authentic, frightening dream he had ever experienced. A moment ago he was certain that he saw the violently disfigured body of Ian Booth lying in bed next to him. Unlike the photo he had been shown by Woody and Stephanie, this body was far more than two-dimensional; it had depth and weight and presence.

Swinging his feet over the side of the bed, David drew in bushels of air. His stomach churned roughly, mixing bile and acid in a noxious concoction known to every person who has been truly frightened beyond all reason. He blinked hard and rubbed his eyes with the palms of his hands. "That was bad," he said aloud, "really bad." Getting to his feet, he swayed for a moment, then walked in uncertain steps into the bathroom, turned on the shower, disrobed, and crawled in the tub. The water ran warm to hot, and David sat, letting the streams cascade over his head and down his back. The dream slowly dissolved into the real world, and the night terror diminished into a manageable memory.

Twenty minutes later David was standing in the kitchen making a cup of tea and thinking about how his life had suddenly turned into a roller coaster. Why him? Why did the FBI and CIA have to choose him? Several hundred people worked at Barringston Relief, and they had to choose him. They had answered that question the first time they met, but the answers provided no comfort. Other questions plagued him. Was this all part of God's plan? Had God placed him in this situation to test him or maybe involve him in some important cause? If so, then what was the cause? Protect A.J. and Barringston Relief so that the work would continue? Or submit to the wishes of the FBI? What was right? What was true? David had no idea which course of action to take.

The tea, an orange pekoe, felt warm and soothing on his throat. David sat at the dining table and stared at the highly polished woodgrain, letting his thoughts run random and hoping to find some guidance. A passage of Scripture popped to the surface of his mind like a submerged cork that had been suddenly released. He wasn't sure exactly where, but he knew the text was from the book of Esther. "Who knows," Mordecai said to Queen Esther, who was being called upon to save the lives of thousands of Jews, "but that you were chosen for such a time as this."

Chosen. Chosen for what? David wondered.

With his teacup drained and the clock on the wall reading 2:30, David cast a wishful glance toward the bedroom and wondered if he could go to sleep again, and if he did, whether the night terror would return. He was tired, his eyes burned, and his mind seemed fogged. He had to sleep. And he had to make a decision—a decision that would change his future forever. *Who knows,* David thought as he climbed back into bed, *but that I was chosen for such a time as this.* Fifteen minutes later, he knew what he would do. Ten minutes after that, he was swallowed by peaceful sleep.

25

"I'M GLAD YOU COULD MAKE IT," DAVID SAID, RISING from his seat and hugging Kristen lightly.

"Your invitation rescued me from washing clothes and dusting my house. It's not very exciting, but it fills a Saturday."

David studied her for a moment and tried to imagine her busy about household chores. He found it difficult to conceive. Kristen didn't seem the type to be occupied by such mundane things as laundry and furniture polishing.

"I've forgotten how lovely it is out here," she said softly. She closed her eyes and turned her face skyward. "The sun feels good on my face." A gentle breeze wafted along the concrete plaza, carrying the fragrance of eucalyptus trees and green grass. The sounds of people strolling along the walk mingled with the bubbling of the fountain behind them.

Balboa Park was the favorite destination of both tourists and San Diego residents who visited the many museums and strolled through the gardens. The area was verdant and lush, filled with the best of San Diego's scenery and architecture. The museums held some of the nation's best displays of aircraft, natural history, and art. There was also something magical about the place. It seemed, to David at least, that the concerns of the real world were prohibited from entering the byways of the park. Only that which was interesting or beautiful was permitted to linger here.

"It's warm for the season," David commented innocently.

"Why is it that I think you've asked me here for some other reason than to discuss the weather?"

David bowed his head and laughed softly. "It's true," he said, turning to look at her. He motioned to the concrete berm that served both as the edge of the fountain's bowl and a seat for foot-weary sightseers. Once seated he slid closer to her and placed his arm around her shoulders. "I want to talk to you about something."

"Uh-oh," she said, her voice betraying her puzzlement. "It sounds serious."

"It is," David replied softly, "but first . . ." He leaned forward and kissed her gently on the lips. At first she held back, allowing the kiss but not returning it, and then her caution crumbled and she eagerly surrendered to the embrace. Gentle lips stroked still gentler lips, and the sounds of the milling crowd diminished to a mere murmur bathed in the bubbling of the fountain. The gentle, heavily scented breeze caressed their skin, and the sun immersed them in soft light. When the embrace ended, they sat in silence and watched a young boy on a skateboard doing tricks on the concrete plaza. A couple, younger than David by ten years, leisurely rode by on bicycles.

"I'm scared," Kristen offered.

"Scared?"

"First you say you want to talk to me and ask me to meet you here, then . . . then this," she touched her lips. "I'm afraid you're going to drop some bad news."

"Not about us," he said. "I need your help, your wisdom. What I have to talk to you about isn't easy for me to say. It affects someone we both admire, and I'm not sure what to do. I'm also concerned that you may end up thinking less of me."

"I'm not sure that's possible," she said smiling.

"I hope you're right." He stood, took her by the hand, and began to walk. They passed through the Spanish-style arcade with its graceful plastered arches. As they walked hand in hand, David unburdened himself. He told her everything about the FBI, the CIA, and their allegations against A.J. He spoke of Ian Booth and his murder and of Mahli. He told her of his dreams, fears, and guilt. As he spoke, Kristen listened in silence, her head down as she took in every word.

"I have resisted this at every turn and in every way, but I'm now being plagued with doubt. I've grown close to A.J. and think he is a wonderful and powerful man. I can't begin to tell you how much I admire all that he's done. He is, perhaps, the most compassionate man I've ever met. I can't bring myself to believe that someone who has invested his life and wealth in the alleviation of hunger could be guilty of such intrigue."

They paused at a rail next to the walkway and gazed down into the recessed area called Zoro Gardens. The gardens were sheltered on the east and west by buildings and a dense grotto of trees, ferns, and other plants that created a small paradise isolated from the noise of traffic and the clamor of tourists. Its beauty made it a popular place for summer weddings. This day it was empty except for a gathering of sparrows that hopped from place to place hunting for fallen seeds.

"But . . . ," Kristen prompted.

"Part of me, a very small part of me," David continued, "wonders if it might be possible. Not A.J., but someone else in the company." Exhaling heavily, he rubbed his eyes. "At times it makes sense. Someone could be so devoted to the cause that they might be willing to undertake . . . unusual methods." He turned to face Kristen. "I know that you're as loyal to A.J. as they come. I admire that, but I have to ask you this for my own sanity: Do you have any reason to believe that these accusations might be true? Could someone in Barringston Relief be involved in computer piracy? Could someone like Roger be involved in covert activities and even murder?"

Kristen didn't answer immediately. Instead, she stared unblinkingly down into the grotto. Looking at her, David could see that her jaw was clenched tightly, her muscles tense, and her eyes slightly squinted. "That is what I was afraid of," David replied softly.

"I can't believe you're telling me all of this," Kristen replied tersely. "This is preposterous. It's unbelievable."

"Just remember, I didn't create this."

"How could anyone suspect A.J.?" she snapped. "And how could you be part of this?"

"I'm not part of it," David objected. "I didn't invite the CIA and FBI to come knocking on my door, but they came anyway, and so far I've refused to help. Not that I could have done anything anyway. What little I did was a disaster."

"I know this wasn't your choice. It's just so maddening, that's all."

"*Maddening* is a good word for it. I hate to ask this again, but I feel I have to: Do you know anything that would give credibility to these accusations?"

Kristen shook her head slowly. "I suppose someone with access to the computers could break into another system, but that would take special knowledge and special equipment."

"What do you know about Eileen Corbin?" David asked.

"Not much. Her work and mine seldom cross over. She heads communications. I've heard that she's brilliant, but I don't know anything more than that."

"What about Roger? Do you know anything about him?"

"I've met him a time or two, once in Africa, but you were there so you know that. He seems to be close to A.J. At least he did that night in Ethiopia. Again, that's all I know."

"I'm sure this sounds like an interrogation, but I don't mean it to," David said apologetically. "What about Sheila?"

"She's an enigma. A.J. seldom goes anywhere of significance without her. If he leaves the country, she goes with him. She lives in one of the apartments, but all that's to be expected. She is, after all, his bodyguard."

"Bodyguard?"

"You didn't know that?" Kristen was surprised. "That's why she's so protective of him. That and she's in love with him."

"You know that for sure?"

Kristen smiled. "It's a woman thing. I can tell by the way she looks at him."

"That's pretty subjective, isn't it?"

"Spoken like a man. Trust me, she's in love with A.J. But I don't think that he's in love with her. A.J. loves his work too much to be distracted from it even by love. Nothing stands in the way of the work."

"Could she be the one the CIA is looking for?" David sounded hopeful.

"Possibly, but I doubt it. I don't know her well, but what I do know leads me to think that she's better at following orders than giving them."

Placing his arm around Kristen's shoulders, David led her down the walk, sidestepping children, couples, and families of tourists wearing Sea World caps or San Diego Zoo T-shirts.

"I have an uncomfortable feeling, Kristen, that something somewhere isn't right. I don't know what it is, or even if I should be involved."

"Now who's being subjective?" Kristen asked. "I can tell you right now that I don't believe for a minute that A.J. has done anything that can be considered criminal, unless caring too much is a felony."

"I know," David agreed. "I appreciate your willingness to listen. I was afraid that when you heard what I had to say that you'd bite my head off."

"I was angry at first, still am, but I can see that you're concerned for A.J. and that you feel the same loyalty that I do. It was unfair for those two agents to put you in this situation, even if they thought they were doing the right thing."

"Being suspicious is their job. I imagine the CIA is extremely embarrassed by all this."

"What are you going to do now?" Kristen asked.

"What can I do? For that matter, who am I to do anything? If I had evidence of wrongdoing, especially where it touches on national security, then I would do whatever was right, but as it stands now, I know nothing and have no way of learning anything. It's pretty much a dead issue. Mahli's my biggest concern."

"I can't believe that he's coming to this country at the invitation of the president," Kristen snapped bitterly. "That man killed Dr. Rhodes, he doesn't deserve to live, let alone come over here pretending to represent Somalia. It's so arrogant for him to demand to see A.J."

"That's precisely my concern," David confided. "I don't believe that A.J. is guilty of any crime, but how will he respond when he's standing within striking distance of Mahli? And if A.J. is everything that Agents Summers and Cooper say, then the situation could be dangerous for everyone involved."

Shaking her head, Kristen said, "A.J.'s not a violent man by nature. He loves peace."

"This is going to be difficult for me."

"You?"

"I'm going to Disneyland with A.J.," she said matter-of-factly. "Part of my job is to record the event on videotape." David felt a sudden rush of fear. In his mind he saw Kristen standing near Mahli, a man he had been told was a killer. "I think we'll all be okay. Secret Service people will be around."

David only nodded. Something about this whole situation upset him and made his stomach tighten in apprehension.

They walked a little farther before he spoke. "I don't suppose it would do any good to ask you not to go, would it?"

"No," Kristen replied quickly. "It's part of my job, and I need to go. But thanks for caring about me."

"Why do you suppose Mahli requested a meeting with A.J.? It doesn't seem right. Surely he knows that A.J.'s aware of his activities."

"Who knows what goes through the mind of someone as loony as Mahli? Why choose Disneyland of all places? He's an egomaniac who lives to serve and amuse himself. Maybe this is one way to rub salt in the wound."

"But all A.J. ever tried to do is help."

"Unfortunately, that carries little weight with men like Mahli. To him, A.J. and the rest of us are interlopers who get in the way of his plans, whatever those may be. It's not uncommon for those being helped to turn on those who offered the help in the first place. You, of all people, should know that."

"Me? How so?"

"Think of your Bible," she said as she took his arm. "How long did it take for the people shouting praises to Jesus during His triumphal entry to turn and cry 'Crucify Him'?"

David nodded bleakly. "Not long—not long at all."

"People are no different today than then. Who knows, maybe we're worse."

"Still," David uttered, "the president and his advisers must know the kind of man Mahli is. Surely, they wouldn't want to be yoked with the likes of him."

Kristen shrugged, "You've heard it before, politics makes for strange bedfellows."

"Yeah, but—"

"No yeah-buts," Kristen interrupted. "We can talk about this all day and night and nothing will change. We're powerless in this situation."

Powerless, David thought. *That's the right word, the perfect word to describe how I feel.*

■ ■ ■ ■ ■

When David arrived home that evening, the phone was ringing. He heard the first ring as he inserted his key into the lock of the front door. He knew that after the third ring, the call would automatically be transferred to his message manager and he would have to retrieve the caller's message, if he or she left one. "Hello?"

"David? This is A.J. I'm glad I caught you. You sound winded."

"I just now arrived home and had to run to catch the phone."

"Been out enjoying the day?" A.J. asked pleasantly.

"Kristen and I went to Balboa Park and then to the zoo. It's been a long day."

"But an enjoyable one, I trust." David felt oddly embarrassed. "Kristen's a lovely woman and smart too. You make a great couple."

"She keeps me on my toes, that's for sure," David replied.

"I'm sure she does. I'm sure she does." A.J. seemed mildly distracted, as if his mind were elsewhere. "Sorry to bother you at home on a weekend, David, but I have a favor to ask. You're aware of my upcoming trip to Anaheim. I'm taking only a few people with me—Peter's going, and Kristen too. The president asked us to keep the group small, something to do with the Secret Service. But now I have a problem. Timmy overheard me talking about the trip with Peter and picked up that we're going to be at Disneyland. Naturally he wanted to go, and since he's never been, I couldn't tell him no. My problem is that I can't keep an eye on him."

"Will the Secret Service allow Timmy to go along?"

"I insisted, and since I'm doing the president a favor by meeting with that . . ." A.J. broke off in midsentence. "The short answer is yes, Timmy can go. Which brings me back to my original problem. I can hire someone to, in essence, baby-sit, but I think Timmy would enjoy the experience more if he was with someone he knew and liked."

"Such as me?"

"Such as you. How about it, David. Would you like a free trip to Disneyland?"

"Sure, as long as I don't have to leave tonight. My feet are killing me."

"Great. You and Timmy will stay with us, but you'll need to

keep him back from the main group. You know how excited he gets."

"Yes, I know."

"He really likes you," A.J. said. "You've made quite an impression on him."

"I think the world of him too."

"David," A.J.'s voice became serious, "this is not an easy situation for any of us. I make no apologies for my avid disdain for Mahli. No, *disdain* doesn't say it. I hate this man, David. I know your belief system finds that repulsive, but I truly hate this man, and I hate the day he climbed out from under his rock. But I have to do this. Much of our work requires close ties to foreign-policy makers in Washington. They listen when I talk and often act when I request it. For that and many other reasons, I owe them a favor or two, and they're calling in my chit. It's time for me to pay a little on the outstanding balance, if you know what I mean."

"I know, A.J., and no one thinks less of you for your . . . sacrifice."

"*Sacrifice.* That's a good word for it all right, a sacrifice. I've made many, but standing shoulder to shoulder with this man will be one of the greatest. The president is going to owe me big for this one."

"Maybe he can get you a break on next year's taxes," David said humorously. A.J. laughed. It was good to hear the tension leave his voice, even for a moment.

"I appreciate this, David," A.J. said a moment later, "and I appreciate all your work. It's good to have a friend these days."

"It's good to have a friend any day," David agreed.

A.J. sighed heavily. "We are friends, aren't we David? Not just employer, employee, but real friends?"

It was an odd question, and David could hear the genuine loneliness in A.J.'s voice. David had always been one to think that the rich and powerful never lacked for company or friendship. His dealings with A.J. had proven how wrong he had been. Men like

A.J., wealthy and committed to a worthy cause, were often lonesome. Very few understood their needs, hopes, and dreams and assumed that the normal anxieties common to most were not problems for the rich. A.J. lived a largely solitary life, consumed by his drive to end world hunger.

"Yes, A.J., we're friends. No matter what, we will always be friends."

"That's good to hear, David. Real good to hear."

"Are you all right, A.J.? You sound down."

"I am, but it's just weariness. I'm going to take a late jog, have some dinner, and go to bed. I'll feel better in the morning."

"Tomorrow's Sunday. Kristen and I were planning on going to church. You're welcome to join us."

"Thanks, but I must say no. I've got a great deal to do tomorrow, including a meeting with some Secret Service agents. They're going to ask a bunch of questions about everyone who's going. You know, to see if any of us have screws loose. But I'll take a rain check, okay?"

"Okay." David hung up the phone, then closed the door he had left open when he had run to answer the phone. Night had fallen, and a cool breeze was blowing into the room, along with a few moths attracted by the light in the living room. A few minutes later, he was seated in front of the television watching a *National Geographic* special on the Great Rift Valley in Africa. The images of Africa brought back the sense of adventure, awe, and even fear that he had felt while there.

The rift, which he had only seen briefly and from the air, fascinated him. In many ways it was a metaphor for human life: Poverty and politics have separated the needy from the suppliers as sure as the Rift Valley had separated the physical land of Africa. *How long would it take to fill in that gorge?* David wondered silently. *However long, it would probably be easier than ending the hunger that fills that country.*

26

THE NEWS OF MAHLI'S ARRIVAL IN THE UNITED States was carried to every region of the country, to an extent that amazed even President Gillian Laine's expert publicity team who had worked feverishly to promote the event as a harbinger of the future peace in East Africa. From newspapers to the Internet, news of the warlord's activities were documented and discussed. Excerpts of his speech before the United Nations were broadcast on every major network, as were the cautiously kind words of the UN secretary-general who praised Mahli for his efforts in Somalia. A careful eye, however, could detect her disinclination toward the man.

When Mahli spoke to the press club in Washington, D.C., he did so in the clear but still accented English he had mastered during his days in a London college. His speech had been well rehearsed and confidently delivered. He made no promises; he asked no favors. He spoke of Africa as the cradle of civilization and as the fountain from which all humanity had sprung. He then promptly accused the Western world of forgetting its past mistakes.

"The black African may no longer be a slave to the wealthy plantation owners of your past, but we have been kept in slavery by the harsh masters of economic servitude. The time has come for the world to grant the simple respect and dignity to East Africans that all men deserve. Our technology may be inferior to the West, but we are still a people of pride who love our families and know the dignity of work. We are a people to be respected, and we no longer request that respect—we demand it." The speech was greeted with polite applause.

Mahli proved himself an able dignitary who, despite his limited experience with such, breezed easily through the crowd of party-goers at a reception held in his honor at the White House. The room had been filled with senators, dignitaries, captains of industry, and military leaders as well as stars and starlets. Mahli stood straight, bowed slightly when the occasion called for it, smiled broadly, shook hands, and discussed African politics fervently.

Not everyone greeted Mahli with respect and admiration. A small group of conservative senators, who could not forget the crimes of Somalia against American military personnel half a decade before, protested his presence in written editorials and hastily called press conferences. Few read the editorials, and fewer still attended the press conferences. The White House answered the critics with a cursory reminder that Mahli had not been involved with the real criminal, Mohammed Farah Aidid. The response was enough to quiet most of the fears of the populace, who had become fascinated by the little man from the little land.

David followed Mahli's activities closely, reading every article in the papers and newsmagazines and watching intently each broadcast of his movements. Watching a *NewsHour with Jim Lehrer* special report on PBS about the Somali's visit, David wondered how such an innocuous-appearing man could draw as much attention as Mahli did. David knew that fact made Mahli all the more dangerous.

Now he was walking the neatly kept paths of Disneyland, keeping an eye on a mildly retarded young man, and watching the closest person he had to a best friend strolling with a man responsible for the killing of a Barringston doctor, among others. Keeping them company was none other than the secretary of state. Around them were three Secret Service agents charged with the protection of Mahli and Secretary Douglas DeWitt. David knew that there were at least three other agents spaced throughout the crowd. And taping it all was the woman with whom David had fallen in love.

The whole outing had been tense from the beginning. Secretary DeWitt had briefed A.J. on Mahli's plan for food distribution in Somalia. A.J., who quickly recognized the self-serving nature of the scheme, seethed with barely contained anger. The animosity A.J. felt for the killer combined with the revelation of Mahli's plan had so angered the head of Barringston Relief that he very nearly exploded in indignation. David could only admire A.J.'s resolve to maintain his composure in front of DeWitt, who rattled on without noticing the tension in A.J.'s jaw or his clenched fists. But David knew A.J. too well not to recognize a burning furnace of bitter rage welling up in him.

A.J.'s anger did not diminish upon their arrival at Disneyland. The two-hour drive from San Diego was made in near silence while A.J. stared out the window of the gray limousine in which David, A.J., Kristen, and Timmy were riding. DeWitt had taken the leased air shuttle provided by the White House to Anaheim. Only Timmy was inclined to speech and asked question after question about rides and candy and Mickey Mouse. David had done his best to keep Timmy occupied so that he wouldn't bother A.J., but it proved an almost overwhelming task. The young man's uncontainable ebullience was understandable. But A.J. never lost his temper with Timmy. Instead, he smiled, reached across the limo's spacious back quarters, and squeezed Timmy's hand.

"You're my buddy, aren't you?" A.J. asked.

"Sure am," Timmy replied.

A.J. grinned for a moment and then returned his gaze to the passing scenery. Only Timmy could not see the anguished soul of the head of Barringston Relief.

David had been able to distract Timmy with a Nintendo Game Boy. "Are you going to be okay with all this?" David asked.

"I'll be fine," A.J. replied. "I want it over with, that's all."

"Do you think that Mahli will get what he asks for?"

A.J. looked at David for a long moment then shook his head slowly. He had the look of a man with a secret he wanted to tell but couldn't. "No," was his simple reply.

A.J.'s disposition was not improved by Mahli's arrival. His long black limousine, driven by a Secret Service agent, had pulled up forty minutes late to one of the many back gates leading to the Magic Kingdom. Mahli exited the vehicle with two men whom he introduced as his personal security guards. He did not give names. "It's not that I don't trust your Secret Service," he had said to DeWitt, "but one can't be too careful. After all, someone might wish to harm me as they did my dear brother." Mahli stared at A.J. when he made the comment. A.J. did not respond.

The two men eyed each other intently. They had never met before, but each knew the other at a deep level, a level that only bitter enemies can reach. David wondered what would happen if Mahli had offered his hand to A.J. Fortunately, he did not. Seeing the two men standing in close proximity was almost comical: A.J.'s tall muscular frame and dark hair pulled tightly back into a pony-tail contrasted sharply with Mahli's short, paunchy body and his graying head. *The ultimate Mutt and Jeff*, David thought.

The rest of the morning and afternoon had been taken up with a guided tour by one of Disneyland's senior guides. Lunch was served in the private dining area next to the Blue Bayou, known as Club 33.

■ ■ ■ ■ ■

David, fearing that Timmy might prove a disruption during lunch, took him to eat tacos at one of the many small restaurants spaced throughout the park. Timmy was filled with the excitement of the day and inhaled his food quickly. "I wanna ride something," he said eagerly.

"I'm still eating, Timmy," David answered. "I can't eat as fast as you."

"Oh," Timmy dropped his head in disappointment for a moment, then began to bounce impatiently in his seat.

"Okay, Timmy, okay. I can't have you exploding here in Disneyland. Why don't you walk . . . listen to me now . . . *walk* over to the Dumbo ride and get in line. Be polite and wait your turn. The line isn't long, so you should get to the ride soon. I'll finish eating and then join you."

"Don't you wanna ride Dumbo?" Timmy asked.

"I think I'll sit here and rest for a little while. You're hard to keep up with, you know. I can see you from here. I promise to watch you on the ride. Okay?"

"Okay."

Timmy left David at the outdoor table and quickly walked to the short line waiting to ride Dumbo. David shook his head wearily, took a sip of soda, and sighed.

"I'll bet he's a handful," a voice said behind him. "Seems like a real special kid."

"He is," David said, turning to see the speaker. It was Woody Summers of the FBI and Stephanie Cooper of the CIA. Both were dressed casually. Woody wore a blue-and-white windbreaker. "What are you doing here?"

The federal agents walked to the other side of the table and sat down. "A little interagency cooperation, that's all," Woody said. "Unofficially, we are part of the Secret Service team."

"I didn't know you were trained for such things," David said coolly.

"It's a complex world, Dr. O'Neal. The FBI, DEA, ATF, and local police often work together. We're protective of our own turf, but we're all on the same team."

"Why do I doubt you're here to protect DeWitt?" David asked.

"We're not. We're here to watch Mr. Barringston and Mahli. I, we," he said nodding at Stephanie, "still believe your boss is our man."

"And I still believe he's innocent." David turned to Stephanie. "I thought the CIA's charter prevented you from working cases in the United States."

Stephanie shrugged. "I'm an interagency observer."

"I see," David said. "Why are you sitting at my table? Aren't you afraid I'll alert A.J.?"

"You haven't alerted him before; I doubt you will now," Woody answered

"How can you be so sure?"

"Let's stop the charade, Dr. O'Neal. You're a man of principle. I think you've been fooled by a very complex man. Your loyalty is admirable, but we are loyal too. We're loyal to the laws of the land, and those laws have been broken. I believe you know that to be true. You also know that we're just doing our job—an important job. You have too much integrity to alert Mr. Barringston, because you know, deep down, that there's a good chance we're right."

"Why show yourselves to me?"

"You would have spotted us sooner or later, Dr. O'Neal. We thought it best to be up-front with you."

David turned toward the Dumbo ride. Timmy had made it through the line and was riding in the gray fiberglass-and-plastic elephant as it rose up and down in the air and spun around its carousel pedestal. Timmy was grinning from ear to ear. He saw David and waved. David smiled and waved back.

"What do you want from me?" David asked.

"Nothing. We wanted you to know we were here and to warn you to be careful. Mahli and your boss have a very stressed history."

"I already know that," David said sharply. Then he softened. "Look, I know you two are doing your job, and I've not been much help to you. But I know A.J., and I believe he's innocent of every accusation you've made. He has become my friend, a close friend. You're chasing the wrong rabbit."

"David," Woody began, "there's a great deal you don't know about A.J. He does a wonderful work, but there is mounting evidence that he is the mastermind behind several international incidents. We've told you about some of them, but there are some things to which you are not privy."

"We've been interviewing a man named Mohammed Aden in Somalia," Stephanie added. "He's worked for both us and for Barringston Relief. We've talked to him before—he was the one who told us about Mahli's brother—but now, because of Mahli's new power, he's been more forthcoming. Aden has placed Roger Walczynske in Somalia and has admitted that both he and Roger were working for Barringston Relief. It's an interesting and violent story."

David sat in silence. Pieces were falling together, and he didn't like the picture.

"Dr. O'Neal, despite our differences," Woody began, "I've come to respect you and hope the feeling is mutual. Be careful. Mahli and A.J. are a bad mix. Watch your back."

"I understand," David said. "I'll be careful."

Woody and Stephanie rose to leave. "I wish I were wrong about all this, David. I really do. But I'm not wrong."

■ ■ ■ ■ ■

"What was lunch like?" David asked Kristen when the group congregated in front of the Pirates of the Caribbean.

"You could cut the tension with a knife," she replied. "Everyone is putting on a good front, especially if I have the camera on them, but there's no love lost in that group."

"How's DeWitt dealing with things?"

"He's the consummate diplomat. I can see how he made so much progress in the Middle East."

"What about A.J.?"

"He's miserable," Kristen said, shaking her head. "He speaks only when spoken to, and he stares intently at Mahli. If A.J. looked at me that way, I'd melt in fear, but Mahli seems to be enjoying it." David thought of Woody's words. He wanted to tell Kristen about the unexpected visit from the federal agents, but he felt that the news would only upset her. Besides, the situation was tense enough.

"Are you able to get the shots you need?" David asked, pointing at the small video camera Kristen held in her hand. It was a small camcorder, barely larger than her hand.

"For the most part, but it's going to take an awful lot of editing to find any footage that'll be useful for PR purposes." Turning her attention to Timmy she asked, "Are you having fun, Timmy?"

A huge grin spread across his face. "Oh yes. We rode Dumbo and Alice in Wonderland and Mad Tea Party. I didn't like the teacups; it made my stomach feel funny." David rolled his eyes and nodded in agreement. "But I feel better now. David bought me tacos to eat and promised me that we could ride on Space Mountain again."

The tour guide had led the group on several rides, including several roller-coaster types. Since dignitaries were involved, they were ushered to the front of the line through side doors. Only one patron in line complained, and he was immediately silenced by an icy stare from one of the Secret Service agents.

"What's the plan now?" David inquired.

"We're going to ride the Pirates of the Caribbean, then tour the Disney Museum. After that we're going to the Small World ride. That'll wind the day up. Secretary DeWitt has arranged a meeting with a few business leaders from Los Angeles. Apparently Mahli thinks he can entice some foreign investment."

"He's a dreamer."

"What about you and Timmy?"

"I thought we would ride the Haunted Mansion, then Space Mountain again . . ."

"Goody!" Timmy interrupted. "Will the Haunted Mansion be scary?"

"Not too scary," David replied patiently. Turning his attention back to Kristen, he said, "Then we'll join you at Small World. If we're not there on time, go without us. Unlike you folks, we don't get to go to the front of the line."

"I'll bet you're glad you brought that," Kristen said pointing at the Game Boy in Timmy's hand.

David nodded and pulled a pack of AA batteries from his pocket, "I came prepared." Kristen smiled. She leaned forward and kissed him on the cheek.

"What did I do to deserve that?"

"Nothing, but wait until you do something," she said with a wry grin. "Gotta go."

David watched as she hurried to join the others and wished deeply that he could go with her. Disneyland would be a magical place for them. Someday he would bring her back, and they would come sans Secret Service agents and government officials. As he watched Kristen make her way through the crowd, he noticed A.J. and Mahli standing by themselves to one side. DeWitt was not to be seen. *Probably in the rest room*, David thought. He watched the two men for a moment. A.J. was peering down at Mahli, who was craning his neck to look up at A.J. Even at this distance, David could see the ongoing tension and wondered what they were talking about.

■ ■ ■ ■ ■

"At last we have a few moments to ourselves," Mahli said coolly as he looked around. Several Secret Service agents were nearby as were Mahli's personal guards. One agent spoke into the small mike he held in his palm. Two other agents were at the door to the men's room, politely turning away patrons.

"Our time is short, so I'll get to the point. I want you to approve my plan."

"My approval is not necessary," A.J. replied coldly.

"No, it's not. I can and will go on with or without your endorsement. It's a good plan, and everyone gets what they want. Your president gets a good image, I get solidified power, and you get to continue feeding hungry people. What could be better?"

"You floating facedown in a sewer comes to mind." A.J. was stone-faced, but Mahli was taken aback.

"What would Secretary DeWitt say if he heard you speak that way?" Mahli let his grin return.

"I could care less. You are nothing more than a murderer."

Mahli actually laughed out loud. "I'm a murderer? So are you, Mr. Barringston, so are you. I know you killed my brother. Not directly. Not with your own hands, but I know you're behind it. It took me a while to put the pieces together, but I did. My brother, Mukatu, was a violent man, a sadist, actually, but he was my brother."

"And Dr. Judith Rhodes was one of my people. You killed her, you little scum."

"She attacked me," Mahli protested. "I have a right to defend myself."

"If she attacked you, she did so with good cause. I only regret she didn't do a better job of it."

Mahli's grin dissolved into a grimace. "Since we're being so blunt, let me tell you how it's going to work from now on. All food supplies to Somalia and Ethiopia will go through me. I see to the distribution. There is no room for discussion here, no debate. You will permit it because if you don't, I'll see to it that more than one woman doctor dies. You'll be picking up the bleached bones of your workers for years. Even now, I have men watching several of your camps, and at one word from me they decimate the people in the camps. The world will think it's the work of a rival warlord, but you and I will know that it was your fault."

"My fault?" A.J. took a threatening step forward and saw a brief glimmer of fear in the warlord's eyes.

"Sorry to keep you waiting, gentlemen," DeWitt said, striding quickly to join them. "I've been out of the country so much that home cooking doesn't sit well anymore." He chortled at his own joke. "Shall we?" he asked, motioning toward the guide standing discreetly by the front wrought-iron gate. "I think you'll enjoy this ride. I went on it once a decade or more ago. It was great then, and I'm sure it will be enjoyable now."

Mahli was grinning once again. He looked at A.J. and shrugged. "I think you see my point," he said. A.J.'s reply was communicated through his eyes, and his message was not wasted on Mahli.

■ ■ ■ ■ ■

The music, redundant and loud, mingled with the machine sounds of chains meeting gears, hydraulic pistons rising and falling, and the clicking of electronic switches. The noise was annoying, and the music, which he had heard cycled over and over again for the last eight hours, grated on his final raw nerve. His back and neck ached from a night spent sleeping on the cold concrete foundation that ran underneath the Small World ride. He might have been a little more comfortable if he hadn't been wearing a Kevlar bulletproof vest. The vest pinched and shifted, making lying down painful. Only the anticipation of the events about to happen made the noise and the cold tolerable.

Roger rolled over on his back, adjusted the mouthpiece of the headset he was wearing, and said simply, "Your turn."

"Got it," Sheila said.

It was part of the planned procedure: Roger would watch the lines of people through a small surveillance camera aimed through a half-inch hole that he had drilled through the wall. The camera was a type used by private investigators and law enforcement agencies that could provide closeup images to a small handheld monitor. Sheila had an identical setup at her position twenty feet away. The Small World ride consisted of boats carrying sixteen people along a fiberglass channel. That channel separated Roger and Sheila.

Roger smiled as he thought of Sheila, her short blond hair now died coal black, her makeup heavy to darken her complexion. His smile widened when he thought of himself with the same makeover. He thought of his own light hair dyed dark and the makeup he wore. He almost laughed out loud, but he hadn't come here to entertain himself—he had come to kill a man.

The plan was simple and had been executed perfectly thus far. A week ago, Sheila and Roger visited Disneyland like any tourist couple. They dressed casually, spent time in the shops, rode the rides, and videotaped everything—especially the uniforms and costumes. It was a simple matter to have the maintenance uniforms replicated. Returning to Disneyland yesterday, they spent the day as any visitor would, but shortly before the park closed they quickly changed into the uniforms. The equipment they brought—the two surveillance cameras, and two 9mm Uzi automatic weapons—fit nicely into a small backpack carried by Sheila. When the park closed, they had worked their way against the human tide of visitors leaving the park and walked to the Small World ride. They avoided the ornate front of the building and made their way to one of the side entrances. Although it was dark outside, it only took a moment for Roger to pick the lock. Once inside they separated, with Roger carefully crossing over the water-filled channel, being cautious not to disturb the robotic dolls that made up the visual aspect of the ride. He took his position underneath the staging upon which the little automatons continuously danced. Roger and Sheila set up a surveillance camera and waited for the sun to rise and the park to open.

There were more comfortable places in the Small World to hide, but the ride, like all the rides in Disneyland, had strategically placed cameras that were constantly monitored by the park's staff. Any movement outside the ride area would alert park security. That's why the next part of the plan had to be done perfectly.

"Tell me again, why do we have to keep surveillance if we're going to be signaled when they arrive?" Sheila said softly into her microphone.

"Redundancy. Things can go wrong," Roger whispered. "Besides, the electronics in here might interfere with reception." Unconsciously, he fingered the pager attached to his belt. The pager was set to vibrate instead of beep.

"How much longer do you think we'll have to wait?"

303

"Can't tell. Who knows what they're doing out there." Roger knew that Sheila's questions were not the results of nerves. He had worked with her many times and had found her exceptionally capable whether she was making coffee for A.J. or pushing someone out of a helicopter. "Are you okay?"

"It's the music," Sheila replied bitterly. "I'll be hearing this song long after I'm dead."

Hopefully, Roger thought, *that won't be today.*

■ ■ ■ ■ ■

Gasping for breath, David struggled to keep up with Timmy as they walked quickly toward the Small World ride. "Hurry, David, or we'll miss A.J."

"Timmy, we're not supposed to ride with them, remember?" David said breathlessly. "A.J. has important business."

"But he promised he would go on one ride with me, and this is our last ride. There they are!" Timmy broke into a jog, with David close behind him. "A.J.! A.J.!" The group turned to see Timmy waving both arms over his head as he ran. Puzzled, DeWitt looked at A.J., and the three closest Secret Service agents stepped toward Timmy. A.J. waved them off.

"What's the matter, Timmy?" A.J. asked with concern.

"You said . . . you said . . ." Timmy struggled to catch his breath. "You said I could go on one ride with you."

"But, Timmy, we were just about to go on this one."

Timmy grinned. "That's okay, this one looks neat." Timmy glanced at the gold-and-white facade with its giant clock with the crooked hands. Just then, the clock began to chime and doors in the facade opened. Toy soldiers dressed in red marched around as the Small World tune began to play. "See, it'll be fun."

"But Timmy . . ."

"You said you would. I wanna ride a ride with you." Timmy leaped forward and hugged A.J. "Please, please, let me ride with you."

Breaking free from Timmy's grasp, A.J. said firmly, "I know what I said, but it would be better if . . ."

"Nonsense," DeWitt interrupted. "Let the boy come along. We've got room on the boat."

Unconsciously, A.J. fingered the small transmitter in his pocket. The transmitter looked like those used to activate or deactivate car alarms and was attached to his key chain. The device felt familiar in his hand. He had just pressed its button a moment before. "Timmy, I . . ."

"I'm sorry, A.J.," David said. "I'll try to explain it to him."

"But, A.J., you promised," Timmy protested. "You told me to never break a promise."

"Come on, son," DeWitt said jovially. "You can sit with me."

"No," A.J. exclaimed. "Sit with David. Sit in the back. David, please."

"Sure," David replied. "Are you okay?"

"Fine," A.J. smiled weakly, clearly concerned about this unexpected change in plans. "Just sit in the back."

■ ■ ■ ■ ■

"Timmy's with them," Sheila whispered seriously.

"Yeah, Kristen and David too," Roger said. "That's not part of the plan. I told you, things go wrong,"

"So do we proceed?"

"We got the signal from A.J., so we go. If Mahli gets back to Somalia, we'll never catch him. And if we don't stop him now, all our work over there will be lost." Roger looked at his monitor. "They're sending the empty boats now. Let's pack up and move. Don't shoot the kid."

■ ■ ■ ■ ■

The Secret Service agents watched as boatload after boatload of people came out of the ride and exited their little crafts. Soon only empty boats were exiting the expansive structure. "The building is empty now; we can go."

Dutifully they boarded the tiny blue boats that rocked only mildly to the side. Two Secret Service agents rode in the first of the four rows available. Mahli, bracketed by his two guards, sat in the second row. Behind them sat DeWitt with one agent and A.J. The back row was occupied by David, Kristen, and Timmy. The boat was moved from its loading area by a broad belt under the water. A second later the boat was floating in the canal, propelled only by the constantly moving current. The craft full of dignitaries cruised slowly along the little aqueduct, passing topiaries of an elephant doing a handstand and a grinning hippopotamus. Growing up in San Diego, which was less than two hours away, David had been to Disneyland many times as a child, an adolescent, and an adult. He knew what awaited them before the boat sailed into the cavernous structure that housed the Small World feature.

Warnings in English, Spanish, and Japanese reminded the occupants to remain seated at all times and to keep their hands in the boat. The warnings were soon replaced with the music.

As the craft entered the building, the travelers saw hundreds of cherub-faced dolls dressed in costumes from all over the world dancing and singing the song. As they moved, the clicking of the servos could be heard mildly echoing off the elaborate backdrops of plywood flowers and mountains.

The music was punctuated by giggles from Timmy. "Oh, look!" he cried. "Look up at the ceiling. There's a doll riding a bicycle on a tightrope. I hope he doesn't fall on us." David patted his leg and motioned for him to calm himself—a task, David decided, akin to trapping a hurricane in a bottle.

DeWitt turned around and smiled at Timmy, then he turned to A.J. and said, "He's a fine young man, Mr. Barringston, a fine young man. He reminds me of my youngest grandson, his behavior, I mean." A.J. offered a limp smile and nodded. "Are you all right? You look pale. Surely you're not seasick on this little bit of water."

"No, I'm fine," A.J. replied. "Lunch didn't sit well with me."

"Me either," DeWitt said, patting his stomach.

A.J. had stopped listening. He turned back to look at Kristen, David, and Timmy. Kristen and Timmy were smiling, David's face showed concern. He cocked his head in a silent question that asked about A.J.'s noticeable nervousness. A.J. winked and smiled to show he was all right. "Still a pretty impressive display, wouldn't you say, David?"

"Always been one of my favorites."

"Oh, A.J., this is great," interjected Timmy. "Thanks for bringing me."

David detected something different in A.J.'s eyes, something he had never seen in his friend—profound fear.

27

IT SEEMED AMAZING TO ROGER HOW CIRCUM-
stances could change one's view of a situation. When A.J. first pro-
posed killing Mahli at Disneyland, and after he laid out the basic
plan, Roger felt the idea was gutsy, bold, and daring. Now, as he
was about to burst through an access panel from underneath the
staging, he wondered if the plan wasn't just plain stupid.

It wasn't the killing that made the scheme difficult, it was the
not killing. Roger knew that A.J. had no hesitancy about murder-
ing killers, but innocents were another matter. If all Roger had to
do was kill everyone in the boat, then the job would have been easy
and could have been accomplished with a spray of bullets or even a
well-placed remotely controlled bomb. But the situation was different. Mingled with the targets were nontargets like the Secret Service agents, Secretary DeWitt, A.J., and now Kristen, Timmy, and
David. This was going to have to be a surgical killing, the most difficult kind of assassination. For the first time in his life, he had
doubts that the innocents could get away unscathed.

The core idea of the plan was brilliant. Roger and Sheila would
suddenly appear in the ride area and begin shooting, targeting the
area around Secretary DeWitt and shouting several Arabic phrases.
To investigators who would come later it would appear that two
Arab terrorists had set out to assassinate DeWitt for his involvement in the Middle East.

What A.J. had insisted on, and what they had practiced a hundred times over the last few weeks, was that DeWitt come through

the attack unharmed. It took a great deal of practice to learn to shoot an automatic weapon like the Uzi and miss. In the bedlam of the attack, Mahli and his guards would be killed. If the scheme went as planned, they would be the only ones dead. Roger and Sheila would then race from the building. The Secret Service agents in the boat were tasked with the protection of their charges and would not give chase. They would be occupied with the wounded and with getting DeWitt out of immediate danger. This would allow several minutes for Roger and Sheila to egress out of the building through one of the emergency exits, dash through a hole cut in the chain-link fence at the perimeter of the park, and make their getaway in a van parked near the fence. From there they would travel Interstate 5 to Interstate 10 toward Arizona, changing clothes once and cars five times. Once in Phoenix they would fly back to San Diego. If everything went right.

The time for second-guessing was gone. Roger whispered breathlessly into his microphone, "Mask." Then he removed his headset and wrapped a bandanna around his lower face, leaving everything above the bridge of his nose exposed so that witnesses could describe a dark-haired, dark-skinned attacker. He knew that Sheila was doing the same thing. The masks were meant to hide their identity, not only from the Secret Service agents who would be called upon to give a description to a police artist, but now from David, Kristen, and Timmy as well. Roger replaced his headset. "Ready?" he asked.

"Ready," Sheila replied evenly.

"On my mark, go. Three, two, one, and go!" Roger rolled out from under the staging and walked quickly along the service passageway behind the stage scenery; Sheila did the same on the other side of the building.

■ ■ ■ ■ ■

Outside, standing next to the Disney employee who operated the Small World ride, Agent Woody Summers leaned back against the thickly painted tubular rail and scanned the waiting crowd again.

Although a federal agent, he was not part of the official protection detail of the Secret Service. Instead, he was there to watch the war-lord Mahli and A.J. Barringston interact. He didn't know what he expected to see. At this point he was grasping at straws. Over the months, he had been unable to get even a simple search warrant to investigate the computer rooms of Barringston Relief or to recruit David O'Neal to help. He was getting no breaks.

He pushed aside his frustration and returned his gaze to the six video monitors neatly tucked into the employee's console. Nor-mally, a Secret Service agent would be stationed at the monitors, but Woody, bored and frustrated, persuaded the agent in charge to relinquish the job to him, allowing one more agent to be stationed at the ride's perimeter.

All of the boats in the building were empty, just as they were supposed to be, except Sugar Bear's boat. *Sugar Bear* was the code name for Secretary DeWitt. Mahli had been given the generic code name *Guest One*, and his two guards, *Guest Two* and *Guest Three*. Code names were a tradition in the service and were used here as part of standard protocol. Woody listened to the Secret Service agents' brief, no-nonsense radio communications through an ear-piece, which was the same issue as used by the Secret Service agents.

As he gazed at the monitors, he first saw the boat with his charges in it and the young man Timmy pointing excitedly about. Then he noticed something unusual. "What's that?" he asked, squinting at the faded image on one of the monitors.

"What's what?" the employee asked.

"Here," Woody pointed at the screen with his finger. "Right here."

The employee, a nineteen-year-old male college student, leaned forward and studied the screen. "Looks like a couple of maintenance workers," he said nonchalantly.

"Maintenance? Did you call them?"

"No, but it could be routine. They often—"

"Move," Woody commanded, pushing the young man aside.

Squinting, he studied the blurry movement of two people walking quickly along the perimeter of the building. As he looked closely, he saw that they were wearing masks. Allowing his eyes to carefully trace down the body of one of them he saw a familiar shape—a shape he had been trained to recognize in a second. "Oh, God," he said. In one fluid motion he brought the flesh-colored handheld microphone up to his mouth and shouted into it, "Intruder, intruder. One right side behind staging; one left side. Gun! Gun! Gun!" Turning to the employee he ordered, "Stop all the boats. I don't want any more boats in there." As he spoke, he pulled his gun from his shoulder holster and raced toward the opening to the building, leaping into the canal when the path was too narrow for him to pass. Stephanie Cooper, who had stationed herself at the ride's exit to observe A.J. and Mahli as they left the ride, watched as Woody ran to the ride's entrance and disappeared into the tunnel. A second later she charged in through the exit.

■　■　■　■　■

David flinched at the sound of gunfire.

The reaction inside was immediate: The agents at the front of the boat stood and drew their weapons, taking, as best they could in the confines of the boat, a shooter's stance. Behind them, Mahli's guards stood, too, in reaction to the agents in front of them, causing the boat to rock. Before DeWitt could speak, the agent sitting next to him pushed him to the bottom of the boat, causing DeWitt to hit his head on the metal grab bar on the back of the seat before him.

The first burst of gunfire came from Sheila, who strafed the stage area to the left of DeWitt, firing over the hunched figures of the secretary of state and his bodyguard. A.J. leaped from his position in the middle of the boat to the back row, yelling at Timmy, "Get down, get down." Before Timmy could react, David pushed him down, and A.J. covered Timmy with his body. David, a half-second later, grabbed Kristen behind the head and forced her down into his lap, then lay over her.

■ ■ ■ ■ ■

Roger popped out from behind a plywood facade of a Swiss mountain town and aimed his weapon on Mahli's row. From his position to the left of the little craft, he had an unobstructed shot at his targets. Roger shouted the Arabic phrase he had rehearsed—"Death to sympathizers!"—and applied a steady pressure to the trigger until the Uzi came alive. The weapon's report reverberated off the walls and backdrops, obliterating for a moment the ubiquitous theme music.

■ ■ ■ ■ ■

One of the agents in the front seat saw Roger and quickly drew a bead. He fired three shots from his 9mm. The first two shots struck Roger in the chest, but the Kevlar vest did its job. The impact of the bullets staggered him, however, causing him to step back. The impact also drove the air from his lungs. He had expected this and continued firing. What he had not expected was that the third bullet would strike him in the neck, severing his right carotid artery. Roger grabbed his neck, then pulled his hand away; his hand was coated in thick blood. He knew he would be dead before help could arrive.

■ ■ ■ ■ ■

As Roger slipped from consciousness, he let another burst of bullets fly, but he was too shocked, too weak to control the weapon. The gun fired endlessly as he fell to the ground, its bullets screaming through the air and destroying dancing dolls and scenery. As he fell, the weapon's aim moved forward from the middle of the boat where Roger had been firing to the front. Four rounds struck and killed the nearest Secret Service agent. The man spun on his feet and fell backward over the front of the ride and splashed into the water. The current moved him along the channel in front of the boat.

■ ■ ■ ■ ■

"Agent down! Agent down!" his partner cried into his microphone. He spun to his right in time to see Roger fall face forward onto the staging, taking several of the robotic dolls with him. Spinning back the other way he saw Sheila—a tall masked assailant with one of the deadliest automatic weapons in the world. He leveled his weapon at her chest and squeezed off a series of rounds. After each shot he quickly adjusted for the recoil and the movement of the boat and fired again.

■ ■ ■ ■ ■

Sheila had seen Roger fire at Mahli. She saw the closest guard take several hits and watched as he fell backward over Mahli. The other Somali guard had been hit, too, and fell sideways over the left side of the boat before slumping backward over the bodies of his companions. She wasn't sure if Mahli had been killed. So intent was she on her aim that she saw neither Roger nor the Secret Service agents killed, nor did she see the remaining agent take aim at her.

Snapping her weapon around, she took aim at Mahli's position in the boat. Her rounds never fired.

The first round from the Secret Service agent struck her under her left arm, an area unprotected by the bulletproof vest. The impact drove the breath out of her; it also pierced her aorta. The next round caught her in the ear. She died as she fell to the ground.

■ ■ ■ ■ ■

"Stay down," DeWitt's agent said as he cautiously poked his head up over the seats. Several moments had passed since any gunfire. With his weapon drawn, he surveyed the situation. Behind him, still huddled as low on the seat as possible and covering their heads were A.J., Timmy, David, and Kristen. In the row beside him, DeWitt was still on the floor. In the row in front of him he could see Mahli's two guards, both dead; Mahli lay beneath them. In the first row one agent was missing, the other stood, slowly swaying, an expression of shock shadowed his face. A moment later his swaying increased until he fell backward across the bow of the boat. One of Roger's bullets had hit the agent in the side. The agent, driven by a rush of adrenaline, hadn't realized at first that he had been shot. Now his life's blood was leaking away inside him until there was insufficient blood pressure to maintain consciousness.

DeWitt's agent was all that was left. As the boat slowly rounded another bend he shouted, "Out of the boat! Everyone out of the boat." Then he unceremoniously seized DeWitt by the front of his shirt and yanked him up off the deck of the craft. Everyone who could move scrambled to follow him. A.J. grabbed Timmy and dragged him onto the staging area. Timmy was crying, wailing, and covering his head. David and Kristen followed.

"Here. Huddle here. Everyone stay down." Alone, frightened, and angry, the agent did what he was trained to do: protect. He turned his back on the small group as they hunkered down next to one of the plywood backdrops. He raised his handgun to shoulder height, holding it with both hands. In rapid motion he forced his eyes to search the area. He saw nothing. Bringing his radio microphone up he announced breathlessly, "Simmons here, we have two agents down. Repeat, two agents down. Sugar Bear is unhurt. We are out of the boat and in . . ." Simmons looked around him for a landmark that would identify their location. He was surrounded by dolls in African dress and hyenas who were laughing loudly and rocking back and forth on their haunches, their paws crossed over their exposed stomachs in a never-ending simulation of a belly laugh. "We're in Africa. Guest One, Guest Two, and Guest Three are down. Condition unknown. We also have two gunmen down, condition unknown. I need backup—now!"

■ ■ ■ ■ ■

Agent Woody Summers heard the report through his earpiece. He responded succinctly: "Understood. Sit tight." Woody raced along the maintenance path behind the animated exhibits as fast as caution would allow, rounding each corner with his weapon elevated and ready to fire. Fortunately, the ride was not as dark as some rides in the park, so it didn't take long for his eyes to adjust, but there were plenty of cubbyholes, access ways, and dark corners in which an assassin might hide, and each one had to be approached cautiously. He estimated that he would arrive at the attack scene in less than three minutes.

Outside the ride two other agents, who had been dressed to blend in with the tourists, took positions, one at the entrance, the other at the exit. They had already cleared the long lines of people away from the ride and were shouting orders to Disneyland guards, who quickly cordoned off the area. In the distance, police sirens and ambulances wailed mournfully.

▪ ▪ ▪ ▪ ▪

"Do you think they're gone?" DeWitt asked pensively.

Simmons shook his head, "I can't say. I didn't see anyone except the two shooters, and neither one of them is moving. I haven't heard anything, but then who could with that incessant song."

Feeling a little more confident that the attackers were either gone or dead, David turned and briefly looked at the others. Each wore a mask of fear except A.J., whose expression was one of profound sorrow. He gazed empty-eyed across the water-filled channel at the still figures lying on the staging, his arms wrapped around the fear-shocked Timmy. It struck David as odd that A.J. would seem so sad at the attackers' deaths. Turning to Kristen he asked, "Are you all right?"

She nodded. "Yes. How about you?"

"Fine, for the moment." David started to rise.

"Stay down," Simmons ordered. "I need you to be as small a target as possible." David complied immediately, squatting in front of Kristen.

"What about Mahli?" DeWitt asked. "Did you see him?"

"It doesn't look good, sir," Simmons replied without turning around. "He was on the floor, or the deck, or whatever you call it with his guards lying over him. His men were pretty shot up. They have to be dead."

"But Mahli," DeWitt persisted. "Did you actually see Mahli?"

"No, I didn't. He was covered by his guard. I assumed he was dead."

"Assumed?" DeWitt exploded. "Assumed? You mean he could be alive? The president will kill me if something happens to Mahli."

"My job, sir," Simmons said firmly, "is to make sure someone doesn't kill you. Keeping your voice down will help me do just that. Besides, no one could have survived that hail of bullets."

"But they were after me," DeWitt said morosely. "They were Arab terrorists seeking revenge for my work with Israel. You heard what they shouted."

"I don't speak Arabic," Simmons replied.

"I speak enough to know that they were after me, not Mahli."

"Well, I'm afraid they got him—"

Simmons was interrupted by a loud voice, thick with accent. He stepped between the huddled group and the direction of the voice.

"BAR-RING-STON!"

A moment later, Mahli, his clothes and skin covered in blood, appeared.

"Don't move!" Simmons shouted, leveling his gun at Mahli.

"Don't be an idiot," DeWitt cried. "That's Mahli, and he looks hurt."

"Stay down," Simmons ordered, lowering his gun only a little. "Sir," he said to Mahli, "you're alive."

Mahli looked at the agent briefly, then quickly raised a handgun and pointed it at Simmons and pulled the trigger. The gun's report echoed through the building; the bullet smashed into the agent's forehead. Kristen screamed, and David attempted to cover her with his body. DeWitt swore and quickly covered his head. It was too late to stop the spray of blood. Only A.J. didn't respond in a panic. Instead, he slowly rose to his feet.

"This is between us," A.J. said firmly, his eyes fixed on his enemy. "Let them go, and you and I can settle this right here."

Mahli glanced around him and then laughed, a devilish, evil laugh that reverberated in the air. "Apropos, don't you think?" he said, waving his gun to indicate the African surroundings. Without hesitation or warning, Mahli aimed the gun—a pistol he had taken from the body of one of his guards—and fired it at a little black dancing doll in African dress. The tiny figure shattered, leaving only a portion of its mechanics clicking and clacking away.

A.J. stepped forward, but not before Mahli leveled the gun at his head.

"You did this," Mahli said coldly. "You set this up, didn't you?" A.J. didn't respond. "First you killed my brother, and now you attempt to kill me. You failed, Mr. Barringston. You failed miserably, and now I'm going to make you pay."

"What, by killing me?" A.J. said. "I've been ready to die for years."

"Bravo," Mahli mocked him. "Such a self-sacrificing soul you are. Unfortunately for you, I'm not impressed."

"What does he mean, you killed his brother?" DeWitt asked timidly.

"Shut up!" Mahli snapped. "Since Mr. Barringston here has no fear of his own death, let us see if he fears the death of his friends. Now who shall it be?" Mahli's mouth separated into an infernal grin, but his eyes were flat, devoid of any emotion except hatred and anger. He eyed the small group slowly. "The woman? Yes, the woman. That's what all this is about, isn't it Mr. Barringston? A woman." Mahli pointed the gun at Kristen's head. "You're angry at me because you think I killed your precious woman doctor. Well, I did kill her and her emaciated friend too. Do you know what, Mr. Barringston? I enjoyed it. I relished it. Unfortunately, I let her die too quickly, but not before she saw her friend bleeding in the sand."

A.J. said nothing, remaining as still as a statue. Only his eyes moved, following every action that Mahli took.

"This woman doesn't move you? Doesn't concern you? How about her boyfriend?" Mahli quickly snapped the pistol in David's direction. David felt his heart stop. Despite his fear, he stood slowly and took one step sideways to interpose his body between Mahli and Kristen.

David watched Mahli closely as the madman suddenly changed his aim from Kristen to him. From Mahli's fearless, indignant attitude, David knew that he and the others would most likely be shot. There seemed little they could do. It was clear to David that Mahli's primary concern, maybe his only concern, was tormenting and killing A.J.

"Maybe Secretary DeWitt should be the first to die." Mahli spat out his words and shifted his aim to the secretary of state who sat on the floor. David watched the man's eyes grow wide. "What do you think, Mr. Barringston? Should it be old man DeWitt?"

A.J. offered no response. Instead he stared with piercing eyes at their tormentor.

"Don't care, huh?" Beads of perspiration oozed from Mahli's ebony skin. "I know. The boy." A.J.'s eyes widened slightly, a sign not missed by Mahli. "Yes, that's it, the boy. You're fond of him, aren't you, Mr. Barringston? You'd be unhappy if the young man got a bullet in the forehead, wouldn't you? You're tensing, my friend, I can see that. You love the boy, don't you? Simple as he is, useless as he is, you love him, and having his brains splattered all over the walls would hurt you. I know just how you feel. I felt much the same way when my brother was tossed from that helicopter with his hands tied behind his back. It took me a while to figure out it was you and your people. I think it's only proper for me to make you suffer the way you made me suffer. The boy it is."

Mahli took three steps back and aimed the pistol at Timmy, who covered his head with his arms and whimpered. "A.J.! A.J.! Don't let him shoot me. Don't let him hurt me!"

Slowly, deliberately, Mahli stretched out his arm, took aim, and began to squeeze the trigger.

■ ■ ■ ■ ■

Woody couldn't believe what he was seeing. Hearing voices, he had carefully, stealthily made his way to within ten yards of the group and hid himself behind one of the plywood backdrops. The music and the clicking of the mechanics of scores of dolls made listening difficult, but he could hear well enough. Mahli was holding the others at gunpoint, including the secretary of state. This was not something they had taught him at the academy. Woody knew what he had to do, and he had to do it now. Then he heard the gunshot.

■ ■ ■ ■ ■

David had heard that motion seemed to slow down in crisis situations. He had found this true once before when he was involved in what turned out to be a minor traffic accident. There was nothing minor about what was happening here. Mahli had pulled the trigger. He did it without blinking or without the slightest change in his sardonic smile. Kristen screamed, and David turned to see where the bullet had struck Timmy. But the bullet hadn't struck Timmy; it had struck A.J. With unbelievable timing, A.J. had stepped in front of Timmy, interjecting his own body between the boy and the bullet. The copper-plated slug struck A.J. just below the sternum. David watched in horror as a small red circle on A.J.'s shirt expanded. A.J. swayed for a moment, but his strength and near superhuman resolve could not keep him standing. He dropped to his knees, then face first onto the platform.

"A.J.! A.J.! A.J.!" Timmy screamed. Tears gushed down his face. No longer afraid for his own life, and driven by love for the man who had loved him so much, Timmy scrambled to A.J.'s side. "Get up, A.J. Get up. Don't die. Who will eat hamburgers with me? Who will play video games with me? Please. Please get up. A.J.! A.J.! You can't die!"

Oblivious to the danger, David sprung to A.J.'s side and pulled Timmy back, and like A.J., interposed his own body in front of the weeping lad. David looked at the bloodstained body of his friend and slowly shifted his gaze to Mahli.

For the first time in David's life, he truly hated someone. For the first time in his life he was facing someone possessed of absolute evil. And for the first time in his life, David wanted to kill.

"What do you think you're going to do?" Mahli said bitterly to David. "Do you think you're a hero?" Mahli raised the gun then quickly snapped the gun to his left. A shot was fired. David flinched and raised an arm in a futile effort to shield himself. The shot, however, had not been meant for him. Instead, a man cried out and fell forward from his position behind one of the plywood backdrops. It was Woody. When the FBI agent hit the floor, his gun slipped from his fingers and danced across the stage.

Mahli walked to the pistol and picked it up, holding it in his left hand while pointing the weapon in his other hand at the fallen agent. "Now who are you?" Mahli asked.

Woody, who had been hit in the shoulder, writhed in pain on the ground.

"I must apologize," Mahli said to Woody. "I was aiming for your head. But don't worry. I never miss at this range." He directed the pistol at Woody's face.

From his position next to the wounded A.J., David watched as the madman took slow and purposeful aim. Without thought, David acted. Springing to his feet he charged the Somali, screaming each step of the way. Mahli spun around and tried to take aim at David, but it was too late. David slammed into the African with all his might, propelling both men back toward the boat channel. A second later they were both in the shallow water.

As they were tumbling into the water, David saw a gun drop into the blue aqueduct. That meant that Mahli was now reduced to only one gun, but he knew that was enough. Clawing madly, David reached for the weapon in Mahli's right hand, but Mahli fought back viciously. Both men stood in the shallow flow, David clutching the wrist of Mahli's upraised gun hand. A round was fired, the bullet impacting noisily in the ceiling. David pushed forward against his attacker, and both men fell under the water again, struggling, wrestling, one out of madness, the other out of desperation.

Seconds passed slowly. Mahli had succeeded in rolling over on top of David, pinning him under the water. David's lungs began to burn and to cry for air. If he had both hands with which to fight, then David knew he stood a chance of freeing himself enough to raise his head above the water, but if he let go of Mahli's arm, then the madman would have a clear shot. It seemed hopeless.

Staring up through water, David saw the out-of-focus image of Mahli grimacing down at him. Then there was another figure, one with red hair. A second later there was a splash and the weight of Mahli was removed from David's chest. He struggled to stand on the slippery floor of the culvert as he gasped for sweet air, but what he saw immediately took his breath away: Kristen was locked in battle with Mahli. David watched helplessly as Mahli raised the gun high in the air and then brought it down on Kristen's head with a sickening thud.

"Kristen!" David shouted.

She slumped face first in the water. The current carried her toward David, who pulled her up and to himself, cradling her in his arms. Blood ran freely from the crown of her head.

"You Barringston people are a challenge," Mahli shouted. "But not much of one." He raised the gun and took aim. David spun on his feet to cover Kristen with his body. A shot was fired, then another. David waited for the pain.

There was no pain, but David felt something in the water bump him. Slowly and leaning against the flow, he turned to see Mahli floating facedown. The water around him turned crimson.

A second later he heard, "Here, let's get her out of the water." David looked up to see Stephanie Cooper reaching for Kristen. "Well, come on," she said. "Anyone who fights like that deserves to be saved."

It took all of his remaining strength, but David, with the help of Stephanie, lifted Kristen out of the water and set her on the stage. "You stay with her. I'm going to check on the others," Stephanie said.

David turned to see the lifeless body of Mahli carried away by the water's flow.

■　■　■　■　■

David rolled A.J. over and cradled his head in his lap. Kristen stood behind him, her hands on his shoulders, weeping softly. Timmy wept unashamedly and repeatedly cried, "Don't die, A.J., don't die!"

A.J.'s eyes fluttered open. His body was limp, his skin pale, and his breath ragged.

Woody sat nearby, his hand clutching tightly his wounded shoulder. Secret Service agents and local police poured into the ride. An ambulance siren wailed outside.

"Hang on, A.J.," David said. "Help's on the way. Just hang on."

A.J. shook his head. "Too late. Sor . . . sorry. You weren't supposed . . . to know . . . not involved . . . my fault . . ."

"Don't try to talk now," David admonished. "There will be time for that later."

"No time," A.J. muttered, then he coughed. Blood trickled from the side of his mouth. "Is Timmy all right?"

"Yes, he's here."

"I'm here, A.J. Please don't die."

Slowly, and with astonishing effort, A.J. raised his hand and stroked Timmy's check. "You be a good boy . . . do . . . your work . . . listen to David."

"I will, I promise, just don't die." Timmy was crying uncontrollably, weeping with great sobs. Tears raced down his face.

Looking at David, A.J. said weakly, "Timmy . . ."

"I know. I'll take care of him," David said, finishing A.J.'s sentence. David's own tears fell unabated onto A.J.'s blood-stained shirt.

"Maybe I was wrong, David," A.J. began. "David?"

"Yes, I'm here."

"Don't let the . . . work die with me. Make sure it goes on. Much . . . good to do. Lives to save. Talk to my father. He knows what to do."

"Just hang on, A.J.," David said urgently.

"Promise you'll try, David. I trust you. I need you. You have the heart for it. Promise."

"I promise, A.J., I promise," David wept openly.

A.J. smiled weakly, "You're a good man, David. Better than me. We both have a heart . . . but you have a soul."

"Oh, A.J., I . . ." David didn't finish his sentence. A.J.'s body jerked in spasms, his eyes blinked once, and his throat emitted a soft gurgling sound. A.J. Barringston, defender of the abused and neglected, was dead.

Epilogue

"DID YOU SMUGGLE A PIZZA IN FOR ME?" WOODY Summers asked David.

David looked down at the man in the hospital bed. Standing next to him was Stephanie Cooper. Seated in a nearby chair was a woman that Woody had introduced as his wife. Kristen stood next to David. "I'm afraid they confiscated it in the lobby. A hungry pack of interns is enjoying it right now."

"Pity," Woody replied with a chortle. "Nothing like a pizza to help a man recover from shoulder surgery."

"I hear you'll be back on duty soon," Kristen said.

"Next month," Woody replied. "Four weeks of R and R here in San Diego, then back to the FBI salt mines in D.C." Everyone laughed. "I think I owe you a word of thanks for saving my life, David."

"Actually, I owe you an apology."

"Apology?"

"You and Stephanie were right all along. It's still hard for me to believe, but A.J., Sheila, Roger, and Eileen were doing everything you said they were. I don't think I'll ever forget that moment in Small World when police removed the masks of the two gunmen. Even with the heavy makeup I could recognize Sheila and Roger."

"I know that wasn't easy for you," Woody said. "And no apology is needed. You were loyal to a man who did a lot of good. He just couldn't recognize the line between good and bad any longer."

"Still, I'm sorry."

Woody nodded his head. "I'm glad you weren't hurt badly. How's the head, Kristen?"

"I've lost all desire to wear hats, but I think I'll be okay as soon as the knot goes away."

"What will happen to Barringston Relief?" Stephanie asked.

"I spoke to Archibald Barringston before I came over here. He said that its operations will be placed in administrative trust under the guidance of Barringston Industries and that an independent executive will be named by the courts. After that, no one knows. The Justice Department is investigating. We'll have to wait and see."

"What about Eileen Corbin?" Woody asked.

"Disappeared," David said. "Without a trace. She did leave behind her equipment though. I think there's some interest in that."

"I guarantee there's a lot of interest in that," Woody replied. "It's a shame really. She is brilliant."

There was an uneasy silence that was broken by Woody. "So what happens to you, David? What do you do now?"

"Mr. Barringston has asked me to stay on. He's also asked me to watch over Timmy for a while. Both he and Timmy have a lot of grief to work through."

"You're going to stay with Barringston Relief?" Stephanie asked.

"As long as I can. There are some wonderful people there, and the organization does a great work. Despite the misguided actions of some, there are still many heroes out in the field saving lives every day. That should continue."

"It will, David," Woody said. "It will. As long as there are people like you and Kristen, it will. Now enough of this. Go get me a pizza. I'm hungry."

TARNISHED IMAGE

Prologue

Sierra de Agua, Belize, Central America
May 15, 1990

PERSPIRATION DOTTED HIS FOREHEAD AND streaked his cheeks. Raising his hand, the young man wiped at his face and grimaced at the act. Every joint was pierced with pain; every muscle protested the movement with ferocious agony. His skin felt aflame, and his head throbbed as if it were an anvil in a blacksmith's shop. A groan, small and pathetic, issued from his parched mouth, passed split and swollen lips, and joined the guttural emanations of the other fifteen patients.

He closed his eyes for a moment and then reopened them, focusing on a large blue-green fly that rested on the white netting that surrounded his bed to keep insects out. The fly was motionless except for its front legs, which it furiously rubbed together like a famished man rubbing his hands over a banquet table. Unfortunately the netting kept out the sweet, light breeze that wafted in through the open windows spaced throughout the ward. The breeze played a lullaby, using the supple leaves of nearby trees as instruments, but the young man could not sleep; he could only wait and hope the disease that incapacitated him would leave as quickly as it came. He doubted that it would, but hope was all that he had now.

He was fourteen and until a week ago was strong and full of the energy of youth. He ran where others walked, and he loved nothing more than playing fusball after school with his friends. Four of those friends were on the ward with him now, and two others had already died. Soccer no longer occupied his mind, just survival.

A movement outside the netting caught his eye. A woman in a white smock stood next to his bed. "How are you feeling?" the woman asked. Her voice, lilting with an American accent, was sweet to his ears.

"Bad, Doctor. Really bad." His voice was surprisingly weak. "Are my parents here?"

"They were, but I sent them home," she answered without emotion. "It's best that they not see you right now. You don't want them to get sick too, do you?"

He shook his head slowly. The effort sent ripping bolts of pain down his back.

"You're a good son," the doctor said. The young man watched as she raised a large hypodermic and removed the plastic cover that protected the large bore needle. "I need to take a blood sample."

He didn't want to give blood. He was tired of giving blood. He wanted to go home and sleep in his own bed. Still, he offered no objection.

The doctor pulled back the white netting and leaned over him. The blue-green fly took flight. Deftly she plunged the needle into a vein just below the crook of his elbow. Moments later she was done. He watched as she raised the hypodermic and studied the red fluid. She smiled and closed the netting. "Try to get some sleep. Maybe your parents can see you tomorrow."

The young man nodded slowly and watched as the woman walked away.

■ ■ ■ ■ ■

The woman in the white smock locked the door behind her. It was the only room in the small outlying clinic that was capable of being locked, and she was the only one with a key. Turning, she faced a ten-by-fifteen room filled with laboratory equipment and a computer terminal. Dominating the center of the room was a broad table upon which rested a large, rectangular glass box that looked like an aquarium without water. A small piece of white paper had been taped to the glass container. It read: Aedes aegypti. Carefully carrying the vial of blood she had just drawn from the teenager on the ward, she made her way to the table and gently set the syringe down.

She felt a moment of sadness for the boy. He would be dead in two or three days. This fact bothered her some, but not unduly; she had, after all, been the one to give him the disease.

She leaned forward and placed her face near the glass surface and closely studied the container's inhabitants. A grin spread across her face. She raised a hand and drummed her fingers on the glass box. A thousand mosquitoes swarmed into frenetic flight within the container. Her grin broadened into a full smile.

Glancing at the blood-filled syringe, she said aloud, "So, is anyone hungry?"

1

La Jolla Shores, California
August 8, 1999

THE AUGUST SUN HUNG HIGH IN THE DEEP TUR-
quoise sky and poured its effulgence down on the beach. David
O'Neal took in a long, deep breath through his nose. The air was
perfumed with the smells of salt water, warm sand, and suntan lo-
tion. It was hot, and David could almost imagine a sizzling sound
coming from the well-oiled bodies of sunbathers who, with no re-
gard for the dangers of skin cancer, joyfully roasted themselves in
the sun's bountiful light. Not David. He preferred to lie on his lawn
chair in the full shade of the beach umbrella he had so wisely rented
from a local stand.

The cry of gulls and terns overhead blended with the gentle
sounds of rolling surf in a relaxing symphony that lulled him to the
edge of gentle slumber; it was something to which he would happily
surrender. After all, this was the first real day off he had taken in sixteen months of steady, grinding, mind-shredding work. Yet, despite
the unrelenting pressure, high learning curve, and sometimes foreign nature of his job, he would not trade one moment of it.

Being the director of Barringston Relief, the largest relief organization in the world, was as fulfilling as it was demanding. Since
assuming the position after the death of his friend and employer
A.J. Barringston, David had traveled to twenty-four countries getting acquainted with the "heroes" who labored in the worst possible
conditions. He had made a return trip to Africa where he spent
time in Rwanda, Republic of Congo, Burundi, and the Sudan. He

also toured the relief work his organization had recently established on the island nation of Madagascar. His travels took him to famine-stricken North Korea where farmland had yet to recover from devastating floods. Several weeks were spent in South and Central America. He walked along the Appalachian Mountains and the inner-city streets of Los Angeles, Dallas, Miami, and New York. Everywhere he went he saw the worst possible conditions; he also saw the brave men and women who faced those elements with passion and aplomb.

David O'Neal had worked with the same tireless passion as his predecessor. The broad expanse of the world and the unrelenting need of suffering people now defined his life, which had once been expressed in church work. The enterprise of relief was now the power that energized his soul. It was his work, his dream, his service and worship. He thanked God for it every day.

Today, however, he was not Dr. David O'Neal, head of Barrington Relief. No, today he was just plain old David, citizen of the beach on a searing hot August afternoon. Through drowsy eyes, he scanned the horizon. Children scampered joyfully along the shore while others built sandcastles with their parents. Thirty yards out in the water, body surfers struggled to find a wave with sufficient energy to carry them in its foamy grasp. It was a futile effort, for the rollers were nearly as still as the air was calm. Only gentle waves made their way to the sand to flop lazily on the shore, spreading diaphanous foam on the sand. That was fine with David. It meant he could relax more and worry less about Timmy.

Like the other children along the strand, Timmy was enjoying the water. David spied him as he raced forward into the ocean, leaping wildly over the two-foot waves like they were moving hurdles. Once the water was waist high, Timmy would boldly leap headfirst into an oncoming wave only to surface, rubbing his eyes and coughing. He was having a great time.

Unlike the other children, Timmy stood just over six feet tall and was nearly twenty-four years old. Despite his adult height and age, he was still a child within. His intellectual and emotional development had been compared to that of an eight-year-old. While many who met the boy-man responded with pity, David often found himself admiring Timmy, for the young man was resilient, strong, and chronically cheerful. Every day brought him new joy and a renewed zest for life. Living was an unending adventure for him. *Not a bad way to live*, David had thought many times. Timmy had known a hard life, surviving on the streets where the other homeless had frequently beaten him. A.J. had rescued Timmy from just such a beating years ago. A.J. was the closest thing Timmy had ever had to a father, and now that he was gone, David filled that role.

Assured that Timmy was well, David once again closed his eyes and waited for the simple sleep of relaxation that he knew was just moments away.

A muted sound, foreign and misplaced, jarred him from his trance. David blinked in confusion. There it was again: a ringing, electronic and annoying. Subconsciously, he glowered and reached for the cell phone he had tucked away in a utility bag he used to carry towels and sun block. He had to search for a moment before he found the small black phone.

"David O'Neal," he said, after snapping open the small folding phone.

"Dr. O'Neal," a tinny and distant voice said through a haze of static, "this is Osborn Scott. Sorry to bother you on your day off."

"No problem, Oz," David said. Osborn Scott was a new addition to Barringston Relief. A quiet, capable man and a driven scientist, Oz—as he insisted on being called—normally stayed to himself, preferring his work to social contact.

"How was your trip to Belize?" Osborn asked. Even over the phone, he seemed distracted.

"Fine, but puzzling. I'm afraid I came home with more questions than answers."

"People still getting sick down there?"

"Yes. It's not an epidemic yet, but it's worrisome. All that our research doctors know is it's viral. But I don't think you called me to talk about Belize. What's up?"

"I need to show you something," Osborn said.

"Can it wait until tomorrow?"

"I think you might want to see this sooner than that." Osborn's voice was tense.

"Is there a problem?" David asked. He could feel his stomach tighten. If Osborn was concerned, then David's life was about to become far more complicated.

"I'd rather not talk about it over the phone."

David sighed. "Okay, I'll be there in half an hour. That's the best I can do."

"That'll be fine." Osborn hung up suddenly.

A puissant feeling of disquiet replaced the sense of peace that had so permeated David a few moments ago, and for good reason: Osborn Scott was the head of C.M.D., the Catastrophe Monitoring Department. If he was as concerned as he seemed, then something monumental and frightening was in the works.

David wasted no time calling Timmy in and packing his things.

■ ■ ■ ■ ■

Seated on the concrete wall that separated the sand from the cement walkway that paralleled the shore, a thickly built man with a marine-style haircut carefully aimed a small camera in the direction of the man he had been assigned to follow and depressed the shutter button. *Click*. The picture was recorded, not on the emulsion of film, but on an electronic chip inside the body of the camera. The image, and the scores like it he had been taking since David O'Neal had arrived at the beach, would not need processing. Instead, the camera would simply be downloaded onto the hard drive of a computer. From there the pictures would be used anyway his boss decided. He had no idea what that would be, nor did he care.

The camera he held was an amazing and expensive item, something he had been reminded of many times by Jack and that pencil-necked geek he was to turn the camera over to. "Ten thousand dollars," they had said several times, as if he were some dumb high school kid who couldn't grasp the concept the first time.

Click. Another shot. *Click.* The assignment was boring. Sitting in the hot sun, dressed in a pair of brown walking shorts and a white tee-shirt, the man waited patiently for his target to position himself so he could take a usable picture. Unfortunately, that meant prolonged periods of inactivity as David lay quietly in the shade of an umbrella. The retarded boy had been much easier to photograph. He hadn't stopped since arriving at the shore and stood in the sun most of the time. His pictures would be the best. The man wished he could say the same for the ones of David O'Neal. He would just have to wait and see.

The thick man watched as David gathered his things, returned the rental umbrella, and walked to the car with the young man close behind. He took another ten pictures and opened a palm-sized cell phone. He dialed a number. An answer came on the first ring:

"Jack, here."

"He's moving," the thick man said evenly.

"Got it." A moment later the connection was broken. Jack was never one for long conversations.

No matter. At least now he could get out of the sun. There was no need to follow David O'Neal. They knew where he was going, and people would be waiting, people with cameras like his as well as video cameras. The phone call O'Neal had received that prompted his departure had been monitored and recorded. The truth was, everything there was to know about David O'Neal was known, and every place he went someone would be nearby, watching, recording, waiting.

Standing, the thick man stretched, yawned, and placed the cell phone back in his pocket. Then he leisurely strolled to his own car.

■ ■ ■ ■ ■

The fifty-three story Barringston Tower cast an ever lengthening shadow on the four-lane downtown street that passed in front of it. David never ceased to be amazed at its beautifully designed exterior. Instead of sterile glass and cold concrete that had become the redundant theme of many mid- and high-rise buildings in the heart of San Diego, the Barringston Tower was adorned with earth-tone pebbled panels. Along each floor were planters brimming with hearty plants. Each time David saw the structure he was reminded of artists' renderings of the hanging gardens of Babylon.

Turning the wheel of his Ford Taurus, David steered the car through the drive that led to the first of two subterranean parking garages. Near the central bank of elevators was a parking place marked with a sign: "Dr. David O'Neal, CEO, Barringston Relief."

A minute later, he and Timmy, still dressed for the beach, were standing at the elevators. Timmy shivered despite the heat of the day. His swim trunks and white tee-shirt were still wet; sand clung tenaciously to his bare feet.

"Thanks for the hamburger, Dr. David," Timmy said as he hugged himself in a effort to ward off the chill left by the ocean.

"It was the least I could do after making us leave the beach earlier than we planned. I appreciate your being a good sport about this."

"You're welcome." Timmy shivered again. "I still feel cold, Dr. David."

"I think you may have picked up a little sunburn. That's why you feel cold."

"A burn can make you feel cold?" Timmy asked puzzled.

"Sometimes, Timmy. I know it doesn't make sense, but it works that way."

"Oh," he replied innocently. "Will it hurt?"

"The sunburn? A little, but I have some stuff to make it feel better."

A soft chime announced the arrival of the elevator cab. The two stepped inside, and David removed a small plastic card from his wallet and inserted it into a slot next to the control panel. Immediately the doors closed, and the elevator began its rapid rise to the fifty-third floor.

"When we get to our floor, Timmy," David began, "I need you to take our stuff to the apartment and put it away. You can take a shower then watch television. I have to meet with someone for a few minutes. Then I'll be up. Can you do that?"

"Sure," Timmy said. "Can I have a soda?"

"Absolutely," David replied with a big grin. "Just be sure to put your wet clothes in the bathroom. I'll deal with them later."

"Okay."

The elevator arrived at the top floor and opened its doors. Timmy stepped out and walked toward the penthouse apartment he shared with David. When the mantle of leadership passed from the murdered A.J. Barringston to David, the Board of Directors insisted that he move into the large flat. David resisted, feeling it was an unnecessary extravagance. It would remind him of his lost friend—a violence he had yet to overcome. Nonetheless, David acquiesced.

It wasn't long before David realized the importance of living in the suite. Directing Barringston Relief's worldwide efforts was not a nine-to-five job. Over the last sixteen months he had averaged working fourteen hours a day when he was in the country and longer when abroad.

The luxurious suite presented some problems, as did the entire Barringston Tower. Visitors often assumed that monies that could be used in hunger relief and other efforts were being spent on the magnificent high-tech building. More times than he could count, David had explained that the building, everything in it, as well as the staff of nearly five hundred was largely subsidized by Barringston Industries. The top ten floors were used rent- and utility-free by Barringston Relief. The thirteen floors below were occupied by Barringston Industries, and the remaining thirty floors were leased to various businesses. The lease money from those organizations paid for the building and the cost of its operation.

Barringston Industries was led by the enigmatic Archibald Barringston, founder of the global construction company that built high-rise structures in scores of foreign countries. It had been Archibald Barringston who, twenty years prior, had given a ten-million-dollar jump-start to his son Archibald Jr., known to everyone simply as A.J. From there, A.J. had guided the relief agency from conception to being the largest such nongovernmental organization in the world.

Monies for the actual relief work came from several sources. First were donations from people around the world. Since almost all of the relief organization's overhead and operational expenses were covered by other sources, more than 90 percent of donations received from individuals and businesses went directly to relief work—more than any other relief organization in the world. Substantial funds were gained from patents on research done by Barringston scientists and engineers. Barringston Relief did more than take meals to the hungry; it was the leader in the development of the bio-technology necessary to end famine and famine-related diseases. Side benefits from this research improved crop production in the United States and other countries. Funds from these products were poured back into the relief work.

The elevator descended two floors, and David exited it into a lobby. The lobby was empty except for a few potted trees and chairs situated around the perimeter. The floor was shared by three departments: the Communications Department, the Political Analysis Department, and the Catastrophe Monitoring Department. A large pair of oak doors led to each office complex. The C.M.D. was behind the doors to his left.

Casually he strolled through the half-dozen cubicles that delineated the work areas and tried not to look conspicuous. Although there was no dress code for employees, and attire ran the spectrum from jeans and polo shirts to three-piece suits, his swim trunks, sandals, and a San Diego Padre tee-shirt were stretching it. David said hello to the few workers who caught his eye. When he had left the beach, he had planned to head straight to his apartment, change clothes, and then quickly make his way to the C.M.D. offices. That plan had changed, however, when Timmy made his disappointment about leaving known by lowering his head slightly, a heartbroken expression across his face. David knew he was being manipulated, but he couldn't help feeling guilty. He made things right by promising to stop for a hamburger and shake on the way home. That had added an additional twenty minutes to the trip. David had promised to meet Osborn in thirty minutes; he was now twenty minutes late.

Osborn's office, a twenty-by-twenty room with a teak desk and credenza and floor-to-ceiling windows on two walls, was in the corner of the tower and overlooked the dense cluster of buildings of urban San Diego. From fifty-one floors up, the view was captivating. Osborn, a stately, middle-aged African-American, was not looking out the window. Instead, peering through small, wirerimmed glasses, his eyes were fixed on his computer screen.

"I'm sorry to have taken so long, Oz," David began, "but things took longer than I expected."

"No problem," Osborn answered without looking up. "Let me show you something."

David walked over to stand behind Osborn. On the large color monitor was a photo of the Gulf of Mexico and the Caribbean Sea.

The picture was detailed, showing mountains, valleys, rivers, and even clouds overhead.

"What am I looking for?" David asked.

Osborn picked up a pencil and pointed at the monitor. The sharpened end touched the glass screen and gave a discernible tap. "Here, fifteen degrees north by about seventy degrees west."

David leaned forward and squinted. "That clump of clouds?"

"Yeah," Osborn leaned back and scratched his chin thoughtfully. "Except it's more than a clump of clouds. It's a tropical storm, a big one, and I think it's on its way to being a hurricane."

"Hurricanes happen every year," David replied. "I don't think you called me here to show me a new one."

"We've already had two this year," Osborn said as he leaned forward and tapped a key on the keyboard. Instantly, the map zoomed out to reveal more of the area. Again Osborn clicked a key, and again the map shrank. David could now see the entire eastern seaboard. "The first two started well out in the Atlantic and moved toward the coast, but each turned north and never made landfall." As he spoke, Osborn traced the paths of the previous storms. "No harm, no foul. This one, however, is sure to hit something."

"Like what?"

"Too early to tell. It's not even a proper hurricane yet, but it will be, and I think it's going to be a big one."

"How can you tell?"

"Gut feeling right now, but this is what I do. This is why you hired me last January. I study catastrophes; it's my science, my passion."

That was true enough. Barrington Relief had been heavily involved in the easing of world hunger. Its considerable resources were aimed at meeting immediate and long-term needs. When the mantle of leadership fell to David, he added another dimension to the work: emergency aid to victims of cataclysm. Every year millions of people were killed, injured, or left homeless by natural disaster. It was David's dream to ease that pain. That's when he hired

Dr. Osborn Scott, one of the highest acclaimed students of catastrophe. His reputation was global.

"So you think it's going to be a problem?"

"Oh, it's going to be a problem all right. I just don't know how big a problem." They both studied the map for a few moments. "If you promise not to tell the world yet, I'll give you my best guess."

"I promise."

"If I were a betting man," Osborn began, "I'd wager that this fellow will reach hurricane status tonight or tomorrow and that it will take a northwesterly track." Once again he pointed at the screen. "Worse-case scenario: It grows to a four or five, plows across Cuba, picks up steam in the Gulf of Mexico, and makes landfall again somewhere around here." He pointed to New Orleans.

"That would be bad," David said seriously.

"That would be very bad," Osborn corrected. "In the next three days, David, people will die, and homes will be destroyed. You can bet the farm on it."

David reached for the phone on Osborn's desk and quickly punched in the number of his personal assistant. A second later he spoke: "Ava, I need you to set up a meeting with the R.R.T. Make it for . . . ," he looked at his watch, "4:30. That'll give everybody a couple of hours to rearrange their schedules."

David listened for a moment, then said, "No, better put us in the big conference room. I'm not sure how long we'll be meeting, so you better arrange for some coffee, water, that sort of thing. Thanks, Ava." He hung up.

"I think convening the Rapid Response Team is wise," Osborn said.

"It can't hurt. Besides, I'd rather be ahead of the game than behind. I'm going to go clean up while you prepare to make a presentation. Bring whatever information you can, and be ready to answer questions. You're the authority on this, and the team will need all you can give them."

"I'll be ready," Osborn said resolutely.

"Don't take this the wrong way, Oz," David said, "but I hope you're wrong."

"Me too," Osborn answered. He paused, then continued, "But I'm not."

■ ■ ■ ■ ■

Indian Ocean
Depth: 21,645 feet

Slowly . . . steadily . . . unfailingly . . . the jigsaw pieces of the Earth's crust moved—not by feet, but meager inches each year. The plates expanded as the fluid rock beneath purposefully produced new crust, and other plates tediously gobbled down the existing shell, melting and blending it with the mantle beneath. Not a day passed, not a minute ticked by, without the ancient ballet continuing.

Overhead rested a four-mile thick blanket of saltwater, always in motion. It was a concert conducted since creation, a dance of endless motion.

With almost intelligent tenacity, the Indo-Australian plate slowly twisted clockwise creating pressures, magnifying stress, subducting with a plate 800 miles east and diverging with its sister plate 1500 miles west. At its center was a portion of crust, 60 miles thick, that fractured and elevated a slab of rock the size of California in a titanic eruption of power. With it, rose 625,000 cubic miles of ocean.

Two minutes after it began, the eons of stress relieved, the ocean floor resumed its sluggish dance only slightly altered, moving in restful moderation.

Not so the ocean.

■ ■ ■ ■ ■

The conference room was a large trapezoid, wider near the double-entry doors, narrower by ten feet at its head. David stood with his hands clasped behind him and faced the gathered executives of Barringston Relief; ten pairs of eyes returned his gaze. Behind him was a large and technically sophisticated projection screen. To his right was a computer terminal.

The room itself had no windows, a purposeful design meant to decrease distractions. The walnut-paneled walls were adorned with pictures of Barringston Relief work around the world.

A large walnut table dominated the center of the room. Seated around the table were the ten department leaders who comprised the Rapid Response Team—the R.R.T. Each was an expert in his or her field.

"First let me thank each of you for rearranging your schedules to be here," David said. "I believe this is the first time we've met like this since the inception of the team six months ago. Two hours ago, Dr. Osborn Scott brought a serious matter to my attention. I've asked him to bring us up to date. Oz, if you would please." David stepped away from the lectern and took a seat.

Osborn, a thin, handsome man, stood and took his place at the head of the table. He carried no notes. Before he began, he paused at the computer terminal next to him and tapped in a command. On the floor-to-ceiling screen behind him a satellite photo appeared in bright colors. He stepped to the side so as not to impair anyone's view.

"This is the latest satellite photo from the NOAA. As you can see, it is of the Gulf of Mexico and the Caribbean." Facing the image, he pulled a penlike device from his pocket and clicked on a small switch. A low power laser emitted a small red beam that appeared as a small dot on the satellite image. Aiming the device at a smear of clouds, he continued. "This accumulation of clouds here is a massive tropical storm that is quickly growing in power and size. The National Hurricane Center has named the storm Claudia. While it's too early to say with certainty, I estimate there is more than an 85 percent chance this storm will grow to hurricane status and do so quickly, perhaps as early as tomorrow morning. When it does, it is sure to cause severe damage.

"It's impossible to predict the track a hurricane will take,"

Osborn continued, "but because of its present position with Venezuela to the south, several Central American countries to the west, Cuba and the Caribbean Islands to the north, we can safely say that some country, most likely several countries, will be adversely impacted by this storm. Someone is going to take a beating."

"How strong a storm do you anticipate?" Kristen LaCroix asked. Kristen was the Director of Public Relations. She was a bright woman with deep red, shoulder-length hair. She was also David's closest friend.

"Prognostication is a tricky business," Osborn answered, "but I think it's going to be a four, possibly a five."

"Please explain," David directed, wanting to make sure everyone understood the magnitude of his words.

Osborn nodded. "Hurricanes are rated on a scale of one to five, with category five being the most severe. Hurricanes are judged by their wind speed and the low pressure cell around which they rotate. For example, Hurricane Andrew devastated Florida, annihilating several towns, cutting a swath of destruction 35 miles wide, and severely damaging even a much wider area. It had sustained winds of 145 miles per hour with gusts up to 175. Before it was done, it left forty dead and caused twenty-five billion dollars in damage."

"That was a category five?" Kristen asked.

"No," Osborn replied. "That was a category four. A five is described as catastrophic and maintains winds of 156 miles per hour or greater with gusts that top 200 miles an hour. In addition, it brings a storm surge of eighteen feet or more."

"Storm surge?" asked Tom Templeton, Director of Inner-Agency Relations. His department maintained communications with other relief organizations worldwide, as well as governmental agencies.

"Yes," Osborn replied. "Most people think that a hurricane's winds are the most dangerous part of the storm, but that's just one segment of the problem. The storm brings a water surge with it.

This surge is like a mound of water that is pushed along by the winds. When the hurricane strikes the shore, this mound of water, which may rise twenty feet above its normal level, instantly floods the surrounding land, engulfing everything—cars, houses, people."

"I take it that category five hurricanes are unusual," Kristen said.

"The U.S. has only endured two in its history. A four is bad enough."

"How bad is bad?" Bob Connick, Barringston Relief's Chief Financial Officer asked.

"Factors vary," Osborn answered. "Much depends on where the hurricane strikes. Developed countries with sophisticated warning systems fare far better than undeveloped countries. Those systems are wonderful when it comes to saving lives, but they can do very little to diminish property damage. To give you an idea of what a hurricane can do, I'll share a few examples.

"On October 7, 1737," Osborn continued, "a typhoon—which is the same thing as a hurricane but occurs in the western Pacific or Indian Ocean—struck near Calcutta and sank 20,000 ships and killed 300,000 people. On October 1, 1893, a hurricane originated in the Gulf of Mexico, just like this one," he motioned to the satellite image, "and moved ashore near Port Eads and the Mississippi coastal region. It took 1,800 lives. In 1900 a hurricane came ashore at Galveston, Texas, and killed 6,000 people. The city was largely destroyed and was later rebuilt—seventeen feet higher than the high-tide level."

"But those all occurred a century or more ago," Bob Connick protested.

"True. Today we can evacuate many of the people, but there is still a horrible price to pay. In September of 1989, not all that long ago, Hurricane Hugo blasted through the Caribbean islands from Guadeloupe to Puerto Rico before ripping through North and

South Carolina. Hugo killed 500 and did several billion dollars worth of damage. And as I said earlier, Hurricane Andrew did over twenty-five billion dollars worth of damage in Florida in 1992 but took only forty lives, thanks to modern technology.

"But don't let the low death toll confuse you," Osborn said, pacing back and forth in front of the looming image of the tropical storm. "These storms are still dangerous, far more so than most realize. November 1995 saw Typhoon Anela strike the northern Philippines with winds in excess of 140 miles per hour. The devastation was unbelievable: more than 600 dead and 280,000 homeless."

"Do we need to tell anyone about this?" David asked.

Osborn shook his head. "No, the experts already know, including the NCEP and other agencies. My concern is Mexico and Cuba."

"NCEP?" Kristen inquired.

"National Centers for Environmental Prediction in Miami, Florida," Osborn answered. "The National Hurricane Center is associated with them. They already have a plan of action for such storms, and they will be monitoring it as well. I have a friend there who will share information with us. As I said, the real problem is Mexico and Cuba."

"How so?" David asked.

"Many parts of Mexico are populated by small impoverished towns. There's a good chance that thousands will not get advanced warning, and even if they do, they will not be able to move out of harm's way fast enough. That will only be a problem if the hurricane doesn't veer north as I expect it to do. Cuba is the concern. While they are familiar with hurricanes—they deal with them every year—one this size may be too much for them, and unlike the U.S. with its freeways and surface streets, the people of Cuba have no place to go. Getting on a boat sure isn't going to help. Those with access to hurricane shelters will be safe, but the others . . ."

David stared at the image of the storm for a moment, then

swung his chair around to face the others. Before him were the department heads of Communications, Medical Relief, Political Analysis, Volunteer Facilitation, Public Relations, Resource Distribution, Transportation Coordination, and his Chief Financial Officer and Inner-agency Liaison. All capable people, each trained and dedicated to the cause of global relief. They were all experienced with heroic efforts for long-term projects: famine and plague. Meeting catastrophe-related needs was something new for them and Barringston Relief. For nearly six months they had been working as a team to provide quick response to stricken areas while working in concert with other agencies and governments. While they had coordinated on several small disasters, this would be their first real test.

Turning back to Osborn, David said, "All right, Oz, break it down for us."

"The following scenario is subject to change," Oz prefaced. "Tomorrow morning, Tropical Storm Claudia will be upgraded to Hurricane Claudia. It will continue to gather strength over the warm waters north of Venezuela and move in a northwesterly direction. I believe it will veer north in time to hit Cuba and hit it hard. The storm will slow over land but will regain its power and intensity once north of Cuba. It will then continue on until it makes landfall on the southern coast of the U.S. The eye wall will most likely hit Louisiana and Mississippi."

"You sound very confident about your prediction," Bob Connick said.

"Call it scientific intuition," Oz answered. A moment later he said, "It's not confidence you hear . . . it's fear."

David stood. "Okay, folks, that's it. I would like to see brief summaries about your departments' readiness in two hours. Let's get to work." Turning to Osborn, David said, "Thanks, Oz, you made everything clear."

"I hope so, David. I have a bad feeling about this. A really bad feeling."

■ ■ ■ ■ ■

Cox's Bazaar, Bangladesh
7:47 A.M. local time.

Akram Kazi felt the loose sand under his feet give way with each step. Grains slipped between his bare feet and the sandals he wore. Pressing his chin down on the tall stack of newly washed white towels he carried, he struggled to make certain he didn't spill his load. It was his job to carry towels from the resort's laundry to the small white shack in the middle of the beach where tourists and traveling business executives freely retrieved them after a swim in the ocean. It was just one of the many services the Holiday Resort offered its guests.

Akram, nineteen, hustled along the sandy beach that ran in front of the hotel. The August heat would soon have the guests lining the shore, sitting under umbrellas to protect them from the fierce tropical sun. Akram hurried. He had many things yet to do, including wiping off the tables of the outdoor café. Already, guests were being seated and eating breakfast. Akram was running late.

Thirty hastily taken steps later, Akram was at the ten-by-fifteen-foot shed. "*Assalaa-mualaikum,*" he said, wishing peace on his coworker.

"*Wallaikum assalaam.*" Zahid Hussein, an employee who tended the shed, returned the traditional greeting, but it was clear he was upset. "It is about time, Akram. I have no towels to give, and already people are asking for them."

"It is not my fault, Zahid," Akram protested. "The laundry was not done with them. I could not bring you wet towels, could I?"

"No excuses. You have made me look bad before our guests. I will not tolerate that."

"The towels were not ready . . ."

"Enough," Zahid interrupted. "Do you see that man over there? The one with the big belly?"

348

"Yes." The man, portly with fish-white skin, reclined on a lounge chair.

"He wants a towel. Take him one, and apologize for your actions."

"But I have tables to . . ."

"Take him a towel, and do it quickly."

Akram acquiesced. Zahid was older and had seniority. Everyone had seniority over him. But that didn't matter. In just two months he would move to Dhaka, the nation's capital, to attend college. It was a fortunate opportunity from Allah, who had already blessed him many times. He could read, unlike 65 percent of other Bangladeshis, and he had a hunger for knowledge. So he worked, saving every taka and paisa, and looked forward to that day when he would study at the University of Dhaka. He longed to be a teacher, like his father before him. Education was the only way his tiny country could climb out of the pit of constant despair and depredation.

Approaching the white man with the big belly, Akram held out a clean white towel in his right hand. Since personal hygiene was done with the left, it would have been an insult to have used it with something so personal as a towel.

"Thank you, young man," the middle-aged man said.

"I offer my apologies for not having your towel ready when you requested it." Akram raised his right hand to his forehead, palm slightly cupped, offering a traditional salute.

"No problem, buddy," the man said.

American, Akram thought. *His accent is American.*

"It's just a towel. Everything is okay."

The man touched his index finger to his thumb to form a circle. Instinctively, Akram looked away. It was an obscene gesture, highly offensive. Of course the American didn't know that. The gesture, Akram had learned, was common in the Western world and simply meant that things were all right. Still, the sign shocked him. Akram had had to learn many things about foreigners since coming to work at the Holiday Resort two years ago. They were always doing something offensive: pointing with their index fingers, showing the bottoms of their feet, passing food with their left hands. It was simple ignorance on their part, and Akram had learned to endure it.

"Thank you for your kindness," Akram said, his eyes diverted to show humility before the guest. "Is there anything else I can get for you?"

"Nope. Nothing at . . ." The American's voice trailed off. "What . . . what's going on?" he asked.

"Sir?"

"Out there, boy, look!" The man pointed out to the ocean. The offensive gesture was lost on Akram when he turned to see the ocean rapidly retreating from shore. "Don't tell me that's normal." The man lumbered to his feet.

"I have never seen such a thing," Akram said, his eyes wide. "The ocean is leaving."

Slowly he and the American began to walk toward the tide line. Looking up and down the beach, Akram could see that other guests and employees were doing the same thing. Curiosity was a powerful force. The beach itself was unique, being the longest unbroken stretch on the planet, but this was something unseen before.

"Look at this, will ya'," the man offered. "Fish and crab for the taking."

Akram had noticed it too. The now-exposed ocean bottom was littered with crabs and other crustaceans. Fish flopped on the wet sand, slowly suffocating in a blanket of air.

"What do you suppose did this?" asked the pudgy man.

Akram shook his head. "I don't know. Maybe I should tell my manager . . ."

"Wait! Do you hear something?"

Tilting his head slightly as if to line up his ears for better reception, Akram closed his eyes and listened. "Yes, a roar, a rumble."

He opened his eyes and looked at the guest. The man's face was drained of all color, his mouth slack, his eyes wide. Again he pointed out to sea and then crossed himself.

"Hail Mary, full of grace . . ." the man began. He crossed himself again.

Akram turned to see what had so terrified the man. "Allah have mercy," was all he could say.

■ ■ ■ ■ ■

80 kilometers SE of Bhubameshwar, India
Altitude 2,200 meters

The Cessna Skylane RG airplane bounced slightly as it passed through a thermal. The pilot, an East Indian named Rajiv Kapur, paid no attention to the bump—his mind was elsewhere. Below him the dark blue of the Bay of Bengal was turning a shade lighter as the plane flew over the shallow waters of the continental shelf. Above him the sky was a crystalline blue. It was a beautiful day for flying and even a more beautiful day to be home celebrating the birthday of his five-year-old daughter, Jaya. Normally, Rajiv would be happy to chart a leisurely course back to Bhubameshwar and then to his home outside the city, but not today. He wanted nothing more than to be with his family.

He checked his airspeed again: 156 knots—75 percent power, just what it should be. The craft was capable of over 160 knots, but that was pushing the engine harder than necessary, especially on a substantially long flight like the one he was taking from the Andaman Islands 735 miles behind him.

A devout family man, Rajiv was proud of the three boys his wife had given him, but Jaya had stolen his heart like countless daughters across the world had done to their fathers. It wasn't that he loved his sons any less; it was that little girls knew the secret passages to a father's soul. Jaya knew those passages well and could melt her normally stern father with a simple glance and a flash from her obsidian eyes. She could manipulate her father like no other, and Rajiv loved it. As he flew, his mind filled with the image of his little girl: smooth, brown skin; coal black hair; bright eyes and a beaming smile. She could laugh in such a contagious way that a room full of adults would find themselves giggling like children with her.

Rajiv arched his back to stretch out the kinks of three and a half hours at the plane's controls. He shifted in his seat and checked his navigation indicators. Not that he needed to. He had been making flights like this one for over ten years. He often bragged that he could fly blindfolded to the Andaman Islands, as well as any airport on the eastern coast of India. Still he was a cautious pilot. Caution mixed with courtesy had made him one of the busiest charter pilots in the area. Next year he hoped to add another plane to his "fleet" of one.

"What's that?"

The voice dragged Rajiv from his revelry. He turned to his passenger, Mr. Julius Higgins of London, a jovial man with shiny white hair and a broad mouth. He and his wife, a woman with hair as dark as her husband's was white, were both recently retired and were sightseeing in India. "I'm sorry, Mr. Higgins. What did you say?"

"That," Higgins replied, nodding out his window. "Looks quite odd, don't you think?"

Rajiv peered across the small cabin and out Higgins's window but couldn't see anything. Instinctively he looked out his own side window. What he saw made his heart stutter. Even from an altitude of over 2000 meters he could see the ocean being drawn back like a blanket off a bed, leaving long streaks in the mud and sand of the ocean floor.

"Have you ever seen anything like that before?" Higgins asked. "I mean, does that happen all the time?"

Rajiv could not speak; he just shook his head.

Higgins turned to his wife who was in the seat behind him in the four-passenger plane. "Wake up, dear. You don't want to miss this. Something unusual is happening."

Groggily Mrs. Higgins opened her eyes. "What? What's wrong?"

"Look out your window," Higgins replied.

"Amazing," she exclaimed. Then she smacked her husband on the back of the head. "Why aren't you taping this, Julius? That's why you have the video camera in your hand."

"Oh, right," Higgins said. A moment later he was pointing the Sony camera out the window. "Try and hold the plane steady, chum."

Rajiv just stared out the window and tried to make sense of what he was seeing. In a few more minutes they would be over land with the ocean behind them and unable to see the drama below. Slowly, Rajiv turned the Cessna and took a course parallel with the shore. To his left was the heavily populated coast, to his right, open ocean.

A gasp came from the back. Rajiv turned to see Mrs. Higgins with a hand to her mouth, her eyes wide in fright. Another gasp, this time from Mr. Higgins.

"What? What is it?" Rajiv blurted.

No one answered. Both of his passengers sat stonelike in their seats, gazing out their windows. The terror in the cabin was palpable. Julius Higgins rigidly held the video camera to his eye. Instinctively, Rajiv leaned to the side to see the monster that had terrified his passengers. The terror of realization struck him hard, like a vicious punch to the stomach. His heart beat rapidly, pounding so hard that Rajiv thought it might burst from his chest any second.

A ribbon of white, sinuous like a snake, raced toward the coast. So long was the ribbon that Rajiv could not see its ends. The line of white tumbled and churned and grew. Without thought, Rajiv banked the plane hard and pushed on the yoke. The craft responded without hesitation, and everyone was pressed back into their seats by the invisible hand of acceleration.

"What are you doing?" Higgins cried out.

"I must see," Rajiv said.

Higgins glanced at the altimeter in the instrument panel. The white indicator arm spun as the Cessna plummeted down. "Are you trying to kill us?" he shouted above the now roaring engine. Rajiv did not respond.

Rajiv kept his eyes fixed on the surface of the glistening earth below and then, after an eternity of moments, pulled back on the yoke. Slowly the plane leveled in its flight. The craft cruised at 175 knots, 100 meters above the now barren ocean floor. Rajiv, consumed by the image before him, was only barely aware that Julius Higgins had resumed taping. He blinked, then blinked again, but it was still there and it appeared to be growing.

A wave. Rising. Building. Charging with locomotive speed. A wall of water. A cliff of ocean.

"Dear, Lord," Higgins said. "It's a bloody tidal wave."

"It's huge," his wife added.

"I'll say. That thing's got to be around twenty-five meters."

Twenty-five meters or better, Rajiv thought. And it was growing.

Again Rajiv banked the plane and raced for shore. This time he maintained his altitude. Urgently he snatched the microphone from his radio set and raised it to his mouth. He keyed the device and began to speak rapidly in Hindi. "Mayday, mayday, 55W with emergency traffic."

"N20355W this is Bhubameshwar tower. State your emergency."

"Wave. Tsunami headed your way." Rajiv's voice was breathy as he struggled to keep his emotions controlled.

"What?" came the response of the air traffic controller.

"I'm forty kilometers southeast of Puri. I see a large wave . . ." Just then the monster of water raced underneath them. Rajiv checked his air speed: 165 knots.

"How fast are we going?" Higgins asked.

Rajiv ignored him and spoke into his radio again. "It's moving at about 300 kilometers per hour! Take emergency action!"

Higgins shook his head. "Three hundred kilometers per hour, and that thing is pulling away. It'll hit the shore in less than five minutes."

Five minutes, Rajiv thought. Five minutes wasn't enough time to do anything. Not enough time to get into a car and drive to safety. Not enough time to seek shelter. Just enough time to pray.

Rajiv watched as the wave raced away from them, outdistancing them with each passing second. The wall of water was rising and racing toward the coast, toward Puri, toward his home. And there was nothing he could do about it.

But he would try.

Pushing the throttle to the stops, Rajiv made a vain attempt to catch the watery behemoth. The engine roared, then screamed in protest. Rajiv did everything to speed the Cessna along—trimming the propeller, easing all flaps—but it did no good. Only a jet could catch the wave of destruction ahead of him. At the moment, the wave was the fastest thing on or above the ocean. Rajiv would arrive moments after the wave struck shore.

Squeezing the yoke tight until his knuckles turned white, Rajiv attempted to will the plane to fly faster. He even pointed the nose down to make full use of gravity. His air speed rose to nearly 200 knots, but it was not enough. He could not descend forever. Soon he would have to level off or die. But maybe that wasn't so bad.

If only he could be there with his family—with his wife and sons and his beautiful Jaya—then maybe he could help or at least hug them one last time. He knew it was a foolish thought, but men were allowed foolish thoughts when their families were in danger.

As the wave approached the shore, Rajiv saw it crest. A second later a spray of white rose high in the air and then quickly rained down. The plane arrived a minute or two after the impact. Below it, rubble bobbed around on the churning caldron of cold seawater.

What had once been houses were now little more than fragments, kindling. As quickly as the wave had arrived, its destructive tide receded, taking with it the debris of buildings, cars, boats, and bodies.

Rajiv was now flying a mere thirty meters above his hometown of Puri—close enough to see detail that would forever be branded in his mind. Next to him Higgins continued to tape. At first Rajiv felt a nearly overwhelming sense of anger at the man for being so unmoved by what had just happened, but that dissolved when he saw a single tear stream down the Englishman's cheek.

Below was utter carnage. The streets were littered with debris as though an atom bomb had been unleashed. The wave had not cared if it destroyed the wood huts of the poor or the fine homes of the rich. Little was left. Bodies of men, women, and children were strewn about; some of them lay naked, the wave having viciously ripped the clothing from their bodies.

Two minutes later Rajiv began circling the plane over a decimated stretch of ground. A missile attack would have left more structures intact. Homes, offices, schools, people had been turned into the flotsam of fate.

"Why are we circling?" Higgins asked softly.

Rajiv did not answer. He stared out the side window.

Higgins sighed. "Is that where you lived?" he asked kindly.

Rajiv nodded slowly and continued to gaze at the wreckage of what had been his middle-class home. Gone was the white stucco house, the courtyard, his family. This was where he had lived. Now gone. All gone.

Below he could see a small yellow tricycle implanted next to a fractured stone wall—the birthday gift he had purchased for Jaya.

Tears came unhindered.